THE KNIGHTS OF PECAN FALLS

STEP TO THE SIDE

GRANT HOLLAND

WESTBOW
PRESS®
A DIVISION OF THOMAS NELSON
& ZONDERVAN

WestBow Press books may be ordered through booksellers or by contacting:

WestBow Press
A Division of Thomas Nelson & Zondervan
1663 Liberty Drive
Bloomington, IN 47403
www.westbowpress.com
1 (866) 928-1240

ISBN: 978-1-9736-2930-6 (sc)
ISBN: 978-1-9736-2931-3 (hc)
ISBN: 978-1-9736-2929-0 (e)

Library of Congress Control Number: 2018906153

Print information available on the last page.

WestBow Press rev. date: 06/25/2018

This book is affectionately dedicated to everyone who is tired of being the villain and desperately wants to be the good guy.

CHAPTER 1

RIBBON CUTTING

"And in conclusion ..."

I know what you are thinking. Those three words do not seem like the best way to begin a book. But a certain butler named James was holding a small stack of notecards at arm's length, squinting as he read. But the speech was not *his* to read. He was merely going over it out loud for Billy's sake. Billy himself would soon deliver the address in front of a small, excited crowd of reporters, dignitaries, the morbidly curious, and other swells.

Right there in a small dressing room, a toothy grin spread out on James' normally sour face. The pleasant smile looked completely out of place on him. But a more polished butler you would not find. He was dressed to perfection. Impeccable as always. His stance may have been a bit forced and awkward looking, but it was all for the sake of his young master.

By Billy's standards, James was one of the ancients; to everyone else, he appeared to be in his late fifties. His hair was combed straight back with more black than gray in it. His thin beard, by contrast, had more gray than black. His rounded tummy was always the first part of him to enter a room.

James continued the speech's conclusion in a rich baritone voice. "I speak for the entire Harris family in thanking you all for coming out on this momentous occasion. On the surface, it looks like a simple ribbon is being cut, but what you are truly seeing are the dreams of many people coming to life. It is a pity that the cameras cannot capture the love of so many being built right into the floors and walls of this beautiful structure.

May the new Harris Civic Center be a place for future generations to develop strong bodies and sharp minds."

James stopped reading and addressed Billy, "This is the part where you take the scissors … Billy?" James repeated the name, but the second time had a touch of irritation behind it. "Billy! Are you listening to me?"

Billy was staring off into space. His gaping mouth looked like that of a Florida largemouth bass. His dangling arms seemed to defy the possibility of an actual skeletal structure. While his butler stood at attention off to the side, he was reclined in a chair facing a large mirror.

The makeup lady had just touched up his forehead to keep it from shining. Now the bib was off. She had collected her makeup and had just departed. The reason for the makeup was something of a mystery to James, since Billy had long bangs that prevented his forehead from ever being seen, even by the cleverest of cameras.

Billy suddenly became aware of James addressing him. With a sudden glance, he pulled an earbud from his ear. Instantly upon release, the earbud gave the auditory impression of a miniaturized band playing rock music on the end of the cord. Looking up at the butler, Billy said, "James. Did you say something?"

James was not especially pleased; he had just finished reading the entire speech for nothing. He placed the notecards on the counter in front of the mirror. "You didn't hear a single thing that I said." He sometimes wondered if there was even a scrap of brain located somewhere underneath that big ol' mop of light-brown hair. *Someday*, he thought, *I'm going to cut off all that hair and find out what his head really looks like. It's probably shaped like a bullet … or a cathedral.*

Billy looked blankly at the butler.

James returned to his ramrod-straight posture and pushed his anger further down where it could not be observed in his expression. His voice remained calm and cautious. "Okay. Let's try this *one more time*. Your parents had written a speech that they had intended to deliver at this event. I was just going over it with you now since you must address the crowd in your parents' absence." James paused and took a deep breath. "Do you know what you're going to say?"

"Oh yeah!" Billy reached over and picked up the oversized scissors. "I was going to say, 'Hey, everyone! Check out the size of this thing!

Sweeeeeet!'" He lifted them high above his head and then brought them back down to his face. "Pretty cool, huh?"

James rolled his eyes. "Just read the notecards. It is all there." He gestured defeatedly toward the blue rectangular cards.

Billy put the scissors back down on the nearby countertop and turned on his familiar whiny voice. "Why can't my parents do this instead of me, anyway? I'm no good at this sort of thing."

"You know why. They were in Japan on business and their plane was delayed. Otherwise, *they* would be here with you right now. Whereas *I* would be back at the house performing duties more becoming a butler." He turned his back to Billy and began to brush Billy's sports coat. "Instead I am here babysitting you."

Billy's fifteen-year-old frame plopped backward into the chair. "And being a general nuisance, I might add." This was not the first time that James had gotten on his nerves—and vice versa.

James' tone was far more professional than his choice of words. "My job is not to make you happy. It is to provide services for Mr. and Mrs. Harris. My allegiance is to them—not you." A strangely condescending tone finished that sentence, very odd for a polished butler of James' caliber.

"Well, if it weren't for my parents, I would fire you faster than you could say, 'Jack—'"

"Frost," James interrupted. He turned slowly with Billy's jacket in hand. In a slower, more deliberate voice, he added, "Sir, if it were not for your parents, I would not be around long enough for you to fire me." He held up the jacket to be worn and smiled a most insincere and menacing smile. "Your coat, Master William," he said in an almost villainous tone.

The jacket itself was stylish and attractive. Someone in Billy's position could easily afford to be chic. But judging from the look on James' face, Billy began to wonder if there could be a mousetrap hidden in every pocket.

Billy angrily got out of his seat and placed his arms through the sleeves. "Whatever. Let's just get this thing over with." He began to make his way to the door when James pointed out the notecards sitting in front of the mirror, waiting patiently to be picked up. Billy gave out an exasperated sigh, grabbed them, and put on a pair of expensive shades. Out the door he went.

Fortunately, James remembered the pair of colossal scissors and carried them himself as he scurried after Billy.

The two of them came out of a side door unnoticed at first and made their way over to the main entrance of the new building. A large red ribbon blocked the front door and was spread out between two handrails. A small podium with a microphone stood opposite.

Billy marched in like a rock star. "Greetings, Luminous City!" People began to cheer and scream. The scene was electrifying. Onlookers crowded together. Several camera crews from local television affiliates were on hand, all armed with their own microphones, hoping to get something to quote later. Members of the printed media were also in attendance. Other well-dressed people stood around excitedly and began to applaud when they caught sight of young Billy Harris, the most talked-about teenager in the country. A string quartet sat to the side, masterfully playing a familiar classical tune.

Billy looked back at James in disgust and got his attention. Leaning over, he whispered, "And what is *that* supposed to be, if you're so smart?"

"To what are you referring exactly?"

"That racket." He pointed at the musicians.

"The world-famous string quartet? Ah, yes. They were hired to perform. They are the absolute best in the business and were far from cheap. We were extremely fortunate to secure their services for today's event. Don't you think they punctuate the festivities with perfection?"

Billy gave James a pained expression. "Well, I think they're terrible. Find out what we are paying them and then double it just to make them quit what they're doing."

"*To quit what they're …?* You want me to send them home? We flew them in from Austria just for the event."

"Of course. Don't you find them depressing? If we wanted to jam on some tunes, we would have wanted something a bit livelier than *Johann Amadeus Beethoven*."

That one took James a second. "Oh. You mean what they're playing? That's actually Vivaldi."

Billy's eyes widened in amusement. "Did you say *'the baldy'*? That's hilarious." He looked back at the quartet and started laughing, completely unaware as to how rude he was being to the performers. "I guess that might explain why all the old composers and songsmiths wore those ridiculous wigs." Billy gave his butler a soft pat on the back and a gentle nudge in the direction of the quartet.

Sadly, it now looked like the butler had an uneasy task to perform. So he started his route toward the musicians and wondered what he was going to say. What did Billy mean, James pondered, when he said to double their expense to make them stop? Did he mean to double it in the sense that he was to offer them the same amount as what they were getting paid now, thus doubling it as a result? Or was he supposed to find out what they were being paid and multiply that times two in addition to what they were already getting? That was enough to confuse anyone. Billy should have clarified what he meant.

As it turned out, James did not have to ask them to stop at all, to his relief. The mayor of Luminous City walked up to the podium and spoke into the microphone. He got everyone's attention and began to make what was intended to be a short speech, the purpose of which was to introduce Billy.

Billy was not listening. What could the mayor possibly say that this teenaged boy would find even remotely interesting? Looking past the powerful camera lights and boom mics, he looked into the well-dressed crowd and saw *her*.

She was standing front row center, literally the girl of his dreams. Her smile was brighter than all the lamps combined. Her simple, elegant dress looked like starlight blinking as she moved. He was instantly smitten. But he was smitten every time he saw her; oh yes, he had seen her many times before. He had carefully memorized the details of her face. Could this be the day that he would actually get the courage necessary to meet her? Overcoming his boyhood fears, He began to approach and unpredictably wandered away from the mayor.

In mid-speech, the poor mayor noticed Billy's brief departure and did not know how to react. He was just about to make a joke about Pimento cheese sandwiches, but now this teenage boy was walking away from his post with everyone watching and was evidently making his way over to have a conversation with one of the attendees. This was rude behavior on Billy's part, even if the sandwich joke was going to be a dud anyway.

5

In spite of this breech of protocol, the cameras kept rolling.

Right over the stumbling words of the speaker, Billy began to introduce himself to the lovely young woman. "Excuse me, but I think I know you."

At first, the young lady did not realize that he had singled her out. But once she understood that, she was startled and a bit nervous. In fact, she was now feeling a slight hint of embarrassment.

In the meantime, the orator had stopped talking and was looking uncomfortable and agitated. He quickly glanced down at his typed program to see if he had missed something on the schedule; but alas, Billy walking away was not part of the ceremony. The other guests in attendance stared at Billy and this young lady. Flashes went off from dozens of cameras. James was horrified, but not altogether surprised. The whole scene was awkward.

Billy continued. "Yeah, that's right. I know exactly who you are. There is no way that I could ever forget the most ravishingly beautiful person in the world. Your name is ..." He paused closing his eyes momentarily and bringing his hand up to his temple. When he opened his eyes again, he snapped his fingers and said, " ...*Chloe Chastain*."

She could not help smiling. "That's right! How did you know that?" The expression on her face was enough to see that she was not expecting any of this.

An overly confidant voice came out. "Oh, I know everything about you. I know that last year you moved to a tiny little town in the Ozarks called Pecan Falls. I know that you are about to start your tenth grade year. And I know that your dad is a very powerful man back there in the hill country."

She folded her arms in a jokingly defensive manner. "That's very impressive. What else do you know about me, Mr. Harris?"

A mischievous smile appeared. Everyone in attendance was watching them and listening to what was being said. But he ignored them all. As far as he knew, it was only him and her, both engaged in a normally private conversation. He spoke to her in a breathy kind of speech that was slower than normal talk. "I know that your favorite color is hot pink. You like to dip your fries in ranch. Your socks never ever match. Your eyes squint whenever you have a genuine laugh. And the date of your birthday sounds beautiful as it rolls right off the libs: April tenth."

She looked away and then back again as she laughed. "That was very sweet, but my birthday is not April tenth."

Undaunted, Billy kept smiling. "Really? What about June fifteenth?"

"No."

"September twenty-sixth?"

"No." She was definitely amused by his incorrect guesswork.

"No? Okay, okay. If I'm *ever* going to guess your birthday correctly, let's do this systematically. January first?"

"No."

"January second?"

"No." She started laughing at this point.

"January third?"

"No."

"January fourth?"

At this point, people were visibly annoyed.

How many years do I have until retirement? James asked himself. The butler quickly made his way over to Billy before his young man could get to January eighth. He spoke in Billy's ear as quietly and politely as he could. "Do you not have a speech to give at this time?" He turned back to the man behind the microphone. "Mr. Mayor, please continue with your gracious introduction."

Billy charged up and gently pushed the man away from the microphone. "Nah, nah. Step to the side, Mr. Mayor-Man. I got this." Momentary feedback made its clumsy song over the loud speakers as the microphones changed their focus. The teenage socialite addressed the crowd. "Uh, HELLO! That's English for *hola*." (And yes, he mistakenly pronounced the hard *H* sound in this Spanish greeting.) His momentary laugh included a brief snort, but no one else thought his joke was funny. He looked down at the slightly bent notecards that he now took out of his pocket. "I have a speech prepared for me to give because my parents are stuck in Japan, but ..." He put the cards back in his pocket and spoke with mock sincerity. " ...but I think that today I am just going to speak from the heart."

James rolled his eyes. *Did he just say 'Speak from the heart'? His heart? Ugh. The Harris' do not pay me enough to listen to this nonsense.*

All cameras were rolling. Photographers were getting their pictures. At that moment, a flash of inspiration filled Billy's empty head. "Yes. This will be from the heart. And right now, my heart is saying that you really don't want to take pictures of me cutting this big ugly ribbon. After all, this building was not built for me. It was built for you – the people of this grand and glorious city of Luminous, the biggest in the nation." He made a large sweeping gesture with his arm. "But since there is no way that all of you can share in this honor, we need to pick out a representative for the people." Billy then turned his focus back to Chloe. "I would like to see Chloe Chastain from the small town of Pecan Falls get over here and cut this ribbon. Who's with me here?" He began to clap, thus encouraging everyone else to clap, confused as they were. "Chloe Chastain, get on up here!" The clapping continued.

Chloe hesitantly tiptoed over to him as if she were crossing the world's shortest minefield. "What are you doing?" she whispered to him.

"I'm making you famous," he said softly. "Tomorrow, every daytime TV show is going to wonder *who's that girl that was with Billy Harris Jr.*" There was a slight mocking voice as he imitated the announcers on television.

Without any warning for James, Billy instantly swiped the overgrown scissors from the butler's grasp and brought them over to Chloe.

She pulled some hair behind her left ear and took the scissors. "What do you want me to do?"

"Just put one hand here on this handle and the other hand here." Billy moved in closely as he spoke. Together, they held the scissors in position on either side of the red ribbon. "On the count of three? One. Two. Three."

Flashbulbs were going off from every angle. But nothing happened. The ribbon was not cut in the least. Billy and Chloe looked at each other with question marks shooting out of their heads. They started to laugh. This solemn and serious ceremony was being turned into something campy and juvenile.

"That's weird. Let's try that again, shall we?" Billy asked.

They came down with the scissors again as before – except this time, they tried it with more force. Again nothing happened.

Chloe was already uncomfortable; this only intensified the sensation. She was just a sweet, simple girl who lived in tiny town and was visiting the big city. Still, she thought that Billy was rather cute. And he was certainly wealthy, the richest kid in America, in fact. Who has never heard of the

Harris' from Luminous City? Chloe tried to remain cool in view of the circumstances. "I don't think these scissors are ever going to work."

"I think you're right. We're not gonna get anywhere with these." He tossed the scissors into a nearby sticker bush. "Enough of this. This ribbon is getting on my nerves anyway." He ripped it from one of the handrails and cleared the path.

Acting on the safe side, the attendees began to clap once more.

Billy spun around to face the audience. "HEY! DOES ANYONE HERE WANT TO GO IN AND SEE SOMETHING COOL?" he yelled.

By then, a few people began to loosen up. A handful of them followed his example and cheered.

"THEN FOLLOW ME, THRILL-SEEKERS! BESIDES, I THINK WE CAN FIND SOMETHING TO EAT IN THIS PLACE!" He turned and jerked on the front door latch to open it. Embarrassingly, the door was still locked. *Locked out? How can I be locked out of my own building? This was poorly planned.*

The butler closed his eyes slowly and put the palm of his hand in front of his face. *I'm sure I'll be blamed for this somehow. What are Mr. and Mrs. Harris going to say about this social gaffe? I wonder if there is any chance that they won't be seeing the footage.*

Just inside the door, a nearby security guard was luckily walking by at that moment and quickly understood what was happening. He scrambled over to pop the door open for Billy and company as if his job depended on it. He held the door open as the crowd poured inside.

Billy's butler walked over and eased into Chloe as if to tell her something in confidence. "You will have to excuse Master William. He really is a nice boy when he's not busy dreaming about being ri ..."

"James!" Billy interrupted. "I think that we have heard sufficiently from you, thank you very much." With a short gesture, he told James to back off a little and then turned his attention back to the door.

The security guard stated in a nervous voice, "Sorry about that, Mr. Harris. I don't understand what happened."

Billy smiled and placed a kind hand on the security guard's shoulder as he walked past. "No problem at all, Graham."

Awesome, the guard thought to himself and smiled. *Mr. Harris just spoke to me. That is pretty cool! I can't wait to tell my wife.* A bewildered expression fell on his face. *Except my name isn't Graham. It's Al.*

Billy was just about to give a tour of the new facility (actually, he was about to give *Chloe* a tour while everyone else was going to be tagging along). But mercifully, a bright young lady named Jodi arrived with her equally energetic fellow at her side – his name was Skip or Chip or something like that. It seemed to be their job to give the tour and they controlled the crowd with a collegiate spunkiness. Billy was all too happy to release the press and other curious members of the crowd into the care of this peppy young couple.

They drifted from the main lobby, with its ornate stonework and potted plants, to the other rooms in the building. There was an Olympic-sized swimming pool, a basketball court, indoor batting cages, a dining hall, and little sitting rooms for tutoring and reading. They even had a pool room with several other games, including darts, pinball, a couple of arcade machines, and even chess. There were also a few meeting rooms including a fairly spacious one that companies or individuals could rent out. Everyone was very impressed and excited about the new building. Chloe's face was especially beaming with joy. Never in her years had she seen anything like it.

At the conclusion of the tour, the crowd was making their way to the dining hall for a specially prepared meal for the occasion. Billy had other plans. He held onto Chloe's hand in a way that was asking her to stay there for a moment.

"Hello," he said in a smooth, flirty voice. "It's about time those stooges left us alone."

"I want to ask you a question," she said as she looked up at him. "You are not at all as you seem, are you?"

"What do you mean?"

"What your butler was saying earlier – you're not really the wealthy and confidant Billy Harris, are you?"

"Sure I am. What makes you ask that?"

"I think that this is all just a dream that you have. That none of this is real. For one thing, it's way too cool."

Billy looked uncomfortable. "Some of it is real. You're real. And I'm real. And I think that that is all that really matters."

Chloe smiled. But then she looked off behind his shoulder and frowned. Pointing at a couple of security guards, she said, "Look over there. What do you suppose they are doing?"

The two guards were darting strangely toward one of the exits. When Billy hollered at them, they both took off running for the door. Billy gave chase; but once the guards were outside, they barricaded the doors with a large metal beam and ran away from the building.

Billy tried pushing the door, but it would not budge. He yelled over at some other security guards to check out the other exits. They discovered that they were all barricaded. "Whatever does this mean?" he asked himself.

"Uh! Billy? You may want to see this," Chloe yelled.

Billy, James, and a couple of guards rushed over to where Chloe was. She had heard a noise and opened the door of a utility closet. Right in front of them was a bomb, just like in the movies. The timer was counting down from four minutes and some change.

Billy sprang into action. "Guards, I want you two to check every door in this building and see if we can't get these people out of here. And find out if these windows are bulletproof – I suspect that they are, but it wouldn't hurt to try." The guards took off. "James, gather all of our guests and make sure that they are in the dining hall. There are plenty of strong tables in there. Make sure that they all get under the tables just in case the roof falls in."

James interjected. "What are you going to do?"

Billy took out his phone and started to type. "Chloe and I are going to stay here and defuse this bomb." He turned his attention to her. "That is if you are okay with that. Are you up for some fun and an adventure?"

Chloe's face changed. She looked determined and tough. Looking into Billy's eyes like a laser beam, she answered, "Let's do this thing!"

The clock was ticking, so James ran off to gather the others to safety.

Chloe began to rummage around in her handbag while Billy searched for something on his phone. He laughed and said, "Those rank amateurs. They are using a T-11 Truger with an electrocoil – and an outdated one at that. I was reading about how to disarm them just the other day. See?" He held his phone up briefly to reveal the directions on how to disarm the explosive. He looked back at it. "If only we had a Phillips screwdriver and a nice pair of wire cutters."

Chloe pulled those very items out of her handbag. "Will these do?"

Billy was stunned. "What is that? A Swiss Army purse?"

She placed the tools in his hands as she took his phone. "Never ask a girl from Pecan Falls what she has in her handbag."

Billy made a mental note of that.

She took a deep breath and looked at his phone. "This looks easy enough. I'll read it to you while you defuse the bomb."

What followed was a textbook example of teamwork. As soon as the next directive came out of her mouth, he did it. An observer might think that this was their profession. As they worked, the clock continued to count down. Two minutes were left. A minute and a half. Occasionally, Billy would wipe away beads of sweat that were now appearing on his forehead. Dramatic music swelled as if this were the climactic scene from an action picture. Less than a minute now remained. With each passing second, the clock sounded a soft – but annoying – electronic beep.

Finally, Billy placed the wire cutters on the last of the cords. Applying a little pressure, he slowly sliced through the red covering on the copper wire. With less than ten seconds left, the beeping sound ceased and the numbers on the display stopped. All was quiet - - even the suspenseful music had ended.

"Whew! I think this is the part when the guy says something astute and funny," commented Billy. He got the attention of the security guards and told them that the crisis had passed. By this time, outside authorities had arrived to open the doors.

Chloe looked up at Billy and smiled. "Do you always have this much fun when you meet a girl?"

"Not usually." His attention was beginning to focus on her again. "Usually, I just ... Actually, there is no 'usually.'"

"I really think I ought to be going." She handed his phone back to him and took two steps away.

"Why? I don't understand why we can't keep doing this." He moved his open palm back and forth between the two of them.

"Doing what?"

"This. You know. Just talking. I mean here you are leaving, but I don't even have your phone number."

Chloe reached over and tapped on Billy's phone. "Yes, you do. I programmed it into your phone already when you weren't looking. And I sent myself a text with your phone, so I now have your number too." She left him speechless as she walked right past him and toward the door.

He watched her as she disappeared out the door. "Girl, you don't play."

Knock-knock.

Billy woke up long enough to roll over. *Go away,* he thought.

Knock-knock. There was the noise again coming from his bedroom door.

Billy opened his eyes and saw the familiar sight of his bedroom. Disappointment covered his face. *You mean all that was just a dream. Figures.* Just in case, he reached over for his phone and began looking at his list of phone numbers. As he expected, no Chloe Chastain. *Phooey.*

Early morning daylight was peeking through his bedroom window. Posters featuring his two favorite basketball players struggled for attention on either side. Morning racket from the birds was now beginning to drown out the noise coming from his ceiling fan.

Knock-knock. Billy's mom opened the door. "Wake up, sleepyhead. It's the first day of school." She walked over to Billy's bed and pulled the blanket off of him.

Billy grabbed another blanket that was hidden between his bed and the wall. He yelled, "Emergency Back-up Blanket!!" He pulled it on top of himself and rolled over.

His mom gave a polite laugh and headed back to the door.

"Hey, mom?" He sat up in his bed.

She stopped and turned to face him. "Yes, babe?"

In his morning delirium, he asked, "You and dad wouldn't ever get stuck somewhere in Japan leaving it all up to me to cut a big ribbon all by myself with an obnoxious butler and a bomb to defuse, would you?"

His mom answered without missing a beat, "No. Never. And certainly not on an empty stomach." She left the room and closed the door.

Billy fell back down on his pillow. It did not occur to him how strange that must have sounded until he was halfway through his shower.

CHAPTER 2

PECAN FALLS

While Billy was busying himself with the details of getting ready for school, this would probably be the best time to introduce you to our fair community. Pecan Falls was hidden away in the foothills of the Ozarks, big enough to feel like a real place to those who live there and small enough to feel like nowhere to those who are just passing through. Time of sunrise? Unknown. That all depends on where you happen to be standing. The town lacked a clearly defined horizon due to the hills all around. But just like anywhere else, the darkness of night surrendered to early day. Slowly, the inhabitants of Pecan Falls awakened from their quiet mountain slumber to embrace the dawn.

From a distance, the town had a modern American fairytale sort of look to it. The nighttime sounds of crickets and bullfrogs were replaced with birdsong. A gentle morning breeze blew through across the top of the woods; as a result, the trees looked like they were cheerfully waving at the kids who were hitting the streets with their paper routes.

Diners and doughnut shops filled up with funny old men with politics on their minds and coffee in their cups. Although they sometimes did not agree, each one was an absolute authority on every subject and had all the problems of the world solved - - at least, in their own minds.

A nearby waterfall contributed something to the name of this community – hence the 'Falls' in 'Pecan Falls.' The other part came from the pecan trees that dominate a large portion of the area. Not too long ago, someone had the idea that the pecan needed to become the state nut.

Scientifically speaking, pecans are not true nuts; they are drupes. But you would still find them in the nut section of your local store. That is like saying that a tomato is a fruit that is grown in your vegetable garden. Matters such as this are not worth splitting hairs over, and those people who do are probably just idly looking for a fight anyway.

There was a small debate on the correct pronunciation of the town's name. If you look long and hard, you might find a handful of old-timers who pronounce the town PEE-kan Falls; but most of the residences prefer to call it puh-KHAN Falls. But again, things like that do not really matter either. No one is going to throw you in jail if they do not like the way you pronounce words around here. Besides, that just means more paperwork.

This particular Monday was the first day of Billy's tenth grade year. Historically, the first day back to school would be an exciting event for him - - a day filled with reuniting with old school friends, hearing about their summers, and figuring out what classes they will have this year, and with who (or 'with whom' if you prefer).

It was fairly routine as the sounds of locker doors slamming shut and hysterical laughter would be returning to the halls of PFHS. But this day was very different for them because this was the first time the entire graduating class would be gathered in one place. Pecan Falls had two middle schools, North and South; so when the tenth graders merge at the high school, they finally got to see all sophomores at once. Half of these students would not know the other half as the year began.

In short, it would be a bit of a thrill.

But if someone had taken the time to stop and ask Billy, he would have bored us all to death with an unending parade of complaints. These complaints primarily fell into three categories, all of which we will address shortly. As the reader, you may reserve the right to your own opinions concerning whether or not Billy is justified in his self-inflicted agony. Nevertheless, the events in this story should bring about a transformation that will hopefully please the reader (not to mention Billy's friends, family, and whoever else has to put up with his nonsense).

If we could peer inside some of these houses on this particular morning, we would find a wide variety of goings-on. For instance, Clayton Peck, one of Billy's closest friends, was carefully placing his favorite running shoes into his ever-present backpack. You yourself may have friends like Clay. This young man stands quite tall for his age - - with his uncontrollable red hair. His clothes do not truly fit him well because he had just hit another growing spurt over the summer (hopefully, the last one for a while since he is already man-sized). Typically, most kids try to squeeze in some shopping time for new clothes just before the school year started up. Normally, his mother would have taken him shopping for new school clothes as well, but that was not an option this year. The shoes that he was loading up were among the most expensive items that he owned. He quickly greeted his mother and hopped on his bike for school. The bike was an old bike that was given to him by his buddy Mike (an unintentional rhyme, I promise you). But it was a good bike – now that he had grown into it – and he took very good care of it. Honestly, it really needed to be in tiptop shape anyway because it was quite a distance from their home all the way to the school. And that is how he got around.

He had no lunch and he has had no breakfast.

In a home on the more fashionable side of Pecan Falls, Chloe Chastain (yes, *that* Chloe Chastain) opened the door of her room carefully. She did not want to make a sound. With shoes in hand, she tiptoed down the carpeted staircase in her usual mismatched socks, her fingers gracefully giving her balance against the ornate railing. Her house was rather large considering that it was just her and her dad living there. She stopped just as soon as the dining room door came within view. She surveyed the situation with laser beam precision.

And there he sat. Her dad, Gregory Chastain, was at the table with his usual coffee and toast, his mind buried deep down within the dimensions of his newspaper. If she is caught, he might have some outdated view about her attire. So this was her big chance. Her goal: to make it safely across the spacious entryway of their house undetected.

She carefully made for the front door. With her hands firmly guiding the knob, she managed to open it without the betrayal of a squeaky hinge. Success. It helped that her dad was listening to the morning news on the radio.

Their fights were the stuff of legends. He was certainly not physically abusive, but father and daughter knew how to abuse each other verbally.

And the last thing she wanted on the first day of school was to get into yet another argument. She sat on the front steps, slipped her shoes on, and jumped into the car that she got on her birthday earlier that summer. So off she went, leaving dear old dad to wonder if she were even coming downstairs.

Elsewhere in this town, Clay's best friend Mike Hairston balled up his trash and tossed it in the air with the perfect trajectory needed for his goal. "Swish." It completed its beautiful arc squarely in the trash can. "And the crowd goes wild!"

"You had better grab your lunch and go, unless you want *me* to go wild." His mother was ready to get him out of the house at long last. She had work to do.

Mike's dad looked up from his breakfast. "Getting ready for the basketball tryouts?"

"Oh, no." He shook his head playfully. "The question is, 'Are *they* ready for *me*?'"

His parents laughingly reacted to his self-confidence, bordering on arrogance.

Mike rushed over and grabbed his lunch and turned to face his mom. "Did you put in extra chips and fruit drink?" This was a question he asked practically every school day.

"Of course; I've been doing that for years now."

"Bye, mom. Gotta go. Clay thinks that he's going to beat me to school." Mike kissed his mother, gave his dad a quick fist-bump, and raced for the door.

His mom looked at him curiously. "Are you really in that much of a hurry to get to school?"

A snarky grin appeared on his face. "Pffff! Not really. I just want to get there before Clay. That's all." Out the door he went.

"Be good today," Mrs. Hairston yelled. But it was doubtful that he heard her due to all the barking coming from their dozen or so dogs.

By this time, Billy was out of the shower and dressed; so this would be a more appropriate time to catch up with the Harris'. His dad, William Harris Sr., had just completed the knot on his tie (*Third time's the charm,* he thought to himself) and walked into the kitchen. Billy was working his way to the bottom of his cereal bowl. Diane, his mom, was making herself some instant oatmeal and instant coffee. William grabbed his usual banana, piece of toast, and water bottle.

"I'm showing off that house today, the one on Maple …" Diane began to talk about her plans for that day. As a real estate agent, she did nicely. Her outfit was professional, but comfortable.

Billy was not exactly following his parents' conversation, an almost impossible task anyway considering the constant thumping coming from that horrible old clothes dryer in the next room. The dryer seemed to be an extension of the rest of the house - - old and stupid. Billy hated the house and the dryer with equal passion. As always, his thoughts returned to his troubles. But he was able to spring back to reality when he heard a gentle knock on their door.

Billy's best friend, Curtis Baker, walked over from his house a few doors down. They have been giving Curtis a ride to school for years. This time-honored tradition was actually running out of time since Curtis would be sixteen-years-old in a couple of weeks and would no doubt be driving himself to school soon enough. "Hey! Anybody home?" That was his usual greeting whenever he knew that he could just open the door and march right on in.

"Certainly not," Billy protested. "You'll just decide to get comfortable and then we'll all be late for the first …" Billy stopped himself nearly in midsentence. His tone changed as he began again. "Wait a minute. Yeah, that's a good idea. Why don't you come in, Curtis, and make yourself at home? We'll get some pancakes started and be nice and late for school. So, HA!"

"Very funny." William was slightly amused. Billy and Curtis were very funny. And when they got together with Mike and Clay, the parents could usually expect some hilarious mayhem.

The four boys have been the best of friends going way back. With two white guys (namely Billy and Clay) and two black guys (Curtis and Mike), William once said that their quartet friendship reminded him of a music group called Booker T and the MG which consisted of two black men and two Caucasian men. A short time later, he had Billy listen to a few of their classic songs. They were okay - - for 'old people music.'

"Let's get going," William said.

"Did you make two sandwiches for my lunch?"

With inquisitive eyebrows, Diane handed him the bagged lunch. "Yeah, yeah. But I don't know where you put it all. You teenage boys have the appetite of a black hole."

"We'll burn it off fast enough," Curtis added.

"Bye, mom." Billy led Curtis out the door and off they went to the truck.

William shrugged his shoulders and winked at Diane. "It's a little early yet, but it appears that we're leaving for school now," he mumbled with a mouth full of toast. "Go figure." He picked up his briefcase and keys, kissed his wife, and soon found himself in his well-seasoned truck. It was not exactly a clunker, but it certainly was not new. It made a loud squealing sound as he backed out of the driveway. Billy used to call it the *Gray Goat* as a joke, but now all he thought about was how embarrassing it was to be seen in it. That fan belt must have grabbed the attention of everyone on their street each time they went anywhere. So not only was the *Gray Goat* an eyesore, but it was also an *earsore* (if we are allowed to make up a word).

It was mentioned earlier that there are three (3) main reasons why Billy was not excited about this school year. The first reason was that he just had his birthday. And it was not that he had a dislike for birthdays; it was simply the positioning of his birthday in the calendar. He was officially the youngest member of his class, and by quite a wide margin. Practically everyone else in his grade would be turning sixteen at some point during the school year. At the earliest, Billy would have to wait for nearly an entire year before he will legally be able to drive to school on his own. He would often imagine everyone in the parking lot laughing at him while his dad delivered him to school each day like a little kid. How lame. It would be one thing if his dad was cool - - but he was not. Absolutely not.

William climbed into the driver's seat and put on his seatbelt. His dark hair showed hints of gray, but it was the gray in his beard that betrayed his forty-something years. Driving down their street, he spoke up. "Curtis, are you ready to start the tenth grade?"

Curtis looked up at him and smiled. "I think so, Mr. Harris." He then glanced down at his watch. "But if I'm not, I've only got about thirty-five minutes or so to get myself ready."

William chuckled lightly and fired back, "You'll be fine. There is nothing scary about Pecan Falls High School. And if you are a little scared, just remember what it says in First Peter 5:7: 'Casting all your care upon him; for he careth for you.'"

Of course, Billy silently moaned in his thoughts. *Right on cue.* Mr. Harris had a quote for everything - - and usually it was from the Bible. Billy was so sick of it. Could he have just one normal conversation with his dad without being thrown verses from the Bible? Billy had nothing against the Bible naturally; it was the way that his dad quoted from it all the time. That was something that you would never catch the other dads doing. Just one more weird trait out of many ...

They went on for a few miles and finally arrived in the parking lot of the school. Mr. Harris pulled in and came to a stop. Billy knew exactly what to expect so he thought about popping out of the truck as soon as it stopped. But here it came, one last quote.

"Before you get out," Mr. Harris began, "I want to remind you both about what it says in Proverbs 3:7. 'Be not wise in thine own eyes: fear the LORD, and depart from evil.'"

Whatever. Just let me out of this ugly truck already before anyone sees me.

Both boys climbed out and thanked him for the lift. But Mr. Harris just stayed put in the parked truck. He opened a book and began to read for a few minutes. What a nerd. What a total nerd.

The school courtyard was not officially crowded yet, but there were quite a number of students already present. An undeniable spark of electricity filled the air as the kids greeted each other. Their excitement was something very real, but difficult to define. Maybe it was just the idea of returning to a regular schedule and the routine of being involved in activities with each other again: football, homecoming, and that sort of thing. Getting back to normal might be a welcome change of pace.

"Well, well, well. Look who decided to arrive!" The boys' faces lit up when they heard this familiar voice. They turned to see Mike Hairston walking their way. Clay Peck was trailing behind him. "We were about to think that you two goons weren't going to show up."

Mike was outgoing and fun, the human equivalent to a fireworks show. Clay was the quiet, sensible, and reliable friend. The four of these boys have been the best of buds since they began school. In addition, they seemed to get along with just about everyone else. They may not have made the best grades in town, but teachers often looked forward to seeing them come into their classrooms.

Clay chimed in after Mike. "Yeah, we've been here waiting on the both of you."

Curtis spoke up with confidence. "Yeah? Well, we're here now so let's get this party started. How does this whole sophomore thing work out anyway?"

"Man, I don't know yet." Mike looked back at Curtis. "I've got to try it on first and walk around in it for a while. But so far, it is looking okay. I know that we aren't seniors and don't come anywhere close to ruling the school, but this year is going to be way different than what we are used to."

A quizzical look came across Clay's face. He turned to look at Mike. "Huh? Why is that? Are you planning on doing anything differently?"

A big grin crept across Mike's face. "You bet! I have decided to turn over a new leaf and be nice this year. I am going to stop making fun of people for the little things that they can't help." He turned to face Billy. "Billy, you should really enjoy hearing that considering all the stuff that is wrong with you. Dude, you're a natural target." Mike laughed teasingly.

That playful joke went way above Billy's head. He was only halfway listening to the conversation anyway. His time was being spent looking back and forth scoping the scene as if he was searching for someone. He became suddenly conscience of the others looking at him so he snapped out of it.

Mike turned to Curtis and gestured over toward Billy. "What's *his* problem?"

"Never mind him. He brought his own personal raincloud to school this morning. See?" He pointed at the space above Billy's head.

Mike laughed. "What's new about that? Sometimes Billy is in a funk. Sometimes he's not. Sometimes, the soup is hot. Sometimes, it's cold."

As always, thoughtful Clay grew concerned. "So what's the matter, Billy?"

Billy rejoined the conversation. "Think about it, Clay. How exactly would you feel?" There was a slight hint of frustration in his voice.

"About what?"

Curtis took over for Billy. "He's busy moping about who his English teacher will be this year. He isn't exactly jumping for joy over it."

Mike reacted instantly. "Phffff! Whatever."

Curtis kept talking without interruption. "But in this dinky little town, there is just no way around it." Turning to Billy, "So you might as well make the most of an awkward situation. You never know, this may turn out to be a blessing for you."

Clay shrugged his shoulders. "Personally, I think it would be cool."

Mike kicked in. "It IS cool! Everything is cool. Just you wait, Billy. It'll be better than fine. It will be stellar."

"That is *exactly* what I've been telling him." Curtis laughed and made a wide gesture toward Billy.

Of all classes, Billy was the least excited about his English class - - and it was not the class itself. It was the teacher. All of this talk about his unfortunate teacher situation was beginning to grate on his nerves a bit. He knew in his heart that the others were right. In this tiny town, *everyone* in the tenth grade has had this man for a teacher. But there was no way that anyone could force Billy to like it. That was not going to happen.

Mike gathered that Billy was getting a little steamed at the direction that this conversation was going and decided to change the subject. He reached up behind Clay and shook the back of his neck as he spoke. "Not only that, but our man Clay here is going to blow them all away at track this year. Just wait and see. When everyone else crosses that finish line, Clay will be sitting there waiting for them with his feet propped up and polishing his new trophies."

The others agreed and began high-fiving each other.

Curtis became interested. "So the coach has finally seen you run?"

Half embarrassed, Clay rolled his eyes a little. "Yeah."

Mike spoke up for his best friend. "Dude! The coach had his eye on him since before Christmas last year. Coach Holton actually came to him! Clay didn't even have to ask. None of us even said a word. It was awesome. And when he came, Clay was running like a hot desert wind!"

Curtis plopped his hands down to his sides. "See? And you were worried about it all this time. We told you. We *all* told you. When are you ever going to learn?"

Clay swayed back and forth a little bit. "Yeah. You guys were right.

It's so cool. Everything is falling into place. This is going to be the best year ever."

The guys liked talking about Clay because it made him feel slightly uncomfortable. When they teased him, his ears would turn bright red with embarrassment.

But now Clay saw an opportunity to redirect the conversation back over to Billy. "And everything will work out for you too. You'll see." He gave Billy a light punch on the shoulder.

Clay was excellent at that. He was the source of support and optimism in the group. And he filled those shoes nicely. Of the four of them, Clay was easily the most likeable, the most concerned, and the most positive. Mike was the loud clown. Curtis was loyal and practical, usually pointing out things that the others did not consider. And Billy …? Well, Billy was just Billy, a walking/talking mess.

Billy was not convinced by Clay's lovely words and hopeful attitude. "Yeah. Whatever."

Mike looked up at a clock on the side of the building. "Come on. We got to get going before we're late."

Honestly, they still had a good twelve minutes before class started, but there was no reason for them to just stand outside – not when they could be grabbing a good seat - - away from the front. All four of them had the same first class together: English, go figure. Billy's stomach turned at the very idea of it. He thought about trying to fake an illness on the first day of school. … and the second. … and the third. There was no way he could pull that off. For starters, he was not exactly a dishonest kind of guy. And in addition, his parents would get wise to him instantly.

The other boys went on while he stood there for a moment, lost in his melancholy. Maybe this would be a good time to mention the second reason why this school year was going to be awful for Billy. As it turns out, his family was not exactly the most …

Hold that thought. We have to stop the story here for just a moment. Someone had unintentionally caught Billy's eye. The young man had spent all this time subconsciously looking around for her. And there she was: Chloe Chastain, in person. She was the undisputed queen of her class. It would come as no surprise if even the kids from Pecan Falls North Middle School had heard of her.

She seemed to move in slow motion. Music followed her as she walked. The colors, the scents, the sounds, everything was taken to the next level whenever she walked by. Now Billy can stop looking all around the place. He finally found her.

Chloe came to the school at Christmas break last year when she moved to Pecan Falls to live with her dad. Billy was instantly smitten with her. She was constantly on his mind. Technically, they have never met. He somehow lacked the courage to introduce himself. On top of that, her dad was one of the wealthiest people in town, employing a sizable percentage of Pecan Falls' residents and other folks throughout the county with his grandfather's industry. The bankable question here is: How does a guy like Billy meet up with a girl like Chloe? Under ordinary circumstances, that would never happen.

Her best friend, Bree, was ever by her side. A host of the more well-to-do boys found themselves on the receiving end of her flirtatious nature as the two ladies made their way through the halls of the school. Chloe seemed to take it all in her stride, talking to Bree and entertaining the boys from her own social class. At this school, sometimes your friends were handed to you by how much money your folks had. But fortunately, that was not always the rule. Case in point: Mike and Clay were best friends and they were from two totally different family incomes.

Actually, this would be a good time to rejoin the story. Chloe, Bree, and these dozen or so rich boys gave Billy a gentle reminder of the second reason why this school year was doomed before it truly started. They all belong to the snooty upper class – and Billy did not. If family wealth were a high-rise apartment building, they were all up in the stratosphere somewhere and Billy felt like he was down in the basement – alone, forgotten, and sitting next to a pile of old rags and empty boxes of laundry detergent. But he remained hopelessly stuck on this girl and he knew it. He was also fairly certain that she would not even give him the time of day - - but he did fantasize about it frequently enough. Billy let out a big sigh and decided to move on. *Does she even know that I exist?* he asked himself. *I doubt it.*

Billy started to make his way to his English class. The boys were probably there now anyway. This school year was already DOA. He thought, *Maybe I could run away and hop onboard a train. I hear Virginia is nice this time of year.*

No sooner did he turn around but the third reason for this year being awful was staring at him directly in the eyes. These eyes of his fell onto one of the fliers on a nearby bulletin board. It was merely an advertisement for the Pecan Falls High School Chess Club. No big deal. But the problem was that it featured a picture of his English teacher's face. His English teacher was potentially the nerdiest specimen in this town. This Chess Club flier featured the face of none other than Mr. William Harris Sr. - - Billy's dad. And Billy had him for first period. He had dreamed of fitting in with the cool crowd, or at least being a *somebody* this year. But with his dad as the English teacher/Chess Club Faculty Advisor, there was no chance of that happening. He had better odds swimming the Atlantic.

CHAPTER 3

HOMEROOM

While Billy was dragging his feet over to his first period class, let us just briefly recap. Behold, the first day of school and everyone was more or less excited - - except Billy. We mentioned that his thoughts have been taken over by three primary 'problems' that seemed to sweep over him for the new school year. The first one that we presented was the idea that he is the youngest student in his class, which means simply that he will be the last to drive (assuming that everyone in his class obtains a driver's license at some point during the year - - an unlikely event, but try telling that to Billy). Next was the fact that he seemed to be stuck on the richest girl in his grade, Chloe Chastain. He was solidly convinced that she would not give him so much as a glance due to his family's apparent lack of material wealth (which may be closer to the truth actually - - but if that were indeed true, it would tell us more about *Chloe's* nature than it does about *his*). Lastly, he is upset because his chess-playing, Bible-quoting, nerdy father just so happens to be his English teacher this year – an experience that will be starting in a few short minutes. Poor baby.

So when he would look at himself in the mirror, a truly cursed boy would be looking back at him. To you and me, his troubles may sound silly and petty; but to him, they were very important. That forces us to wonder if our own problems look petty from an outside observer - - but this book is not about us (directly), so on with the story …

With a great deal of reluctance, Billy entered the classroom. He scoped around. Some desks were already occupied and others were filling up quickly. Over by the windows on the far side of the room, he could see his three friends saving him a seat and waving him over. He looked at the front of the classroom and there sat his dad, looking at something through his reading glasses quietly. The name 'Mr. William Harris' had been drawn on the marker board in his dad's all-too-familiar, left-handed (and remarkably neat) handwriting. Billy sighed. *Well, here I am finally face to face with the situation I have dreaded all summer long*, he thought. *I will now be known as Mr. Harris' son. Before the day is out, a prominent member of the 'proud crowd' will probably write 'Loser' on my forehead with a permanent marker – and in full view of everyone. I'm sure that this entire nightmare will seem funny to me when I'm grown. ... if I survive.*

SIDE NOTE: A classmate could probably write the entire Preamble to the Constitution on Billy's forehead and no one would know. His bangs were quite long and fell prey to earth's gravitational pull – like curtains for the eyes. He should still try to enjoy having hair while he was able since all the men in his mother's family were decidedly bald. But maybe we should ask ourselves the same question that was on his mind: Would he find all of this funny when he is grown? Answer: When he is grown, he will probably have other things on his mind rather than how his dad was his teacher back in the day.

"Billy! Over here!" Curtis was flagging him down, standing and waving his arms around like some shipwreck survivor on an island.

Billy thought about the unwelcome attention Curtis drew. Just to get him to stop if nothing else, he made his way across the room, plopping himself down into one of the seats. He sat behind Mike against the wall. The windows on that wall provided Mike and Billy with a perfect view of the trees and the nearby hills. The bad part was that he might struggle to stay awake when that sun beat down on him. Curtis was next to Billy and Clay sat in front of Curtis. Together, they formed a tight defensive box, a phalanx ready for academic defense.

Curtis looked at Billy and frowned. "What's been chewing you? Still all weirded out about your dad?"

Billy's reaction had a sharp and ugly sound. "What do you think?!" He looked up and gestured toward his dad. "This is so stupid and embarrassing. Did you see that ridiculous Chess Club flier out on the board? Why does my dad feel the need to put his geeky face on stuff?"

William Harris sat motionless as he read. In his mid-forties, he still had all of his hair. It was mostly dark with just a hint of grayness about it. Most of his gray had settled in a goatee. On this day, he had forgotten to trim it before school and it was showing some unusual length off of his chin. He actually looked rather youthful for his age (probably due to clean living), but the constant stream of teenagers coming in and out of his classroom would only see him as *old*.

"Just look at him," Billy added. "With all that gray in his beard, he is starting to look like a Schnauzer."

Clay slowly got to his feet and was gawking out the window. "Whoa. Guys, check out the sweet ride." Before he could finish his sentence, the others could hear the purr of the engine as a car pulled into a nearby parking spot. Billy and Curtis chimed in with a similar reaction.

"Whoa."

"Nice."

Mike squinted his eyes as he peered outside. "Who is that?"

One of Pecan Falls' wealthiest students climbed out of his new candy-apple red European import. From head to toe, Wesley looked like someone had spent a great deal of money on his wardrobe. Hair perfect. No trace of acne. The girls were always talking about him. In many ways, he was the guy that the others wanted to be; but even then, most would just settle for having the car. This is the guy who seemed to have it all. He would definitely be the guy who gets the girl if this were an 80's movie.

Curtis did not say anything about it, but he noticed that the only thing missing was the arrogant walk. One might think that a conceited swagger would come with the part; but Wesley failed to project an aura of self-confidence. In fact, his walk could nearly be described as humble. Most of his classmates could not see it through all that money. Underneath it all, he felt that this family's financial abundance created a huge gulf between him and most of the other students. Sadly, he was right.

But in the world of the sophomore class, Wesley was still one of PFHS's most eligible bachelors.

Mike was not positively impressed. "Phffff. Oh, him. Figures. Rich boy alert." With a great deal of sarcasm, he began to speak to the car's occupant knowing that his words were never going to cut through the glass and land on Wesley's ears. "Okay, we all see you now. Bravo. You can stop waving your money around in front of us." Mike sat back down in his seat as he turned his back to the window. "It is a pity that this isn't springtime. I could take a can of soda and pour it on the front of his hood. Then after school, there would be so many bees buzzing about his car, he wouldn't be able to distinguish it from a bee hive." Mike let out a slight laugh and sat back in his seat. "In fact, make a note of it, Clay, and we'll do that come next April."

Clay smiled. "Mike, you don't mean that."

Billy turned around and sat down in his seat also, glancing up at his dad. *This is going to be miserable*, he thought. But someone walking in suddenly caught his eye. He experienced a sudden rush of panic. "Oh no. There she is."

Clay turned to see. "There who is?"

"Chloe Chastain. Should I say something to her? What should I say?" Billy spoke now in almost a whisper - - an unnecessary precaution since everyone else was being loud.

Curtis raised an eyebrow. "Nothing. She is completely out of your league. Don't take this the wrong way, my friend, but she is caviar and you are ketchup."

Mike nodded in agreement. "Dude, steer clear of her type. She is the queen of trouble."

At that moment, something new occurred to him. His face went pale with end-of-the-world fright. "Oh man! I wonder if there is ANY possible way to keep her from knowing that her English teacher is my dad. I don't see any reason for her to know that. I wonder if that little known fact could just stay buried."

Mike's comment did not offer much hope. "I think your chances are quite high considering that *she doesn't even know you exist*."

Curtis' voice nearly matched Mike's. "I doubt it. I mean it could mathematically happen - - but you are kinda busy making a thing out of it. Why don't you just relax and see what happens? You know, you're being pathetic over this whole thing." The school bell rang in the middle of Curtis' sentence.

Mr. Harris casually rose from his seat and stood before the class. "Alright. That's the bell." The students began to hush as the teacher greeted the students. "Hello, sophomores. Allow me to welcome each of you to

Pecan Falls High School. As you already know, I am Mr. William Harris and I teach tenth and eleventh grade English." A sneaky, but warm, smile crept across his face. "I know that all of you are very anxious to get back in the classroom after a long and exhausting summer."

A few students gave a nearly silent chuckle. If Billy heard any laughs, he would think that they were laughing *at* his dad rather than at his joke. *Ugh! My dad thinks he is soooo funny. My life is such a tragedy*, he thought. *I seriously wonder if anyone has literally died of embarrassment.* Sitting there in his seat, Billy imagined a team of policemen standing over his dead body lying in the middle of the classroom. As someone covered him with a blanket, a medical examiner turned to the other officers and said, "This has to be the most acute case of embarrassment I have ever seen."

"But before we get started, I will take roll." William looked curiously around at the students. "I already know a few of you. The rest of you must be patient as I learn your names. You know the drill. I'll call your name and you reply appropriately. Timothy Aldridge?"

"Here."

"Curtis Baker?"

"Here."

Billy was momentarily startled at Curtis' loud reply. He should have expected Curtis' name to be called early on, but he was too occupied with his mental complaining to anticipate the sound of his friend's voice.

"Chloe Chastain?"

"Here." The sound of her voice was like that of an angel to Billy. He did not know whether to be terrified or raptured.

Billy's dad continued to call name after name. The students replied. Some students wanting to be different replied with "Present." One bold young man replied with "Yo!" But Billy was ignoring them. He was shifting in his seat trying to get a better look at Chloe Chastain. At one point, he was leaning forward with his chest almost laying across the top of his desk. In doing so, he accidently knocked a few school supplies off and onto the floor. Honestly, few people even noticed. But he falsely felt that everyone was looking at him - - including Chloe. *Rats! She is only going to know me as the guy who dumped his stuff in the floor.*

At that awkward moment, his dad called his name from the roll book. "William Harris, Jr.?"

Billy was still picking up a couple of items that he dropped when his name was called. For a split-second, the timing of his name being called out looked like a dad publically chastising his son for his clumsiness, although he knew even then that that was not the case.

Billy was again embarrassed. Any chance of him distancing himself from his freak father had just poofed into smoke. It will probably be the headlines of whatever school paper PFHS may have. "Here." His cry was squeaky and barely audible. He must have taken his voice out of gear for a moment. He tried a second time, but louder. "Here!"

Curtis leaned over and whispered to him. "Smooth, William Harris, Jr."

Clay looked confused. "*William*? I thought your first name was *Billy*."

Billy looked across at him. *Are you being serious?*

A few more names were called. Further down the list, Mr. Harris called out, "Wesley Porterfield the Third?"

As Mr. Harris called out the name, the well-dressed young man who drove up in the sports car opened the door and stepped in. Mike disgustedly thought that it looked like Mr. Harris was giving him a big introduction as he walked in the door. It might have made a nice entrance, but the young man looked a little nervous when the class looked over at him.

"Uh … That's me. Uh … *here*."

Chloe smiled and her face began to blush a little.

"Mr. Porterfield, the bells ring at 8:30. Today is the first day, so I'll let it go. But be on time tomorrow."

"Yes sir."

"Have a seat please. There are two here in the front and one there on the side." Mr. Harris continued to call out the roll as Wesley inched his way over to the seat at the side of the room.

Billy looked as though he were in pain. *Oh yeah. This school year looks like it is off to a smashing start. How could this get any worse?* His thought was about twenty seconds too soon.

Finished with calling the roll, Mr. Harris put the roll book down and spoke as he turned the corner around his desk. "Before we jump into things, does anyone have any questions for me?"

Mitch, a popular football player on the second row, raised his hand and Mr. Harris called on him. "Last year, the teacher made us read a couple of books for class. Are we going to have to do that this year?" Judging solely from his tone and facial expression, one may deduce that Mitch would rather not have to read anything at all.

"Oh yes. Two books and a play." The majority of the students let out this tired moan. "In fact, I'm going to pass out the first book right now." The moan got even louder and Mr. Harris picked up a box full of paperback books.

I don't know how it happened, but this day just got worse. I'll bet dollars for butter beans there isn't a single picture in any of these books.

Rather than announcing the title of the book, Mr. Harris made his way over to the young man who asked the question and handed him the first copy. He assumed – and rightfully so – that this guy would make the announcement to the rest of the class. And rather loudly.

The young man fell backward in his seat as he read the title out loud. "*Pride and Prejudice*?!" Nearly everyone in the room reacted negatively. One boy nearly collapsed onto the floor. The only exceptions were one boy in the back row who had wasted no time in going to sleep and two weird girls on the front row who excitedly stiffened their backs at attention, looked at each other with thrilling smiles, and silently started mock-clapping.

Mr. Second Row spoke up again. "Excuse me, Mr. Harris. But isn't this a girl book?"

Mr. Harris continued to pass out books as he seemed to be looking for a polite response. "I would say '*Yes, this is a girl book.*' But I would venture further to say that this is probably the most girl book you will ever read in school." More moaning followed. "I know that that is not exactly what you want to hear, but that is exactly why we are reading this one first. We're getting it out of the way. But to make up for it, we'll be reading Shakespeare's MACBETH around Christmas. You'll find some ugly witches, a few ghost sightings, and buckets of gore in that one. And for you guys out there, next semester we are reading Homer's *The Odyssey*." It sounded like that was supposed to get the boys excited; all it did was generate more moaning. "As always, we have a you-break-it-you-buy-it policy on these books. If they get destroyed or damaged while in your care, you'll have to replace them. I took some quick notes on where everyone is sitting. Plus, these books are all numbered, so I know who has which one. Many of you can download the book for free on your electronic devices.

Whatever is more convenient for you. If you choose to do so, you can then return this paperback copy once I have seen your device. Just so you know, I am actually quite familiar with ALL filmed versions of this story and have written the quizzes to feature things not brought out in the various films and videos - - so you cannot fool me by seeing the movie. … although I guess that they could be used as helps." He had just finished passing out the books. He put the box on the floor next to his desk and turned back toward the students. "But who knows? You may decide that you like *Pride and Prejudice* after all. It has happened before."

Billy wanted to vanish. Maybe he would get lucky. Perhaps a member of the school staff would interrupt class and tell his dad that there was a bad mistake and that he would have to switch classes.

His dad continued. "In addition, you can also expect weekly vocab tests, two research papers, and oodles of grammar."

Clay leaned over toward Mike. In a low tone, he asked, "Are we being punished?"

Mike wrinkled his nose and looked back at him. "Dude. What if this were our *easiest* class?"

Clay rolled his eyes as he settled back into his chair.

Billy had heard from older students just how awesome of a teacher his dad was. The report was that he was funny, he really knew his stuff, and he made it easy for the students to learn. Strangely enough, a high number of them even used the word *cool* to describe him. Either these kids were pulling his leg or they were delusional. There was no way that Billy could see these pleasant rumors as being true. All he could see was his nerdy dad. Each minute brought with it more agony. His face grew hot and was turning several shades of red. Everything that his dad stated made him want to crawl deeper and deeper into a hole.

His only relief came at last. The bell rang and the students scrambled to their feet to leave. Billy did not even wait for his friends and disappeared as soon as he could. Avoiding eye contact with Chloe, he made a direct path to his locker. While he was fooling around with his stubborn lock, he sensed someone's presence next to him. He looked up to find Justin standing there.

Justin was a distant friend of his, like a satellite friend. They didn't hang out, but they certainly knew each other. He was a tall, skinny, handsome-ish, goofy kind of guy with big blonde hair that hung down nearly over his eyes in sheepdog fashion.

"Hey, Billy."

"Hey, Justin." If Billy sounded less than thrilled, it is because he was not yet planning on talking to anyone. He was still recovering from what he thought was that horrible ordeal called 'first period.'

"So, what is it like having your dad as a teacher?"

"What?" Billy was surprised. Was this Justin's idea of diplomacy? Did he leave his manners and common courtesy in his other clothes? "What kind of a question is that?"

Justin did not understand. "What do you mean?"

Billy's lock finally unlocked for him. He opened his locker door and turned looking at Justin directly in the eyes. "I haven't seen you in months. And now here you come along with 'What's it like having your dad as a teacher?'"

Justin raised his hands as if Billy had pulled a gun on him. "Nothing, man."

Billy turned back to his locker and began getting books out for his next class. "Because if you're looking for a fight, you can go pick on someone else."

Justin started to look frustrated. "Come on, man. Just answer the question, please."

Billy was intrigued. What was Justin up to? "Why? Why do you need to know? Are you like working for the school paper or something?"

Justin was reluctant to answer. Finally, he slouched down and admitted, "Because my girlfriend asked me to find out."

Billy shook his head with a crooked grin on his face. "Huh? Let me get this straight. It isn't really *you* who wants to know. It's your nosey girlfriend? I knew that she is usually all into other people's business, but really?"

Justin started to relax a little and smiled. "That's right. And I told her that since I knew you that I could find out all subtle-like. You know. … under the radar." Justin was trying to act smooth while he was speaking. He failed.

Billy rolled his eyes and gave a soft laugh. "Yeah. You have a gift for being discreet. It stinks."

Justin straightened in a defensive pose. "Huh? I stink at being discreet?"

A serious look fell across Billy's face like a heavy curtain. He looked directly at Justin once again and said in a slow, deliberate tone, "No. Go back and tell your girlfriend that having my dad as a teacher stinks."

CHAPTER 4

FROZEN DINNER

Early that particular evening, he was glad to be safe at home and away from all the drama that comes with high school. But just because he was back in his domestic sanctuary, that did not mean that he was sitting on easy street. Perhaps soon, he could stop complaining and start having a little fun (especially after he learns the truth about who he is). But for now there was still the ordeal of getting through dinner with his mom's prying questions. Obviously, he knew that she meant well; she was just being a mom. Nevertheless, he had no desire to relive this horrible day through a series of inquiries, no matter how innocent her intentions were. He wondered if this was how a dartboard felt just before the darts started flying.

"So Billy, how was your first day of tenth-grade?" There in the dining room, Diane kept looking down at her plate. By this time, the whole family was digging into some of her tasty lasagna with garlic toast on the side.

There it was. The conversation starter was thrown out like an angler casting his line. He decided that he would not to look up from his plate either. Maybe if he simply answered the question quickly, he could avoid any long term conversational commitment. He chose the quick and easy method – few details, fewer words, over and out.

In retrospect, it might have been a good idea for him not to say anything at all. We are only a few short chapters into this book and all Billy has done thus far is gripe about stuff. And over what? So what if he could not drive before anyone else in his grade? And who really cares about how rich or how poor his family is? And what is the big deal about his dad being his teacher anyway? And honestly, reading a classic nineteenth century novel is not going to kill him. He needed to get over it. Besides, no one wants to hear all that complaining. If he kept this up, everyone reading this book is eventually going to put it down and find something else to read. Then they would be missing out on all the cool stuff that happens to him later.

Besides, there are many worse things that can happen to a guy. In fact, that list could get rather long quickly if we pursued that idea. For instance, he could be chased all over the school by a deadly robotic woodpecker with bionic wings and laser beam eyes. Let's be practical. Someone could light a stick of dynamite and force him to swallow it – after all, classmates can be cruel. Or he could find himself out in his own front yard in his underwear in full view of his neighbors. *Okay. That actually happens later - - but no more spoilers after this.

Billy answered his mom's simple and polite question. "Fine." He had no intentions of telling his parents about not qualifying for the track team. This was just another disappointment on top of an already miserable day.

Diane looked up at Billy and then across at William. "That was scarcely informative. I was hoping for more details. Let's try that again." She cleared her throat in a theatrical fashion and then repeated herself as if it were a well-rehearsed speech. "So how was the first day of tenth grade?"

He was clearly not getting out of this one. But there was no way he was going to mention how awkward it was to be in a classroom with his own dad as the teach. It was bizarre enough just to have his dad in the same town - - driving around and stuff, flaunting his particular brand of shameful peculiarities, the undisputed champion of embarrassing weirdos. "Not so fine. I tried out for the track team today, but I didn't make the cut. I think I'm going to try to get on the basketball team with Mike tomorrow - - that is if the coach likes me."

In a reassuring voice that was anything but reassuring, William spoke up. "Well, if that doesn't pan out, you could always check out the Chess Club," he mumbled with a mouth full of bread.

"Yeah, dad. I know." He rolled his eyes. That would certainly do it. He could join the Chess Club and hang out with his dad and all the geeks of Pecan Falls High School. No thank you. That would be deliberately racing toward social suicide in high gear.

"Well, I'm not going to pressure you. But you are a strong player and you already love the game. I think you'd enjoy yourself. Plus, you might get a kick out of our colorful little group."

"Whatever. I just … don't … I mean they're probably all nice people and all that, don't get me wrong. It just sounds a little nerdy. No offense."

To Billy's relief, his dad did not take that the wrong way. "Please. Psalm 119:165 says, 'Great peace have they that love thy law and nothing shall offend them.' I understand. But you are always welcome to join us, just the same."

Why won't these people just be quiet? he thought to himself. Billy had had enough of this nonsense. Between his mom's nosey investigation and his dad's persistent needling, he wondered if he could just have a nice quiet dinner. It was time for a change.

"FREEZE!!" he yelled. Everything in the room stopped. His mom sat there frozen in time with her knife and fork cutting another bite of lasagna. He looked over at his dad who was making a hilarious face as he stopped chewing his food. He was also in mid-blink, which gave him a dull-eyed effect. Everything was instantly silent. Even the clock stopped making its usual noise; Billy had not even noticed that it was ticking at all until it had stopped. "Cool! Did I do that?" From all indications, his simple command had managed to stop time. Weird. He had never been able to do that before.

Billy got up from the table to check this out a little closer. He approached his mom and waved his hand in front of her face. No reaction. He did the same thing to his dad with the same effect. Neither of them appeared to be breathing. They were as still as statues. Just how far did this go? He wandered over to the window and looked outside. Mr. Baker was walking his dog right in front of their house, both in mid-step – frozen in place. Looking up, he saw a couple of birds frozen in mid-flight as if they were in a photograph. Returning to the table, he took another bite from his toast and thought about taking a picture of his dad's doughy face with his phone.

"Is there anything I can do for you?"

Billy's heart skipped a quarter note as he jumped out of his seat. He looked over in the kitchen and saw James, the butler from his earlier dream. "Dude! That's not even funny! You just scared the fire out of me!"

James' responded with as much sarcasm as he could without losing command of his butler image. "Begging your pardon, Master Billy, but it is *you* that keeps dragging me into your dreams and your daydreams."

"Is that what this is?"

"Look, I don't know. I just work here." He turned to go back into the kitchen.

Billy got up from his seat and began to follow him. "Well, how come I have a butler in all these dreams? Am I supposed to be rich or something? At least, in my dreams?"

"Why do you want to know? It isn't real."

"I'm asking because if I were actually rich in my dreams – and I suppose in these daydreams too – I wouldn't be sitting here subjecting myself to this boring line of questioning."

James had made his way over to a cake and began to cut it while Billy was talking. "Oh? And if you had great riches, just where would you be having dinner tonight? And with who?"

"What are you saying?"

James put the knife down and looked up at Billy. "Well? This is your fantasy. Make it happen."

The first thing Billy noticed was that he was suddenly outside on a gorgeous sunny day. He was sitting at a small circular table among many in an outdoor restaurant. He turned in his seat in an attempt to find out where he was. He discovered a thick network of five-story Mediterranean houses. The narrow streets were actually made up of dark greenish water with the occasional pedestrian bridge crossing these thin waterways. Long, skinny gondolas were gliding slowly through the water and were being manned by men in black and white striped shirts and operating long poles to push them along. The other tables in this dining area were occupied by beautiful young couples all focused tightly on each other. Every one of these couples looked like they could be the subject of a pukey made-for-TV movie that Billy's grandma was always watching. A small army of pigeons were on patrol looking for something to eat under the tables.

Softly, Billy said to himself, "Okay. I am either in Venice, Italy, or someone left the tub running."

He heard a feminine laugh. He turned back in his seat only to realize at that moment that Chloe was sitting across from him. Her eyes were smiling right back at him. She was dressed comfortably and looked like a million bucks. Actually in Italy, she would look like a million *lira*. That's not right either. On second thought, better make that a million *euros*.

Unsure of himself, Billy began to speak. "This is really cool. I've never been to Venice before. I've only seen it in movies. Was this my idea or yours?"

Chloe kept smiling the whole time, but looked at him with a sideways glance. "Well, as much as I would love to take credit for this, it wasn't my idea. But I simply love it. Thank you for bringing me here." She reached over and put her hand on his.

"Uh, it was nothing. Literally nothing."

She laughed again.

"I'm a little fuzzy on what has led us up to this point. Have we ordered yet?"

"Yes," Chloe replied in a flirty voice.

At this moment, James appeared at the table with something in each hand. "Alright. Here we are. Here is a salad for you ..." He laid one down in front of a delighted-looking Chloe. "And here is one for you, good sir." The other one was put in front of Billy. "It is at this point that I generally tell people to enjoy their salads, but I'm afraid that you won't have time to eat them. Sorry folks."

Billy did a double take. "Huh? We won't have time to eat them? Why not?"

"Because your mom is about to ask you another question, which means that this daydream is about to come to an end." He turned to Chloe. "My apologies to you, signorina."

Chloe was clearly disappointed and refused to look at James.

Billy was puzzled by all of this. "So what you are saying is that we really aren't here?"

"Uh ... no."

"And I do not have the power to freeze time."

"No. And in fact," James looked at his watch to start a countdown, "your mom will ask her next question in five, four, three ..." He only mouthed *two* and *one* like they do on live TV following a commercial break.

"So, do you have any classes with Curtis this year?"

Billy let out a depressing sigh as he continued picking at his food. "Yes. Three." He looked up at the ceiling fan as he went through the list. "We have English, Biology, and Spanish 1."

William butted in. "Ah, Spanish. That should prove to be very useful. And cool."

Billy was not easily convinced. "What is so cool about Spanish?"

"'What is so cool about Spanish?!' Always remember ..."

Oh no. Here it comes. Another display of dad's nerdiness.

"El camino al Corazón de una mujer esta escrito en español."

Billy rolled his eyes. *Great. He can even quote in other languages,* he thought to himself. He let out a big sigh, waited a few seconds, and then asked, "Is that from the Bible?"

"No. That would sound more like, 'En el principio era el Verbo, y el Verbo era con Dios, y el Verbo era Dios.'"

The sarcastic machine kicked on. "Oh yeah. I can totally tell the difference." Billy's face betrayed his thoughts of being surrounded by abnormal people.

William raised an eyebrow at his son, then turned back to Diane. "Just so you know, he gets his good looks from me, but his sarcasm comes from you."

His mom looked disturbed. "I don't think that you should be telling him that, that that you said earlier." Diane objected.

"And why ever not?"

"What if he goes around telling that to all his friends?"

Billy was nearing the end of his lasagna. He could only assume from her tone that his mom knew enough Spanish to understand all that - - whatever that was. He did not know what was said and he certainly could not repeat it even if he tried. "Mom, I honestly don't think that'll happen."

She added another comment. "Besides, your statement is not even true."

"It's okay, mom. I didn't understand a single word of it anyway."

William spoke up. "It is too true. It's very true."

"No. It isn't."

William faced Billy and leaned in a little as if he was telling him an important secret. "Well, it's *mostly* true."

Billy shrugged it off. "You couldn't prove it by me since I have no idea

41

what you even said!" Billy was completely okay with not knowing. He just wanted to move on at this point.

His mom interjected. "Well, *I* think that the road to a woman's heart is in Italian."

Billy had seen this odd behavior before. "Can we just change the subject please?"

William leaned toward Billy again and addressed him in a way that he could be heard by Diane. "Listen to my words, son. Listen, learn, and reflect. If you want to do well for yourself, do exactly what I did. Marry a girl with a big Italian family. The food is always *magnifico*."

Billy was now ready to beg. "Mom! Dad! I implore you! Can we *please* just change the subject?"

William picked up his glass to wash down some of Diane's yummy lasagna. But just before his drink reached his mouth, he managed to redirect the conversation with a simple statement. "Sure. Billy got his copy of *Pride and Prejudice* today."

Instantly, Billy regretted his request to change the subject.

Diane gasped long and loud. It was as if she was deliberately sucking all of the oxygen out of the dining room air. "*PRIDE AND PREJUDICE*?!"

Billy could feel it down in his sinews. A new can of worms just opened up.

"I looooooooove that book. You are going to enjoy it soooooo much." Diane's voice took the same tone it always did when she described some overpriced fancy French coffee or some new foofy bottle of expensive scented hand lotion.

Flatly, "Great, mom."

She found herself pointing to a stack of his books on the counter behind him. Right on top was the book in question. "Is that it? Ooo! Let me see!"

Whatever was I thinking? he asked himself. *I wasn't even TRYING to hide it. I know better than that.* Billy passed it to her and she handled it delicately - - like it was a baby bird.

"Awww. This was my all-time favorite book as a teenager. I once read it five times in one semester." She reverently passed the book back over to her son. "I just couldn't get enough of it. My mom eventually bought me a copy of *Jane Eyre* just to get me to read something else." Diane laughed lightly as she recalled these events of years gone by.

Billy calmly set it down on the table in front of him. But he seriously thought about poking the book deep down in the trash can – or maybe the garbage disposal – or the paper shredder. Maybe he could donate it to a local scout group who needs help starting a campfire.

William's voice had a very different tone about it. "Diane, this isn't helping him. In fact, your behavior is probably going to scare him away from the book."

Diane went back to her plate as if her behavior was perfectly normal. "Nonsense. I'm just glad that he has to read something wonderful in school this year."

Billy's eyes got wide and then returned to normal as he spoke. "Yep. Boy, am I lucky?!" There was definitely a hint of sarcasm there.

"What you could do," William leaned in, "is read it the way you did with *Animal Farm* last year. We'll order some pizza and have Curtis over and you two read it together. Or have Mike and Clay come over as well and the four of you all take turns. It'll keep you awake as you read. And it is far better than lying about having read it when you really didn't."

Billy gave a little chuckle. "Why don't I just invite the whole class over?"

Diane sat up as if a wonderful discovery had been made. "Why not? I don't care if you invite a few people over. If you want to make a big thing of it and if it helps you at quiz time, what's wrong with that?"

Hmmm, I might have to consider that, he thought to himself. *It really would be easier than reading it by my lonesome.* "May I please be excused from the table?"

William looked over at his plate. "Finish your drink and you can get up."

Billy reached for his drink but accidently knocked the glass over instead. His sweet tea poured right onto his copy of *Pride and Prejudice*. Billy leaped up from his seat to clean his mess. He pulled the book out of the puddle of tea and began to dab it with a paper towel. But it was too late to salvage the book. It had gotten too wet – and sticky. True, it was still readable; but how could he return the book to the school after it had been that wet. When it dried, it would be difficult to close or to stack up with the others.

William shook his head. "Well Billy, you remember the school policy. *You break it – you buy it.* When we're done here, I'll run you over to the book store."

Way to go, genius, he could hear him say in his own head. *Smooth move. The first day of school and I have already damaged school property. Not to mention a waste of sweet tea.*

CHAPTER 5

THE PRONOUN

About the same time that Billy was bathing his book with sweet tea, Wesley Porterfield the Third was looking around the house for his mom. He found her as she came down the stairs, keys in hand.

She was counted on to give her son the usual spiel. "I'll be spending tonight with my sister in Memphis and she will be taking me to the airport tomorrow. I'll be in Philadelphia all next week and then on to Florida. Your father will be in sometime tomorrow and will be here until the thirtieth. I'll be back sometime at the first of next month. You should be fine here tonight; but if you need anything, you can always call Juanita. You know where her number is."

Wesley's mounting disappointment was hard to mask. "I don't know why you have to go on this trip at all. Mom, why don't you just stay here with me?" What he did not say was that he felt the only reason why she was skipping town was to avoid being with her husband - - and as a result, she was going to miss spending time with Wesley.

She stopped walking toward the door, sighed, and turned to face him. "I know. This isn't very fair for you, is it?" She took a deep breath and glanced up at the ceiling as if the words that she was looking for were somehow glued up there. "Sometimes people just get along better if they don't have to see each other. But I want you to know that your father and I love you very much. And whatever happens is not because of anything that you did or didn't do ..."

For the next few minutes, Wesley listened patiently as his mom rambled on trying to make things right with her empty words. It was all the same patter, identical to the stuff he had already sat through a hundred times before. It played back like endless reruns of some ancient television show – and with about the same amount of feeling.

Her bags were already in the car and her mind was made up. She chattered some last minute instructions, climbed in her car, and drove off with Wesley standing helplessly in the doorway. Void of any signs of life, the house stood behind him. Logically, if a person were scared, there would be something to be scared of. In his case, it was the presence of nothingness that made him uncomfortable. The emptiness was as frightening as any tangible threat. Irony?

He felt he was part of a sentence with no subject and no verb. Just him in the middle, one little pronoun in the center of a blank page the size of the ocean. In search of a verb. Desperate for someone to read that page. Living a life that was grammatically incorrect.

He cursed softly and went back into their humongous house. The house itself was filled with all the cool stuff that his parents *thought* would make Wesley happy; but it was hard to feel happy amidst the deafening quiet. What good is any of this junk if there was no one to share it with?

So he went back to the pool table where he had been prior to his mom's departure. He picked up the pool cue and looked at it intensely. But rather than resuming his game, he felt something swell up inside him. Rage was irrupting from deep within. It was something that he could not seem to control - - something that he did not *want* to control - - something that was now controlling *him*. He brought both of his hands together at the base of the cue and brought it down like a club as hard as he could across the top of the pool table. The narrow end of the cue broke off at once and shot off somewhere toward his right. As the broken end bounced on the floor, Wesley had hit the top of the table again with what was left of the stick. He hit it a third time, each time cursing as the stick made contact with the table. In the process, he somehow cut his thumb. He set down the broken stick and looked curiously at the cut. His fury had left him just as quickly as it came.

This was not really like him at all. He was generally a mellow kid. Honestly, his own actions startled him for a moment. With shaking hands, he looked at the broken stick and the fresh nicks on the table. "Well, I guess I'll have to answer for this," he said to himself. But then he caught a glimpse of a picture frame on the fireplace mantle. The photo inside the frame had all three of them sitting around each other in a beautifully shaped triangle. The fake smiles on their faces seemed to tease him, even at this distance. He thought about it and shook his head. "Nah. They won't even notice."

There were bandages in the bathroom. After tending to the cut, he calmly returned to the pool table. Pieces of the cue stick were scattered about; so he gathered them up and stood them up in the trash. He again approached the pool table and casually racked the balls up for a new game. He selected an identical cue stick from the rack on the wall.

"Alright. You start," he said to no one. "Stripes or solids?" He leaned over and hit the cue ball. The familiar cracking sound of the impact was the only noise in the entire house.

Later that evening, the bookstore was not especially crowded when Billy and his dad arrived. The store itself would be closing inside a half-hour. William pointed out to Billy where the store would keep copies of *Pride and Prejudice.* This particular book was easy to locate. Not wasting any time, Billy rushed over to the shortest checkout line. He looked up and, to his astonishment, there she was. Chloe was walking past the store window. Naturally, Bree was with her. They must have been visiting the upscale clothing store next door.

"So who's the girl?" This rather harsh feminine voice came from behind the checkout counter.

Billy had not been paying attention and he suddenly realized that he was now up to the register. Fortunately, there was no crowd behind him.

"I said, 'Who's the girl?'" The checkout lady was looking right at him. She was an older middle-aged woman with way too much eye makeup, a raspy voice, and a name tag that said *Midge*. With a name like that, Billy thought that she might be married to a guy named *Vince* or *Ernie*, perfect bowling league names, probably stitched onto their bowling shirts in tight little ovals. Midge had a double chin. Her hair seemed to defy any one-color tradition. Her fingers sported more rings than Saturn and she smacked her gum as if this job was not particularly interesting. You could tell that she was probably high-maintenance emotionally and unquenchably nosey by nature. She looked like the type that could generate plenty of drama on social media.

Being caught off-guard, Billy stumbled over his reply. "Huh? Do what?" What was going on here? Could she have seen him staring at Chloe? Was he gawking at her and not being discreet about it? He did not even know this lady and here she was teasing him about Chloe.

"The girl? The one you are trying to impress?"

Billy decided to employ a bluff and see if it would work. "I don't know what you are talking about."

The lady began to scan the book's barcode. *"Pride and Prejudice.* Teenage boys don't generally come in here looking for a copy unless they lost a bet or there's some girl that they're trying to impress."

Billy gave out a nervous laugh and pretended to be cool. It may sound like a novelty, but he was going to try telling the truth this time. "No. It isn't like that. I need this for school."

The checkout lady's face returned to its previous lack of expression. "Sure thing. Whatever you say, Romeo." She then informed Billy what he would owe for the book.

Billy stood there not knowing what to say. He dug in his pocket and paid the lady, but he could not just let her presumptuous comment go unanswered. "No. Really. It is required reading." Even as the words were spilling out of his mouth, he was wondering why he was defending himself. He did not owe her an explanation. He was only there for a few seconds anyway, however long it would take to run in, buy a lousy book, and scram. He certainly was in no mood for this idiotic checkout counter small talk.

She poured the money down into the register drawer. "Hey, you don't have to worry about me. I don't judge." She loaded the book and the receipt into a flimsy plastic bag with the bookstore's name and logo on the side. As she held out the bag for him, he noticed her bright red fingernails. He wondered if that shade of red even existed in the natural world. He usually only saw that color on classic cars.

Unsure of how to react, he took the bag from her and darted for the door. *I hope I never have to come in here again*, he thought to himself. *That lady scares me.*

The door dinged as he walked out.

Chloe and Bree were heading into the diner next door. He wanted so desperately to follow them in and introduce himself. It is true that he had just finished eating at home, but this place had the all-time best ghost pepper cheeseburgers. He wanted to march in there and say something charming, to hear them laughing at his jokes, to be interesting and cool, and to become a part of their wonderful world. And there they were just a few feet away and going into the diner. And there he was. An awesome opportunity had just presented itself.

"Hey! Come on!" His dad had rolled the truck window down and was getting his attention. That's right. His uncool dad was with him. That ripped it right there. Fantasy over.

Oh no! The greater nightmare struck him. What if the girls actually saw him in public with his dad? In addition, he was their English teacher. And everyone knew that bumping into one of your teachers out in the world is weird.

Billy watched the girls laughing their way into the diner. Then he himself made his way over to his dad's ugly truck and climbed in. The passenger's door made that same horrible sound that it always made whenever it opened. It needed some kind of grease on the hinge. The motor finally rolled over the second time that his dad turned the ignition key. And it roared loudly - - and not by design.

Billy looked at the hole in the dashboard where a radio used to sit. He then looked down at his hands. He pulled the new copy of *Pride and Prejudice* out of the bag and peered at it. He was sure that it was supposed to be a good book, but he already had a rough idea that it was not something that he himself would enjoy.

Luckily, the girls never saw him. That was good. He would probably die from shame if they saw him climbing into that old truck with his dad, the English teacher.

Reality had once again played the cards that were dealt.

CHAPTER 6

THE PITY PARTY

Since before *time immemorial* (a.k.a. July 6, 1189), those throwing a pity-party have pulled up a chair only to discover that it is a table set for one. As touching as their sad story may be, no one wants to attend a party where the host is going on and on about their pathetic problems – especially if those problems really do not stack up. By remarkable contrast, there are some who live truly horrible lives and yet manage to lighten up the room with their sunny smile and marvelous attitude.

Fortunately for the reader, this coming-of-age fable contains so much more than just one enormous pity-party. In fact, Billy has no idea just what a blessing he is about to receive. But until that happy moment arrives, he has chosen a sad path indeed. But we shall indulge him solely for the purpose of good story-telling.

Side note: The funny thing is that we all despise seeing this behavior in *other* people, and yet we all feel justified when we demonstrate it ourselves. We do not want to hear it, but we expect everyone else to listen whenever we get a raw deal. To constantly seek that kind of attention is not merely impolite to those around us, but is also unhealthy behavior for ourselves. Sadly, some of us are that way all the time. None of you are going to be called out by name, but you should probably know who you are. Now back to our story already in progress …

The next day began enthusiastically. Still getting into the swing of things, students enjoyed their second day of school. Some of that pleasant energy was still being transferred around the campus. And then there was Billy, offering counterpoint to everyone else's cheery disposition. Along with a new copy of *Pride and Prejudice*, Billy brought with him a major attitude problem into his English class. But other than that, he did his best to muddle through the first half of the day. He joined the other students in eyeing the clock during the concluding Geometry class; that bell was all that stood between them and lunch. At the climactic moment when the bell sounded, it looked more like someone had tossed in a grenade as everyone sprang into action.

For our four boys, there was a secret routine that occurred every day at lunch. The school had lunches available naturally, but Mike, Curtis, and Billy had always been in the habit of bringing their own – partly because of their friend. Clay had nothing. Maybe the cause was originally financial – we do not know – but for whatever reason, Clay never got the school lunches. His friends had always looked after him since they were little tykes. They had secretly agreed to bring something extra in their lunches each day and give it to Clay claiming that they were not as hungry as all that. So there were actually four lunches among the three boys. That way, Clay had a lunch as well. Whether Clay was wise to their little scheme or not, the others did not know. But the extra food was always accepted with gratitude and little fanfare.

TUESDAY

As most of the students did, the boys had the customary habit of sitting at the same table each day. But here they were in a different school, so their new table would have to be selected. On Monday, in true helpless fashion, the boys did not know where to go, so they had lunch under a tree - - which worked out surprisingly fine. (Perhaps the ants were out having their little nails done and left them alone.) But Tuesday came. Curtis and Mike arrived first and scouted out a place where the boys could eat and draw as little attention to themselves as possible. Almost instantly as they sat, Billy found them and sat down as well. Clay walked in from the far side of the room, smiling and empty-handed as usual.

"Hey guys!" Clay was always very chipper. The most likable of the four, he had a natural way of lifting any mood with his positive outlook. Because he came from a home that was the least affluent by far, the boys found that his optimistic quality shined all the brighter. And in spite of what others may consider setbacks, people seemed to bask in the warmth of his being.

"Hey, punk!" Mike smiled back and gestured at one of the seats. "Come here and sit down, you."

The others repaid his greeting with the usual, "Hey, Clay."

Billy held up the additional sandwich. "Clay, I've got an extra here if you want it. I think it is ham, but don't hold me to it. There are two here, and I can't eat them both." He grinned and added, " ...well, maybe I can – but I'm not going to. So you might as well eat up."

Excitedly, "Hey! Thanks."

Curtis chimed in. "And you're more than welcome to my banana."

"Here's a fruit drink and some chips that I don't want." Mike finished up the round.

"Cool. Thanks."

Mike pulled a cookie out of his lunch (he always ate those before his sandwich). As his best friend, he understood that Clay was not the type to toot his own horn; so whenever Clay had big news, it was up to Mike to draw this to the attention of others. "Hey, Clay. Tell Curtis about your big plans." That was all it took. The others would take it from here.

Both Billy and Curtis looked up with interest. "Big plans? What's going on, big guy?" Curtis asked.

Clay sensed some shyness coming on. Talking about himself always made him a little uncomfortable. But because it was just the guys, he proceeded. "Well, it's like this - - I know we're only sophomores, but I am already thinking about college. There is simply no way that my mom and I can afford that. Sooooo, I am hoping to get a track scholarship." The others reacted with the appropriate amount of encouragement as he took a deep breath. "If I work really hard, I really think I can make it happen. And if not, then at least I gave it my best shot."

Curtis was the first to react, "Awesome. If anyone can do it, you can. But if that doesn't work out ...?"

"Then I'll see about getting into the military and maybe they will send me to college whenever *they* decide I can go – or however that works."

Billy wrinkled up his nose inquisitively. "I thought you wanted to be a cop like your dad. You've been talking about that since who-knows-when."

"I know. I do, but the military sounds cool too. I would still like to do something along those lines. Maybe I could be part of the military police or something. But until then, I am going to pour all of my attention into track. I would like to go college and a track scholarship might be my best ticket."

Curtis' genuine excitement for Clay was made evident in his words and his tone. "It sounds like you've got it all figured out. It'll be great to see all that happen. But I doubt that you'll have to go down the military route. That track scholarship is practically in your pocket." He shifted his attention toward Billy. "So, do you have any plans yet, Billy?"

Billy was still stinging from the ordeal of his dad being his teacher. This negative mindset was something he could not seem to shake - - nor did he want to. "Plans? Me? Sure I got plans. I plan to get stinkin' rich any way I can so I can get out of this nowhere town." He bitterly took another bite from his boring old sandwich.

True to form, Clay suddenly became conscience of his good fortune in light of Billy's bad. "Oh, uh ... Billy. I'm sorry that you didn't get selected for track this year. I really wish you had made it. It would've been fun beating you to the finish." He gave a brief chuckle.

Billy shrugged. "Don't feel bad. I also found out that the football team clearly doesn't want me either. Oh, and apparently they began practices sometime during the summer. Who knew? But no regrets. That might be in my best interest anyway; they would probably clobber me senseless on the first day." He took another bite. "Yep. I'd be flatter than a pancake out there on the gridiron."

Billy was not always this way. But his friends were quickly getting used to his 'poor little me' attitude. Generally, Curtis talked him through it, Mike was irritated by it, and Clay showed the most sympathy. So Clay was not going to let it go that easily. "Well, keep trying. You'll find something."

Mike's voice suddenly exploded with energy. He walked across to Billy's back and put him in a loving headlock from behind. "Well, *their* loss will simply be *our* gain. Don't worry about my man Billy here. This afternoon, I am personally going to escort him to the basketball tryouts. It's in the bag."

"That's so right!" Billy finally grinned and pretended to toss an invisible basketball in Clay's direction. They laughed.

WEDNESDAY

It was again lunchtime. In a repeat performance, Clay came over to the table where Curtis, Billy, and Mike had been eating. But this time, he had something on his heart. "Billy, I'm sorry that you didn't make it on the basketball team." Without comment, the others handed him the extra parts of their lunches. "Don't feel bad about it though. Basketball is kinda a dumb game anyway."

"Do what?!" Mike acted as though he were horribly offended and turned sharply at Clay. "What are you talking about? Basketball is the bomb. It's only the best game there is or ever was!"

Clay really did not have a problem with basketball, but he knew that he could get a rise out of Mike - - and that the exchange had the potential of being hilarious. "Uh, not really. Not when you sit down and analyze the game."

Mike sat stunned. The comical look on his face announced that the time was ripe for a nice little halftime speech. "I see that setting the record straight is long overdue. Child, allow me to enlighten you. Consider that an entire team works hard together … dare I say *unified* … as one mind to get a ball in a hoop that is high off the ground in the face of skilled opposition. It's a lesson in teamwork. And that is just *one* amazing point. Shall I go on? I've got a fist full of 'em."

Clay was ready for him. "Of that, I have no doubt. And all this stuff may be true. But no matter how hard you try to make a basket, the ball will always fall out the bottom. That sounds rather counterproductive to me. Until some engineering genius figures out a way to plug up the bottom of that net, that big ugly ball is *always* going to fall through - - at which point, members of the *other* team then end up with the ball. In the wonderful world of getting things accomplished and seeing the fruits of your labor, please explain how that does not feel like a total waste of time."

"Dude! The 'fruits of our labor' as you call it are sitting up there on the scoreboard." Mike pointed up at some imaginary scoreboard as if there was one right there in the lunchroom. He then leaned into Billy and thumbed over to Clay. "This coming from the guy who runs around in circles."

Billy and Curtis were not worried about this kind of trash talk and even found some of it amusing. Clay and Mike were best friends and frequently found themselves in similar comical arguments. In fact, to even call these conversations *arguments* would be grossly inaccurate. Sometimes they were so good, you would swear they were rehearsed.

What started this conversation to begin with was the revelation of Billy's inability to join the basketball team. Curtis decided to return to the central topic. "So what is your next move?" he asked Billy. "Are you coming with me today to meet the baseball coach? He is building up his team."

Billy perked up a couple of degrees. "Pffff! Absolutely. That was *always* in the plans."

Curtis matched Billy's sudden burst of enthusiasm. "That's right! No one can stop the Baker and Harris show!"

Billy rang in. "That's what I'm talking about! With us together, how could anyone say no?" They gave each other a fist bump and started to laugh, keeping students passing by at a nice comfortable distance at all costs.

THURSDAY

"Hey Billy. I'm so sorry you didn't make the baseball team." Clay was genuinely concerned, but even *he* was starting to sound redundant right there in the lunchroom.

Billy plopped down in his seat completely oblivious to his lunch. Shock was easily read on his deadened face. "I'm still trying to figure out what happened. I was all ready for this. Everything was on my side, ya know. It was like ... the planets were all lining up. I mean I didn't expect the whole town to turn up and applaud, but I honestly expected to do *okay*. Then all of a sudden ..." Billy brought his hands together, then spread his arms out widely, and made an explosion noise with his mouth.

Clay's eyes squinted. "Yeah? What happened?"

His voice surrendered to feelings of desperation. "I don't know. It just wasn't my day. Everything that could've gone wrong went wrong. It was like I had never even seen a baseball glove in my life. The entire time I was out there, I felt as if I was outside my body watching me make a total fool of myself. You missed what was truly one of the most horrible events of my life. It was almost as bad as finding myself in my dad's English class."

Mike was finding all of this difficult to believe. "I don't get it. You would think that if nothing else, the coach would let you do some bench-warming. Or you could take a crack at being the water boy. Something. And the same thing goes for the basketball and football coaches." His eyes got wide. He leaned into them and whispered, "It's like a weird anti-Billy conspiracy."

Billy sighed. "Honestly, I wouldn't be at all surprised if the coach would never let me in the park to see a game. All the folks collecting money for admission will probably have little copies of my picture so they will know to turn me away at the gate. The entire team will probably think that I am some kind of bad luck charm or something. And after the week that I've had, I am starting to believe it myself."

Mike turned to Curtis. "No kidding. Curtis, you were there. What really happened?"

Curtis suddenly looked nervous and uncomfortable. It was as if his blood was being replaced with ice water. He initially opened his mouth but there was no sound. He looked over at Billy, back at Mike, then back at Billy. He proceeded to speak in a slow, cautious voice. "Billy, I'm your best friend. And I think that it might be wise to look toward the future and forget that yesterday ever happened."

Billy was now way past frustrated. "Ya know, guys, I'm seriously starting to wonder if I am good at anything at all."

"Don't be that way," Clay said. "You're great at plenty of things."

"Oh yeah? Name *one thing* that I am good at."

For a moment, all four sat in silence.

Mike was really no good at encouraging people, but he took a stab at it anyway. "Uh, you …" He stumbled some more as he started a sentence that had no preconceived ending. "Well, whenever you … walk into a room … you have the natural ability to … lighten up the mood with … your disarming …" He turned back to his lunch. "Just forget it. I got nothing."

Clay ignored Mike's little joke. "Curtis is absolutely right. Forget about yesterday." He popped up out of his seat and looked around the room.

"There has to be plenty of other things around here that you can do. I'll go check the bulletin board." He spotted one loaded with announcements and walked over for a closer look. In no time, he was out of earshot.

A thought came across Curtis' mind. What if Clay came back from the board with no ideas at all? But was that the point? Curtis spoke up. "I don't know why you are trying so hard to be a part of a team around here anyway. Is it really that important that you try to define yourself with a group of some sort? What's so wrong with you just being you for a while? A complete original – at least until you can figure out the score around here? Is that so bad?"

Billy shook his head. "Dude, I need to do *something*. I want to look back on the high school experience as having done things. I don't want to be one of those guys who has nothing listed by their name in the yearbook."

A curious look struck Curtis' face. "What was that? What did you just say?"

Billy sighed. "I said that I don't want to be one of ..."

"Yeah, yeah, yeah. I heard you the first time," Curtis interrupted. He then burst out in mock-excitement. "That's it! That is *exactly* something you could do!"

"What is?"

Curtis continued, "You just mentioned the yearbook. Join the yearbook staff." He sounded very proud of himself for this most brilliant of ideas.

For some reason, Billy did not like that idea at all. *How idiotic*, he thought. *Maybe Curtis is trying to make a joke.* "Very funny," he replied with a smirk. "I don't want to be one of those guys that reports about what *other* people have done; I want to be one of those that gives them something to write about. I want to be the guy that stands out. I want to do something that gets noticed."

Curtis felt that it was time for a reality check. "*Popularity?* Is that what you want? I think 'popularity' might work against you. You don't want to be known as the dude who was rejected by every organization on campus."

Oversensitive Billy took another ungrateful bite from his sandwich.

Mike was ready to talk about something else. He leaned all the way back. "Okay guys. I have no intention of spending the rest of my life talking about your silly problems. This entire conversation is going nowhere. We all know what you are really really good at. Why don't you take a shot at that Chess Club?"

At the word *chess*, Curtis reacted. "Yes! That's *exactly* what I've been saying from the first! But try getting that through his thick head bone."

But while Curtis was talking, Billy already started in with his negative clarification. "No, no, no, no. Not a chance."

Mike kept pushing the point. "Dude, there is no reason known to man or beast why you shouldn't jump at this. You play Chess."

"*You* play Chess too." Billy and Mike had begun to raise their voices a little but not enough to disturb anyone.

"Hey genius, any monkey in striped socks can move the pieces around. But you are actually decent at it. In fact, you kill me all the time. Your pieces do laps around mine and make them look stupid. And in nothin' flat, you've got my king up against a wall."

"Whatever. I am not going to Chess Club and that's that."

"Give me one good reason why not."

"*Because my dad!*" Suddenly Billy became aware that his voice was getting fairly loud. He nervously looked around and fortunately no one other than Mike and Curtis seemed to have heard him. Billy took a deep breath and calmed down a bit. In a softer tone, he added, "Look. It's embarrassing enough to have my dad here to begin with. I'm not going to *hang out with him* at school. Can you imagine what a total loser I would be if I suddenly started doing that? Besides, I don't want to be branded as one of those hopeless chess nerds. I want to go my own way, thank you very much. I want to be with a different crowd. A better crowd."

"You mean the *proud crowd*." Mike looked at Billy with a stern expression.

There was a moment of silence. In that time, Mike's words stung and Billy took offence at this. "You're out of line. It's not like that."

"Oh, it's *exactly* like that." Mike's piercing gaze met with Billy's eyes. "You want to hang with that Chloe Chastain and her little rich disciples."

Perhaps Mike was right. And perhaps deep down inside, Curtis was agreeing with Mike. But Curtis played the loyal friend and came to his defense. ... sorta. Turning to Mike, he said, "Will you take it easy on him?"

As always, Clay's timing was spot on as he returned with news from the school bulletin board. Unaware of any present tension, he sat back in his previous seat looking down at some notes he made. "Okay. Assuming that you are still avoiding the Chess Club, here are some more options. There is mention here of a tennis team."

Ever the clown, Mike was more enthusiastic about making jokes rather than helping Billy. "A tennis team! That's a great idea - - that is if he can tolerate all that *racquet*!" He began to laugh. The others looked annoyed at him.

Clay looked down again at the list he wrote. "There is also the golf club."

This time, it was Curtis who made the obvious joke. "Golf *club*? Are you trying to be funny? Do they actually call it the 'Golf Club'?"

Billy was not really amused but even he had something to say on the subject. "HA! Could you see me playing golf all of a sudden? In golf, you have to hit a little ball and then go chase after it. At least in bowling, you use a big ball to knock things down - - and then the ball automatically comes back to you. Golf is too much work."

Clay lowered his list in defeat. "Well, that is what it says on the bulletin board."

Billy rolled his eyes. "With my luck, I would do something to tee-off the golf coach." Billy leaned in toward Clay's list. "What else is there?"

FRIDAY

The four of them sat motionless at the lunch table, the other three looking at Billy as if someone had just died. Although the lunchroom was a fairly noisy place, they felt the discomfort of silence around them like a soundproof blanket.

After a few moments, Clay broke the silence. He spoke softly and with a great deal of caution. "Let me see if I understand you correctly. You couldn't get on the yearbook staff?"

Billy could only shake his head in shame.

Curtis was trying to be sympathetic, and yet he was perplexed over this entire scenario. "The yearbook staff? No one gets booed away from the yearbook staff. If nothing else, they need stooges to run out and hustle up some ads …" Curtis paused and looked at Clay. " …ads for the back pages of the yearbook. This makes no sense."

Clay always managed to say something positive in any situation; but today, he was at a loss.

Mike's voice was slow, deliberate, and a bit horror-movie freaky. "It's like there is a curse on you. It's like you aren't even supposed to be here." He looked over at the others. "I'll be honest with you guys, this is starting to creep me out."

That was it. Billy began to sound a little upset now. "Can we please do me a huge favor and stop talking about what a pathetic loser I am?"

For once, Mike was in total agreement. "Yes! That is an excellent suggestion. All we've done for the entire week is talk about you and your silly problems. Personally, I'll be glad when you *do* find someplace to belong. We'd get to stop hearing you whine all the time. It was old way before it got old."

The four boys ate their lunch in relative silence and said something occasionally. After a while, they were back to smiles and talking about video games and some funny things that made them laugh. The half-hour got away from them and soon lunch would be over.

Before they knew it, the bell rang. Students all around the room began to get up from their seats, toss their trash in appropriate places, and headed to their lockers to get all they needed for the next class.

Curtis was going the opposite direction from Billy. He yelled out, "Hey! You still coming over tomorrow?"

Billy looked back. "Yeah. Just give me a call in the morning." Billy had been planning on spending Saturday with the Bakers. They thought about going over to the falls again before the weather started to get chilly, but they usually just played it by ear.

Curtis and Mike went off to catch their next class. They were both ready to dismiss the fog that came with having lunch with Billy this entire week. He was not a killjoy or anything; but of their little tightknit quartet, Billy was the one most likely to drain all the energy out of the room.

Clay was about to dash off and leave Billy moping, but he stopped in his tracks. Something was on his mind, so he ran back over to where Billy was standing. Clay placed a gentle hand on Billy's shoulder. His voice was direct and loving. "Hey, do you want my advice?"

The short and honest answer to Clay's question was a firm negative; Billy really did not want his friend's advice at that moment. On some level, he was having too much fun feeling miserable. But that automatic response thing inside did his talking for him. "Sure."

"Go check out the Chess Club."

As soon as he said the word *chess*, Billy was already backing off. But Clay managed to keep his attention.

"No. I'm serious. You're a natural. I only wish that I could play chess as well as you do."

Billy shot back. "You're kidding me. It is so embarrassing to have my own dad as my English teacher – *English* of all things. That's bad enough. But now you are asking me to spend *more* time in his classroom? Think about it. How would *you* like it if *your* dad was your teacher?"

Suddenly Clay went from being serious to being really serious. "I would love it."

Billy instantly felt ashamed. He should not have said that. Right away, he wished that he could have taken it back. "I'm sorry. Of course you would. I don't know what I was thinking. That wasn't very sympathetic of me."

Clay was not in the mood for this conversation right now. Plus, he needed to get to his next class. "Well, *sympathy* was last year. This year, I'm all about picking up the pieces and making something good of myself. All the self-pity in the world isn't going to bring my dad back. Besides, you and I both know that he's in a better place now. You should really try to focus on something more than feeling sorry for yourself. Your big plans for this school year should include not being sad just because you *think* your life is unfair. Just chew on what I said for a while." Clay walked away. " ...and think about that Chess Club," he yelled back at Billy.

Well, that could've gone better, Billy thought to himself. But what if Clay was right? It just occurred to him that someday he will be looking back at his tenth grade year - - and what would he see? Moodiness? No one likes to be around people who are always ...

Billy stopped sharply. *What's that?* Something on the bulletin board caught his eye and it was enough to make him put on the brakes. It was the exact same flier for the Chess Club that he saw earlier. Only now, someone with a marker had come along and drawn on his dad's face. The image of Mr. Harris' head now had on an enormous pair of glasses, a couple of stray teeth hanging out of his mouth, large curly hair, and an arrow going through his head.

Billy silently rushed over to it and ripped it from its tack. Standing there staring at it, a number of emotions began to overwhelm him. He first felt anger, but that was quickly replaced with a cage of embarrassment and ridicule. How he wished that he could simply step into some thick fog and disappear as if the two of them were not related at all. But fortune was seldom kind. His dad was too well-known for that to happen. And now, his nerdiness was put high on a shelf with lights on it for the entire world to see. "Oh, dad," he said softly. "Dad, you seriously have no idea how much it hurts to see the students making fun of you this way. Do you even realize just how much of a weirdo you can be? Why do you let people make such a fool out of you? This is so embarrassing."

The bell rang announcing the start of fifth period. He was now officially late. Billy secretively loaded the flier into his backpack and dashed off to class. But as fast as he was going, he could still not outrun what he had seen. And although the flier was hidden away in his backpack, it became an enormous distraction; his mind kept turning back to the vandalized face on the Chess Club flier.

What was he supposed to do about this? What could he do really? As he sat in his next class, he looked around the room at the faces of the other students. One thing he knew for certain: someone here is out to make his dad look like a fool. The Harris' had an enemy somewhere. But who?

CHAPTER 7

WITH ONE WORD

It was a strange feeling. His bones even felt weird, especially his shoulder blades. Uneasiness covered him like a second skin. Half afraid, he stayed close to the walls as he walked, but he still felt exposed, still felt the weight of what he was hiding in his backpack.

Physically, Billy went to the remainder of his classes; but his teachers should have recorded his mind as *absent*. His head seemed to be rolling around inside his backpack staring up at the altered face of his dad on the Chess Club flier. And although it was tucked away at present, just the idea that it was out there messed him up. The picture might as well have been painted up on a building downtown like a mural.

While that was going on, Billy simultaneously tortured himself by looking around at the other students, all the while trying to figure out just which of these villains it was who drew on his dad's face. The very thought of his dad having enemies around him felt eerie, a chilling sensation and one that he could live without. And although Billy did not relish the thought of his dad being his teacher, he was more than a little worried *for* him. In fact, this worry was growing by the minute.

Whoever could be making fun of his dad? And why? Was it just one guy? Maybe it was a small group of them. What if this was something big? What if there were a tremendously large network of anti-Mr. Harris club members, like an opposing camp. For all he knew, they could be well-organized and popular. Another thought: Whoever it was would probably take on Billy just as easily and just as quickly as they would his dad.

This was a living nightmare. How could this be happening in a small town like Pecan Falls of all places? They were only one week into this new school year and Billy was already having thoughts of putting a hundred miles between him and these halls. What other horrors awaited him? What could he possibly …?

Oh no, he interrupted his thoughts again. *Another one!* He rushed over to another bulletin board where yet another Chess Club flier had been marked on. This time, his dad had horns, angry eyebrows, and fangs. Rather than ripping the flier from its tack, he calmly pulled the tack off and repositioned it elsewhere. He took the first flier out of his backpack and gazed upon them both. Is this the work of the same person? How many more of these idiotic fliers are on campus? There was only one way to find out. He bolted toward his dad's classroom.

Walking about a mile a minute, he came around a corner precisely as Justin was coming around the other side. They nearly collided, which *would* have been funny if we could add some sound effects (maybe the sound of bowling pins being knocked down).

"Finally!" Justin exclaimed. "I've been looking everywhere for you!"

"What do you want, Justin?" he replied rather impatiently.

"My girlfriend was wanting to know if you were the one drawing all these funny pictures on your dad's face." Justin had barely finished the question before Billy walked away from him in angered silence. "Dude," Justin said disappointingly. Now it seemed he had to return to his girlfriend with nothing to report.

School was out for the day, but William Harris was still at his desk. A half-dozen students sat around his room. All was silent except for the soft sound of a Claude Debussy tune playing in the background. The desks had been arranged to face each other to support the vinyl cloth chess boards. Three games were currently in play. The handsome pieces were tall and made of tough plastic with green felt on the bottom of each piece.

Mr. Harris had just finished grading papers and brought out his phone to text his wife.

I love you, Mrs. Harris.

A moment later, the silent reply came. *I love you too, Mr. Harris. Would you still love me if I suddenly grew an exoskeleton?*

You're weird.

Out in the hall, Billy approached his dad's classroom cautiously trying not to make a sound. He remembered seeing that the Chess Club meets on Mondays, Wednesdays, and Fridays. He knew that there was a good chance that they were there. And he was right. He had no intentions of disturbing the club or drawing attention to himself. But he had to talk to his dad about these fliers. How many of these horrible sheets did he post? How extensive was their placement around campus? And how easy would it be to collect them and have them mercifully and humanely destroyed?

He stood by the door trying to get his father's attention without being noticed by any possible chess-playing oddballs.

His dad finally saw Billy waving at him from the hallway. William's eyebrows popped up and he awkwardly waved back wondering if Billy had just stopped to surprise him and say *Hi*. But Billy made it known that he wanted to speak to his dad, so William got up from his seat and joined him just out of visual range of the game-playing students. He looked down at Billy's sad face.

Mr. Harris usually liked to keep the mood light. But on this occasion, genuine concern could be heard in his voice. "Hey Biggin'. What's wrong?"

Billy had no idea how to articulate what he was feeling. He knew that anything that he could say would probably just sound corny. So instead, he chose simply to lift up the two vandalized fliers that had caused him such a painful afternoon and let *them* do the talking. Deep down inside, Billy already knew that his dad would make light of it. He would not be as negatively affected by the fliers. But Billy did not expect his dad to actually laugh at them. He was astonished by his father's good-humored reaction.

William pointed at one of the fliers as he chuckled. "I really like that one. It's funny. But I think the funniest one is the one over by the Chemistry lab. In that one, my face is covered in spots. I have a thermometer in my mouth and a hot water bottle on my head. Great stuff."

"Huh? You knew about these?"

He stopped laughing and stood up straight. "Sure I do. I think they're hilarious."

"Hilarious?!" Billy was stunned. "You aren't embarrassed or even a little worried about these?"

William laughed again. "No. Of course not. I'm the one who drew these."

Billy's eyes nearly leaped out of his head. "YOU did this?" His voice nearly broke. "Why?"

William's voice sounded like years of experience talking. "Well, I've been teaching long enough to know that someone would eventually come along and do this anyway. So naturally, I always like to beat them to it. That way, I can control what is done. Besides, I think I do a much better job than these amateurs."

Billy's face contorted into a comical grimace expressing the need for clarification.

So William continued. "Think about it. Would you rather see one of the students do this or have me do this to myself?"

Billy hated it but at times his dad's argument was unexpectedly sound. He never would have thought that up in a million years. He searched for words. "Uh, okay ... But I don't see why you would want your picture on these at all." He held up the fliers together in one fist.

"Well, it is only for the benefit of new students and transfer students who want to play chess. They don't know who I am at first, but they'll recognize me in the hall and ask me questions about it." William looked down at Billy and noticed his expression. It was obvious to him that his son was still uncomfortable with the idea. "You really are bothered by this, aren't you?"

Billy felt dumb. He had been worrying all afternoon about his dad being made a mockery by one of the students (or a large organized network of students); and as it turned out, his dad was making fun of himself all along. Now there was a plot twist that came out of nowhere. All Billy could do was hang his head down. "Yeah, I guess so." How could he tell his dad that having him at the school all the time was a major source of embarrassment to him? Fliers or no fliers.

William paused for a moment. He then spoke reassuringly as if he found a solution. "Well, I'll tell you what ... I guess I can go around the school and take them down; I usually do anyway after the first month. But you're going to have to learn how to laugh at yourself. Don't become one of those people who are offended by everything easily. Remember Proverbs 17:22? 'A merry heart doeth good like a medicine: but a broken spirit drieth the bones.' Don't go around looking for things to bring you down or steal your joy. Keep it happy. Keep it positive."

Billy had the sudden urge to leave - - although he did not know where he could go. He just had a premonition that he was about to get stuck doing something that he did not want to do. "Alright, dad. Look, I'll catch up with you later."

"Wait. Since you're here anyway, you ought to come in and try the Chess Club." William made a quick and friendly gesture toward his classroom.

Billy quietly looked around the room. "I don't think so, dad. This doesn't really look like my thing."

"I know. They're too *nerdy* for someone as cool as you. Well, I certainly won't pressure you. But I still think that you should try it out since you're here. And if you don't like it, you don't have to come back."

"Yeah, no. These people are too ... weird."

William straightened his back to reach is full height. "*Weird?* So you think these ordinary, fun-loving students are *weird?* You don't even know them. Whose standards are you measuring them by anyway? Are you qualified to declare who is *weird* and who is *cool?*" Suddenly, William's face changed. Anyone with half of an eye could easily see that an idea just came to him - - and it was a sneaky one too. "You know, I *could* get you in this room and playing chess in roughly a minute by saying just one word."

A nervous smile crept onto Billy's face. He would not admit to it, but he was intrigued. "No, you can't. Impossible."

"Oh yes, I can - - with just one solitary word. In fact, I can go back in the room, sit at my desk, and say one word and it would be as good as done. In addition, this one word isn't even in English. What would you say to that, tough guy?" William smiled knowingly from ear to ear. He was not bluffing.

Still, Billy foolishly doubted his dad. Just what strange magic did Mr. Harris possess? Billy knew one thing: he was *not* going to enter that room. His only course of action was for his legs to carry him back down the hall and straight out the door. "Nah. There's no way that'll happen."

"Do you mind if I try?"

Billy was feeling awfully sure of himself. He was not going in that room. No force was able to make him budge. "Sure. I'd like to see you try. But I still say that it's impossible."

William's same sneaky grin remained unchanged. "Okay. Just stay right here. Don't move." He slowly backed away from his son as if he was balancing a hot cup of coffee on his head.

Billy let out a quiet, disbelieving laugh. "Yeah. Okay, dad." He rolled his eyes. This was total nonsense. If he were the betting type, this would be easy money.

William casually walked back to his desk, sat, and picked up a pen again as if he was going to be entering grades in his grade book. His return went completely unnoticed by all students. Without even looking up at anyone, he said just one word. "Alejandro."

A boy with black hair instantly popped his head up from his game, looked over at Mr. Harris, then looked at the door, and saw Billy standing there. A huge smile appeared on his face and his arms flew up in the air. "Bienvenidos. Welcome sophomore!" He sprang from his seat and rushed over to Billy.

A sudden rush of terror overpowered Billy. *Huh-oh!* he thought. He nervously looked for a polite escape, but the young man managed to get to him first.

"You *are* a sophomore, right?" The student with a slight accent was already ushering Billy into the room. He must have possessed some uncatalogued superpower for controlling other people's movements.

"Uh, yeah." Confused, he now magically found himself in the front of the classroom.

His dad secretly smiled. Billy had fallen for his little trap. Now it was all a matter of time. *Good,* he thought to himself. *He needed a place to belong.*

Alejandro excitedly turned to the others. "Hey, guys! We've got a sophomore here!" The others in the group did not bother looking up. Unimpressed, they kept playing their games. The boy turned again to Billy. "What's your name, sophomore?"

Billy was too stunned to think about anything other than answering the question that was put to him. "Uh, Billy. Billy Harris."

"Uh Billy Billy Harris? That's a funny name. Kinda redundant." Alejandro stopped sharply and quickly put his twos and twos together. "Un momento. Billy Harris? As in *William Harris Jr.?*" He turned to address William. "How about it, teach?"

Finally, Mr. Harris spoke up. Pointing a pencil his way, "Billy is my son and has been all his life. You can tell because we have the same cowlicks."

With a sly smile, the boy replied. "Well, there is no reason to apologize for that, Mr. Harris." He turned to address Billy. "But just because you have the same cowlicks as the teach, don't think that that entitles you to any special privileges. You can lose games as well as any of the rest of us – maybe better. ¿Comprende?"

Billy nodded apprehensively.

Alejandro faced the rest of the group in introductive mode. "Hey! This is Billy the Sophomore."

Right on cue, four of the remaining students all said in bored unison, "Hello and welcome to Chess Club, Billy the Sophomore."

Billy thought, *Oh no. This is weirder than I imagined. A chess-playing cult.*

The young man directed Billy around the room by placing his hand on Billy's back and giving him a friendly shove. "So, do you already know how to play chess or would you like us to teach you?"

This was a dangerous question. Any way he answered, it was like committing himself to something that he would rather not do. Nevertheless, he felt a little flushed by this pointed insult. He answered in a rather defensive tone. "I *know* how to play chess, thank you very much."

"Good! That means that you can sit down and start playing. And this is great news for us because your presence here gives us an even number. Now everyone here can play. But first things first; let me start with the introductions. As you heard, my name is Alejandro. And I am the Chess Club welcoming committee."

"…self-appointed." A boy with dish-water blonde hair spoke up in a somewhat playfully sarcastic tone. He had blue eyes and a superhero t-shirt on. His teeth broke through a crooked smile.

Alejandro did not look back at who spoke - - in fact, he did not even gesture towards him. He simply said, "And THAT is Joey. Watch out for him; he likes to sneak up from behind with his rooks."

Joey gave Billy a welcome smile and waved. "We already know each other. Welcome fellow sophomore."

"Hi, Joey," Billy said with recognition.

As Alejandro spoke, he made his way behind a boy with long black hair and maybe an earring or two under there somewhere. The beginnings of a beard were growing on his face. The largest student in the room, he was dressed in such a way that would discourage people from messing with him. Alejandro put his arms on the young man's shoulders and continued his introductions. "And THIS big ray of sunshine is the lovable – but misunderstood – Quotes." As he said the name, Alejandro made hooks out of two fingers on each hand and bent them as he said 'Quotes.'

Billy did not know what to make of that. "Quotes?"

Alejandro corrected him. "Oh, no, no. It's pronounced ..." He theatrically repeated the hand motions. " ...Quotes." For a moment, he could detect an expression of worry on Billy's face. "Nah. Just kidding. You can say it anyway you want. Quotes will let you know himself if he doesn't like the way you say it." He turned to face the senior. "Isn't that right, big guy?"

Quotes grunted.

Billy managed a smile and began to nod his head. "*Quotes.* That's a cool nickname."

Alejandro explained. "Well, he needed a good nickname in the worst way. His parents actually named him *Electron*. They said something about receiving a negative charge from him when he was born. So when people pronounced his name, they often motioned quotation marks by bending their fingers. So now we just call him Quotes." Alejandro leaned closer to Billy to talk softly in his ear. "Actually, Electron isn't exactly a bad name, all things considered. His sister's name is Pineapple Yogurt. We are guessing (or rather hoping) that his parents were on something prescribed by physicians at the time." He backed into his original posture and voice. "Give folks the benefit of the doubt, right?"

Billy smiled. "Well, personally I think it is a cool nickname."

Without missing a beat, Alejandro led him away to continue the introductions. "Whatever, brah. There will be plenty opportunities to offend Quotes later, trust me." He pointed to the next kid. "*This* character is Eugene. He's really a special case. And Eugene actually *is* a nickname as well."

Billy was not sure if he heard that correctly. "*Eugene* is your nickname?"

Eugene turned to him sharply, smacking on some gum. With a big smile, "Yeah! ... on account that I was born there."

"Eugene, ... Oregon?" Billy thought about rubbing his eyes. *There better not be a quiz over all these names,* he pondered.

"Born and bred," he replied.

Alejandro pulled Billy in and whispered in his ear. "Another warning. Watch out for him. He's got jokes."

Billy hoped he would never discover what Alejandro meant by that.

Eugene leaped up and made a wide sweeping gesture to his chair as if it were a prize on a game show. "And you, Mr. Billy Sophomore, may have my seat. That'll be my punishment for losing this terribly-played game."

Alejandro bumped Billy into the sitting position. "Cool. Check you out. No waiting. No long line. You're already in a game. That must be some kind of record."

William sat quietly in his seat, looked at his wristwatch, and smiled. It might have taken a little longer than he had anticipated, but Billy was about to play a game against one of these so-called nerds – and, in some weird way, enjoy himself.

Alejandro drew his attention to the student sitting opposite of where Billy now sat. "And this is your new opponent: Maggie."

Billy practically did an old-fashioned double take. "Uh ... You're a girl?!"

The *girl* he was referring to was not smiling. "Oh, you're good. You must've seen one in a movie." If first impressions count for anything, this was going to be a stormy game. In a bitter voice, she continued the *compliment.* "Your powers of observation do you credit, *sophomore.* I'm not sure if I'll be able to beat you and your keen intellect. Apparently, nothing escapes you."

Overhearing this exchange, William knew that his son was in mortal danger. He did his best not to grin.

Billy instantly found himself issuing an apology. "I'm sorry. I just didn't expect to see a girl in Chess Club."

"Uh, 'girls.' Plural." The voice came from the girl sitting next to Maggie.

Billy already felt like an idiot. Now it was completely confirmed. "Uh, sorry." He lifted his hand in a polite wave. "I'm Billy."

71

Her tone matched that of Maggie's. "Yeah. That's the rumor going around. I'm Berly."

"Nice to meet you." Billy tilted his head slightly. "I've never heard of the name Berly before. Is it your last name?"

"No. It is short for my first name, Kimberly."

"I thought Kim was short for Kimberly."

Maggie interrupted. "Yeah, yeah. It's your go, detective."

Billy looked down and noticed that Maggie had already arranged the pieces in their starting positions while he was talking to Berly and making a general fool of himself. His opponent had taken the initiative to make the first play by moving a pawn forward. He responded by picking up his knight and hopping it over a row of pawns.

He sensed something awkward and strange and it did not take long to discover what. He turned to see that Eugene was staring at him. Eugene sported a corny grin as he smacked his gum and waved his hand. Billy spoke up. "Hey! I thought that Alejandro said that my presence here give the club an even number. But it doesn't. There is an odd number in here and Eugene is just sitting there grinning at me."

Alejandro felt that he had to explain. "The numbers add up just fine. You see, I was counting our Chess Club president, Rodney, who is absent today."

Without warning, everyone except Billy, Mr. Harris, and Quotes suddenly exclaimed, "LONG LIVE RODNEY!" Their voices were loud and in perfect unison. This caught Billy completely off guard; in fact, he quite nearly jumped out of his skin.

In a normal voice, Joey had this to say, "I think he had to get another allergy shot after school. But don't worry; I'm sure he'll be here next time. He hardly ever misses Chess Club. You'll want to meet him."

Allergy shot? Billy thought. *Well, that is something he can't control.* But Billy could not help but sound a little sarcastic as he said, "I can hardly wait."

Eugene made an attempt to verbally communicate amidst his loud gum-smacking. "Thanks for coming today, sophomore. This might be a stretch to the ol' imagination, but some students want very badly to come to Chess Club, and yet they don't. They think that it is inhabited by a whole flock of weirdoes. Ha! Can you believe that mess?"

William looked up from his desk in silent amusement.

Billy was somehow conscience of his father's peering eyes. He fully concentrated on not returning his gaze and answered, "Really? Weirdoes? Where would anyone get an idea like that?" He was unaware of how much guilt he was projecting at that moment.

Eugene blarted out a loud laugh. It sounded like a horse stomping on a bagpipe. "I like you, Billy Sophomore. You're funny."

Quotes growled.

Just a few short minutes ago, Billy was pacing the halls worrying himself sick over the display of a few artistic interpretations of his dad's face. Now, he was in the very den of the chess freaks. So much for popularity. Out of the frying pan …

CHAPTER 8

THE DRAGON

Maggie cracked her window a smidgen and tightened her grip on the steering wheel. Glancing over at Berly, she said, "You've been unusually quiet. I hope there is no special reason for that."

Since the first day of the new school year, Maggie had been giving Berly a lift home each afternoon. The two girls had gone to the same church all their lives and had been friends since before they could remember. Maggie was a year older and in her junior year. On this day, they considered themselves unnaturally blessed because the two girls managed to sneak out of Chess Club without having to listen to one of Eugene's awful jokes. They quickly found themselves headed back home.

Maggie tried again to make a connection. "Hellooooo? Earth to Berly."

"Huh?" Berly snapped out of her little trance. Up to this point, she had been blankly staring out the window at nothing in particular – houses, trees, mailboxes, people walking their dogs. "What was that you said?"

Maggie kept her gaze forward. "I was just mentioning how quiet you've been since we left the school. You're breaking with tradition – not that I'm opposed to it; it's just a little …" Her eyebrows furrowed. " …scary. Should I run you by the hospital or call your mom?" She grinned, amused at her own joke.

"I'm sorry." Berly shifted in her seat and brushed the legs of her pants a couple of times as if there was something on them. She looked forward again and pulled her brown hair back and adjusted her glasses.

Maggie lightly laughed. "It's not a problem. It is just that you have been much more talkative on the other days." She looked up at a green traffic signal and drove straight through, making a visual sweep of the intersection as she went. "In fact, I normally have a hard time shutting you up." She punctuated her next question with a funny facial expression. "Girl, what's that all about?"

"I don't know. I guess I've just got something on my mind. That's all," she shrugged.

Another few seconds of awkward silence ticked by. Maggie already had a rough idea of what was on Berly's mind. This uncomfortable subject matter did not have to be pursued. But just to clear the air a little, she decided to throw a comment out there just to see how Berly would react - - and to prove that Berly was not fooling anyone. "So, that was Mr. Harris' son."

Berly's eyes widened. Could this be mere polite chitchat? Or was Maggie reading her mind? She wondered just how obvious she was.

Maggie added a question. "Did you know him from before?"

"No, I di ..." Her voice squeaked a little bit, the human equivalent of a clarinet. She started again. "No, I didn't actually. He must have gone to Middle School South. Since I went to North, I would've missed him." She turned her attention back toward the passenger window. "It still feels so weird to be in a school where I only know half of the kids in my own grade."

"Well, I don't care if he *is* Mr. Harris' son. He totally missed the Chess Club orientation meeting and I'd be willing to bet that he has no earthly idea about any of our weird little traditions. And what's even better, I don't think that I am going to fill him in at all. To watch him trying to figure out the routine is going to be quite hilarious, that is if his daddy doesn't tip him off first. The Chess Club could use a few laughs - - and I *don't* mean from Eugene's horrible jokes."

"I don't know. I thought Mr. Harris' son was kinda cute."

Maggie briefly rolled her eyes. "Okay. I'm going to pretend that I didn't hear that."

"What? Did I say something wrong?" Berly turned to look at Maggie.

"I'm still trying to figure out *what* he is. He's too clumsy to be a swan, so we can mark that off the list. And I'm pretty sure he isn't an oyster."

"You don't think he's cute? Not even a little bit?"

"They're all cute from the proper distance. If you want them to stay cute, you'll have to keep them there."

"So you don't like the guy."

Maggie exhaled. "I didn't say that. Mr. Harris' son probably has many fine qualities. He may just be a diamond in the rough. After all, high school boys are a work-in-progress. It's just …" Maggie's sentence trailed off. There was something that she was obviously thinking but not really knowing how to say.

Berly's voice switched over into an impatient tone. "Okay, okay. What is it about him that you have a problem with?"

Maggie defensively glanced over at her. "Nothing. It's just that he doesn't fulfill my *List of Absolutes*. That's all."

Berly wrinkled her nose up. "*List of Absolutes*? And just what is that?"

"My *List of Absolutes*? Uh, how can I best explain it?" She searched her mind for a fitting explanation and came up short. Nothing was said for a few seconds. "You know what? Maybe this is something that I need to show you. Why don't you call your mom and find out if you can come over to my house for an hour or so?"

Berly's voice sounded cautious and amused at the same time. "What are you doing? Are you trying to sell something?"

"Me? Certainly not. It was just an idea that I had and I'm rather proud of it – that's all." She gestured down at Berly's phone. "Go on. Get your mom on the phone and see if you can come over."

Berly got excited as she pulled out her phone and started dialing. "Cool. Can I see Sir Lancelot while I'm there?"

"Absolutely."

Berly made the call and squared everything with her mom.

The walls of Maggie's room were painted a light pink color and her bed was covered in pink blankets. Other than that, this was not the bedroom of a princess. Her walls featured some strategically-placed posters of her heroes and favorite works of art. Marie Curie was over by the window. Van Gogh's *Starry Night* was above her bed and Albert Einstein was sticking his tongue out behind her bedroom door. An M. C. Escher calendar hung above a table that she used as a desk. She had taped pictures of Amelia Earhart and Mae Jemison along with a dozen or so notes in her handwriting all around the edges of her mirror. But when Berly walked in the room, her eyes were drawn to Sir Lancelot who was resting in a glass tank across from the bed.

"Can I hold him?" Berly was very excited.

"Sure. Go sit on the bed and I'll bring him over to you." She approached the tank and slid the lid back. Her bearded dragon had been sleeping, but woke up when the girls walked in the room. She reached in the tank and picked him up, tail whipping nervously as she pulled the reptile out. She brought Sir Lancelot over to the bed and set him down directly in front of Berly. "Calm down, baby. I want you to meet somebody. Sir Lancelot, this is Berly."

If the bearded dragon was genuinely excited to see Berly, he did not let his feelings show. He retained his blasé countenance and blinked his golden eyes.

Berly was fascinated. She gently rubbed the top of his head with her fingertips. "He feels so cool. He isn't slimy at all. Actually, he feels kinda dry." She stared intently at the bearded dragon's neck and beautiful scales. "He's a handsome one. Look at all that amazing detail. He's so neat looking."

Maggie sat next to Berly and smiled. She was obviously proud of her new pet. "The younger ones are all spazzy; but since he is older, he's all nice and chill. He likes to cling to my shirt and go to sleep while I'm watching TV. And he is very affectionate. Some say that he likes my warmth, but I know better. He loves me." She briefly turned her comments to the dragon. "Don't you, sweetie?" She handed Berly a piece of kale. "Here. Put some of this in front of him and see if he'll eat it."

Berly looked up at Maggie. "So what is this list again?"

As soon as the question hit her ears, Maggie got up from where she was sitting. "Oh! That's right! My *List of Absolutes*! I have it right here." She began to rummage around in a drawer and pulled out a steno pad. "This is simply a list of requirements that I have made up for anyone who I may want to date. These are essential qualities that I am looking for in a guy. If a guy wants to ask me out but he doesn't meet these qualifications, I don't even waste my time. And honestly, it's not exactly fair to be wasting *his* time either — as mean as that may sound."

This started to sound a bit weird to Berly, but she knew that Maggie usually had a level head on her shoulders. "I've never heard of anything like that before."

"That's because I made it up." She threw her arms in the air as if she just performed a magic trick and then resumed her normal stance. "It's just a list of things that I feel are important." She handed it over to Berly's eager hands.

Berly began to look at the pages curiously. "Well, what brought all this about?"

Maggie did not often talk about what happened last year, but Berly had been her friend from the beginning. "You remember Garrett. We started dating and it was very cool at first. Thankfully, we never did anything that we shouldn't or anything like that; but when it was over, I have to admit that I was hurt. And so much of that pain could've easily been avoided if I had a lick of common sense. Looking back on the experience, I discovered that there were some things about him that I would not normally tolerate. In fact, I am horrified at myself for letting it go as long as it did."

"I liked Garrett."

"Yeah. I thought I did too. Fortunately, it wasn't one of those things that freaks out the entire school like that time when Becky broke up with Trevor."

"Oh? What happened?"

"Well, the most popular girl in my grade broke up with the most popular boy. When that happened, everyone was getting involved and choosing sides. It was so dumb. The student body was practically divided, but not really divided if that makes any sense. It was just a lot of unnecessary drama and stupid gossip. That is exactly why I won't date anyone that I go to school with again – not in high school anyway. It's just too much trouble." She pointed down at her list. "See? That one is number four." She went back to petting her dragon. "And that is why I would never think about dating Mr. Harris' son; that plus he's not my type."

Sir Lancelot bit into a piece of kale. The girls forgave the beardy for chewing with his mouth open wide. Reptiles are not known for their devotion to common table manners.

Berly looked up from the list. "So you don't think that I should go out with him?"

"Whether I do or don't is of no consequence. Look, this is on *my* list.

You need to make your own. You may not feel as strongly as I do about some things. Likewise, you may be very passionate about something that would never even occur to me." She stood up and walked over to a chair. "Actually, I need to redo mine. There are some items on here that are more *preferences* than *absolutes*. I think I should probably clarify that by making two lists."

"What's the difference?"

"Well, I would prefer for my guy to be taller than me, but I am not making it a requirement. I could work around issues like that. But I won't even think about going out with a guy who hasn't put his faith in God. Our relationship would be built on a crumbling foundation. Yep. Doomed from the start."

Sir Lancelot too frowned at the thought.

Berly continued to glance down at the list. After a moment, she said, "You're pretty strict on yourself, aren't you?"

"I don't think so. Some girls we know are so incredibly eager to get into a relationship that they will date any dude with a pulse. Then when that blows up in their face, they catch the next dude on the rebound. It adds up to a lot of heartbreak, a lot of tears, and a lot of drama." She reached down and gave Sir Lancelot a gentle pat down his back. "I only have one heart, so I don't need to go looking for people to will eventually ending up kicking it around the room. That is something I don't want to mess with."

Berly's eyes drifted off. She seemed to be lost in thought.

Maggie knew exactly what her friend was thinking. She knew it was not easy. It was not easy for anybody; all the wondering, all the waiting. It seemed like it would be forever. Besides, boys were always too busy thinking about unimportant things. They were always seeming to be interested, but they were distracted away from girls as well. Or did God wire boys differently for a reason? Maybe it was part of God's plan? Maybe their timing was just merely off for their own protection? That thought had occurred to Maggie before. With all these older brothers, Maggie knew something about how boys think.

Berly now began to wonder if she were one of those girls. Was she wanting a boyfriend so desperately that she was willing to risk falling for some nice-boy-turned-creep? Was she going to be obsessed with someone now who she will one day despise?

Maggie spoke as she walked over to her mirror and pulled off one of her many handwritten sticky notes. "I know it takes a little self-discipline. I honestly think that it is easier for me because I have four older brothers. I don't get all moonstruck over boys because I have to deal with them all the time. But take my advice and make your own list." She crossed back over toward Berly. "And when you do, be sure to pray over each issue. Search the Bible for ideas. See what God tells you. In fact, one of the awesome things about this list is that it'll give you and God something to talk about while you are waiting for Mr. Right. And listen to this …" She began to read the note in her hand. "'Delight thyself also in the LORD; and he shall give thee the desires of thine heart.' He wants you to have the very best. But we need to make sure that we want the things that are best for us and only God can tell us what that is. This also says, 'Commit thy way unto the LORD; trust also in him; and he shall bring it to pass.' Remember He is not going to adjust His timing to fit what we want our schedule to be. We need to put all our trust in Him." [Psalm 37:4-5]

A cynical smile drifted onto Berly's face. "Have you ever shown this list to your parents?"

Maggie let out a brief laugh. "Actually, I did."

"So? What did *they* think about it?"

"My mom thought it was an excellent idea. She also offered a few suggestions. Some of it was just her talking like a mom. But a couple of her ideas were really good. She gave me a few things to think about. I am still taking them under consideration. I might add one or two of them. After all, she has gone down some roads that I haven't; I keep having to remind myself of that."

"And your dad?"

"Oh. Well, he thinks that I should add one about not dating until I'm thirty."

The girls both laughed. Sir Lancelot had just finished eating his kale and was too full to laugh.

Maggie walked back over to the bed and picked up Sir Lancelot. Looking right into the beardy's eyes, she said, "But until that happy day when God brings Mr. Right to me, I still have you, Sir Lancelot. Don't I, baby?" She kissed him on the top of his head and returned the dragon to the glass tank.

Berly exhaled as she was thinking aloud. "I wonder if Billy has a girlfriend."

Maggie did not turn around to look at her friend, but kept looking at the dragon. "If you are so curious, you could always ask Justin's girlfriend. She would know. And if she doesn't, she can usually find out for you. She constantly seems to be in everybody's business."

"Pfffff. Tell me about it."

Maggie walked over and sat on the bed next to Berly. There was a moment of silence.

Finally, Berly confessed. "Okay, this is embarrassing. Justin's girlfriend knows who everyone is and what they are doing, but I can't for the life of me think of what her name is."

Maggie started laughing. "I was thinking the exact same thing. What *is* her name anyway?"

"Good grief! I know it. I just can't think of it."

"I can't either."

Both girls were now in hysterics and stayed in silly mode for several minutes. Sir Lancelot responded by climbing over a long, flat rock and resting directly under his favorite heat lamp. He chose to ignore the teenage conversation as he closed his eyes and quietly enjoyed a warm nap.

CHAPTER 9

A DREAM COME TRUE

As much as Billy would hate to admit it, he actually *did* have fun attending Chess Club that Friday afternoon. To him, there was a kind of beauty to be appreciated in the endless possibilities and dramatic struggles within the dimensions of the chess board. The game came naturally to him, and yet that did not protect him from getting bested all over the place by Maggie. He was quite impressed. He had never met a girl who played chess before; and now, he had met two.

He must not know very many girls.

But confidentially, you did not have to be *good* at chess to be in the club; you just had to show up and play - - and even then, that is up for debate since Billy still has yet to see this *Rodney* character who they all claim is the president of this organization. In Chess Club, there were no dues to be collected, no interviews to be made, no physical exams to endure, and no trial basis to wait out. At this point, he was seriously thinking about going back Monday afternoon. Why not? Besides, Billy did not have anything else at that time. Without his trombone slide, no other group seemed to want him.

At this point, the only thing that bothered him was that he did not want to go home and listen to a bunch of *I-told-you-so's* from his dad (which, by the way, would not happen).

But that was Friday. Let us now focus on Saturday. The redefining moment of his life unexpectedly came crashing down on him just around noon. This would be Billy's pivotal day.

His parents had a dirty little secret. They have been living a clandestine existence outside of their son's ability to observe. The reality is not at all what Billy had been led to believe, but he was about to be set wise to who they actually were. His big toe was about to kick the rock-solid truth.

As you may recall, he was supposed to be spending the day over at Curtis Baker's house. But life rarely follows the script. Since the Baker's only live a few houses down from the Harris', Curtis and his mom came over to pick him up around eleven o'clock that morning. They scared up some lunch and were on their way back to the Baker's when something unplanned happened. The boys were horsing around in the back of Mrs. Baker's car when someone accidently flung Billy's copy of *Pride and Prejudice* right out the car window. Yep, it was Billy who tossed it. He did not mean to; they were just being silly. The true friend that he was, Curtis could always be counted on to laugh hysterically at Billy's expense. When they went back to retrieve it, they quickly discovered that a stray dog had found the book before they did. Billy tried to get it back, but sadly the dog had more important plans for the book and ran off with it. This led to an amusing conversation between the boys that went something like this ...

Billy: Can you believe this weakness? That dog is straight up dumb.

Curtis: Dude, don't you be hating on that poor animal. You were the one who chunked your book out the window. Don't do stunts like that and then blame the outcome on some innocent dog. He's just a dog being a dog.

Billy: You kidding? Did you see how that dog ran? He even runs like an idiot.

Curtis: Might I remind you that that *dumb* dog is out there somewhere with *your* book while you stand here all empty-handed and empty-headed?

Billy: Your dog doesn't act like that.

Curtis: Naturally, because my dog is a genius. Sheriff is a border collie. And for your FYI, border collies are the smartest breed there is. He can think rings around mutts like that with half his brain tied behind his back.

Billy: Oh? Border collies, huh?

Curtis: Yeah, all the way. He is the Einstein of the canine world. You would never find Sheriff chasing cars or barking at squirrels. That might be fine for other dogs, but my dog is far too sophisticated. He prefers to chew up the newspaper or maybe a science magazine. In fact, the other day, he chewed up a very interesting article on clean energy.

Billy: Okay. You had me going until you said that. Why did you name him Sheriff anyway?

Curtis: Because he would round up all the cats and put them in jail, of course.

While they were 'cracking wise' with each other, they decided to swing by the bookstore and give Billy a chance to buy another copy of Jane Austen's novel for his dad's class. With the others waiting in the car, Billy marched right up to where the book would be, grabbed a copy, and worked himself over to the registers. He was horrified to discover that the only person manning the registers was that crabby lady from the other night: *Midge What's-Her-Face.* He took a deep sigh and got in line.

Midge picked up the book to scan the barcode. "Same book?" She gave him an unamused sideways glance.

"Uh, yeah."

"Different girl?"

Billy rolled his eyes.

He made his purchase and climbed back in Mrs. Baker's car. "Good grief! I haven't even gotten past the first chapter of this book and this is already my third copy."

While Billy was inside the store, Mrs. Baker received a phone call. As it turned out, they had some family that unexpectedly arrived at their house. Afternoon plans were suddenly altered. Now Billy found himself headed back home with Mrs. Baker at the wheel and a disappointed Curtis riding shotgun.

Mrs. Baker apologized. "I'm terribly sorry that you can't stay over tonight. I didn't plan on having my family come over. I swear they said they were coming the next weekend."

Curtis smiled and took a stab at some humor. "Yeah. That makes no sense. But don't worry. We'll have our revenge someday. We'll go over and crash at their house unexpectedly."

"That's okay, Mrs. Baker. These things happen. There are other nights." That happened from time to time. Billy had learned to accept it. There were no bruised feelings.

As they approached the Harris' house, Curtis peered out the window and noticed something odd. "Did you call and let your parents know that you're coming home?"

"No."

"Well, whose car is that?" Curtis pointed out the window toward a strange car in Billy's driveway.

Billy looked out and squinted his eyes. Indeed, there was a third vehicle in their driveway. "Huh? Where did that come from?" It was a handsome black car that appeared to be right-off-the-lot new. In fact, it seemed to have what his dad called a *showroom-shine*. "I don't know anything about that," he said as he shook his puzzled head.

Mrs. Baker brought her car to an easy stop just shy of the Harris' house.

Curtis laughed again. "What if your parents decided to buy you a new car and surprise you with it? And what with you only being fifteen and all? Adding insult to injury, my friend."

Billy was not laughing. It was painfully clear that Billy's family did not have that kind of money. Besides, the car that sat there was a bit too nice – too mature – to be driven by a teenager just starting off behind the wheel, especially considering that Billy would not even be able to drive on his own for another year. And if they did happen to get him a car, he was hoping for something a bit sportier-looking than that anyway. This was more like something that a successful businessman would drive. Very classy.

But Billy did respond to Curtis' pitiful joke. "That's doubtful. With our limited sources of income, that isn't going to happen anytime soon, I assure you." With that, Billy opened the door and climbed out of the car. "Thanks again for the lift, Mrs. Baker."

"Not a problem," replied Curtis' mom. "We'll see you later, Billy."

The boys made their usual farewell comments and the Baker's drove off leaving Billy alone with his duffle bag and a brand-spanking new copy of Jane Austen's illustrious novel. Billy studied the strange car as he walked past it. *Wow. This is nice. Wherever did this come from?* No, this was certainly not a car for a high school student. He looked back toward the house and saw that a yard rake had been left leaning against the wall under the carport. He had been told to put that back in the shed. *If I don't put that away now, I'll never hear the end of it,* he thought. He grabbed it and took it into the backyard where it was supposed to go.

Then a horrible thought came to mind. *Oh no! I'll bet that whoever that is with the car is an old chum of mom and dad's. The last thing I want is to listen to someone telling me about how big I've gotten or how I must've been too young to remember them.* Billy decided right then and there that he would sneak in by way of the back of the house. If he were extra quiet, he and his duffle bag might be able to make it to his bedroom completely unnoticed. They were not expecting him to be home anyway. For all they knew, he was out parading all over town with Curtis. So ... HA!

Upon coming to the door, he removed his shoes, stepped into the house, and gently closed the door behind him. He looked around the living room and listened closely to determine his parents' location. It sounded as if they were seated at the dining room table. But then, he heard the strange man's voice. He did not recognize the voice at all; the accent told him that this man was not from anywhere around Pecan Falls – probably from the northeast.

"...$5,000 to your Haitian orphanages and that extra $900 to their water project. The Chinese Bibles were $2,800."

What is all this? What are they talking about?

"The figures for the construction of that building in Croatia are not yet in, but when they are, I will email that information to you. All in all, the money that you have sent to charitable organizations for this quarter is just above $400,000."

Billy's jaw dropped. *Do what? Am I in the right place?* He quickly looked around the room to make sure. Same old furniture. Same marks on the walls. Same awkward sixth grade school photo of him that sat on the piano. Sure enough; he was in his own house. Then to prove it even further, he heard the voice of his mom.

"Four hundred thousand dollars to charity." She sighed deeply. "Not so long ago, that used to sound like a lot of money; now we barely even miss it. Let's see if we can increase that amount for the next quarter."

WHAT?! Billy suddenly felt as if his whole body were about to explode. *Our family has money? Not just money, but MONEY?! Big money?* He wanted to scream in a very non-masculine way. It was with great fortitude that some inner strength kept him quiet. It was hard. Billy had this uncontrollable impulse to bite into a phonebook. Instead, he tiptoed over to the other side of the room in order to find out what else was being said.

His dad spoke up. "That is the least we can do considering how much God has blessed us. It keeps coming in faster than we can give it away." He let out a light chuckle. "The most amusing part of this whole thing is that it doesn't have any meaning unless you *can* give it away."

The unknown man sounded amused. "Might I just say that finding creative ways to give away large sums of your money is quite an entertaining diversion for me actually? It's rather fun, to be perfectly honest with you. Not many of my bosses have shared your generous attitude."

Diane spoke. "We only ask that you handle this with your usual discretion, Lewis."

"Naturally. So nothing has changed? Your son still doesn't know?" He reached over for another brownie.

Diane had taken a sip of her sweet tea and set the glass down. "Nope. And we want to keep it that way for a little while longer. I know that you probably think that we're out of our minds."

Billy hung on every word spoken. But his thoughts were also buzzing around like bees in a hive. First, his family had incredible wealth. Secondly, his parents were giving away large portions of this money to parties unknown. And finally, all of this information was being kept from him. Any one of those three concepts had the ability to knock him over, but now all three of these discoveries were colliding inside of his head like cars in a demolition derby.

"Actually I was thinking about how refreshingly wise you two are. It can't be easy, living under this level of wealth and trying to raise a son. I know some kids handle it well - - but some don't."

Oh, please; let me try, Billy thought.

Diane looked down and shook her head. "We just didn't want to take that chance. This is our son that we are talking about."

Billy wanted to get a better look at this guy they called Lewis. He crept along the wall of the dining room and slowly peeked around the corner. At this angle, he could make out the back side of this guy's business suit. He also had a bald spot and a slight comb over in the middle of his salt/pepper hair. Not wishing to be seen, Billy backed up a little.

Lewis was speaking with a strong New England accent. "It would take a lot of resolve to raise him 'normal' as you said earlier."

Diane reached over for William's hand as she spoke. "Lewis, while we have you here, we've been praying about that project that we mentioned last time. William and I want you to go ahead and proceed with those plans. We don't care how much it costs. Just pay out and make it happen. Those people need that hospital. That village is just too far from a major city and it's big enough to require medical services."

Lewis grinned. "I thought you might say that, so I took the liberty of drawing this up." He pulled a document out of his leather satchel and scooted it across the table. "What do you think of this?"

As William and Diane both looked over the pages, Billy peeked around the corner again. His curiosity was getting the best of him. He thought that maybe the smart thing to do would be to just quietly go back to his room, or even return outside and let his parents' business be their business. He also thought how hysterical it would be to just casually walk into the kitchen, make himself a drink, and watch everyone squirm. But he chose rather to get a better look.

Lewis felt that there was something going on behind him – a sensation of another presence in the room perhaps. He glanced over his shoulder to see what it was. But he saw nothing. All was normal.

Billy sat against the wall thinking to himself. *That was a close one.*

William tapped his finger on the pages. "This looks good. I like this." He looked up to address Lewis. But in his peripheral vision, he thought for a split second that he saw Billy's nose and bangs disappear around the corner. His expression changed from business-like confidence to sudden worry. When Lewis looked over at him, his face again changed to a comically nervous grin.

Diane was still looking at the document. "So do I. Let's go with this."

The business was concluding so Lewis began to load his paperwork back into his small briefcase. "Do either of you have any questions about the report?"

Still wide-eyed and scared from seeing what appeared to be Billy's profile, William's voice cracked as he answered. "No. I don't think so."

"Everything looks fine to me." Diane spoke as she looked up. Her eyes flashed wide. She saw the sleeve of Billy's shirt through the doorway; and then it was gone as quickly as it had appeared. Her face dropped.

She looked at William and William looked back at her. Both of them knew what the other was thinking. When they looked back at Lewis, they saw the exact same thing. Across the living room, they could easily make out Billy's unmistakable reflection in the glass on one of the picture frames. They were clearly busted.

Unaware of anything wrong, Lewis had just finished gathering all of his things as he spoke. "Well, it sure is always a pleasure to come here to Pecan Falls for your quarterly reports, but I've got a plane to catch ..." Lewis looked up at them and stopped. He noticed that they both had pained looks on their faces – almost like guilt. "Is everything all right?"

They both spoke. "What? Oh, everything's fine!" "Of course. We're great. We're all great." Diane and William then burst out of their seats to escort Lewis out of the house as Billy retreated around another corner to keep his presence from being discovered.

Diane spoke up with a loud voice. "Well, we would love for you to stay longer, but since you're in such a hurry to leave ..."

William echoed Diane's sentiment. "That's right. We'll have to do dinner or something the next time you are down."

At this point, Diane and William each had one of Lewis' arms and was walking him out of their house and right up to his rented car. He was talking just as quickly as they were walking. "I understand. When I get back to New York, I'll prepare an update on that project in Africa as well. So if you need me over the next two weeks, leave a message with the office. I'm scheduled to be in Dallas later this week and Seattle after that." They must have been walking quickly because Lewis now found himself sitting comfortably in his car.

William hurried a reply. "I'm sure everything will be fine. Thanks for coming over."

"Give our love to Sharon when you get back. And have a safe flight," Diane added.

Lewis started his car. "Will do. Bye." Looking slightly baffled, he backed out of their driveway and disappeared down the street.

William and Diane stood staring at Lewis' car and waved. They were still waving after the car was out of sight. Neither of them wanted to turn around. After a few seconds, they stopped and turned toward the house. As expected, Billy was standing in the doorway. Even at that distance, they could see a hundred questions forming in their son's mind.

Both parents looked as uncomfortable as anyone Billy had ever seen.

There were an awkward few seconds because they were wondering how much of Lewis' visit had been overheard. Just because he happened to be there at the end, that did not mean that he heard anything important. Diane decided to pretend that everything was normal as they walked back to the house. "So how was school today?"

"Uh, today is Saturday. We didn't have school. And if we, dad would probably be there too."

William looked down at Diane and shrugged. "That's fair," he said.

Their son pointed up the road where they last saw Lewis' car. "Who was that man?"

They blankly looked back at Billy. Diane turned her innocent voice back on and spoke. "What man?" After another second, she acknowledged the earlier presence of the car that was now gone. "Oh. Him? Uh ... that was just Lewis." She sounded like Billy should already know the guy from a hundred earlier visits, just some friend-of-the-family. "How about some orange juice?"

William followed her lead like a trained dolphin. "Orange juice? That sounds great, honey! I would love a glass of orange juice." They both started for the door again but were stopped by Billy.

"But dad, you hate orange juice. What's going on around here?"

In a defeated voice, Diane exhaled slowly and turned to William. "I think this may be a good time."

William agreed. "I think you're right." Glancing back at Billy, he said, "Let's go in and talk."

Billy walked back inside and prepared himself for some excellent news. Diane wondered how they were going to be able to explain this in such a way that was going to make sense. William was wanting another one of those brownies. This should be interesting.

CHAPTER 10

THE BACKSTORY

For those of you who may have slept since reading the last chapter (and a couple of you who slept *during* the last chapter – you know who you are), let us take quick inventory of the situation. So far, this kid has done nothing but complain. He honestly believed that all of life's problems would be solved by having a substantial amount of wealth. He failed to understand that having incredible riches can *cause* as many problems as it can resolve. But now it seemed that everything had changed. A few short minutes ago, Billy accidently discovered that his parents were in fact *giving away* more money each month than he had ever hoped to see in his entire lifetime. What's with that? They certainly had more money than anyone else in Pecan Falls and perhaps the entire county – which, in and of itself, was not saying much. But what does this all mean? Could this be exactly what he had wanted and prayed for all these years? Have all of his dreams just come true? Even the weird dreams with that annoying butler? Where did this sudden wealth come from? How far could this money go? And more importantly, how can Billy use this to his advantage and start living a completely different life?

William poured himself some sweet tea and reached for the brownies on the table, leftovers from Lewis' all-too-brief stopover. Billy sat in the same seat once occupied by their guest while his parents settled in across the table from him.

William suggested that they begin their conversation with a prayer. This was not Billy's idea and his heart was not especially into it, but he knew that it would not hurt anything. In the prayer, William spoke of clairvoyance and something about wisdom. Clear understanding. Blah, blah, blah ...

When he was done, Billy's mom said, "We should begin by saying that we never had any intentions of deceiving anyone - - but we do want to keep this a tightly-held secret. People are entitled to keep private information private." Diane's hands waved around as she spoke, a habit of which she was often teased. "Our finances are no one's business but our own."

William had just taken a sip of his tea and returned his glass to the table. "And we do not want you to take this the wrong way, but the easiest way to keep it a secret all these years was to leave you out of it - - especially when you were small."

Something deep inside Billy wanted to take offense at this last remark. It was an open invitation to begin a full-volumed trip to Dramatown, but he decided against it. After all, they were right. Small children have the habit of telling everyone everything they know. When Billy was a little boy, he was no different. He would give perfect strangers a full report on all their earlier activities. A real blabber mouth, that boy.

Diane continued the thought, waving her hands frantically in the process. "Besides, when all of this first happened, you were just coming out of diapers. After a lot of prayerful nights, we decided that we would rather have you grow up *this* way rather than as a rich kid who always had everything handed to him."

For the past five minutes, questions by the thousands were running through Billy's whirling head. Now, only one question came out of his mouth. "So why do you keep working?"

William was rather relieved that Billy's first question was an easy one. With a simple shrug, he answered, "Because we both enjoy what we do. I love to teach and your mother enjoys the real estate business."

"But if we have all this money, why are we living the way that we do? Why do we go on living like *this*?" Billy waved his hand in the air indicting the house and all that was in it.

Diane and William were both only slightly insulted. They spoke in unison. "Living like what?"

"Like this? Why can't we live it up a little, like rich folks?"

Diane's eyebrows descended as she peered directly at her son. "Okay, let's get something straight right now. There is a great big world out there, young man; and compared to the way most of the world lives, we *do* live like rich people. In fact, compared to many people in *this* country, we live like rich people indeed. We may not be living like the super rich, but this has been far from real poverty. In fact, no one under this roof has ever known what real poverty is, what it feels like in a personal way."

Billy raised his arms and his voice to a certain degree as if he were looking for a reason to be mad. This was his way of redirecting the conversation away from the sermon at hand. "I can't believe that you two have been lying to me my entire life!!"

Diane was aghast. "What lie? When have we ever lied to you?"

"About this. About us being rich."

William answered back. "We never lied about that. When have we ever said that we weren't rich?"

"But you let me think that we were poor."

"Uh, when have we ever claimed to be poor? Look, I don't remember ever discussing our financial status with you. To my knowledge, this is the first time that it's ever come up."

"I don't get it. Why do we keep living in this dinky old house? Why do we have these beat-up vehicles? How come we are still using this worn-out dryer from the 80's?"

William pulled up his hands in order to count the answers to these question on his spread-out fingers. "Well firstly, we think that this house is the perfect size for us; we don't need anything bigger than this. Secondly, the cars work just fine with a little maintenance. And as for the dryer ..." He suddenly stopped counting and looked over at Diane with his eyebrows all furrowed. "Actually, I have no idea why we don't get a new dryer. That one in there is the pits and we should probably get rid of it."

Diane turned to face Billy. "To put it simply, this is the life that we live. We have been living off of the money that your father and I make from our jobs. We are not depending on the money from the company. That is separate. You see if we begin to live lavishly, people will naturally suspect that we have this money. It wouldn't be a secret anymore. One thing that you must consider is that keeping the money a secret frees us to do great things with it."

This statement made no sense to Billy. What was so awful about people knowing about the money? "*Great things*?! What would be greater than getting a new car? Or a game room? Or our own swimming pool? Lots of people have those things and they're not rich. We actually *are* rich but we have nothing but junk."

Choosing to 'pick his fights,' William ignored that last jab and nodded his head in agreement. "That's true. And we are not opposed to having some things like that. But we don't live off what we call the 'big money.' We pretty much live off the money that we earn from our jobs."

Something his mom said earlier confused him greatly. "Then what did you mean by doing great things with it?" He had a feeling that his parents were about to fill his ears with a lot of noble talk.

"We are talking about helping other people."

"But shouldn't we help ourselves first?"

Diane started to give Billy a stern look. "No. God takes care of us. We never have to worry about things. *He* looks after us nicely. God is way more qualified and way more able to take care of all our needs. Much more than we are."

Billy would never recognize this on his own, but his voice was becoming rather defensive. He was desperately wanting to win an argument that was already lost. "Well, doesn't God help other people too?"

"Oh, yes. Absolutely." Diane waved her hands like an orchestra conductor. "But the *Creator* is nothing if not *creative*. And sometimes, He uses us and our money to do just that."

As far as Billy was concerned, this conversation was going nowhere. He wanted to end it now and go buy something big, like a car. Yeah. That would be nice. Surely they were rich enough to push away from the table, terminate this boring Q and A session, and go do something fun for a change. But he proceeded with the next thought. "So what you are essentially saying is that we continue to live like poor people for the sake of appearances and give out large sums of money to random folks in secret?" He looked irritated and smug as he leaned back in his chair with his arms crossed.

That was the wrong thing to say. A brief look of shock flashed across Diane's face for only a split second. "We *aren't* living like poor people! When are you going to understand that?"

William and Diane continued their gallant speeches, tag-teaming

94

back and forth as a strong united front. Diane waved her hands around as if she were hailing a taxi. But Billy heard very little of their passionate discourse. In situations like this, his mind seemed to wonder - - especially when distracted by such incredibly awesome, out-of-this-world kind of news. *We're crazy rich*, he kept thinking.

How idiotic. Rich kids like him should not have to sit there confined to a chair, listening to his parents go on and on about nonsense. There were about a gazillion other places that folks this rich should be. He ought to be parking a yacht somewhere in Monte Carlo or jet skiing off the coast of Greece. He could be throwing a swanky party on the top floor of a skyscraper in Manhattan. Cruising around the brightly lit streets of Tokyo in a fully-loaded sports car would be kinda cool. It might be fun to pay scads of money for small portions of yucky food in some restaurant in Paris – and then make them take it all back – and the whole time dressed like an oil baron with the biggest cowboy hat he could buy. But no. He had to live in stupid ol' Pecan Falls. In fact, it just occurred to him how dumb that sounded. Pecan Falls. The name conjured up images of a clumsy chef dropping a lousy Thanksgiving pie.

Naturally, Billy remained in the room with his preachy parents. But in his new daydream, he was imagining how it would feel to be out joyriding in a sporty European car shaped like an angular wedge. His clothes were all top of the line right down to his socks. His hair was slicked back and completely under control. His complexion enjoyed a total lack of acne for once. The route he was taking took him through the countryside, past a large gate, and up to a dignified three-story mansion. Horses played on the estate behind the house.

That car was being driven as hard as he dared considering the gravel. His ferocious driving techniques would make certain that everyone in the house would know that he was coming up the driveway. Right in front of the main entrance to the house under some fancy portico, the car came to a grinding stop - - as if he were trying to park that roadster on a dime. A few peacocks ran out of his way with some encouragement from his blaring car horn - - one peacock going so far as to take flight up to a low branch on a nearby tree.

A man with a fine suit and white gloves came rushing out to the car. Somehow Billy knew instinctively to sit there and wait for this man to open the car door. With a low muffled click, the car door was released. A small choir of interior sounds reminded him that the keys were still in the ignition. That was not *his* problem. He stepped out onto the gravel and rose to his feet. Now for the first time, he could see the face of the man who opened the door. It was James of all people, that impertinent butler from his dream several days ago. "You?!" he said in a disappointed voice. The butler made a frown at the reaction to his face.

Billy awoke from his daydream, seated at their dining room table with a brownie in his hand.

William leaned over to Diane. "I don't think Billy has heard a single word that we've said for the past minute."

"Sure, I have." Billy said in a defensive tone. "The last thing you said was, 'And that is precisely why we are keeping it a secret.'" *Thank you, automatic repeat-what-was-last-said brain feature; you have saved my neck from many a tight spot.*

His parents looked at each other with a sense of disbelief on their faces.

"Wait a minute." Something just occurred to Billy. "You have always taught me about the importance of tithing. If this is such a big secret, how can you tithe without it being seen by somebody? I'm sure that if someone dropped ten percent of this kind of money in the offering plate, it would certainly get noticed. It would give the whole show away."

William spoke up. "It is true that tithing is very important to us. So here is what we do: we tithe ten percent of what I make as a teacher and what your mother makes as a real estate agent. With the company money, we don't. But we have set up a system in which ten percent of the corporate money actually does go into faith-based charities and mission work. There are inner city projects that we finance. We bring fresh water to people in villages that do not have access to it in foreign lands. There are always lots of opportunities for ..."

Blah, blah, blah. You just lost me again. We seriously need to talk about something important. Like: wouldn't it be cool to tear down that sad back porch and replace it with a large game room? I could invite all of my friends over and play video games on a thousand-inch flat screen TV. Pump up the sound on a set of subwoofers and we would be all set. Actually, let's do this thing right. We should get rid of this ramshackled old rattrap and build something descent - - some place where we can stretch out and really throw down some parties. That would be crazy. Wait a minute! What am I talking about? I'd bet my parents wouldn't even allow me to buy a used air-hockey table.

Billy sensed a quiet moment. His parents had stopped talking again. It was time to throw out a question as if he had been listening this whole time. "So when did we become rich?"

"Well, that all depends on your definition of *rich*," Diane said. "We've always been rich."

"That's right," William added. "Paul writes in Second Corinthians ..."

I knew it was coming, thought Billy. *We can't have a conversation without tossing a Bible verse into the mix.*

"...'For ye know the grace of our Lord Jesus Christ, that, though he was rich, yet for your sakes he became poor, that ye through his poverty might be rich.' So in short, Christ had all the riches of Heaven and took on poverty so that we being born in poverty might become rich. But the riches that He is talking about are not the riches of the world. In the end, that stuff doesn't matter."

Diane jumped in. "A lot of people preach that it is God's will to make us all rich in this life. That simply is not true. Whether we had this money or not, our mission is the same: to win people for Christ."

Billy was rolling his eyes. "That was not at all what I meant. I was wanting to know when it was that we found ourselves with all this money. Did you guys win a lottery or something?"

This time, both his parents looked offended.

Diane replied, "A lottery?! You should know us better than that. A lottery is meant to raise money by taking it from the poor. Sure, some lucky person might win; but think of the vast number of people who *don't* win. They are pouring in money that they cannot afford to lose and end up throwing it away rather than buying the things that they need."

"...or what their families need," William added. "Plus, when people are taken in by the lottery, they are essentially saying that they do not have faith in God's ability to provide for them. It is an attempt to get-rich-quick apart from God's providence. These poor folks are acting outside of God's direction by throwing away the money that they've worked hard for. Honestly, it's tragic."

Diane then turned to William adding a little side note. "Besides, I wonder just how 'lucky' the lucky winner actually is. They are probably swamped with greedy family and friends after word gets out. The winners are usually paraded around on the news and on social media; and they themselves make a big deal about their winnings to everyone they meet. Enter the moochers. Soon enough, they have more kin than they ever dreamed about having, and these chiselers all think that they are entitled to part of it. It's sad. They're probably better off tossing that money into the fire."

William added, "HA! It'll burn up someday anyway."

Billy was now getting a little frustrated. All he wanted was a simple answer to a simple question. He did not mean to start a series of sermonettes. "So where *did* this money come from?"

William looked over at Diane. "Well, that's a long story."

Diane began to tell the tale as if she had been subconsciously practicing it for years to prepare for this moment. "I had only one uncle and I was his only niece. When I started dating your father, my uncle took a huge liking to him too and made him feel like part of the family. But my uncle didn't have any other family besides us and he left the company to us when he passed away."

"Wait. What company are we talking about?"

William asked, "Well, we have mentioned him before. Do you remember what his name was?"

"Sure." Billy searched in his head. "It was ... Tony Crowe. Right?"

Diane looked at Billy's eyes in earnest and spoke the next sentence very slowly. "That's right. My uncle was the founder of Crowe's Sporting Equipment."

Billy felt the floor open up under his feet. *Crowe's Sporting Equipment? This cannot be. This is huge. They are known all over the globe. You pretty much know when a sports personality has become famous because he or she starts appearing in Crowe advertisements.* "Crowe's Sporting Equipment? Are you serious?!" he yelled.

Neither of his parents seemed weirded out by that last earth-shattering revelation. They were both very calm actually. But when Billy reacted the way he did, they both looked at each other with an amused smile. They knew that this was huge news to someone in Billy's shoes – shoes he got at Crowe's Sporting Equipment we might add.

"I'm not sure that I ..." He stopped himself and jumped to his feet.

He walked over to the refrigerator and back. He did not know exactly what to do with himself. He tried to sit back down, but he only popped up again, like toast in a toaster. "Uh ... Are you sure about this? Crowe? We own Crowe? Because Crowe is huge. This is ... *huge*. No. There is no way. It's ..." Billy slowed down and took a deep breath. "Crowe?"

William's eye narrowed with concern. "Hey, are you okay?"

"Uh, no. Not really. I'm freaking out a little. This is ... This is big. Really big. Do you know how big this is?"

His parents nodded. "Yes, we know how big this is," William said laughingly. "To be more precise, we know exactly how big this is. We could tell you, but you would probably freak out more."

He went over to the sink, got some water on his hands, and splashed some on his face. "I'll be okay in a little bit."

Diane and William looked at each other with worry. After pacing the room and mumbling something to himself for a minute or so, Billy returned to the table and sat.

"Okay. I don't think that I'm understanding this. How can you possibly run a huge company like Crowe's Sporting Equipment and live here in Pecan Falls and doing your little joke jobs?"

That was unfair and uncalled for; but his parents looked through that unintentional insult and found what Billy meant to ask. William put his glass down, which by now was just ice anyway, and began to explain. "We don't. We have people that run the company for us. But we make many of the big decisions from here. And Lewis stops by from time to time to go over the reports. Your great-uncle knew exactly what he was doing when he hired these specific people and, for the most part, those key people are still with us today."

William and Diane continued to explain some of the inner workings of the company; but honestly, all Billy heard were the long list of excuses as to why they could not use this money to live large. When his folks had finished, they asked if he understood everything. He told them that he did in order to get them off his back. Right now, Billy just wanted to be alone to think about all of this. It was too much to process.

Wow! Crowe's Sporting Equipment. Dude!

In a few minutes, the conversation was over. Meeting adjourned. His mom started on some dinner and his dad began to do battle with that old clothes dryer. Billy found himself plopped onto the couch and reached over for the remote. He had absolutely no idea why he turned on the TV; he certainly was not going to be thinking about anything but this money for a long time.

The events of the past hour were quite the game-changer. This was huge. They were global. Generations of famous athletes had their day in Crowe stuff. And now, Billy was the heir apparent to the Crowe company fortune. But what could he do about it? There were so many things that he had always wanted but could not afford. Now, things were different. His parents just did not understand. Well, maybe it was *he* did not understand *them.*

No. This time it was all them. His parents were just weird. With all the stuff in the world that there was to buy, how could they go on living the way they were? This was dumb. It was beyond dumb.

After clicking through a few channels, something caught his eye. It was an infomercial for something called the 'Twelve-in-One Super-Flex Body Builder Set.' *See? Something like that would be so cool to have. And we could easily afford it. That would be nothing considering how much money we are sitting on. Stuff like that was so expensive before today. Now, we have so much money that there is no way that little amount would even be missed. I doubt that mom and dad even keep up with amounts that small.*

Wait a minute. Billy had an idea.

It's time for a change.

CHAPTER 11

EVEN RICHER

If you have never read it before, it is going to sound like some complicated riddle. But it makes perfect sense. The Apostle Paul once wrote, "For that which I do I allow not: for what I would, that do I not; but what I hate, that do I." That simply means that we often find ourselves doing exactly the thing that we do not want to do and vice versa. Tragically, when people tell us flat out not to do something, our subconscious immediately begins to figure out a way to make it happen. We justify our actions to our parents and friends by saying that we 'forgot' or that our disobedience was somehow 'an accident.' We try to sound as innocent as possible. But if we would be completely honest with ourselves, we know that we could have done the right thing if we wanted to. Our mind wants to obey for the purpose of appearances, but our will has other plans for our bodies. And most of the time, our disobedient selves win out.

In Billy's case, he was told not to tell anyone about their big family secret. Unfortunately, this may be more secret than Billy can handle. Money of this size is awfully hard to hide. He had never had to walk around with something this heavy on his back before and he may collapse under the weight.

If his life were being played out on a movie screen for an audience, they would all be shaking their heads. "It's only a matter of time," they would say. "It isn't a question of *if*, but of *when*."

An entire week had come and gone and Billy had not told a soul. ... yet. It was not so much that he believed in keeping the family business in the family;

he just had not yet figured out a way to properly tell anyone. How would you bring that up in polite conversation anyway? "Hey guys, guess what! I just found out that my family is rich beyond my wildest dreams." Pitiful. They would certainly think all this was merely a product of his overactive imagination. He had a much better chance of convincing them that he was the most popular kid at school; and that would take nothing short of a miracle to happen. If they were ever to believe him, he needed tangible proof. Something concrete. Something incredibly expensive and frivolous. And it just so happens that that proof should be arriving at his house very soon.

So in the meantime, Billy was thoroughly enjoying yet another one of his wealthy dreams. This time, he found himself relaxing in a fancy lawn chair just outside his fantasy house on a well-manicured estate. He was outfitted appropriately for tennis – but with the addition of an expensive pair of shades. An unused racquet was resting within arm's reach on a small table next to him. Soft music was being played from speakers probably hidden in the bushes nearby.

As he sat, he sensed James approaching him from behind. James carried a small silver tray and dressed sharply, appropriate of a butler with his level of professionalism.

In a voice as relaxed as the music, Billy let out a deep sigh and then spoke. "James, this is the life. No responsibilities. No work. No school."

Matching Billy's tone, James mockingly continued the list. "No challenges. No purpose. No opportunities for personal growth."

Billy had more than a mere hunch that James would disapprove. Call it a premonition, but it was obvious from James' voice. From the comfort of his chair, Billy scarcely cared what his blowhard of a butler thought. "Judge all you want," replied Billy. "Even your snide little remarks won't dampen my mood today."

James' middle-aged brow wrinkled up in interest. "Why? Because of your wealth?" James looked around at the extensive acreage and back again at the house.

Billy raised his head up slightly and looked at the house over the rim of his sunglasses. "I know, I know. It's excessive, but it's home." He let his head fall back to its original reclining position.

"You know that none of this is real, that this is just nothing more than one of your elaborate dreams, right?"

A large grin found its way onto Billy's face. His eyes however remained concealed behind those expressionless shades. "That is where you're wrong, you old grump. This is so much more than your average dream. What you see around you is all quite nice - - but when I wake up, I'm even richer. So hate all you want."

Favoring his right eye, the butler tilted his head to one side and looked at the young man. "I am not altogether convinced that *richer* is even a real word – not even when comparing the sweetness of two chocolate cakes."

"Don't be a brat, James. You *could* find yourself a butler in someone else's dream."

James rolled his eyes as if to say that was the corniest thing he had ever heard.

Billy nearly interrupted himself with an additional thought. "Oh. By the way, Jaaaaames, I've been meaning to ask you a question. Do you have an actual last name? Or is it just James?"

The dream butler appeared uncomfortable – or more uncomfortable than usual. "Why do you ask?"

"Oh, I was just curious."

"It's *your* dream. Don't *you* have a name for me?"

"No, not that I am conscience of. Come on and tell me. I'm dying to know."

James looked straight forward and remained expressionless. "I would prefer to keep that to myself if it is all the same to you, sir."

Billy removed his sunglasses in a gesture of great interest. "Why?"

"You will probably find it amusing."

"No, I won't. Now tell me, what is your last name?"

With a great deal of reluctantcy, he took a deep breath and stated, "It is Butler. My name is James Butler."

"BUTLER?! Are you serious?" Billy started snickering in manner suggesting a hyena on laughing gas.

James exhaled an irritated-sounding sigh and pushed forward his next sentence, trying to ignore Billy's tone. "Begging your pardon, but in the end, what makes you think that your earthly wealth is any more real than the riches you dream about? People spend their entire lives building up a vast fortune, only to lose it all when they die. A life in constant pursuit of riches is a wasted life indeed. But living a life to further the Kingdom of

God is paying it forward. Those are the riches that do not get burned up in the end."

Billy ignored James' words as James had ignored Billy's. "I don't have any idea what you are talking about and I don't care. But I do have a question for you."

James seemed unwilling to change the subject, but he straightened up knowing that he had slid out of character for a moment. "Sir?"

"Do you know anything about English literature?"

James gave an involuntary tug at his vest and straightened his back. "I am fairly versed in the field of literature. Why?"

"Are you at all familiar with a book called *Pride and Prejudice*?"

An excited grin displayed James' flawless teeth as he eagerly answered. "*Pride and Prejudice*? Naturally. Jane Austen's quintessential work is an essential read and one of the finest in the English tongue."

"I don't like it."

James' smile disappeared.

When Billy noticed the change on the butler's countenance, he could not help but give a little laugh. Billy had set him up on purpose. Although James only existed in Billy's dream, that was no excuse for his rude behavior.

The butler simply cleared his throat and tried to think of something polite to say. "Well, it isn't exactly Tolkien, is it, sir?"

He had scarcely finished his sentence before Billy was changing the subject again. "Just what is *that* anyway?" Billy pointed at the tall cold drink resting on James' tray. "That there with the weird color."

"What?" James looked at where Billy was pointing and quickly acknowledged the drink. "Oh. This? This is your breakfast, sir. Your 'power-drink' if you please." James went back to looking proud of himself.

Billy reached over and picked it up. The clinking of the ice was somewhat muffled by the thick drink. Describing the color would force this book to take an unwanted concession to the vulgar. An unusually thick straw protruded from the rim right next to a huge stalk of celery, a distracting sight. Rather than looking appetizing, it possessed a repelling quality.

James continued. "I thought that you might be needing it this afternoon for your tennis lesson which is in …" He looked down at his watch. " …just a couple of minutes."

"My tennis lesson? What time is it anyway?"

"It is one o'clock in the afternoon."

"One o'clock in the afternoon?! Why am up so early?"

James struggled for the right words to keep from repeating himself. "Sir, your tennis lesson ..."

Billy was not in the mood for some nasty-looking drink and placed it back on the tray. "You drink it." He got up out of his seat and grabbed the tennis racquet. "So. Has that top-dollar tennis instructor from Europe arrived yet? How does she look?" Billy began to look around the estate with great interest for anything that resembled a beautiful woman standing on a tennis court.

With that simple question, James suddenly grew uneasy.

Looking down a grassy slope, Billy spotted a tennis court. But he was not expecting to see this. A man clearly in his sixties was warming up. He had a prominent bald spot, a white beard under a pink face, rather short shorts, and long white socks. Billy was horrified.

James looked like someone was about to pop a balloon in front of his face. "Uh ... in my defense, you asked for the *best* tennis instructor in the world."

"No. I asked for the *best looking* tennis instructor in the world." Billy glanced back down at the court and then returned his gaze to James. He tried to speak again but the words did not come. He felt as if some invisible force was keeping his mouth from working. He focused all his efforts and drove the words out of his mouth. Success! "That's a GROSS OLD MAN!"

At once, Billy's entire body shook, waking himself up from his dream. It did not take much time for him to become aware of his actual surroundings. Everyone in his entire English class had turned in their seats and was looking right at him. Being the focus of the class' attention was only made worse by the uncomfortable silence that accompanied. It was not one o'clock as James had said; it was only first period - - the beginning of what he could already tell would be a long day indeed. *Wait 'til I get my hands on that butler*, he voiced in his head. After a lifetime of awkward moments, one might think that he was prepared for this sort of thing – but no.

The silence was mercifully broken by his dad. "No. I don't think that is correct." Mr. Harris was of average height; but at this moment, he seemed abnormally tall. "Actually, I don't see the words *gross old man* here at all." Some of the other students started to snicker. This certainly was not Mr. Harris' intention. "Billy, try it again please."

"Uh …" Billy had to think and think quickly. He searched his mind for the name of the lady in their silly novel. By some enchanted miracle, the name actually came to mind. Glorious recollection. "Elizabeth Bennett?"

More students laughed.

Mr. Harris looked saddened. He wanted to help his son, but anything that he could do would probably make the embarrassment worse. "No. Curtis Baker, would you care to try?"

Billy met Curtis' eyes. Curtis shook his head and gestured down to his open grammar book. "Uh, it is a run-on sentence."

"And how would you correct it?"

I'm such an idiot, Billy thought to himself. *I don't even have the right book out.*

Curtis continued his answer. "I would put a period after the word *behavior* and capitalize the *S* in *strange*."

Billy sank in his seat. He would give nearly anything to become invisible at that moment. His uncertain eyes turned over to Chloe. She glanced over at him for a split second and giggled silently to herself. He knew from how hot his red face felt that he must be shining like a stoplight.

"Very good. That is absolutely correct. Thank you, Curtis." At that moment, the dismissal bell rang and startled him – he actually jumped causing more laughter from those close to him. Mr. Harris raised his voice so he could be heard over the sound of books slamming shut and students climbing out of their seats. "Don't forget to read chapters four and five of *Pride and Prejudice*. If you didn't read it over the weekend, make sure you have it done by tomorrow. Otherwise, I'll see you at the game tonight."

Mr. Harris' voice changed its projection. Rather than addressing the class entire, his words were zeroed in on one person – Chloe Chastain. "Chloe, I need to have a quick word with you."

Under normal circumstances, Chloe would have kept walking as if she could not hear him. That is exactly what she would have done to her dad, whether she looked at him or not. But this time, she had been looking directly at Mr. Harris as he said her name. They both knew that she heard him clearly. Luckily, his voice was not especially scary; in some ways it was kind, but professional and stern.

There was only one thing to do. She rolled her eyes and dragged herself up to his desk. "Yes, Mr. Harris?" She seemed to rest most of her weight on her left hip.

He sat down and handed her one of her recent quizzes. "I need you to get this one signed as well. This is the third one that you have failed." Mr. Harris took off his reading glasses and laid them on his grade book. He turned in his swivel chair to face her. "The material is not that hard. The quizzes are designed to be easy as long as you have read the material."

"Yes, Mr. Harris." She grabbed the quiz, never making eye contact with either the teacher or the quiz.

Mr. Harris knew that she was not really listening; she was far too fidgety. But he wanted to help her. He took in a deep breath and proceeded. "Look, it takes just a few minutes here and a few minutes there and you'll have it. If you need any help with this, I'll tell you what you can do. My son Billy is going to have a few students come out to our house and they're going to read the next couple of chapters together. This will keep their focus on the book and they actually discuss what they have read. You can bet there will be something to eat and there are more than a few laughs along the way; but they always have a good time and they'll end up earning a good grade on their quizzes. There are already about a half-dozen students planning on being there and that number may increase. If you are at all interested in something like that, just talk it over with Billy. He can give you the address and the correct time to come over."

Chloe seemed to be getting more uncomfortable with each passing word. "I'll think about it."

Nearly everyone in her class had already left by now. Mr. Harris' second period class was coming in and finding their seats.

Mr. Harris instinctively knew that he had lost this round. "Okay. But if I get any more grades like this one, I'm going to have to call your dad."

Chloe's irritation was coming through her voice. "I get it. Can I leave now?"

Mr. Harris nodded. Like a basketball player, Chloe quickly tilted around on her heel and wasted no time leaving the room.

Bree was waiting for Chloe in the hall and was the only one who could see the desperate look on her friend's face. Chloe was irate. She did not even look at Bree as they marched over toward their lockers.

"I hate this stupid class!"

CHAPTER 12

ALL THE MONEY IN THE WORLD

"Classic!" Mike tilted his head back, almost in hysterics, while the rest of the lunchroom went about their business. "That bit that you did in English this morning was *Classic Billy*. I am not the kind of guy that keeps a journal – and I'm not about to start now – but I am tempted to run out and get one just to record this honey-sweet moment." Mike gave Billy a gentle punch in the arm as he laughed. "Yep. You may never be called on to rise up and do something heroic, my friend; but I will be remembering the day that you had the guts to call your dad a 'gross old man' in his own class. What makes it really funny is that your dad is actually a sweet dude – a far cry from being gross."

"I did NOT call him a 'gross old man,'" Billy said defensively. "How many times do I have to tell you that?"

Curtis looked over at Billy with a mock concern. "You aren't planning a repeat performance anytime soon, are you? Or maybe some other, more noticeable stunt?" His eyebrows shot upward as a thought came to mind. "Billy, are you planning a food fight?"

With sandwich in hand, Billy lowered his arms and looked up at Curtis. His eyes betrayed his feeling of worry. "So, do you seriously think that anyone noticed what happened?" he asked.

Even as he asked the question, his answer came. His gaze fell over onto another table where some students were enjoying their lunch. One of the boys seated over there had just imitated Billy waking up in class and all other occupants at his table were in stitches. Kids from surrounding tables had seen it and were laughing as well. Others were explaining what had happened to those who were not there to see the spectacle for themselves. The whole thing was greatly exaggerated, and it only got worse the more people were acting out the incident. But it felt painfully accurate from where Billy was sitting. *So this is popularity*, he thought to himself. It had a stinging feel to it. Billy looked back at Curtis. "Maybe I should just move to Mars or something."

"Mars?! Don't be ridiculous." Curtis held up a bag of grapes. "You can't find *these* on Mars."

Billy chuckled. "Maybe I can take some with me."

Clay trotted over to their table and sat. "Hey Billy. What was all that about in English class today? Were you like asleep or something?" The others passed over the usual lunch items over to Clay.

"Yes. Of course he was. It was *English* class, wasn't it?" Curtis clarified between bites.

Mike continued the sentence. " ...and when he woke up, he also woke up everyone else who was asleep in class." Mike turned to Billy with a comically irritated voice. " ...INCLUDING ME, thank you very much! Talk about inconsiderate ..."

Clay's tone was a bit more caring. "So was this some kind of scary dream?"

"Scary? No, not really. It was more of a reoccurring dream."

"So what is this reoccurring dream about?"

"Well it's ..." Billy stopped and chuckled. He was rather embarrassed to talk about it. Even he had to admit that the entire thing was silly - - and not fascinating enough to talk about during lunch. Usually, they would be talking about the latest video game, a soon-to-be-released superhero movie, or some cool thing that happened over the weekend. Honestly, he really wanted to talk about all the money his family had and all the high-tech gadgets that he would someday buy.

He was still struggling with the idea of having all that money and he felt that talking about it with his friends might help him. Sharing this news had become a minor obsession with him. He wanted to leap up on the table and announce it to the entire school. Or better yet, he wanted to tell one person in particular, just one. But she was busy with her friend Bree.

Besides, Billy and Chloe have not even meet before, technically speaking. He imagined what kind of introductory line he could use. *Hi there. I'm Billy and I have a considerable amount of dough. I'm kinda new to this whole being-rich thing, so I thought maybe you could go with me this afternoon and teach me how to spend large sums of money.*

But his folks told him to keep it a secret. So he decided to stay on topic – which, at present, was his explanation of his peculiar dream from English class.

"You see, there is this butler. And he's really rude and obnoxious."

Mike drew up his hand. "Whoa, whoa! Hold up. A butler? So who does this butler work for?"

"Uh, me." Billy had naturally thought that was understood.

Mike turned on the most fake accent he could work up. "Oh? You have a rude butler in these dreams, do you? Well, *la-tee-dah.*" Mike and Curtis began to snicker, an act out of character for the two teenage boys.

Clay interrupted with his usual thoughtfulness. "Hey guys, this is not a laughing matter."

Curtis suddenly straightened up. "You're absolutely right." Leaning slightly over to Mike, he said in a matching tone, "Good help is *so* hard to find." At this, everyone except Billy began to laugh.

"Yes. Tell us more about this insufferable butler," Mike added. "Does this guy have actual skills or is he just some trendy slice of Eurotrash?"

"I don't even know what that means," Billy said as he moved his plastic spoon back and forth in a small cup of chocolate pudding. "But I do know that I don't want to talk about this anymore." He was not mad exactly, but it probably would not take much to get him there. A momentary awkward silence remained at their table while the rest of the room continued with their lunchtime chatter.

Clay swallowed what was in his mouth and washed it down with his drink. His eyebrows furrowed in thought and he broke the silence. "I don't think that I could ever get used to having a butler, no matter how much money I had."

Billy raised his head. This was suddenly a strange direction. All he could really think about today was his family's money, a subject that he was forbidden to discuss. Perhaps he could talk about his money without having to admit to anything. "Really? That brings up an interesting question. Hey, track star, if you had an unlimited amount of money, what would you do with it?"

"What kind of money? The buy-an-awesome-car kind of money or the buy-a-private-island kind of money?"

Billy smiled. "I mean the buy-a-whole-string-of-private-islands kind of money."

Clay was not given a chance to answer right away. Mike muscled in on this interesting topic with his immediate answer. "I know what I would do. I would buy a house with twenty bedrooms, a built-in recording studio, an indoor AND outdoor pool, and a home theater system that would tell folks outside that something inside was going down. In addition, I would have a different ride for each day of the week. Boom!" In retrospect, this was a peculiar response from Mike since his family was certainly better off financially than most people in Pecan Falls.

Finally, someone who gets it, Billy thought. "Now you're talkin'!"

But Mike was not quite through. " ...and on the rare occasion that I was seen walking by, people would naturally step to the side because they'll see who they are dealing with."

Billy agreed. "That's right. 'Step to the side.' I like that." Billy pointed in Mike's direction, resulting in a short series of intricate handslaps.

Curtis gave Mike an odd look. "Dude, your family *does* have money."

"Yes. My *family* has money, but that isn't *my* money. My money would have to be something that I have built up on my own. I don't want to ride on what my folks have done."

That was a little harsh. Billy felt like Mike was preaching directly at him – which was far from the truth. There was no way that Mike could have possibly known about the Harris' prosperity. Billy sank in his seat a little bit, but no one noticed.

Clay was not quite sure about this. He looked over at Curtis and asked, "What about you, dude? What are your thoughts?"

Curtis was not prepared for the question. "I don't know. I never seriously thought about it before. I guess I would want to spend some time weighing my options before committing to anything. There could be some pretty big consequences, you know ..."

"Pffff!" Mike rolled his eyes and turned his attention back to his lunch.

A thoughtful look graced Clay's face as he said, "I know what I would do."

Clay came across as the simpleton of their quartet. He made okay grades because he had to work for them. Things did not come easily for this boy. But when he began a statement with that certain tone, you knew that he was about to lay down something important, something precious, something that you did not want to miss. Clay had a way of commanding their attention with his purist of sincerity.

He continued with his answer. "Every year, my mom buys a calendar for the kitchen and every year it has the same theme: Australia. She has a deep fascination with that place." He paused for a moment and looked down at the table. "It has been very hard on mom since the Lord called my dad home. And now that my sister is married and moved to Texas, it's just mom and me. I've noticed many times that when mom gets a moment to sit down, she stares at that calendar. Down in Australia, they have snowy mountains perfect for riding horses. They shoot fireworks from a bridge by a big fancy opera house that is shaped like orange pieces. They even have an enormous red rock in the desert that shines bright when the sun is setting. There are animals there that you just cannot find elsewhere – unless you go to a zoo. And out in the water, Australia has the finest coral reefs and colorful fish in the world. Mom has never said anything to me about it, but I know that she would love to go someday and see this place for herself." Clay looked back up at his friends and took a deep breath. "So if I had the money, I would take her there. I would take her to Australia."

Mike was enchanted along with the others, but he was not entirely satisfied with Clay's response. "That's cool and all, bruh, but that isn't really an answer to the question. That is what you think that *your mom* would want. What about you? What would *you* want to do if you had the money?"

Clay shook his head. "Nothing. I'm cool. I don't need all the money in the world. I just want enough money to make sure that stuff is taken care of, you know. My life has never been about fancy cars or a big mansion – and I'm pretty sure that it never will be. I don't need stylish, trendy clothes or the latest electronic thingamajigs. I'm more about having a roof over my head, clothes on my back, and food in my tummy."

There was not much to say after that. They were all too familiar with

Clay's living conditions and they all knew that he was right. Curtis lifted up his soda can and said, "Three cheers for Clayton Peck." And he meant it.

But that did not change the way that Mike and Billy felt; they just had to remember to be more sympathetic in what they said.

All the way across the room, Chloe and Bree stood up from their table. Billy noticed immediately because he was already keeping a light level of surveillance on her at all times. At once, he dismissed whatever Clay was saying and began to zero in on Chloe. Last year, he knew that he did not stand a chance with her. A poor boy could not possibly hope to move into her circle of friends. But now he was the uninitiated richest kid in town. It was time for him to start playing the part.

"Hello? Earth to Billy." Mike waved his hand in front of Billy's face.

Billy snapped out of whatever trance that he was caught in and turned to acknowledged Mike. "Huh? Do what?"

Mike laughed it off and repeated his question. "Dude, I just asked you what you would do if you had that kind of money."

What indeed? Now that he had that kind of money, what was he waiting for? A mischievous smile stretched across Billy's face. "What would I do? Watch and take notes, plebe." He stood up from the table and walked away from his perplexed friends as if something monumental was about to take place. All that stuff about him waking up in class was suddenly out of his system. It was time to go meet Chloe Chastain. Batter up.

CHAPTER 13

SETTING A TRAP

Geographically speaking, the distance over to Chloe was a short walk – just to the far side of the lunchroom. No problema. But the area that he had to traverse was populated by a bunch of noisy students. The room itself seemed to be in motion from their busy presence. He looked at all the kids getting up, switching seats, throwing trash away, a little 'rough play' happening, inquiring about getting seconds from the lunchroom ladies. This place was alive with activity. How was he going to do this? How could he make a good impression on her? And how can he do this without looking like an idiot in front of his friends? The possibilities for failure were endless. This would be a little bit tricky. He closed his eyes.

For a few seconds, he imagined the same scene but in a totally different setting. The lunchroom had faded from sight and was replaced in his mind with the ruins of an ancient and proud throne room possibly in a fictitious South American empire. Jungle overgrowth surrounded the rock walls. Fallen tree limbs and a thick coat of leaves partially covered the uneven stone tiles of the floor. Four guards, the only others in the room, were at attention, two on Billy's left and two on his right. Short steps on the far side of the room led up to a beautifully carved wooden throne sitting in front a mosaic mural made of semiprecious stones; the meaning behind its pictorial representation escaped him.

"Behold, our queen!" one of the guards shouted. The four dropped down to one knee and bowed their heads in unison, spears in hand. Billy nervously looked back and forth at them with no idea what to do.

Chloe appeared from the side of her throne, regally made her way up the steps, and sat. She was wearing a gown of gold. Her hair was also tied by a golden ribbon. Exotic makeup adorned her eyes. She looked across the vast room at Billy and spoke. "Brave peasant, you have saved our kingdom from the killer swarm. My people and I are grateful. What do you ask of your queen?"

Humility and boldness collided in his short answer. "Only that I be allowed to kiss her virtuous hand." (He was unsure of what etiquette demanded. Just to be safe, he used the third person pronoun when speaking to royalty.)

Showing no emotion whatsoever, she replied favorably. "Then approach."

That was easy. A little too easy actually. *This must be a trap*, he thought. He briefly looked around the room. Perhaps this place was filled with hidden dangers. But where would these unseen perils be lurking about? Caution was in order. One possibility hatched in his mind.

To test this theory, he picked up a small pebble and tossed it about eight feet in front of him. The moment the pebble hit the floor, he heard a rope snap somewhere above his head. In an instant, a large black weight in roughly the shape of a pyramid came crashing down on the floor where the pebble landed. The solid iron weight was as tall as Billy and completely covered a six-by-six foot square area on the floor. Amusingly, the weight even had the words 'TEN TONS' stenciled on the side. (While he was having the fantasy, it never even occurred to him that these people would have to be using the strongest rope ever.)

Queen Chloe tightened her grip on the armrests. Maybe that trap was too obvious. She studied him as he made his next move.

Billy's feet barely touched the floor as he slowly walked around the weight, always on the lookout for more traps. Each and every step was executed with the upmost care. One mistake could cost him dearly.

He stopped in front of a large patch of suspicious-looking palm leaves. Why would they be on the floor in such a way? He squinted at it closely, always thinking. Maybe … With a great deal of self-assurance, he lifted a rather heavy stone and tossed it onto the palm leaves. The entire carpet of palm branches collapsed into a deliberate pit. A loud roar came from the floor of this well-dug hole. He walked over and looked down inside to discover the presence of a rather angry tiger. Only moving his eyes, he looked up at Chloe and thought, *Very cunning. Tigers are from the other side of the world. Its presence here is a mystery. Very impressive. Maybe I underestimated her abilities.*

The next few minutes were made up of even more traps: a jar filled with deadly snakes, flame-throwers, darts, a hoisting net, a spray of bullets, slicing laser beams, a large blade that swung like a pendulum, a layer of toy jacks that would explode on impact. Somehow, Billy managed to thwart them all. Thanks to the marvel of chromosomal modification, there was even an eight-foot-tall Dionaea Muscipula (that's a Venus Fly Trap, for those of you …). He defeated that thing in short order - - and *without* the aid of a volleyball-sized house fly.

Chloe protested in her head. *How could this be happening?! I've thrown every cliché in the book at him!* (She may have just answered her own question.) Chloe briefly closed her eyes, shook her head, and pounded her fist onto the armrest. *What a miserable time for our freeze-ray to be out for repairs*, she thought. Through it all, she maintained her poker face.

But as far as Billy knew, she was enjoying herself. Maybe she was starting to appreciate his keen intellect and his strong masculine features. His rugged good looks and endless charm only added to the effect. He was the portrait of the perfect man.

And finally, there he was. Only a few feet from her throne. He marched triumphantly up the steps to her seat and took her by the hand. But wait! What was this? He turned his head to look more closely at something that caught his intuitive eye. *One more trap?* he thought. *How could I have missed that one?* He let go of her hand and got to his feet. He spied something tucked on the floor and against the wall about forty feet away.

He rushed over to it and knelt down. As he stood back up, he carefully turned around to reveal a small mousetrap in his hands. Rather than disarming the minor mechanism, he walked carefully with it past all those reminders of other failed attempts to trap him. He approached the tiger pit and tossed it down inside. He heard the mousetrap snap followed by the sad sound of the tiger yelping.

"Now where was I? Oh, yes. The queen …" He hurried back to the steps where he had just sat and retook her hand. But what would he say? He needed to think of something sweet and memorable. How could he sound smooth and intelligent? Ah, yes. Here it came: "Greetings, ma'am. Why don't you tell me your life's story and I'll see if I can't write myself in as a major character?" He bent down to lightly kiss her on the hand.

She broke a vase over his head.

Yep. He did not see that one coming. Where did a vase even come from? It was not there before. Maybe she had a secret stash of them somewhere for emergencies.

As he lay on the steps in a semi-conscious state, the queen rose to her feet and began to shout. "You arrogant fool! Did you seriously think that that mousetrap was set for you?! Did it never occur to you that we may be trying to catch a mouse?" She stepped down and addressed those in attendance. "GUARDS! Take him away!"

This was enough to break Billy out of his spell and back to reality. He was still standing there next to his buddies in the noisy lunchroom. He had only been standing there for a few seconds, but it was getting awkward. *No time to dawdle*, he thought. *Lunch is nearly over. If I'm ever gonna make this work, I'd better book.* So he pushed himself on with Chloe in his sights.

This time, it seemed that *he* was the one walking in slow motion. His own theme song (heavy on the bass) was playing in his head, like he was watching himself in a movie. An unaccustomed feeling of confidence poured over him, the master of his fate. He totally owned this moment. Now that his fantasy of dripping with money was a reality, how could Chloe resist? (Just keep an eye open for any random vases. Just saying …)

He was unyielding in his quest. There were to be no interruptions. But while he was walking, some silly student crossed in front of his path. Rather than colliding with this faceless person, he gracefully managed to avert disaster with a sweet ninja-style circle thing and quickly went around her. He was even able to make a pithy remark as he went around. He said, "Step to the side, lady. Man on a mission." Shrewd and clever, this boy. That could have gone bad for him. Now, no other impediments remained between him and his target.

Chloe and Bree were laughing about something as they threw their trash away. Billy advanced, but the girls only became aware of him once he invaded their personal space. The two of them looked up at Billy with an almost unwelcome expression. Billy ignored it and continued thinking about his business.

He stood there in silence for just a moment, long enough to be weird. He knew that he could not just stand there gawking at them, so he began to speak – sorta. "I, uh ..." Perhaps he should have thought this talking part through in advance, but he honestly never thought that he would get this far. "Chloe? Could I have a word with you?"

Chloe was confused and uncomfortable. "Uh, I guess." The two of them stood to the side slightly away from Bree. *I wonder if this has anything to do with that horrible reading party idea that Mr. Harris was talking about,* she questioned to herself. *I hope not.*

Okay, he thought. *Here goes nothin'.* Billy closed his eyes, took a deep breath, and opened his eyes again. He thought he was going to be smooth. He was not smooth. "I, uh ... I've been watching you for some time. Oh, uh, not in a creepy way or anything ... I just wanted you to know that I think you're really cool and stuff. I know what you probably think about me, that I just come from a poor family - - well, not exactly poor, but that we don't have a lot of money and stuff - - and not that you would spend any time thinking about me anyway. Uh, I'm sorry. This is really awkward, I know."

Should he tell her the truth about the money? His parents were not fooling when they told him not to tell anyone. But why not? Their reasons were dumb anyway. After all, what would it hurt? Besides, he has never so much as exchanged greetings with Chloe before and now he seemed to have her complete attention. That is so cool. And this could potentially lead to something awesome.

"Anyway, I've come over to tell you a little secret." He leaned forward toward her ear, nearly whispering. "We are just pretending to be poor. We – that is *my family* - are actually quite wealthy and I know that kinda puts us on the same level now. So I was wondering if we could hang out sometime." Clearing his throat, he now resumed his original posture and voice. "Maybe you could invite me over and we could get to know each other a little better ..." He had absolutely no idea how creepy he sounded; he thought what he had said was just fine.

Chloe's face lit up, sending Billy's heart up to the sky. A huge smile flashed across her face. "OH! I think that is an awesome idea, Jimmy!"

"Uh, Billy." In spite of the name fumble, Billy was becoming even more hopeful at this point. Just in case, he did take just a split-second to look around and make sure that this was not just another dream. Whew! At least, that atrocious butler was not anywhere to be found. That would be the worst.

"Yeah, Billy. You're sweet." There was a perkiness to her voice as she spoke. Her eyes seemed to sparkle as she looked at him. "Why don't you let me check my calendar and I'll get back with you?" By now, Chloe was tilting her head slightly and twirling her hair with her fingers.

The effect was not wasted on Billy; he was raptured. This sort of attention was really more than he had ever expected. Nervously, he began to back away from her. That single conversation was enough to make this whole day epic. "Okay. Cool. That sounds great! I'm looking forward to it." As he was backing up, he managed to bump into the corner of a table. But no harm done. At this point, he was virtually floating back to his seat.

Chloe was either amused by this display of clumsiness or she acted like she was. But then she suddenly felt Bree's hand firmly grab her arm as it spun her around. Bree was now looking at Chloe square in the eyes as if she was going to instigate a stern reprimand. "Are you kidding me? What do you think you're doing?"

The cheery smile on Chloe's face quickly melted away and was replaced with a chilly expression. "Relax, Bree. Do you know who that guy is?" She turned her face in Billy's direction and back again.

"That's Mr. Harris' son, isn't it? I think his name is Billy."

Chloe answered Bree with shifty eyes. "Oh yes. The ridiculous son of our even more ridiculous teacher."

Bree's eyes gestured over in Billy's direction. "So what did *he* want?"

Chloe chuckled. "I don't even know. He said something about his family being rich or something. Can you imagine? And then he said that he wants to hang out with me – or at least that is how it sounded."

Bree too began to laugh. "You've got to be putting me on. Billy Harris?"

Chloe brought the eraser on her pencil up to her mouth as she stared slightly beyond Bree's head, deep in thought. "*Rich boy* wants to play? Well, I think that I can arrange a little fun at his expense."

Filled with curiosity, Bree studied her friend's face for answers. She could have asked Chloe what she meant by that, but she knew that it would do her no good; Chloe liked to have her little surprises. But if Bree knew one thing about Chloe, it was that she had something elaborate cooking up in her wretched little brain. She was nothing if not theatrical.

While that was going on, Billy was making his way back to his usual table. The other three boys were silently watching him as he returned. But before he made it back, Justin popped up out of nowhere as usual and stood right in front of him. Justin's long bangs flopped over his eyes as he came to a complete stop. With a jerky head motion, his hair resumed its precarious position hovering just above the level of his eyes.

"Hey man," he started. "My girlfriend saw you talking to Chloe Chastain just now and *she* was wondering if you like her, like in that way." Although they could not be seen, you could tell that his eyebrows went up and down a couple of times in an obvious effort to imply that maybe there was some electricity between Billy and Chloe.

Justin and Billy have always been casual friends but this was getting annoying, but not half as annoying as having to deal with Justin's girlfriend directly. Though attractive, her voice sounded like the piccolo part in *Stars and Stripes Forever*. And to put it politely, the more inquisitive side of her nature just had to go. So rather than answering the question outright, Billy decided to avoid it altogether. "Justin, why does your girlfriend care so much about what *I* am doing? Aren't *you* her boyfriend? Shouldn't she be more interested in *you*?" *Ha! Gotcha!* Billy thought to himself.

With that comeback, Justin was momentarily silenced. Whatever Billy's intention was, it worked. Justin looked immediately distracted. "Hey! That's right. What's going on around here anyway?" Justin did an about-face on one foot and made a straight line back toward his gossipy girlfriend.

Back at the table, Billy sat and noticed that all three of his friends were following him with a silent gaze. Billy became conscience of this rather quickly. They all seemed either irritated or insulted by his brief encounter with Chloe Chastain.

"What?!" he inquired as he looked around at them.

Curtis, Mike, and Clay looked away as if they did not want a good shellacking.

As Billy was sitting defensively with his friends, Chloe and Bree were carrying on what they considered a normal conversation just outside the lunchroom. But this was interrupted at the sight of Wesley Porterfield the Third. Chloe was always scoping the place for him anyway.

He never once asked for this power, but Wesley had the ability to turn Chloe from a condescending snob with an acid tongue to a giggling, boy-crazy girl-child. Their routine meetings were the highlight of her day; but for Wesley, they felt more like an all-too-frequent inconvenience. The poor rich boy saw her at the same unfortunate moment. *Here it comes*, he thought. *My timing is so terrible.*

"OH! There's Wesley," Chloe said in midsentence. "Wesley! Over here!" She immediately rushed over to his side. Bree rolled her eyes as she followed in tow.

Wesley held back his irritation and managed to greet her flatly. "Hello Chloe. Bree." He knew exactly what to expect. Luckily for him, lunch was almost over and he would have to scurry off for his fifth period class. He never imagined that he would actually look forward to Geometry class every day; but if it were not for his happy thought of going to class, Chloe would no doubt be expected to ramble on in her obsessive and flirtatious way.

"I'm sorry you haven't been able to get in touch with me lately. But the truth is too many people had my number and were bothering me day and night. It has been a huge mess. I still have no idea who has been passing my number out. I don't even know these people. Anyway when I got upgraded - - that is why my phone got upgraded - - I simply got a new number in the process. So if you are trying to call, that old number that you have is out and a brand new number is in."

"So *that* was it. *Now* I understand." Wesley's sarcasm was completely wasted on her. But Bree caught it and knowingly smiled behind her friend's back.

Chloe was in control the whole time. In a marvelous display of multitasking, she continued to talk as she grabbed Wesley's notebook and began to write. At some point, she broke from her narrative long enough to say, "There it is. And you can call or text me anytime, day or night." And then there it was: her cutesy little wink.

As the bell rang, Wesley held up the notebook in acknowledgement. "Got it. Thanks." He then walked off in a hurry.

Chloe spun around with her hair flying and looked back again at poor

Bree who had been invisible during the past minute. "See that? See how much it pays to advertise?"

Wesley turned a corner and tore Chloe's new phone number out of his notebook. He then stopped a random boy walking by and handed the number to him. "Here," he said to the bewildered kid. "This girl has a crush on you so start texting her. But don't tell her who you are; she likes to figure these things out on her own. Enjoy." Wesley then left this young boy with a puzzled look on his face.

CHAPTER 14

REWIND

So far, Billy has managed to keep his family's big secret from his three faithful friends. In fact, the only person he has told in confidence is Chloe; and she only told her best friend Bree. But facts are facts; Billy's parents told him specifically not to tell *anyone* about their wealth. So in Billy's mind, that meant that he was not to run all over creation spouting out the news to any stranger who would sit down and listen. He felt that his close friends (or anyone he was trying to impress) were exempt from his parents' command. Nevertheless, partial obedience is *still* disobedience. This is almost sure to come back to haunt him. Fortunately perhaps for him, neither of these two girls believe Billy's earth-shattering confession - - so it looked like it did not even matter.

But it matters.

We know that the boys were having a conversation at lunch and that Billy got up to talk to Chloe. But what was happening elsewhere at that exact time? Let us rewind this story about ten minutes and turn back to the beginning of this lunchtime dialogue. Billy, Curtis, Clay, and Mike were sitting at their usual table in the lunchroom. Clay had just said something that got Billy thinking. Looking across the table at Clay, Billy asked, "Hey, track star, if you had an unlimited amount of money, what would you do with it?"

Clay looked across at him with interested eyes. "Huh? What kind of money? The buy-an-awesome-car kind of money or the buy-a-private-island kind of money?"

Billy smiled. "I mean the buy-a-whole-string-of-islands kind of money."

But we have already heard this conversation. As the reader of this story, you now have permission to step back away from them just a little bit. Turn around and walk down between the columns of tables. Across the aisle and down about three rows, Berly and Maggie were having their own lunchtime talk. Maggie's back was turned to the boys, but Berly had a clear view. She was especially watching Billy Harris.

When Billy first visited the Chess Club, Berly thought that he was somewhat cute. Along the way, Berly had managed to develop a strong crush on Mr. Harris' son. That *crush* only grew stronger with each meeting. Billy had yet to miss a single Chess Club event that entire week. Completely oblivious to these facts, he passed through her mind constantly. She now spent a great deal of her time looking around and keeping up with his whereabouts whenever possible. She was trying hard to play it cool, but she kept looking at the boys – and Billy in particular.

"Do you think that I should go talk to him?"

Maggie stopped chewing and looked across at Berly with unimpressed eyes. "May I assume that, when you use the word *him*, you are referring to Billy Harris ... again? We never seem to talk about anything else anymore." She rolled her eyes, took another sip of her drink, and put it back on the table. "I have this dream that I dream all the time. In it, we are back to having normal conversations like we used to, conversations that weren't centered on the English teacher's goofy son."

"Look at him. He is over there talking to those other three guys he is usually with. Do you know any of them?"

Maggie shrugged. "Not really. I know that they are all from the same church." She had another bite from her salad and then gestured in their direction without looking. "That tall redhead – the one who is talking right now – I hear that he is really amazing at track and field. In fact, they say that he is so fast, his competitors can't even catch him with a zoom lens. I myself heard Coach Holton say the other day that that guy could take Pecan Falls all the way to State this year. Now *that* would be kinda cool." Just because these two girls were in the Chess Club, that did not mean that they were anti-athletics. They had an incredible amount of school spirit and supported their school in whatever way they could. "If Coach Holton can take him to State and redhead can finish well, maybe our school could make the state paper or even the news. We could get some serious exposure. I imagine that most people in our state don't even know that there *is* a Pecan Falls. We're not exactly on the road to Branson, you know."

"Do you know that guy's name?"

"I think it is Clayton ... something. I don't know the other two guys." She took another drink from her soda can.

The noise in the room was considerable, but Berly sat in uncomfortable silence. She could not hear what the boys were saying, but she watched them like a hawk as this Clay character was talking about something serious. She turned back to Maggie and asked, "So do you think that I should go over and introduce myself to his friends?"

Maggie thought that Berly's behavior was bordering on *creepy*. "You do what you want to do. I know you well enough to know that you aren't going to listen to me. And yet, go figure, you keep asking me for my opinion - - all the time. But answer this question for me please: Did you bother to pray over this first? I mean God may not want this for you as much as you want this for yourself."

Under ordinary circumstances, those words would have probably bothered Berly. But today, it was like water off a duck. Her focus was directed on Billy Harris. *Billy Harris.* All of a sudden, that name actually sounded pretty to Berly. And through her eyes, everything in the room pointed at him as if he were the vanishing pointing in an art project. The other students, tables and chairs, the lunch trays, nutrition posters – they were all just mere window dressing around the main attraction.

Clay looked quite serious as he spoke. Then one of the others seemed to ask him a question and Clay looked like he was answering. Then the third friend raised his drink in the air and said something as if he were making a toast.

Berly pushed her lunch away and looked directly at her friend. "Well, my timing might be lousy; but if this is not what God wants, then maybe *He* can find a way to prevent it. In the meantime, I don't see any harm in simply walking over there and introducing myself. It's not that big of a deal. It's just talk."

"I hope you're right," Maggie said as she moved on to her banana pudding. "But I have a feeling that a good *I-told-you-so* will be in order."

Berly stood up and stepped away from her seat. She took in a deep breath, clinched her fists, and then shook her fingers out again. Looking at her target, she could see that he was not fully engaged in their talk anymore; instead, he seemed to be staring roughly in her direction. The thought of that affected Berly. Was he staring at her? It looked like it. She felt her back tingle.

One of his friends snapped him out of his trance and Billy seemed to answer a question. He then stood up victoriously. With a pleased look on his face, he actually began walking toward Berly.

Her heart began to race. Both of her knees seemed to lose their strength, so she directed a small portion of her focus on keeping her knees in place. Instinctively, she began to rub the palms of her hands together. Whatever was she going to say? *Did* she have to say anything? Maybe it did not matter since *he* was coming over to *her*. Surely, that meant that he was going to be doing the talking. *Just act naturally*, she said to herself. At last …

As he got close to her, she took a small step into the aisle to greet him. But when she did, Billy responded by doing some smooth spin move on her. As he went around her, he said, "Step to the side, lady. Man on a mission," and kept walking.

Huh? Am I seeing his more playful and humorous side? she wondered to herself.

But then he kept walking. In fact, he went right up to that Chloe and her friend. In a moment, he was talking to her alone. Berly now became painfully aware that she was standing up for no reason, waiting to speak to someone who clearly was not going out of his way to speak to her. She retreated back to her seat. Her legs felt weird anyway, as if they had lost all their strength.

This caught Maggie off-guard. "Back so soon?" she asked. "That didn't take long at all. You scarcely made it away from the table." She turned and saw what was happening. Billy and Chloe were having a pleasant chat just past them. She returned her gaze back to Berly, who looked like she was about to shatter. At this point, she remained silent. She closed her eyes, shook her head, and inhaled deeply. Her eyes opened again. "Berly, I'm sorry. I didn't mean anything by that."

After about thirty seconds of watching them, Berly shrugged. Her sudden nonchalant demeanor was completely faked. With half-closed eyes and a dismissive voice, she admitted, "She's pretty." Another ten seconds went by. "You can't really blame him." She stopped staring now and focused her attention on keeping the swelling tears from running down her cheeks.

Maggie set her spoon down and looked across at her friend. The youngest in her family and the only girl, she had often wondered what it would be like to have a younger sister of her own. Now she knew.

Berly removed her glasses and laid them on the table. She rubbed her eyes and spoke again. "At least now I know the truth. It is much better this way. Yes. It is better that I know now, before I ..." In one glorious motion, she wiped her escaped tears and brushed her hair back behind her ear. " ...before I make a complete fool of myself." Then she quietly got up and walked briskly to the restroom. Maggie trailed in after her.

After school dismissed that day, both girls went back to Maggie's house. After entering Maggie's bedroom, Berly took off her rather stylish glasses and threw herself face down on the bed in a state of embarrassment. "Oh my stars! I can't believe that just happened."

Maggie followed her in the room and closed the door. "Are you back to that again? I've already told you five thousand times, no one noticed. According to my watch, it is now time to move on."

"I came so close to making myself look like a scary stalker chick."

"The term 'scary stalker chick' may be inaccurate; I wouldn't call it that. All you were going to do was introduce yourself. That sounds harmless enough. But then again, God may have just saved you from yourself. Or maybe the timing was just not right. Look, we don't know what was going on."

Berly rolled over on her back and looked up at the ceiling fan as it made its hypnotic circles. "Do you remember how the wicked witch would disappear in *The Wizard of Oz*? A burst of flames, clouds of thick smoke, and then she would be gone. I would give anything to have that ability at times."

"Don't be ridiculous. Do you realize how much attention you would bring to yourself? Then when the smoke finally cleared, I would be sitting there alone with everyone staring at me as if I set off a smoke bomb.

Then I would spend hours in Mrs. Dunbar's office answering two million questions. Friends don't do that to each other."

Berly laughed. "Yeah. How thoughtless of me."

Maggie walked across the room to her glass tank. "Look, if you can't keep it together, I'm gonna stop having you over here. And that means no more Sir Lancelot." Maggie reached in and pulled out her bearded dragon - - with a little overactive tail wagging on the dragon's part.

Berly had not been crying, but she began to wipe imaginary tears from her face in an overdramatic fashion for comic effect. "Sir Lancelot. I forgot. I can't let him see me this way." She reached out her arms to receive him. Sir Lancelot tolerated her gentle petting for a few seconds and then enjoyed the warmth from Berly's arms – a nice warm place to rest. "I'm just glad I found out that Billy likes Chloe. I guess I did manage to avoid an awkward situation."

Maggie shook her head. "Stop making such a big deal about this. We are talking about meaningless crushes. For all you know, Billy could lose interest in her overnight. Stranger things have happened, you know." (Honestly, this was exactly what Maggie was thinking about Berly's crush on Billy - - but she was not going to share that out loud with her dear friend. Maybe like a bad case of the common cold, this crush just had to run its course.) "And by the way, I am going to warn you right now. If you ever use the term *true love* when talking about these silly crushes, I'm going to take my beardy from you and throw you out into the hallway with no mercy."

Berly laughed at the thought. "Well, it won't come to that, I promise you. After seeing him with Chloe today, I am done worrying about Billy Harris permanently."

Maggie knew her friend better than that. Berly might have believed her own words, but Maggie was not so easily convinced. Nevertheless, she played along. "Good. Because the Bible tells us three hundred and sixty-five times not to worry. That is once a day for every day of the year."

"Yeah? What about leap year?"

For the equivalent of two musical beats, Maggie stared off into space with an amused grin. "If you only worry about things one day every four years, I guess that would be an improvement for you."

Berly looked down at Sir Lancelot, but she was talking to Maggie. "I really wished that I could be more like you. You don't ever seem to worry about anything." (Actually, she could have been talking to the beardy.)

"Me? I worry about stuff all the time. In fact, check out this trick." She reached behind her and grabbed the Bible off of her desk, held it up with the spine facing down, and let it fall open. "See? Cool trick, huh? It automatically opened to Matthew chapter six. Weird, isn't it? That's because I go there frequently."

Berly's right eyebrow went straight into its curious position. "So what is the big deal about Matthew chapter six? Does it contain some magic potion for worrying?"

Maggie picked up the Bible with one hand and the bearded dragon with the other. "Well, I have pretty much made this chapter my second home. The words to it return to me all the time like the lyric of a song that I have heard over and over. Chew on this while Sir Lancelot and I read: 'Therefore I say unto you, Take no thought for your life, what ye shall eat, or what ye shall drink; nor yet for your body, what ye shall put on. Is not the life more than meat, and the body than raiment? ...'"

Maggie continued to read and Sir Lancelot occasionally blinked his eyes. She read about how God takes care of the birds and dresses up the flowers. And of course, God places a much higher value on His children than he does on birds and flowers. We are special to Him. God knows exactly what we need and He provides for His own. She only interrupted herself to explain to Berly that, unlike Sir Lancelot, we are not like pets to Him. We are His children, His treasure, His masterpiece. Maggie finished reading with verse 34. "'... Take therefore no thought for the morrow: for the morrow shall take thought for the things of itself. Sufficient unto the day is the evil thereof.' Bottom line: Stop worrying. God is watching over you." She closed her Bible and placed Sir Lancelot back into his nice warm home on top of his favorite rock.

Berly wanted so badly to listen to what was being said. She truly understood that worrying was a stupid waste of time. In fact, she could easily have made these comments herself to any number of her needy friends. This time, wisdom was being presented to her as if it came giftwrapped. She knew this because Maggie was reading this wisdom from God's Word, and that was not something that you can argue with and expect to get very far. For countless generations, people have been arguing with the Bible and trying to disprove it; and they always fail. But the truths that are in it are just as relevant today as they were at the time that the Bible was written.

But for whatever reason, this whole Billy thing had made her lose her mind. She was not normally like this. Apparently, her mental stability had gone on vacation. Her head might as well have fallen completely off and rolled down a flight of stairs. To make matters worse, she should have kept her next comment to herself, bless her heart. "I wonder what Billy is doing right now."

Maggie laughed. "Girl, you are hopeless."

Actually, it is a really good thing that they could not see what Billy was doing at that precise moment. They would have found him on his hands and knees crawling out on his neighbor's diving board trying to retrieve his endangered copy of *Pride and Prejudice*. This time, the book was currently sitting precariously at the end of the board above nine feet of water. His three friends and his neighbors were all laughing at him as he nervously tried to save the book from a watery fate.

How it got there will remain a bit of a mystery to us. But one thing that is no mystery is that this was not going to end well. Midge at the bookstore could prepare herself for another visit from her new best customer.

… as soon as he dried himself off.

CHAPTER 15

THE TIGHTROPE WALKER

This whole situation was cracked. There sat Billy who was potentially the richest kid in Pecan Falls (and perhaps in all of Western Civilization) with all of his fantasies and hopes tied to a vast fortune. And the only thing standing between him and his goal was an enormous granite wall – complete with barbed wire strung out along the top and graffiti painted all over one side. And somewhere in this big picture, his unfair parents were busy building that wall. Otherwise, he could become what some circles might call a 'gentleman of leisure.' In case you are wondering what that means, imagine a life of travel, checking in and out of hotels, dressing up for expensive meals, making appearances at *the club*, etc ...

Of course, one aspect of this unlikely scenario is that our young man here felt like a superhero. He and his family now had a double life. He had one somewhat normal identity by day; but by night, he was ... Actually, he was the same at night. Even though he was unable to do anything with it yet, it was still cool knowing that it was there. Someday though, he would be of age and maybe he could get his grubby hands on some of that coin. Just the thought of this made him want to get up on a table and do a jig. If you were going to live under intolerable conditions, this was the way to do it.

In the meantime, he was doing an extraordinary job with his self-control and not exploding. Especially during the Chess Club meetings.

Maggie brought her bishop all the way to Billy's side of the board. "Checkmate." She pleasantly gave her opponent a satisfied grin and extended her hand. Billy accepted her handshake. "Good game," they each said to the other.

That was kind of a rule at Chess Club. If you win, you are to offer a handshake and say, 'Good game.' If you lose, you also offer a handshake and say, 'Good game.' Either reaction should be the same. This was merely a lesson in good sportsmanship. The students needed to learn that people do not like a sore loser or an obnoxious winner. Otherwise, they may never get a return game.

Mr. Harris always said, "If you lose a game, that doesn't make you a loser. If you win a game, that doesn't make you a winner. How you behave after the game is what determines if you are a winner or a loser." The students took this message to heart - - which is great because this little saying applies to more in life than just chess. There is something to be said for winning and we should always strive to win the prize, but most of our learning comes from losing. Embrace both with eyes on Christ.

Somehow, Billy had survived the embarrassment of yesterday's loud outburst in his dad's class. But he was still distracted by his lunchtime victory. He had now officially met Chloe Chastain in person – and it felt great. But that was not going to help him here. He had to try to concentrate on the game in front of him.

The usual cast of characters were sitting around Mr. Harris' classroom and playing their games quietly. Billy switched seats to play Alejandro this time. Berly was not saying much at all during Chess Club these days; the more her crush on Billy intensified, the more quiet she became. Mr. Harris had just finished grading his students' papers and had gotten all caught up. So for the next few moments, he took full advantage of this opportunity to text his wife. The conversation went as follows:

I love you, Mrs. Harris.

I love you too, Mr. Harris.

Would you still love me if I were terribly rich, drop dead good-looking, and abundantly talented?

But we ARE rich.

William silently laughed to himself. Then he stopped. Something about that message did not seem right. He reread it. Was that an underhanded putdown?

Just when everything was going well, Eugene could always be counted on to break the silence. "Does anyone want to hear a funny joke?"

With the exception of Mr. Harris and Quotes, the response was a unified 'NO!' But Quotes looked right at Eugene with eyes that said, "Do not even proceed with this joke."

Eugene remained optimistic, even though the notion of his telling another joke was coolly received. He searched the room, looking for a friendly face. He finally met eyes with the unfortunate Billy. This visual connection completed the circuitry required to lighten Eugene's joyful anticipation. "Hey! Sophomore! *You* want to hear something hilarious, don't you?"

Every day, it was a new joke (or should we say a *different joke?*) and they would often bounce around from genre to genre. Some were predicable knock-knock jokes concluding with a bad pun. Others involved the quantity of people from various demographics being recruited to change a lightbulb. There were plenty of jokes involving a cast of people of varying professions walking into a bar (with animals sometimes standing-in for the humans). Still others were giving far too much credit to the size of the listener's mother that the whole concept seemed scientifically impossible – not to mention insulting. And let us not neglect the ones questioning the whys and wherefores for that ambitious road-crossing chicken. All these jokes had one thing in common: they were all terrible.

Billy felt like refusing Eugene's unsolicited request, but he could never turn anyone down. "I guess so." With these simple words, Billy was losing some serious popularity points with his fellow club members.

Typical rapid hand animation kicked in as Eugene exploded into joke-telling mode. "Excellent! You won't be sorry. This will kill you, it's so funny." He interrupted himself for a brief moment of hysterical laughter and then recovered. "A knight got tired of playing chess - - that is to say the knight off of a chess board, one of the pieces. So he decided to leave the game and make it on his own to seek his fortune, you see. So he got this job in a circus, you see, as a tightrope walker of all things. So it's *now* his first night and he is standing up high on the platform, you see. He is about to step out onto this tightrope when the ringmaster yells up at him, 'Watch out for that third step! It's a doozy.'"

No one laughed.

"Don't you get it?"

"Uh, no. I guess not."

Eugene might have showed slight signs of frustration, but having to explain his jokes was as second nature to him as telling the jokes in the first place. "It's easy." He picked up a knight off of the board and began to illustrate. "You know how the knight moves. It takes two steps in any direction and then a third step to the side." As he spoke, he moved the knight two spaces forward and then another space to the right. "If he were on the tightrope, he would be fine for the first two steps, but that third one would send him to his death. And down he would go." He lifted his right hand high above his head and brought it down again onto his left hand, whistling the noise as if it were falling. "Wasn't that funny?"

Billy had no idea what to say. He understood the joke now that it was explained. It just was not funny at all. He decided to engage in a polite chuckle. The other attendees turned and gave Billy a piercing look of disapproval. They feared that any sign of laughter on their part could be interpreted as a request for more jokes. They wanted to discourage any of this sort of encouragement and Billy felt like an idiot for laughing.

Eugene was the only one doing any real laughing - - even snorting on occasion. But even he realized that he was alone in his opinion. He eventually stopped, folded his arms, and leaned back in his chair. "Rodney would've found it funny."

Quotes sat quietly as the others loudly exclaimed, "LONG LIVE RODNEY."

Again, Billy did not join in with the chorus. He just looked around cautiously. "Yeah. Where *is* this Rodney anyway? I've been coming to Chess Club faithfully for a number of weeks now and I have yet to meet this local myth you call *Rodney*. What is his excuse this time? Someone pushed this dweeb into his own locker?"

Berly volunteered, "He had a nose bleed earlier today and I think he ended up going home."

Billy rolled his eyes. *Whatever. This guy has to be the nerd to end all nerds,* he thought to himself. "Well, I'm not convinced that this imbecile is even real. He always seems to be conveniently missing during our meeting times. That's some president we've got in here."

Sitting across from Berly, Joey turned to face Billy. "What are you talking about? He's in here all the time. We see the guy each and every day. Where have *you* been?"

"I have *never* seen this guy." Billy punctuated the word *never* by tapping his hand on the desk.

Joey went back to his game. "*We* see him all the time. In fact, we never *not* see him."

Mr. Harris said nothing but made mental acknowledgment of this obvious abuse of the English language. The double-negative card might be played in Spanish club, but not in his English room. He let it go.

Alejandro snapped his fingers in front of Billy to regain his attention. "Are you going to move sometime this year?"

In an apologetic maneuver, Billy turned his focus back to the neglected game pieces on the board in front of him. "Oh. Sorry." He stared at the pieces for a few more seconds and finally reached for one of his rooks and brought it forward. Billy decided to change the subject. "Has anyone in here ever thought about doing something to promote the Chess Club and try to get some more people in here?"

Strangely, Alejandro replied as if they had been on that subject for some time. "Give it up, amigo. I've been telling them for months what they should do, but no one listens to me."

To perfectly illustrate Alejandro's statement about being ignored, Billy kept on topic. "Well, what do you normally do?"

This conversation had repeated itself over and over again, but Maggie decided that it would not hurt to humor the newcomer. "We put up fliers on the bulletin boards. When the junior high kids have their open house toward the end of the year, we set up a booth. Every couple of years, we have t-shirts made up."

"Don't forget the yearbook photo," Alejandro sarcastically interjected.

Maggie gave Alejandro a knowing look that he immediately returned. She added, " ...that is *if* the yearbook staff remembers to send over a photographer." Apparently, this was a sore spot with several members of the Chess Club - - Maggie and Alejandro in particular. Perusing last year's PFHS yearbook in a vain search for the Chess Club page might reveal reasons for their disappointment.

Quotes looked as if he would have shattered a glass cup in his hands if he had one. He said nothing - - which came as no surprise. (Billy had yet to hear Quotes utter a single word. But he already ruled out the idea that the imposing senior had no vocal chords because the big guy had growled at him a few times.)

Without sounding irked at all, Alejandro chimed right in. "I've told them over and over exactly what they need to do. No one ever listens to me though." Again, his words remained unacknowledged.

Joey shook his head, looked down at the chess board, and sighed a deep sigh. With a defeated tone, he said, "I bet Rodney would know exactly what to do."

In a surprising twist, Billy alone exclaimed in a very loud voice, "LONG LIFE RODNEY!!"

Everyone turned and looked at him in startled amusement. Berly's eyes widened as she peered his way.

Again, Billy was pinned under the weight of staring eyes. Since the first day of school, all he did was attract unwanted attention. All was silent - - except for his accelerated heartbeat. He would almost swear that he could actually *hear* his face turning red. He did not even know if ears could pick up something like that. Was the human body capable of doing that? Perhaps he merely imagined it.

Mr. Harris looked up from his desk to see what Billy was hollering about while the others looked at each other. Joey met Maggie's eyes and motioned his head toward Billy. Quotes squinted his eyes to see what reason Billy may have had for that outburst.

In an amused voice, Alejandro chuckled, "Where did *that* come from?"

Billy had no idea what that was about either. Again, the correct usage of the Chess Club traditions had escaped him. In his usual attempt to fit in, he once again singled himself out. It was the same comical song that seemed to provide the soundtrack to his life. Billy tried to imagine what it might feel like to sprout wings and fly out the window. In a hopeless effort to escape the awkwardness, he returned to his game - - one that Alejandro would eventually win.

CHAPTER 16

FREIGHT TRAIN

Clayton Peck employed everything that he had learned up to that point. Breathing techniques, posture, balance, all of it was working together in concert as he focused on his goal: getting himself across that finish line as soon as humanly possible. Sweat poured from his hair and made the usual patterns on his running clothes. His cheeks were enormous red splotches and his mouth formed a tight circle. He sucked air into his nose and pushed it out his mouth at the rhythm set by his feet as they hit the track. His side was beginning to hurt, but that sensation went largely ignored. Matching the robotic speed of his legs, long arms chopped through the air like machetes. Matching his body, his mind also had a singleness of purpose as all his thoughts were on that one objective. Nothing else mattered. Nothing else existed.

Side note: If some film producer ever decided to adapt this book into a movie, this shot would have to be done in slo-mo with some pounding music. Sweat flying. Face dramatically contorted. The whole shebang. This imagery is a given however for our intelligent and literate readers. Isn't that right, class? But back to the story …

Coach Holton excitedly thumbed his stopwatch as Clay crossed the line. He was wearing exactly what you would expect from a high school track coach: gray t-shirt, thigh-length shorts, whistle hanging from his neck, PFHS baseball cap. If anyone in Pecan Falls ever saw him in anything else, it would make all the papers. "Freight! Freight! Come check out your time! This is absolutely incredible! You just get better and better with each practice."

Clay was slowing down. He was excited about seeing his results and trotted over toward the coach.

Coach held up the watch. "Freight, come here and check this out."

The tall redhead stopped and looked at the coach with an expression of both surprise and amusement. "What did you just call me?"

"*Freight*. Did I get it right? That *is* what your last coach called you, isn't it? That's what he told me. *Freight Train*."

Clay was embarrassed and flattered. "Yeah. He said that I reminded him of a freight train. When I build up my speed, I can't be stopped. ... or that is what *he* said anyway."

"I like it. It sounds mighty cool. I think it should stick. Do you mind if I call you that?"

Clay let out a little laugh. "Nah. I guess not." He glanced over at the stopwatch. "Whoa! Does that say what I think it says? Is that even real?"

Holton did not say it out loud, but he looked at those numbers and looked over at Clay. If this kid were capable of this sort of thing as a tenth grader, what would he be doing as a senior? This sophomore has a very real future ahead of him. It was going to be a pleasure to watch him mature and develop into a genuine athlete. Every high school track coach dreams of having a future Olympian in his program and he felt strongly that he was looking at one right now. He shook his head. *Wow.* If this was the sort of thing that he could expect over the next three years, he was going to have to look up some coaches that could take Clay to the next level.

Just a few seconds earlier while Clay was running, Curtis was observing his friend's progress from high atop the bleachers. "Wow! That's our boy! Look at him go!" He smiled, shook his head, and sat back down on those aluminum bleachers. "He is flying!"

Echoing Curtis' fervor, the leaves on the trees were already beginning to turn orange as if nature itself was busy cheering on their favorite redhead. It was a gorgeous day for it, the first cool day after a hot and humid summer. A gentle breeze came along, almost challenging him to a race. *Come on, Clay. Let's see what you can do. Try to outrun me.*

Chess Club had ended for the day and Billy was catching up with

Curtis. He used every other step on his climb and hopped his way to the top. "How's Clay?" Billy inquired.

"Take a peek down there and see for yourself, but you'd better be quick or you'll miss it. Clay is that blur crossing the line now."

The four boys had plans in a little bit. When practice was over, Curtis was going to take Clay over to get some pizza. When Mr. Harris got all his work done, he was going to be dropping Billy off there as well. Mike was just a phone call away and would also meet them there.

Curtis added, "That boy is like lightning! I cannot wait until we start to compete. I wouldn't be surprised at all if he goes all the way to state this year. Clay is on fire!"

Clay flew across the finish line and the coach took note of the time. After exchanging a few words, Coach Holton showed the results to Clay. Even at this distance, Billy and Curtis could tell that Clay was excited. After the short talk with the coach, the two boys saw that Clay was making his way off the field to get cleaned up.

Both boys got up from their seats. They were remarkably proud of what their tall buddy was able to do. They knew that Clay received a lot of encouragement from his mom, but they were always there to support their friend in any way that they could.

Speaking of encouragement, Billy remembered something that he wanted to show Curtis. He pulled a small stack of fliers out of his backpack and handed one over for approval. "Here. Take a gander at this and tell me what you think?"

Curtis reached over to get a better look. The bright yellow flier was an open invitation to anyone who wanted to come to the Harris' house for a reading of the next two chapters of *Pride and Prejudice*. It contained information about when and where it would be and a little something about how it would help the students out during quiz times. And naturally, the flier also mentioned something about food. If this function did not provide something to eat for teenagers, they could understandably have a riot on their hands.

Billy pointed down to the flier in Curtis' hand. "Consider *that* your formal invitation, Curt."

Curtis gave Billy a quick sideways glance. "Excellent. Reading all the required *Pride and Prejudice* chapters for the next week? You really know how to throw a swinging party." A slight tone of sarcasm could be detected in that last comment - - but certainly not in a mean-spirited fashion.

Billy neatly returned the other fliers to his backpack as he spoke. "Well, I'm going to put these up on all the bulletin boards – mostly where the English classes are and probably a few around the lockers." He paused as he zipped up his backpack. "I just remember how easy it was last year when the four of us read together. This year, I thought I would open it up to whoever wanted to come. And who knows? Maybe we can liven up the book a little. It might even be funny – but I doubt it."

"Yeah. Good luck with that. But you can count on me to be there if it means grazing over your dad's grilled burgers. Being ready for the next quiz ahead of time is always a bonus – but those burgers take priority. That is enough to justify going to a Jane Austen party. ... sorta."

"A 'Jane Austen party?' Uh, let's call it something else, shall we?"

Curtis started laughing. "Hey, dude! Remember last year when your dad had that fish fry out at your place?"

Billy remembered all too well.

Curtis began to laugh so hard, he could scarcely finish his sentence. "I don't remember if the fish was any good or not. I only remember that every stray cat in Pecan Falls showed up to see where that smell was coming from." <insert laughter>

"It was embarrassing is what it was. I didn't realize our town had that many cats."

"I remember seeing a cat show up - - and then another. Then I looked up and here come a hundred cats."

"There wasn't a hundred."

"Okay. Ninety-nine then."

"There was less than a dozen."

"No. There was *at least* a dozen. Maybe *two*." Curtis was doubled over with laughter once again. This was becoming a bad habit with him.

That didn't sound right, Billy wondered. *Was that even the right verb? Is it 'there <u>was</u> less than a dozen' or 'there <u>were</u> less than a dozen'? Oh no. I'm starting to sound like dad, the grammar police. Time to change subjects again* ... "Hey! Guess what!" Billy seemed excited all of a sudden.

"What?" Curtis was snapping out of his laughing tirade and was once again acting like what would pass in those parts for a normal human being.

"I asked Chloe today if we could hang out sometime and she actually ..."

Curtis interrupted with his annoyed voice turned way way up. "Chloe? Again with this girl? Dude, I am telling you for your own good, stay away from her."

Billy protested. "Dude, what are you going on about this time?"

"Chloe is just another one of those mean rich girls. She is going to tear you in half like a ticket stub. Take a good look around, friend. We have no shortage of girls at this school, so why don't you run along and find one that is nice and fairly normal?"

"Pffffff. Whatever." Agitated as usual, Billy turned and walked off.

"Dude, where you headed?"

"I'll catch up with you over at Anthony's for that pizza. I'm going to see if Mike is done with basketball practice. If it's alright with dad, I may hitch a ride with him. See you there."

Curtis' head tilted to one side as his friend walked out of earshot. "Touchy," he sang mockingly to himself. He turned to walk back toward his rendezvous point for Clay. He pondered over the possibility that this was how the entire school year was going to go. Why is it that Billy could not see what was going on here? Why would this Chloe show Billy any attention at all? Was she just toying with his head?

But Curtis was always the one to approach each scenario from different angles. He paused this train of thought and stepped back in his mind. Was he truly being fair concerning Chloe? For all he knew, there may be something going on here that was legit. He should not add any turmoil to an already-tense situation. Curtis may have to take the high road to reach that lofty place. Yes. Silence may be in order. Plus, it would help the pizza digest.

This video game had gotten old a while back. Wesley Porterfield the Third finally turned off the game and set the controller down next to him on the Oriental rug. He climbed up out of the leather recliner and looked around the game room at his cold, inanimate companions. A pool table. A pinball machine. Dart-board. Air hockey. Loneliness. All this stuff was supposed to be fun, but everything he saw reminded him that he was alone. The pool cues stood in perfect alignment on the wall rack mocking the pattern of prison bars. Wesley was in his own gilded prison, as it would seem. A well-furnished cell is still a cell. What he would not do to have an annoying sibling or two.

Sra. Teresa had cleaned all day and made dinner for him. Now his housekeeper had gone to her own home for the evening. As Wesley understood it, his mom had gone back to Massachusetts to visit family and his dad was on a business trip somewhere in Thailand. Or was it the Philippines? Maybe it was for the best; his parents did not especially get along with each other when they were in town. They moved to Pecan Falls at the beginning of last year - - but it seemed that Wesley was really the only one of them who was spending any time there. He wanted to yell across this spacious house to see if anyone would respond. He refrained because he knew that only the silence would answer him.

He stepped out of the game room and playfully skated across the hardwood floor in his socks toward the front of the house. That floor was highly polished and the setting sunlight came through the windows and blindingly reflected off of it as it would on the surface of a nearby lake. He was tastefully surrounded by expensive pieces of abstract art and weird modern furniture. A tall grandfather clock stood in the corner disapproving of all these modern artistic choices. The piano bench beckoned for someone to sit and make beautiful music resonate from the baby grand. The overhead crystal chandelier had been turned on. The teardrop shaped prisms were pretty, but no one was there to share the spectacle with him. The worst thing about loneliness was that there was no one there to share it.

He placed his hand on the cherry railing on the stairs. Should he go up? Should he go eat what Sra. Teresa made first? Should he pass the long hours tonight in front of his mindless television? Should he wrestle with this Jane Austen book? He honestly had no idea. He wanted to call someone and talk, but he did not know anyone in town who he felt like calling. It struck him as being humorous that he was alone in this great big house, but he felt that he was stuck in some invisible traffic jam - - unable to move. Ultimately, he sat on the stairs and looked at the trees just outside the windows.

After a few minutes, he grabbed his car keys, slipped on some shoes, and exited through the side door. There must be some people somewhere in this town.

CHAPTER 17

THE PRICE OF A PIZZA

"Good! It's empty." Mike led the way from the front door to their favorite booth. The four boys darted across the room to the far corner and scooted around the circular corner table down at Anthony's Pizzeria, a popular hangout that locals lovingly considered a historic landmark. The table itself was big enough to easily accommodate all four of them; but it never occurred to these man-sized kids that they looked like little children scrambling for their favorite seats. But this has been their thing since they were little boys and they were not quite ready to grow out of this particular habit yet.

Anthony's was still pretty much the same place that it was when Billy's parents were kids - - and probably many years earlier. It had the same checkered floor, vintage pinball machine, and an out-of-order jukebox full of corny old songs. The owner played CD's of those timeless tunes on the overhead speakers. Most of the songs that were played were from the 1950's and 60's, but some were as 'recent' as the 80's. As Billy and his friends were walking in that evening, the particular song being played was encouraging energetic young people to attend an event called 'the hop.'

After sitting, the quartet looked around the room to properly assess the situation: a couple of members of the braces brigade, an aging metal-head working the pinball machine, a table populated with five squealing ten-year-old girls chaperoned by some lucky dad with a growing headache, a young family with preschoolers plus a toddler, nothing unusual. When the waitress came along, the group ordered their usual soft drinks.

Billy spent most of that night grinning as if he was following the conversation; but in reality, he was contributing very little – and almost nothing of any intelligence. The reason for his vagueness was understandable; he was trying to work up a way to tell his friends about his family's wealth. That was all he wanted to do and he decided that tonight was the night. His parents had strictly forbidden him to share their family secret to anyone; but he had already spilled the beans with Chloe, so why should he not tell his closest and dearest friends? These were guys that he could trust.

He had already made up his mind that he was going to do it, but how? *Oh. By the way, guys, my family is filthy, stinking rich.* No. That was like ripping medical tape from a hairy arm. Should he hint at this information with subtle references like inching his way down into a chilly swimming pool? Or should he jump right on in, as if he were performing a cannonball? (Perhaps these swimming pool analogies are inappropriate considering the recent fate of his third copy of *Pride and Prejudice*.)

He *could* do exactly what his parents told him to and just keep this information to himself. After all, the reason they did not tell him earlier was because they feared that he could not resist the urge to tell others. Like that would happen.

His mind wandered. Billy glimpsed down at the floor's checkerboard pattern and subconsciously began to imagine giant chess pieces moving around on the linoleum tiles. He wanted to move his rook down, but first they would have to scoot one of the tables out of the way. The thought was amusing to him.

"Well, what do *you* think?"

Apparently, Mike had been talking to him – but for how long? Billy blinked away his daydream. "About what?" Time to play it cool.

"About what we were just talking about. Dude, were you drifting off again? Billy, I swear," Mike exclaimed. "Sometimes I think that one of your tires isn't aired up all the way."

Clay jumped in to save his daydreaming compadre. "We were talking about this silly old song that is playing." He pointed up at the speaker in the ceiling tile. Apparently the song had changed since they sat down.

Billy tilted his head slightly to catch of few bars of this ridiculous music.

Curtis was used to Billy's absentmindedness and decided to fill him in. "The age-old question on the table is as follows: 'Is the thing eating the people actually purple in color? Or does it only eat purple people, thereby keeping people safe who *aren't* purple?'" By now, the sped-up saxophone solo was playing.

They all looked at Billy as if they were about to have their heads filled with knowledge from the master. Of course, it was all done sarcastically.

"Well? What *do* you think?" Mike was being comically pushy. Curtis joined him in mock anticipation. Clay was trying not to laugh.

"I'm sorry, guys. I can't seem to focus on anything tonight."

Mike was not surprised. "Oh, that much we already knew. And what's so different about that?"

Billy took a deep breath. Okay. Here it comes. "Well, since you brought it up, there is something on my mind that I'd like to share with you guys."

The boys looked at each other, not knowing what to expect. Whatever news Billy had to share may be alarming. But the boys were not too alarmed. Billy sometimes would start off an announcement that way and it was usually just a big deal over nothing.

"Well?" Curtis pretty much spoke for the three of them.

"You guys know how …"

"Here you are, boys." The waitress leaned forward and placed their pizza on the table. "One extra-large pizza with pepperoni on one side and everything except pepperoni on the other. Anything else?"

Billy was irked. He had been trying to talk about their fortunate finances all night, and now *this* interruption. In addition, he did not even remember them ordering the pizza yet - - but whatever. Maybe he was just not paying attention. But he was cool with it; theirs was still the best pizza in town. He also wondered how it came to the table so quickly; after all, they had to cook it. He must have been playing mental linoleum chess longer than he thought. Strange.

The boys sat in silence while they scarfed down their first piece each, burning their mouths as they went.

About midway through, Billy began with a question. "You know how we were talking the other day about what we would do if we had all the money in the world?" After their reply, he continued. "Well, we do." He found himself chuckling. It felt weird to finally say it.

"Huh?" The boys looked at each other with confused gazes.

"Yep. You heard right. We actually *do* have all the money in the world."

Clay was not one to pick out other people's inaccuracies as they spoke. He preferred to politely let others talk. But he broke out of character and responded to Billy's statement. "No, we don't. We have just enough to cover this pizza."

"I'm not talking about the four of us. Just me." Billy began to nod his head in a proud way. "Well, not just me. It's my parents and me." Billy frowned at his own sentence and tried to correct himself. "Uh, my parents and I." *That doesn't sound quite right either*, he thought.

The boys were silent. They all stared at him. They were not even chewing the food that was in their mouths.

"So, what do you guys think of that? Pretty cool, huh?"

Curtis was trying to speak (and not laugh) while taking another bite of his pizza. "Your family doesn't have *all* the money in the world. But I'm sure that they get by just fine."

Billy's face dropped slightly as he got more literal. "No, not *all* the money in the world. But we have *most* of the money in this county."

Mike rolled his eyes. "Well, that's saying a lot. All the money in this county could fit comfortably inside that broken jukebox over there."

Billy was unaware of the general effect of his voice, but the others could tell that he was growing more defensive with each passing comment. "Guys, I'm not *even* foolin'. We're incredibly rich."

A sly grin snuck onto Clay's face as he turned back to his pizza. "Oh yeah. You're sooo rich."

"We are."

The boys were silent. Clay, Mike, and Curtis took turns looking at each other.

Ever the one to speak up first, Mike addressed his comment toward the other two. "Are you thinking what I'm thinking?"

"I think so," Clay replied.

Curtis did not have to think twice about it. "Well, I'm pretty sure that I am."

Billy was starting to get a little concerned about these comments being made *about* him and not *to* him. "What? What are you all thinking?"

Hesitatingly, Curtis spoke in a concerned voice. "I know that we were the initial ones to suggest this, so it could be our fault. But maybe those kids in the Chess Club are not the best influence on you."

"What?! What do *they* have to do with any of this if you don't mind my asking?"

Clay ignored Billy and turned to Mike. "I was wondering if it was too late for him to join the band."

Mike filled him in. "Man, it is never too late to join the band. They're *always* looking for folks - - as long as they know which is the business end of an alto sax." (Actually, what Mike was saying was not true; there was indeed a cutoff date. But that is not relevant to the story.)

Clay asked a question in his usual sincerity. "Yeah, but didn't you hear Billy earlier? He said that he has no idea where his trombone slide is."

Billy was getting more annoyed with each passing comment.

Curtis got excited. "I can tell you where it probably is. It's probably under the bleachers at the middle school football field. He spent half of every football game last year climbing down those bleachers whenever he dropped his slide between the seats. If we're lucky, I'll bet that we can not only find Billy's slide but also dozens of other slides from other clumsy trombone players over the years. Those things would be a whole lot easier to find than a bunch of clarinet reeds."

Mike jumped in. "Dude! We can sell that stuff and make some real money. It'll be easier than picking up those stupid pecans!"

This actually sounded rather logical to Billy, but he was certainly not going to agree with them. Besides, he was not done getting angry yet; how can they just talk about him with him sitting right there in front of them? How rude. He was just about to say something regrettable when he was interrupted.

A light came on inside Mike's head. "Is this anything like the time we were in the third grade and you had us dig up your backyard looking for Spanish gold?"

This amused Clay and Curtis, but Billy swayed his head as he explained, "Okay. That was just a little misunderstanding."

It was Curtis' turn to expose their friend. "Oh? Kinda like that time that we were on our way to Memphis and saw those low-flying crop-dusting planes and you swore that our country was under foreign attack."

The boys were on a roll now.

"Dude!" Clay just remembered something. "What about that time last year when this old man came in from out of town and was visiting the church."

Curtis and Mike pointed at each other in remembrance and laughed hysterically. Mike tried to finish the story. "That's right! And Billy thought that the old geezer was Ronald Reagan."

Billy sighed in irritation. "Not Ronald Reagan. It was Nixon. And in my defense, he looked just like the guy."

Clay tried to speak over the laughter. " ...maybe from the back pew."

Mike's voice definitely rose above the laughing. "There is no way that that old man could've been Nixon. Nixon died before we were born. And the *only* reason I know that is because I remember looking it up at the time."

At this point, one might ordinarily think that these boys were getting way too loud; but no one really let it bother them. Between the table with the squealing girls and the speakers playing something called *Shotgun* by Junior Walker and the All Stars, three of these boys never even slowed down.

Billy felt that it was time to maintain some sense of control again and bring them back to indoor voices. "Guys! Guys! Listen! I'm telling you the truth."

Laughter changed to light chuckling. As Billy began again, the others responded by subconsciously leaning forward as if they were receiving top secret information.

"I recently found out that our family is the richest in town by like a mile."

Clay asked, "If what you are saying is true, then how did your family gain this sudden wealth?"

Curtis' eye got wide with sarcasm. "Do your parents print it in the backyard shed?" The other boys snickered.

"Of course not. And it isn't exactly sudden. Apparently, we've had it for some time. My parents just never told me about it. I found out by accident just the other day."

Clay's question was not answered, so he tried again. "Yeah. But where did it all come from?"

"Well, we own a very well-known company."

Their eyebrows all scooted up their foreheads. "Oh?" Mike asked, "What company? Have we heard of it?"

Billy was hesitant. He had already said way too much. But if he did not reply, they would assume that he was making all of this up. "Crowe's Athletic Equipment," he answered.

Once again, they all stared at him in silence. No sound came from their table. The only sounds came from the kitchen, the silly girls laughing a few tables away, and that old-timey song. Then all at once, they exploded with laughter.

Billy was getting ticked again. Why would they not believe him?

"Step to the side, gentlemen," Mike announced. "Here comes Billy Harris Jr., heir to the greatest throne in the athletic world."

The boys were still in hysterics.

Billy was mad. He had been completely honest with them and they were all acting like he had made it up. He wondered why did they not believe him the way that Chloe did. Maybe he was learning who his real friends were - - and maybe these real friends were not sitting around the table with him at that moment.

Right on time, their waitress arrived with the bill. "You boys want this in four ways as usual?"

Mike spoke right up. "Not this time. Hand the whole thing over to our friend Mr. Rockefeller over there. He's sitting on a bundle."

Billy ended up with the check in his hands and was looking at it. "Uh, I can't pay for all of this."

Curtis was as amused as the others. "Huh? What do you mean? You just got finished telling us that your folks make bank, but you aren't even good for the price of a pizza?"

Clay looked up at the waitress. "I think you had better split this up like you usually do."

Curtis spoke up again. "Yeah. But Billy, that would've been awesome if you were rich."

"We are!" In spite of some encouraging words from Earth, Wind, and Fire coming over the speakers, Billy felt nothing like a shining star.

"Sure, sure." They pulled their money out and in a short amount of time, their business with Anthony's Pizzeria was concluded, including the gratuity.

The familiar sound of the cowbell hanging on the door filled the air announcing the arrival of another potential patron. Mike's face dropped. "Oh no. There goes the neighborhood." He was looking over at the entrance. Standing in the open door was Wesley Porterfield looking around the room. The young man stepped in and saw the four boys. With an eager smile, he strode over in their direction.

"Quick, get up." Mike gave Clay a light shove encouraging him to move. "Let's get outta here. Those video games aren't going to play themselves, ya know."

As a reflex action more than anything, the others complied.

"Hey guys!" Wesley greeted them with those perfect teeth behind that perfect smile. But he noticed they were getting up and his smile faded a little. His eyebrows furrowed. "Are you guys leaving?"

The others responded politely to him, but Mike's voice rose above the others as the official spokesman of the party. "Yep. We were just leaving. But if you want …" Mike gestured at their mess. " …this table is available." He then rudely ushered the other three straight out the door and onto the next phase of their evening. And with that, they were gone.

Looking like a complete stooge, Wesley helplessly watched the others leave - - and with them, all hopes of friendly conversation. He turned to look down at the mess on their table and then sat in a much smaller table next to theirs. The waitress came along, took his order, and also left him to sit there all alone. Over the next few minutes, all the other groups of people in the room left. Above his head, singer Ricky Nelson came over the speakers crooning some sad old song about an entire town where lonesome people go. Wesley could certainly sympathize.

CHAPTER 18

THE INTERROGATION

Following its customary habit, the sun came up and went back down a few more times over the next few days. In fact, that entire weekend came and went faster than a 20 G centrifuge. Billy went to school on Monday as expected and he had fun with his friends. But these supposed friends of his were no closer to believing his outlandish (but true) story of immeasurable wealth than they were the previous week. If only he had some sort of concrete proof ... If only *the item* would be delivered ... That'll show 'em.

Tuesday arrived - - and with it, more of the same. That day was pretty much like the rest with Billy bouncing his way from class to class like an academic scavenger hunter complete with a quiz in Algebra. He found the concept amusing that such grotesque wealth was his as he glided unseen amongst the common folks. On the plus side, he would occasionally get an unexpected smile and a friendly wave from Chloe. She even said *Hi* to him once as he made his way to his seat in first period. That was reason enough just to go to school. It almost made up for having to endure his dad's embarrassing presence.

There was no Chess Club on Tuesdays. That afternoon, he found himself back home that much sooner. At this point, Diane made her way down the hallway and into the living room where Billy had been playing a video game. A pile of clean clothes was tossed onto the couch right next to where Billy sat. His mom ran her fingers through the top of his hair as she walked by. "Dinner will be ready in a few minutes and I need you to fold these clothes for me."

"No problem, mom. Just let me finish this level. I'm almost done." He continued to play.

"Don't forget," Diane turned and pointed at him as she entered the kitchen. She was finishing up a big pot of spaghetti and was about to start toasting some garlic bread in the oven. "Yeah, he'll forget," she softly said to herself.

William came into the kitchen through the side door under the carport (their house did not have a garage). From his facial expression, his wife could easily tell that something was weighing on his mind. "Where's Billy?" he inquired.

She gestured toward the living room. "He's in there. Follow the sound of the video game. Hey, don't be long. Dinner is about ready. Do you want some sweet tea?"

"That would be great. Thanks." With undertones of subtle hinting, William said, "Oh, and you might want to see what showed up today. It's out on the carport."

As he exited the kitchen, Diane curiously tossed her hand towel on the countertop and went to peek outside the door. "Huh? What is that?" she asked herself. Upon closer examination, she had her answer. "Oh, Billy. Whatever were you thinking?" She walked back into the house. "I guess William is going to handle this one."

William found Billy lying all the way back on the couch playing his game. "You may want to turn that off now." That was William's way of telling his son to get off the game system.

Billy had heard that voice many times before. The *smart* thing to do would be to comply and quickly turn it off in spite of possibly losing his achievements. He did the smart thing for once. Was it because dinner was ready or was there something else? Was this going to be one of *those* talks? William pulled his legs around the coffee table and sat down right in front of Billy. Yep, it was going to be one of *those* talks.

"Uh, Billy? Something was delivered to our house today. Do you know anything about this giant box out under the carport?"

Momentary amnesia set in. "Box? What box?"

William pulled an invoice and his glasses out of his shirt pocket. With the glasses perched on the end of his nose, he unfolded the invoice and began to read. "It is something called the 'Twelve-In-One Super-Flex Body

Builder Set'. Do you know anything about it?" He returned his readers to his shirt pocket.

Billy was suddenly filled with excitement. "Cool! It's here already?! Yay!!" He looked at his dad and noticed that he did not share his son's excitement over this great news. He quickly reverted back into his earlier interrogation mode. "Uh, that's really cool. Thanks, dad."

"So you *do* know something about this."

"Well, I … uh …"

"You ordered this without first consulting your mother or myself?"

"Well, I *was* going to tell you before it got here - - and after all, we *are* rich, and I just thought …"

We may want to interrupt our story at this point for a quick little public service announcement. As in many such dramas that have unfolded throughout the ages (especially between father and son), there are two sides to each story. From William's point-of-view, their son had used money that was not his to buy something rather expensive – and without permission. From Billy's perspective, their family had more money than they knew what to do with anyway. So what possible harm would it cause to buy something nice for once? Plus, he could then be able to prove to his buddies that, all along, he was telling the truth, the whole truth, and nothing but the truth. And as a bonus, he would get the last laugh and some exercise equipment. In reality, his dad was speaking to him in a calm voice. But if we were to ask Billy, he would claim that his dad "flipped out" on him. Whatever.

An objective observer may be inclined to side with the parents this time. But poor Billy was going into the parental interrogation process, a place where perhaps you too could sympathize. In truth, they were sitting peaceably in their living room; but in an emotional state, he was sitting in the proverbial hot seat. In many ways, it felt like an old gangster movie or one of those trashy old dime novels with the two-fisted police detective, always saying something tough and funny. So let us visit their conversation as if we were actually watching it in an old movie – at least from Billy's perspective …

*The nighttime scene was shot in stark black-and-white –
probably occurring sometime in the late 1940's. Billy was in*

a back room at one of the San Francisco police precincts. He sat blindfolded in an uncomfortable seat under a hot lamp. Sweat was pouring from his bruised brow. He heard the creaking sound of the door opening. The door itself had a frosted window with the room number painted on the other side.

Police detective William Harris Sr. walked in wearing a white dress shirt and an ugly tie, his sleeves rolled up to his elbows. He closed the door, loosened his tie, and unbuttoned the top button as he spoke. "Did you miss me, you cheap punk?" He hung his hat on a nearby hat rack next to a framed photo of President Truman.

Billy looked very nervous and frightened. His breathing was heavy as he wondered what they would do to him. William, on the other hand, looked mean and nasty. His breathing was normal – except that it smelled like black coffee and a dead cat.

With trembling voice, Billy courageously, but fearfully, posed a question. "When can I get something to drink?"

William walked over to the chair where Billy had been put. In a voice that was manically relaxed, he answered, "That is completely up to you. Any time you are ready to start singing, I'm ready to start listening."

"All I want is a small cup of water."

"You don't get a drop until I hear your story – all of it. And I better like what I hear. You listening, twerp?"

Back in the Harris' actual living room (with color), William leaned forward. In a non-threatening voice, he said, "So, would you like to tell me exactly what happened? And from the beginning?"

Billy rolled his eyes. William interpreted this as disrespectful, but he let it go this time. *Pick your fights*, he thought to himself.

Billy spoke as if this entire offence was no big deal. "The other day when I learned about all our money, I saw an ad on TV for the Twelve-In-One Super-Flex Body Builder Set. And since we were rich and all, I borrowed your debit card and ordered it. If we are as rich as you and mom say, it really shouldn't matter."

William remained characteristically calm. "Billy, all that big money is tied up with the corporation. We don't have access to it with …"

"…THIS CARD!" Back in the police interrogation room, the black-and-white William held the debit card up to his rough face. His other hand was stroking the five-o'clock shadow on his chin. It felt like sandpaper. "The only money here is what your mother and I make with our jobs. We cannot afford the Twelve-In-One Super-Flex Body Builder Set with that account! How are we supposed to pay the bills? Now thanks to you, we're gonna have to move some money around."

Blindfolded Billy squirmed desperately in the interrogation chair. "I didn't know! I promise I didn't know!" he cried. The chains on his handcuffs jingled as they scraped across the armrests.

Golden sunlight was coming into their living room and lighting up William as his spoke in an instructive, loving way. "Well, just so you know, even that corporate money is not truly ours. Everything in the world belongs to God; we're just borrowing this money in a sense. We're trying to be good stewards with all God's blessings." He looked down at the packing slip in his hand. "And this is a major purchase. Did you even pray about this first?" He looked back up at his son.

Interrogation room Billy was on the verge of tears now. "No. I guess not. I honestly didn't know that that was required."

"Required?!"

The door opened up behind William. Diane walked in. She was wearing a knee-length skirt with a matching jacket over a white blouse with a sort of ruffled collar on it. Her head sported a funny old-fashioned hat with a fishnet veil over her thickly lipsticked face. (The lipstick would be a deep red color if this were not a black-and-white movie; color film was quite pricey back in the forties.)

William continued his comment. "It's not required necessarily. Things like the Twelve-In-One Super-Flex Body Building Set can be a blessing to us, but it can also be a curse."

"Here's your drink," Diane said as she handed William a tall glass of tea.

"Thanks, doll." He took a few large swallows.

In his own blindfolded way, Billy could hear Detective Harris swallowing his tea. The young man's lips seemed drier than ever at the sound.

She crossed the room and slinked down into a couch by the window next to a free-standing ashtray that had not been cleaned out for a while. From there, she could see the lights from the boxy houses that populated the sloped streets between them and the Golden Gate Bridge. Traffic quietly crossed back and forth across the towering icon. To her right, Coit Tower presided over the city. And across the bay, Alcatraz.

Billy felt that he was about to die of thirst. This was absolute torture. He may have preferred going over to Alcatraz. But now he had confessed; maybe now they'd let him drink something - - or better still, let him go.

Instead, Detective Harris simply put down his drink and got to his feet. As he spoke, he walked in creepy rings around Billy's chair. "You? Humpf! A hungry fifteen-year-old who can eat an entire acre of food a day and still weigh in at a buck and a quarter—you think that buying this expensive toy is going to give you the body of a lumberjack. You poor naïve child. That doohickey that you just poured all that money into is just a thing and will be burned up one day. What do you think of that, you green hooligan?"

Billy tilted his head in thought. It was evident that he was listening.

Detective Harris stopped right in front of Billy. Maintaining his loud, angry voice, he kept working on him. "For your own spiritual health, I advise you to review First John 2:15-17 ..."

Billy thought, *Oh boy. Here it comes – the unavoidable Bible quote.* Anyone wearing a pair of grammatically-sensitive goggles would be able to see the words coming out of William's mouth, traveling through the air, going into Billy's left ear, and coming out his right.

William said, "First John 2:15-17 says, 'Love not the world, neither the things that are in the world. If any man love the world, the love of the Father is not in him. For all that is in the world, the lust of the flesh, and the lust of the eyes, and the pride of life, is not of the Father, but is of the world. And the world passeth away, and the lust thereof: but he that doeth the will of God abideth for ever.'"

Billy glanced up at the clock on the wall. *How much longer is this going to take?* he asked himself.

Actual William returned to an upright position, a sign that he was finishing his talk. His eyebrows arched up and he opened his outstretched hands as he spoke. "Look, we are not opposed to you having nice things like the Twelve-in-One Super-Flex Body Builder Set ..." *Whew, that's a ridiculous name,* he thought to himself. "But we need you to understand that junk like that won't last."

157

Interrogation William jabbed his sharp pointy finger into Billy's boney ribcage. "What we DON'T like is that you used this card without our permission. And if this happens again ..."

Billy tensed up. Even with the blindfold on, one could tell that he was listening to every word.

"...we'll have to take away your phone,"

Billy shook his head in remorse. "No."

"...your game system,"

Billy's cry was a little louder this time. "NO."

"...and your other electronic devices."

"NO!" Billy began to weep uncontrollably.

"And in the meantime, the Twelve-in-One Super-Flex Body Builder Set will have to be returned."

Pleasant William lifted his hand and began to count on his fingers. "Okay, just as a brief review, let's run over our list of facts. Number one: we do not have a large amount of money in this account. Two: this is the money we make from our jobs and the money that we live off of."

Interrogation William was now in Billy's face. Occasionally, some spit shot out of his cruel mouth as his roared. "Fact three: you do NOT have access to our big money. Fact four: you used our debit card without permission and you will be punished if this happens again."

Billy's mom walked by and rubbed her fingers though the top of his hair once again as she asked, "Would you like your glass of tea now?"

Billy answered in a normal tone. "No thanks. I'm good. I'll just have mine with dinner."

"And fact five: The Twelve-in-One Super-Flex Body Builder Set is being sent back. Does all of this sound about right to you?"

Blindfolded Billy could take no more of this. "YES! YES! ANYTHING!" He was in complete agony. Beads of sweat dripped from his nose and were being absorbed into his shirt.

Somewhat satisfied, the rough detective stood straight and tall. Looking down on his suspect, he said, "Good! As long as we are clear on a few things."

At that moment, they were interrupted by the sound of a loud clumsy buzzer that filled the stale air in the interrogation room. Protected behind a small cylindrical cage, a cautionary red light came on (well, the black-and-white movie version of a red light). Highly alarmed, William spun wildly around to observe the light. "What now? Who could that be?"

Diane looked up from her makeup compact to see what was happening.

In the real world, the harmless sound of the doorbell reached their ears. "Oh. Someone is at the door," William stated.

This was Billy's golden opportunity. "I'll go see who it is." He sprang from his seat and darted for the door, never looking back. Hopefully this timely interruption could declare this conversation finished. *There was no reason for dad to go bonkers on me like that,* he thought as he rushed to the door. He did not care who it was, but he was very glad to exit from these proceedings.

But once he opened the door, this young man would receive the surprise of his life.

CHAPTER 19

A WELCOME GUEST

Billy opened the door wide to the tune of the squeaky hinges. To his complete astonishment, there she stood. Chloe Chastain was looking as cute as ever from the nearly golden hair on her head down to the pink socks that peeked out over the top of her shoes. "Hi," she said in a bright voice as she clung to her big frumpy purse.

Was this another one of Billy's weird dreams? He quickly looked around the room to see if that nuisance of a butler was standing in the corner laughing at him. No, the coast was clear. Maybe this was not a dream.

Just last week, Billy had conjured up enough courage to introduce himself to her and now she was standing at the front door of his house. Half of his brain was saying, *No way! Is this really happening?* The other half was looking beyond her at the sporty number she was driving. He was guessing that she was either sixteen already or she had one of those hardship licenses that allowed her to drive straight to school and then straight home. *My house is NOT straight home for her*, he thought. He pondered these things as he silently stood in the doorway gawking at her like he had never seen a girl before. It suddenly occurred to him that all of his troubles seemed to be washing away. First, he learned about his family's fortunes and now his dream girl was on his steps. Now all he needed was to find a way for his dad to retire from teaching and he would be on velvet.

Following an uncomfortable amount of time, Chloe offered the greeting again. "Hi?" Her questioning tone indicated that it was now *his* turn to speak.

If Billy was a very articulate person at all, he certainly did not show it now. "Uh … Hi. This is a surprise."

"Yeah. Sorry about that. I was just passing by and I thought I'd check out where you live."

Billy was caught off his guard. "Where I live?" *Oh no*, Billy thought. *She practically lives in a big cool palace. I live in this horrible old shack that was probably old when Kennedy was President. I don't suppose that I could talk my way out of this one.* "Where I live? Oh, that's easy." Billy began to point toward one of the far away hills. "You go down to … uh, uh."

The nose on Chloe's face wrinkled up and she looked confused. She brought her hand up and revealed that she had been looking at one of the fliers that he put out for the *Pride and Prejudice* reading. "But what about the address on this?"

Side note: It would occur to Billy in retrospect how dumb it was to put their actual home address on a flier and post it all over the school. That makes it easy for truly bad people to use that to their own evil advantage. What is keeping someone from leaving him a package on his doorstep, ringing the doorbell, and then running away? Billy would find the box, open it, and get hit in the face by a boxing glove on the end of a spring. He needed to start thinking about things like that. And now, back to our story …

Her voice sure sounds cute when she speaks, he thought. But that momentary euphoria lasted nearly a full millisecond. Immediately after, he was thrown into full panic mode. Billy stumbled through. "Well, this … this is where we live as well. But, you know, just during the week … because it's closer to the school and all. We actually have a … much larger … well, you know how it goes. I don't mean to bore you with details."

Something about this was amusing to Chloe. After another brief awkward pause, Chloe began again. "So? This is where you live?"

Billy began to stall. He was hoping to say something clever, but something cleaver did not come. "Yes - - in a manner of speaking." *This is so painful*, Billy thought. *But at least mom and dad aren't out here to embarrass me.*

His parents appeared in the doorway. "Billy? Who is your friend?" asked Diane inquisitively.

This was not really the moment. He himself was not precisely sure of what he wanted his guest to think. He did not want Chloe to think that he did not have any parents at all – as if he may have just hatched out of an egg or something. But at the same time, he did not want his parents anywhere around. Parents at a distance would be nice. Billy choked out the words, "Mom, this is Chloe. Chloe, this is my mom."

A warm smile beamed from Chloe's pretty face. "Mrs. Harris." She turned to William. "Hello, Mr. Harris."

William was not sure what to make of all of this. But politeness is always an appropriate measure. "Chloe," he replied nicely. But he could not help thinking about their brief conversation the week before. He would have described her attitude as *unreceptive*, maybe even *hostile*. And now she was here at their home talking to their son. It all seemed quite innocent, and yet very suspicious.

Diane got tired of waiting for Billy to be polite. "Well, don't just leave her out here. Ask her to come in." She directed her attention to Chloe. "We were just about to have dinner. Maybe you could join us. We've got plenty." Diane and William retreated back into the house and disappeared around the corner into the kitchen.

Billy followed suit. "Yeah. Please come in."

Billy led the way as Chloe entered. She seemed rather scared to touch anything, always clinging to her oversized purse. The first thing that she noticed was a rather old piece of table-like furniture against the wall in the entryway. It featured an uglyish blue glass bowl. Above it was a print of an old painting – a ship struggling in some high waters. Across from it was a painting of a couple of horses running across a field of tall grass. Billy was fortunate to have missed the contorted face that Chloe made when she saw the paintings. It was not exactly pop art.

The entryway opened up into a fair-sized room. "Right in here is the living room. I was just about to ..." *Uh-oh!* Billy saw the pile of clean clothes on the couch. He was supposed to be folding them. How embarrassing! He rushed over to the pile and grabbed the bundle. "Here. Let me just get these out of the way." He scrambled down the hall with the clothes tightly gathered in his arms, presumably to some unseen bedroom.

Undetected by Billy, a pair of his boxer shorts fell out and landed on the floor behind him.

Chloe noticed though and snickered softly to herself.

"Something about this doesn't feel right," William said softly to Diane. The both of them were in the kitchen and could not be heard by either Billy or Chloe. William was at present getting an extra plate for the table.

"Why? What's wrong?"

"Well, it's this Chloe. I told her earlier that she needs to be working harder in my class. She did not look especially receptive to what I was saying. Or at least, that is the impression that I got. And now suddenly she appears at our door looking somewhat interested in our son. To my knowledge, she hasn't had much interaction with Billy - - if any." He realized that he was sounding a bit too concerned. He shrugged. "I don't know. It just strikes me as being odd."

Diane did not look up as she was spreading garlic butter on toasted bread. "She seems like a nice girl to me. But I don't know these kids like you do. Still, I'm not sure if I like this anyway."

Her reservations took his interest. "Okay. What are *you* thinking about?"

Diane started to say something and then stopped herself. Then, she shook her head as if she was going to just say what was on her mind. "Well, she came over uninvited. When I was a teenager, girls didn't just make calls on the boys. It's like they're chasing them. Girls seem just way too aggressive these days. I'm not sure if I like that."

William smiled and took the spaghetti toward the table. "That's no mystery to me. You never had to chase any boy. You were too busy being chased *by* them."

Diane gave him a sarcastic smirk.

Chloe looked around the living room for a quick assessment of her surroundings. It was your typical Cold War era house. The carpet looked old, but not near as old as the house. The ceiling was blown with a random amount of glitter. She felt as though she had just stepped out of a time machine. She was tempted to ask Billy what year he thought it was.

After tossing the clean clothes onto his parents' bed, Billy rushed back into the living room. To his horror, he noticed a pair of his plaid boxer shorts on the floor in front of Chloe. She obviously had seen them. He nervously picked them up. "Uh …" He did not have the first idea of what to do. There was no precedent set that he knew of on what proper etiquette would dictate. So he unthinkingly began to tuck them into the front of his pants. "Sorry. They must've slipped. That doesn't usually happen." His joke was not funny. He then directed her attention to the table under the horse painting. "Here. Would you like to set your purse down over there?"

"I think I'll just hang on to it for a while. Thanks."

"Okay. Would you care to have a seat?"

"Thanks." They both sat on the couch.

Needless to say, what followed was a series of long awkward pauses between Billy's painful attempts at small talk. He finally decided to take an unconventional topic of conversation.

"I heard a great joke last week. Do you want to hear it?"

"Sure."

Suddenly, Billy seemed a little less nervous as his arms became more animated. "Okay. There was a knight who was tired of playing Chess."

Diane stepped into the room and apologized. "I don't mean to interrupt, but I'm putting dinner on the table and I was wondering if you had decided to stay for dinner. I don't know what your plans are."

Chloe replied in an unusually cheery voice. "That sounds great. Thank you, Mrs. Harris."

Billy made another attempt to start the joke. "Right. There was this knight and he was tired of playing Chess. So he joins a circus. At the circus, he gets a job as a tight-rope walker. And the ringmaster yells up at him, 'Hey you! Be careful up there!'" Billy was unaware of this, but he proceeded to demonstrate his donkey-like laugh. Clearly, he was proud of himself and his corny joke.

Chloe's face was blank.

"Isn't that funny?"

Honestly, Chloe did not understand the joke - - which is no surprise. Billy killed it. The joke was not that funny, even in its funniest form; but he destroyed it. Had Mike been there, he would have followed it up with a remark about Billy not quitting his day job.

Chloe did not want to tell him the truth. She did not have to. Her face communicated that message easily enough.

He tried to explain it to her – which made things worse. "You know? The knight is like 'bum, bum, bum.'" Each time he said 'bum,' he moved his hands - - first two toward her and the third one to the left. He repeated the move. "Bum, bum, bum. Well, technically he could go 'bum, bum, bum.'" This last time, his hands moved right instead of left. "You know, forward and then to the side." He struggled hard to illustrate how the knight moves on a chess board, but to no avail.

She did not even know that one of the pieces was called a knight; she probably would have called it a 'horsey.' Wide-eyed, Chloe was shaking her head. "Sorry. You lost me."

"Oh." Billy was just about to apologize for the joke when his mom saved the day.

"It's all ready if you two would like to come on."

"Coming!" Like a little kid, Billy leaped up off of the couch. For a fleeting moment, Chloe was fearful for her safety.

In order to get to the dining room, she had to take a step up - - but it was not actually a full step. It was more like a part of the floor to trip over. The color of the carpet might bring to mind a vision of chocolate syrup mixing with melting vanilla ice cream. Against the wall was a strange architectural device; it was a partial wall that stopped about waist-high. Then from there to the ceiling, it was a series of round wooden columns which may have been fashionable once long ago. At some point in the past, this whole section may have been an actual wall. But anyone who may have known what the house originally looked like was probably dead by now.

The dining room was not actually a separate room. It was more like an extension of the kitchen. The two were separated only by a small bar that had a couple of tall stools. A roll of paper towels hung from under some cabinets directly above the bar. The dining table was a rather old piece with matching chairs. Plates, silverware, food, all were on the table. A ceiling fan was at rest overhead. Whoever installed the ceiling fan somehow missed the true center of the ceiling.

Chloe thought that there might have been some ongoing feud between the architect and the construction crew. Maybe the Hatfield's designed it and the McCoy's built it. She half-expected little clowns to start pouring out of the cabinets. *This is how horror movies begin*, she thought to herself.

Diane welcomed her to the table. "We're having spaghetti and garlic toast tonight. I hope that is fine." Her flattened left hand settled onto her right in a sideways prayer formation.

Chloe tilted her head and returned a warm smile. "It will be perfect, Mrs. Harris." Across the table from the kitchen was a large window and another small table. Chloe walked over to it and carefully laid her gargantuan purse on top. She then took the closest seat. Billy sat next to her. Diane sat across from Billy. William sat between them at the head of the table with his back to the kitchen, the bar, and those hanging paper towels.

As he sat, William began to explain. "Chloe, we have a habit of saying grace before we eat." He directed his gaze at Diane. "And you did it last time so I guess it is my turn." They all bowed their heads. Chloe awkwardly followed their example. "Almighty God, we thank you for giving us food to eat and for the ability to share it with our company. May we always be found in Your will. In Jesus' name, Amen."

During the short prayer, Billy discreetly looked up at Chloe. He then saw that she had noticed him doing that. Embarrassed, he looked down again. His face turned slightly red. But was he embarrassed because she saw him looking at him or because his family was having prayers? Or a combination of the two?

In a sweet southern voice, Diane announced, "Alright! Everyone dig in." She leaned into the table toward Chloe. In a tone directed at her, she said, "We're not much for putting on airs, so whatever you want, just help yourself or just holler for it."

What Diane just said was proper and innocent enough. But just the same, a slight sense of humiliation ran up Billy's vertebrae. "Mom …" Billy said this in that singsong way that gives two syllables to one syllable words.

Diane was scooping out some spaghetti onto her plate and stopped for a second. She wondered if she had said something wrong. If so, she had no idea what it was. She was just being nice. Maybe she was not being formal enough. Maybe they should have changed into their Sunday clothes.

William spoke up. "Well, I certainly worked up an appetite today." Like most dads, he was something of an amateur comedian. Whether he wanted to or not, something less than serious was bound to come out of his mouth. "While I'm at it, I may just get seconds on my plate while I'm getting my firsts. It'll save me a lot of time."

"Dad!" There was that tone again. Did William say anything that would embarrass Billy? It became clear to his parents that, if Billy did not relax soon, dinner was going to be a horrible and uncomfortable experience. There would be nothing that his parents could say or do that was going to be fine with him. What did Billy want? To put his parents in conversational handcuffs while everyone sat eating in silence?

Billy knew that this was a mistake. If he was going to convince Chloe that they were wealthy, it could not be done at the dinner table in their house. How could he maintain the fiction that they were rich? Except they *were* rich. He was confused.

Diane lightened the mood. "Chloe, do you like spaghetti?"

"I do actually." She smiled and took a small bite.

Diane smiled back, revealing the lines on either side of her smile that she herself refused to acknowledge. "Good. Billy here loves it." She gestured at him with her empty fork.

"He sure does," William added with his booming voice. "I'll never forget, we were at a restaurant once when he was only about three years old ..." He interrupted his own story with a slight chuckle.

"Dad!" Another scolding voice came from their irritated son.

William's eyebrows arched in a defensive face. "What? It's just a harmless story."

Diane knew where this story was going and it was a cute one. But trying not to laugh herself, Diane again came to the rescue. "William, maybe this isn't really the best time for that story."

"Oh. Uh, okay." William went back to his meal, not saying anything. In fact, it was quite obvious that Billy was not going to allow either of them to speak during the duration of the entire meal. Everyone awkwardly ate. The only sound to be heard was the sound of forks against the plates and maybe the sound of Billy's slurping up some spaghetti in his mouth.

William and Diane kept thinking about the cute story about when Billy was just a little tyke. After a number of seconds of this, William somehow blurted out in a cute, high-pitched voice, *"For a big pile of shoestrings, this is really yummy."*

Both parents broke out into a short, uncontrollable laugh.

Billy's fork clanged against his plate as he forced it down. "Please stop! Are you two trying to make me look dumb?"

William looked up to see the glaring face of his son looking at him; it was filled with anger and embarrassment. Under ordinary circumstances, William would not put up with such rudeness. But something held him back. One possible reason was that he honestly had no intention of deliberately embarrassing his son – especially in front of company; the punchline just slipped out. But the real reason for his restraint was what he now saw. Across his son's angry face was a long red streak of spaghetti sauce that Billy obviously did not know was there. As a good father, William decided to help out his son. Quietly, he motioned toward his mouth once he got Billy's attention. "Uh, Billy, you may want to …" William made a little circle on his face with his finger.

Billy's ticked-off mind was made up. "Dad. Please."

"No, you don't understand. I think you really need …"

Billy closed his eyes and spread his fingers out on his raised hand. "Dad, could you just …"

At this point, William had done what he could. Amused, he resigned himself to Billy's obviously superior wisdom. "Uh … Okay. Fine with me." He turned his attention back to his generous helping of spaghetti and garlic bread, washing it down with a glass of sweet tea.

Chloe had spent most of this time taking small bites from her plate and glancing up at her big ugly purse. But at this moment, she looked over at Billy. Billy felt the gaze and looked back at her. That was when she noticed the streak of spaghetti sauce on his face as well. She wanted desperately to laugh. Under much self-control, a simple smile crept on her face. Billy thought that the smile was meant for him - - little did he know.

It was not too long before Diane looked up from her plate and noticed the tomato-based streak making a trail across Billy's cheek to the side of his mouth. Her eyes got wide accompanying a rush of motherly panic. Fast on her feet, she thought of a less direct approach than William's. "Oh, Billy. I don't think that I put any napkins on the table. Would you mind getting some for us, please dear."

"Yes, ma'am." Slightly irritated, Billy got up from the table to get some.

As he walked toward the kitchen, Diane added, "Oh, I just remembered;

we're all out of napkins. You'll have to pass out some paper towels for everyone."

"No problem." That was fine with him. They used paper towels most of the time anyway. In fact, paper towels were what he initially thought that she meant. Billy walked up to the bar behind William's seat. The little showman inside of him could not resist. In a loud genie-style voice, he grabbed the first one off of the hanging paper towel roll and gave it a strong quick jerk as he announced, "Four paper towels coming right UP!"

The roll began to spin quickly – much faster than he intended. Far more than a mere four were coming off. Billy's sharp action sent paper towels in a long connected line tumbling onto the countertop and then spilling into the floor. It continued to unroll. It spun and spun and spun. This was a one-in-a-million sort of event. Long afterwards, William and Diane would be referring to this as the Miracle of the Paper Towels.

Billy was stunned. He stood there motionless. His disbelief paralyzed his ability to say or do anything. The only thing that they could hear was the nearly silent sound of connected paper towels rolling into the floor. Hundreds of paper towels seemed to be everywhere and in a short amount of time. And yet, the roll continued to spin.

Everyone knew what was happening. It was surreal. After about twenty seconds of continuous unrolling, Diane proposed a question to Chloe. "So you are one of William's students too?"

"Yes, ma'am."

"Chloe. That's a lovely name. What's your last name, dear?"

"Chastain."

"Chloe Chastain. Any relation to Chastain Enterprises?"

"Yes, ma'am. Gregory Chastain is my dad."

"Oh?"

The roll of paper towels kept spinning and getting smaller and smaller as it unrolled. The first one in this long connected train was still in Billy's hand. And yet he stood there in silence marveling at this unnatural phenomenon. These paper towels were breaking all the laws of physics.

"Allow me," William said to Billy as he took the end of the paper towel roll from Billy's hand. William then tore off the first four and begun to pass them out to the others. Soon after this, the last of the paper towels broke free from the roll and it stopped spinning. A mountain of paper towels now lay between William's seat and the bar. Billy quietly and slowly made his way back to his seat next to Chloe. No one said a word. No one laughed – although it was hard not to. All was quiet.

Is this a dinner or a séance? Chloe amusingly asked herself.

Billy was still stunned. Without presenting any excuse or explanation (because he had none), he reached over for the can of parmesan cheese. He held it over his plate and tipped it over. The lid fell off and into his food. A ton of cheese followed, covering the lid and everything else on his plate.

Every ounce of Chloe's self-control was required to keep her from snickering.

Billy was again humiliated. But maybe he could salvage his dignity. He slowly turned to face Chloe. "I really like cheese."

Chloe sprang from her seat. "I have to go now. I really have got to go." She was desperately trying not to laugh. She grabbed her big ugly purse and made her way out of the dining area and toward the front door. Billy chased after her hoping to persuade her not to go.

From the table, William and Diane could hear him begging her to stay. But soon, they heard the door close. They sat silently. They were not sure if they just witnessed something funny or tragic. Perhaps both. If they were going to laugh, it would have to be later. They would not dare laugh in front of Billy at a time like this. They gave each other a look that they recognized all-too-well. They would be as supportive as possible to their son.

A minute or so later, Billy re-entered the room with a defeated expression on his face. He sat down and stared down at his food. A mountain of parmesan cheese (with the buried lid) sat victoriously over his spaghetti as if it were a show of strength. All was silent. He picked up his fork and began to push most of it off onto another plate.

William felt badly for Billy. Diane wanted to say something encouraging. She searched her head for wisdom. She turned to William; usually, he had the perfect passage of Scripture to say at these times. His mind drew a blank. He did not know what to say any more than Diane did.

Billy broke the silence. "That could be the most embarrassing moment of my entire life."

William sat frozen. He just stared at Billy. Diane's eyes began to swell with tears. One thing that both parents knew was that when one member of the family was hurting, they were all hurting. No one faces their problems alone in this house. They were all to unite as a strong family, a single unit. Constantly learning and adapting to these situations as parents was a skill they had been practicing now for fifteen years. Whatever this was, they would face it together.

Billy put down his fork, looked right at his parents, and said, "I hope you two are proud of how you behaved." He got up and left the room.

Diane and William were both caught way off-guard. Diane nearly said something, but she was too stunned to speak; she felt like the air was knocked out of her. William's eyebrows shot up into his forehead somewhere. They quietly looked at each other. After a dramatic pause, William made a descending trombone noise. "Whaa! Whaa! Whaaaaaa!"

Diane gave him a rebuking smirk. "This will be one for you to write down in your journal."

He responded with another fork of spaghetti and said, "Yeah. I can't wait to throw in that bit about the paper towels."

Chloe slammed the door shut behind her as she marched into her home. The entire time, she clung to that big purse of hers. "This is going to be so bad." She began to laugh to herself.

"Chloe?" Her dad rose from his computer and peeked from the door of his home office. "You seem to be in a chipper mood today." His short hair was black on top and gray on all sides as if he belonged in a comic book. His straight eyebrows rested over penetrating brown eyes. He was home from work and had already lost his tie for the day. He had taken off his shoes, but was still in his socks.

Chloe was indeed in a good mood. But some of her joy departed as soon as she saw her dad. She was in no mood to talk to him at this point. ... or ever. Still, to avoid a fight, she pretended to get along a little. "Yeah? Well, you know me. Every day is a party, I guess." She did not waste any time finishing up what could be a civil conversation. She turned her back on him and began to walk toward the stairs.

It was later than her usual time home. He had just finished eating, and as far as he knew, her dinner was getting cold. "So, where have you been this whole time?"

Honestly, this question was more of a courteous inquiry than anything else. But that is not the way Chloe saw it. She was convinced that he was trying to muscle in on her business. *Always having to pry*, she thought. *Why can't he just leave me alone for once?*

She sighed deeply. In a stabbing voice, she said, "Well! If you must know, I was at Mr. Harris' house." Knowing suddenly that he would not let that go, she increased her speed toward those stairs.

Gregory Chastain's nose wrinkled up. "Wait a minute. Who is this *Mr. Harris?*" There was something about this whole thing that did not seem right to him.

She stopped at the foot of the stairs and turned quickly to face him, visibly irritated. "He is my English teacher. He has a son that is my age and I think he likes me - - the son, NOT the teacher." She knew that she would have to clarify that last point. Chloe began the march up the stairs. Gregory followed her - - usually about four or five steps behind.

"So do you like this boy?"

"No."

Gregory was getting confused rather quickly. "Do you actually like this man's class?"

Enough with the questions already, she thought. "Certainly not! I hate his class."

"Really? How are *you* doing in his class?

She tried to answer the next chain of questions as if it were no big deal. If she was lucky, the answers might float right on by and her dad will be none the wiser. "Not so good, I guess. He had a talk with me about my poor grades." She made a dramatic guttural sound. "Whatever."

Still following Chloe, Gregory pursued this matter. "Well, I'm confused. Why would they invite you over to their house?"

Chloe was becoming more agitated with each question. She raised the volume of her voice. "They *didn't* invite me. I just showed up." They were up on the second floor now and she found herself in front of her bedroom door.

"But ..."

Chloe walked into her room and spun around on her pivot foot fast enough to impress a basketball coach. "Look, dad. I've got a lot of work to do, so if this little Q and A session is winding down ..." Her speech was interrupted by her phone. She pulled it out of her pocket and saw who it was. "I'm going to have to take this one. But you know how that goes." She closed her bedroom door as Gregory simply stood there, disappearing from her sight.

In her garishly decorated bedroom, she immediately picked up her phone and began talking to Bre. "Where have I been? Girl, you would not believe me if I told you. By the way, do you like comedy? Why? Because I am about to put one together that is going to bring down the house."

Outside of her door, Gregory was standing there perplexed. His mind was working in overdrive. He descended back down the stairs and returned to his study. Walking all the way around his desk, he stopped in front of a picture of Chloe back when she was ten. He picked up the bronze picture frame and looked at his daughter's face for a while. It was a beautiful photo of her taken on one of their trips. Taking a pen out of his pocket and a small pad on his desk, he began to write something down. "Mr. Harris - - English teacher." Maybe it was time to introduce himself.

Hours had gone by. It was now late and Billy's parents were about to watch the news. Billy was still upset over the events earlier, but he had chilled out a bit. His parents had a brief talk with him - - but that did not make him feel much better. At this point, he was choosing to be mad.

"It's time for you to head off to bed," his mom said peeking in his door.

"Fine," he said with a bit too much tone. Billy put down the controller for the game that he was playing. After sitting on the floor for so long, he stood straight up. He nearly knocked the light on his ceiling fan with his fists as he stretched. His shirt rose above his pants as he stretched, revealing part of his tummy. Then he noticed something unusual about his reflection as he looked in the mirror. *That's strange.* With furrowed eyebrows, he reached down and pulled the boxer shorts out of his pants that he had tucked in there earlier. *How did that get there?* For a moment, he was very confused; but when he remembered what happened, he became extremely embarrassed. In anger, he chunked the shorts against the wall. *Nice. Now she is going to think that I am losing my mind.*

CHAPTER 20

KIBITZING

More for comic effect than anything, a sign on Mr. Harris' bulletin board read 'No Kibitzing Allowed.' This rule was not strictly enforced. *Kibitzing* is talking during a game of chess – especially offering unwanted advice about the game in progress. But for the most part, everything was quiet during the club meeting on Wednesday.

Quotes was looking down at the chess board while Billy was looking around. *How strange*, he thought to himself, *to be in a room with such odd people and no one is making a sound*. Normally, there was no telling what someone was going to say next. Other than the endless tick-tock of the clock on the wall, the only sounds to be heard were coming from outside the room: a car rumbling by, the occasional bird singing, the air conditioner kicking on and off.

Berly paid little attention to her game or the person she was playing against, this time Alejandro. Her mind was on the young man who was sitting next to her opponent, Billy. She carefully looked around without moving her head and gently took off her glasses, setting them on the desk next to the chess board. Her hair was different. She had decided to wear eye makeup this particular day in a desperate attempt to get Billy's attention.

Billy did not see her; but Maggie did. Like a good chess strategy, the entire rest of the afternoon was already playing out in Maggie's mind. They would march back to Maggie's house where Berly was expected to go on and on about how she cannot seem to get Billy to even acknowledge her. Maggie would then fill her ears with talk of being true to herself and not trying so hard to get noticed. *I'll be so glad when this Billy fever has finally subsided*, she thought.

Billy's opponent was especially quiet. In fact, it had once again occurred to young Harris that he had never even heard the sound of Quotes' voice. ... ever. Was Quotes even capable of human speech? One would think that if someone were to be called 'Quotes,' that they must first say something that was quote-worthy. Ironic?

Billy could tell that Quotes was a full head taller than the other kids and looked like he had started shaving in the first grade. Maybe he should be feared. Did he look like the type that would torture small animals when he was little? Poor guy. *Hey! I wonder if he has ever killed a guy*, Billy thought. *Nah, that would be silly. He wouldn't be here in school with everyone else if he had. Whoa! Maybe he is wearing one of those detection devices on his ankle. Cool.*

Still, Billy now considered it a challenge. Could he get Quotes to say anything? This may require some thought. How about trying some old fashioned small talk?

"So Quotes ..." Billy began in spite of the silence. "If I remember correctly, your actual first name is 'Electron.' That doesn't sound very *positive*." Billy instantly regretted his decision to speak.

Quotes silently looked up from the chess board with dark, annoyed eyes that burned with fire. A low growl began somewhere down inside his barrel chest and come up through his neck and out of his closed mouth. Billy wondered how sharp those unseen teeth were. Maybe they were made completely out of metal. Quotes seemed to be preparing to crash his enormous hands onto the table, totally demolishing it into splinters and chess pieces flying in all directions. Billy was already anticipating the screams of the other students.

Fortunately, that did not happen. But that low rumbling sound he made was enough to make Billy's face tickle from the vibration. With a nice resonance like that, perhaps Quotes should join the PFHS choir - - that is, if Quotes were able to articulate words.

The words 'oscillation' and 'frequency' had jumped into Billy's mind; funny the random things you think of before you could potentially die.

Maybe Quotes could move to the coast and get a job at a lighthouse as the foghorn.

Eugene spoke up with bright enthusiasm. "Hey! I've got a great joke for you all!"

Everyone in the room seemed to moan in unison.

He dropped his smile. "Now that's not fair. This is a good one."

Berly broke in and saved the day. "Uh, not to interrupt one of Eugene's classic and hysterical jokes, but has anyone seen Rodney today?"

"LONG LIVE RODNEY!" Billy was not caught off guard anymore. Over the past few weeks, he had become accustomed to their weird outbursts - - not that he understood them.

"I think today is the day of Rodney's big competition," Joey answered back.

Billy turned to Joey. "What competition?"

"Rodney is big into robotics. He built this robot dog and is entering it in some big robotics show over in Memphis. His robot dog is cool looking enough, but I don't think it will do well though."

Alejandro continued looking down at the chess game as he added, "Nah. It doesn't really do anything cool. All it ever does is bury screwdrivers in the backyard."

Billy had had enough of this nonsense. "I am so sick of hearing about this Rodney. What kind of a club president is he anyway? I have been coming to Chess club three times a week since the middle of August and there isn't a trace of him anywhere – not even a lousy fingerprint. In fact, I haven't so much as seen a picture of this Rodney - - and you all act as if he actually exists. And his reasons for not being here are always something out-of-this-world nerdy. If this guy actually lives and breathes as you all say he does, then he must be the reigning king of sad nerds everywhere."

"Alright, smarty-pants," Maggie interrupted. "What would you like to see done? How would you change things around here if you were president?"

He did it now. He had to think of something smart. "Well ..."

They wanted for his statement with eager anticipation. (Actually, they were being sarcastic.)

"...have you considered new and creative ways to draw more people in here?" he suggested.

Berly spoke, but she also went back to her game and moved her bishop. "We did have that day where we played Chess outside on the benches to attract people as they walked by. We also got some fresh air in the process. That was actually kinda cool, that is until Rodney had that sneezing fit."

Billy nearly laughed. "Humpf! Not surprised."

Alejandro's head was resting, propped up on his hand, as he spoke through a *punched* face. "I keep telling everyone, I know exactly how to bring more people in. But no one will listen to me."

Joey flew back in his chair acting exasperated. "How can we possibly attract people to Chess club with Eugene telling these lame jokes? I mean we got one newcomer recently: Billy. But he doesn't count because his daddy is running the club."

William did not look up at them. He pretended not to hear the comment.

Billy was surprised at what Joey had said. Did they honestly believe that he was there because his dad is the faculty member in charge of the Chess club? His dad had nothing to do with it. In fact, it was because his dad was there that he did not want to be a member in the first place. Actually, why was Billy even still here with these weirdos? His own actions made no sense to him.

But it was Eugene that was insulted. "Hey! My jokes are good! For instance ..." <More moans.> "You've all heard the one about the rooster sitting on top of a henhouse with a roof like so?" Eugene brought his flattened forearms up together making the shape of a roof. "Which way does the egg roll?"

Maggie saved them all from hearing Eugene deliver the punch line. "Yeah, yeah. Roosters don't lay eggs. That joke was brought over with the Pilgrims."

Eugene was delighted. "Exactly! But if you put a panda bear on top of the exact same roof and he's eating Chinese food, *then* which way does the egg roll?"

Silence. Maggie turned quietly to Joey. Joey glanced back at her and smiled. Did Eugene just tell a funny joke?

"Give up?" Eugene was beaming. "Huh? It went down his throat." Eugene began to laugh obnoxiously, almost snorting.

Berly looked over at Eugene in surprise. "That's not the joke."

Eugene stopped laughing. "Huh? What do you mean?"

"I've never heard that joke before, but even *I* know that that's not the answer. It's so obvious." Berly looked at the others in the room. "Did you all catch it? The joke was in the question itself. The joke *is* the punchline."

The others nodded. Eugene was confused.

Joey turned to Eugene. "Dude! Panda bear."

Nothing.

Maggie added. "Chinese food."

Eugene still did not get it.

It was Alejandro's turn to explain. "You mentioned panda bear and Chinese food. Then you asked 'Which way does the egg roll?' Eggroll."

Eugene sat in stunned silence for a minute. After a moment, he smiled. "Oooooh! Eggroll!"

The rest of the room seemed to fall back in their chairs in relief.

"I don't believe it," Berly said. "We all got one of Eugene's jokes before he did. Now *that* is actually funny."

Eugene stopped laughing. The entire compliment of the room finally enjoyed one of his jokes - - everyone except Eugene.

The orange sunlight was coming through the blinds and into William's classroom when it was time to leave. The Chess boards were put away and the group was walking out the door. They were making enough noise to drown out the sound of the approaching visitor.

He was dressed immaculately in a charcoal gray pinstriped suit and a red silk tie. His dress shoes hit the linoleum tiles of the hall with a certain amount of bold confidence and seemed to echo throughout the acoustical corridors. His hair was neatly trimmed and he was sporting a handsome watch on his wrist. The fine-looking middle-aged man marched up to the classroom door just as the Chess Club members were exiting. There was another door, but they were all using the one closest to the teacher.

The students leaving found him hard to miss. *Who's the dude?* they thought.

The man spoke through the crowd of students. "Mr. Harris?"

Struggling to see who was speaking to him, William answered. "That's right. Can I help you?"

"Yes. My name is Gregory Chastain."

Suddenly, Billy took an enormous interest in this stranger. This must have been Chloe's dad. Billy was headed down the hallway with the others - - except he was rubbernecking trying to get a better look at him. What business could this man have with his dad? Is this about Chloe's performance in the class, about her coming over to their house, or some financial business that he was not aware of?

William responded. "Oh yeah. Chloe's dad?"

"Yes. Do you have a moment?"

"Certainly. Please, come in." At this point, the students had all cleared out and the two men stood alone. Billy's curiosity got the best of him. He lagged behind as the others left. Approaching the door closer to the back of the room, he got down on his hands and knees. Crawling, he made his way into the room unnoticed. He had to know what they were talking about, so he found a cozy place on the floor where he could not be seen. But it was close enough to make out what was being said.

"Have a seat." William pulled one of the student desks over next to his own.

"Thank you." Gregory Chastain was amused to be setting himself down in a student desk after all these years as William took his usual place. "Sir, I will be brief. My daughter told me that you had a conversation with her about her grades earlier this week. I would like to see her tests scores if I can."

William was confused. "Of course." He got up from his seat and walked over to his filing cabinet. In just a few short seconds, he returned with a file. "But if I'm not mistaken, I believe you have seen these already."

"I haven't seen anything from her all this semester - - not in *any* of her classes."

William opened her file and placed it in front of Gregory. He flipped through some papers and spread them out so that they could clearly be seen. "Here, we have two quizzes, a test, and a number of homework assignments. The homework assignments are a bit incomplete which accounts for the grade that she received. The quizzes and the test have been sent home for your signature. See?" He began to point at the name *Gregory Chastain* written in cursive. "There? And there?"

"That is *not* my signature." Gregory was plainly upset.

William took a deep breath, the kind that you could hear across the room. "Oh. I see." Mr. Harris took another deep breath. "Well, I imagine that your daughter has quite a bit of explaining to do to her father."

With that said, William was really hoping to gain Gregory as a strong ally. Maybe together, they can reform Chloe's attitude. A teacher's job is so much easier whenever the parents are onboard; but it can also be a nightmare if the parents work against the teacher.

Billy could hear every word from where he sat. This was quite a revelation to him. It sounded like Chloe had a bit of a defiant streak to her. It reminded him of a conversation that he had with his dad a couple of years ago. His dad warned him about girls who were rebellious against their fathers. "Son, try not to get too involved with girls like that," he said. "If they dislike their own dads, they will eventually dislike their husbands as well. If you think that their own fathers find them unmanageable, how effective do you think you will be as a husband? Of course, the same can be said about the boys. If you treat your mother with disrespect, you will do the same to your wife. So I better not *ever* catch you sassing your momma. I gotta think about her interests, but I'm also looking out for the welfare of my future daughter-in-law. So you treat them decently." That message stuck with him.

But this doesn't apply in this case, he thought to himself. *Boys and girls are different today than they were in dad's day. Chloe is proof of that. And besides, what if her dad was a major jerk?*

After William made the assumption that Chloe needed to explain things to her father, Gregory reached into his inside pocket and pulled out a small note pad and jotted something down. "Suppose you let me deal with my daughter in my own way."

So that was it. William had a feeling that he would not find an alliance with Mr. Gregory Chastain, the CEO of Chastain Enterprises. William had already been under the impression that Mr. Chastain was a difficult person to get to know. And more often than not, the teacher already knows how the parents are anyway because of how their kids behave. Parents and kids would both deny it; but oftentimes, if you know one, you know the other. Kids are frequently younger versions of their folks.

Gregory laid the note pad down in front of William, but never taking his hand off of it. "I will strongly encourage her to do what she is supposed to do in her classes – including yours naturally. In the meantime, here is a sample of my handwriting." He moved his hand away revealing what he had just written.

William looked down at the pad. But he did not see a signature. It was a dollar amount. He frowned. "I don't think that I understand."

"I think that you do."

"Sir, this is a lot of money."

Gregory returned the note pad to his inside pocket. "Well, let's just say that it is very important to me that she makes good grades."

"That's very important to me as well, but I'm afraid that she is going to have to earn her grades herself. I cannot be a part of anything like that."

Gregory made some casual body language as he spoke. "You don't have to answer right away. Why don't you take a few days to think about it, huh?" He stood up from his seat and adjusted the legs on his pants. "But don't take too long to think. My generosity only lasts for a little while." He reached in his pocket, pulled out a business card, and dropped it on William's desk. "Just call when you change your mind." He left the room and disappeared down the hallway.

William had stood up when Gregory did. Now he sat back down at his desk. He picked up the business card, read it, and released a slight laugh of amusement. He placed it into Chloe's file and returned it to his filing cabinet. It had seemed funny to him that Gregory should be offering him that money. Normally, that much money would have seemed like a large sum; but to Mr. Harris, it was a sad joke. If Mr. Chastain had any idea how much money the Harris' had, he would have been embarrassed to make that offer. In spite of the Harris' enormous wealth, the accumulation of earthly riches was never really that far up on William's priority list to begin with.

As soon as it became evident that Gregory Chastain was totally gone, Billy popped up from behind one of the desks near the back. "I cannot believe the nerve of that guy."

William was caught off-guard by Billy's presence, but he was able to keep from acting surprised.

Billy continued, "Chloe's dad actually offered you a bribe? That's incredible!"

"What do you think you're doing? How long were you hiding in here?" William sounded a little upset, but not exactly furious.

"Not long. I just came in to see how much longer you would be. I heard you two talking, so I snuck in and got comfortable over there on the floor."

This report was partially true, and William knew it. "Naturally. Your coming in here and laying low like that - - it's all quite innocent. First, you conveniently overheard our conversation with Louis and now this. Someday, this sneaking around is gonna get you hurt."

Billy was not really in the mood to talk about his possible indiscretions; he would much rather talk about Mr. Chastain. "What *he* is doing isn't exactly innocent. Can he go to jail for offering you a bribe?"

"Pfft! Please. Even if he could, I wouldn't report him. It would be a classic case of his word against mine. ... or maybe ours. But can you imagine just what that would do to everyone? Especially for his daughter? I'm not out to hurt anybody and put them through the wringer."

Billy was shaking his head. If he were impressed by the way his dad handled the situation, he was not about to admit it. But he said it anyway. "I wanna know how you were able to keep so calm. I wanted to belt him one – right in his smug face!"

As William spoke, he was gathering his things to take home. "I know exactly what you mean. Let me show you something." He stopped what he was doing and walked over to his marker board. With a marker in his left hand, he wrote the word, *MEEK*. The cap was placed back on the marker and he set it down on the tray. With his back to the board, he thumbed over his shoulder at the word and asked, "Do you know what this word means?"

"*Meek*?" Billy looked puzzled and searched his brain. "I thought I did. But now that you bring it up, I guess I don't really have a clear definition for it."

"*Meek* simply means to have the strength to hold yourself back and not doing something that you might regret later. Jesus demonstrated that quality better than anyone. What does it say in Philippians 2:8? 'And being found in fashion as a man, he humbled himself, and became obedient unto death, even the death of the cross.' He could easily have gotten down from up there; but He was strong enough to stay and allow Himself to die that way. That is true meekness. Does that make sense?"

Billy looked past his dad with squinted eyes. "I think so. I guess what you are saying is that you could've easily knocked Mr. Chastain's block off, but you held yourself back. Personally, I would've liked to have seen you knock him down on his can. Is that it?"

For a long moment, William was quiet - - almost dumbstruck. He pondered the question for a second.

Billy waited patiently for a reply.

Finally, William shrugged his shoulders, grinned, and said, "Yes. That is *exactly* what I am saying. I could've rung his bell – but I didn't."

His son rolled his eyes in harmless disbelief. *Whatever,* he thought to himself.

At this point, Billy's phone chimed. Someone had just sent him a text message. "Oh. That's my phone."

Immediately, William's phone buzzed as well.

They both looked at their phones. It would seem that someone sent them the same message. It only took a couple of seconds for each of them to read it. The news was not good.

William flashed a started glance at his son.

Billy's face suddenly lost all of its color. His voice shook with fright. "Oh no! Clay!"

"Let's go! Now!" William left his stuff there on his desk and the both of them darted out of the classroom and headed straight to the truck.

CHAPTER 21

THE BEST OF US

Imagine this: you and your family are on a road trip. You look up ahead and see that a tunnel is on the approach. Honestly, the road seems to disappear into the side of a hill. It may look like you were going to crash; you might even get a little nervous. In a matter of seconds, everything goes from sunny and bright to weird and dark. After a few seconds, your eyes adjust and you can see some to a degree. The road might take a slight bend and you are unable to see the other side of the tunnel. Because someone had to dig out that tunnel to begin with and a fair amount of traffic is passing by, you have faith that your car will arrive safely on the other side. And indeed, you soon find yourself safely back in the warm sunlight having survived the experience.

Life is a bit like that. God allows us to go through tunnels. We keep moving, keeping our focus on the road. We trust that God is leading us and we appreciate the light that much more when we finally reemerge. In the process, we come that much closer to His objective.

Our characters have now been thrown into a tunnel. This tunnel is dark and deep and cold.

The message that Mike sent to William and Billy did not say much. It only mentioned that Clay was hit by a car, his injuries were serious, and that they were taking him to County Hospital. Pecan Falls had an adequate medical facility, but in serious cases like this, it was better to take the short drive over to County.

William and Billy arrived in no time, but the ride seemed long. Using the side entrance, they were instantly greeted by a nervous-looking Mike. Conversation began as they powerwalked to the ER.

"Mr. Harris! Thank goodness you two are here."

"Did you see it happen?"

"No. I was there, but I didn't actually see it."

Billy asked as they walked, "What *has* happened?"

"Medically, we still don't know. But Clay was riding his bike home after track practice. He stopped at an intersection; and when the lights were in his favor, he proceeded to go. Then here comes this car." Mike slowed down. He could not continue telling any more while they were walking. "Someone was texting while driving and ..."

Billy and William sensed that he had stopped walking. They rushed back over to him. William put his hand on Mike's back. "And that's when he was hit?"

"No. It wasn't like that. He wasn't hit exactly. Um, he was ..." Mike chocked up and was searching for the right words to say. He finally looked up at William's eyes and continued. " ...run over." He corrected himself. "No. He wasn't run over exactly. His legs got caught up in the bike. His legs and the bike were run over together - - together, if you know what I mean."

Billy's jaw dropped and tears swelled up in his eyes. "Together? You mean ... What? His legs and the bike?"

William's eyes closed momentarily as he let it sink in. He opened them again with a singular purpose. "Where's Maxine?"

"She's down in the waiting room. I've been with her pretty much all this time. I came down here to look for you guys."

The three of them began moving down the hall again, matching their earlier speed – and maybe a little more. At a point where the halls intersect, they found themselves being joined by Diane, Curtis, and Kathy Baker, Curtis' mom. They were rushing in from another entrance, but to the same place.

William greeted them as they walked. "Excellent. You're all here. How much do you know?"

"Everything Maxine knows," Diane answered, "which isn't much. We just got off the phone with her."

"I've been on the phone with Clay's sister," Kathy added. "Of course, she can't do anything right now in Texas with those two-year-old twins. But Maxine asked for us to keep her posted, so that's what we're doing."

William's voice became sweetly sincere under the circumstances. "Well, I'm glad you're here. Maxine is going to need both of you at a time like this."

The doors to the ER waiting room opened. Maxine ran over to Kathy and Diane in a three-way hug. She was clearly crying. Her voice was terrified. "Diane! Kathy! Thank you for being here!" After crying for a minute and saying something about her 'baby', she reached out and clasped William's hand. She gave Curtis and Billy a kiss on their cheeks. Mike was not exactly overlooked because he had been with her this whole time. The pastor and his wife were not yet there, but were on their way.

Diane asked, "Is there any new news?"

Maxine kept wiping away fresh tears as she spoke. "Not yet. But Clay is pretty messed up back there. Right now, I'm waiting for the doctor to tell me how bad it is."

"Try not to worry." Kathy's voice was strong and peaceful. "These are talented people here and they know their jobs. And don't forget that we serve a great God."

Everyone there was concerned beyond words for Clay, but their hearts were currently going out to Maxine. The past few years have been rough on her. The permanent bags under her weary eyes were very pronounced. Her frizzy hair was of no particular color. Her daughter's husband had been stationed in Texas, so she had already been missing her daughter and her two grandbabies. Life had been a struggle even before her husband passed away. But this ...

She fought back the tears as she replied to Kathy's statement. "I know. Thank you." She sniffled into a worn tissue. "I was just thinking about Phillip. It's been two years since God called him home. And now ...." Maxine fought to finish her own sentence. "And now my sweet Clay is back there and I don't know what's going to happen." Her hands covered her sobbing face.

The moms were crying with her. The boys were frozen. Even William was without words.

While the ladies were crying, Mike got the others' attention and signaled them to step to the side. William, Curtis, and Billy complied.

In a low tone, Mike began to confide in them. "I overheard her talking earlier. It sounds like with all the stuff that is changing, some of this is covered under her insurance. But some is not. And some of it is only good to a point. It's all very confusing and weird. She seems to make too much to be covered but too little to pay for things. I don't get all this financial stuff, but whatever it is, it's crazy."

Billy looked around the room. "They'll be paying this off for a long, long time."

Mike added, "Oh, you missed it. Maxine was just commenting that she can't even afford the transfer from Pecan Falls Medical out here to County. Even the ambulance ride costs a minor fortune for these people."

William looked up and noticed Principal Dunbar and Coach Holton looking around. He raised his hand and his voice just a bit. "Hey! We're over here."

They saw him right away and hurried over. In just a minute or so, the two of them were brought up to speed. Mrs. Dunbar took Maxine's hands in hers and voiced her loving support as Holton walked over to William and the boys.

Their private conversations were interrupted by the presence of the doctor. He was a tall good-looking fellow, probably just shy of forty. The grim look on his face was very telling. "Mrs. Peck?"

Maxine and the others rushed over. "Yes? I'm Mrs. Peck."

"We need to talk. Won't you please come and have a seat?"

Quickly, the entire party found themselves sitting around the doctor – not standard procedure (and probably breaking some silly policy somewhere), but under the circumstances, he knew that she could use the support. Maxine sat between Mrs. Dunbar and Kathy and they held hands. Diane stood behind her with her hands on Maxine's shoulders. But the doctor's focus was naturally on Maxine.

The doctor proceeded delicately. "As you know, there was extensive damage to both of your son's legs. Right now, his condition is stable. We have stopped the excessive bleeding and that much looks good. He lost a lot of blood – and I mean a *lot* of blood. But we have some that we are giving him at present. We fixed a dislocated shoulder and glued the cuts on his chin and over both eyebrows. The rest of him is pretty banged up with scratches and so forth. He will be quite sore from bruising." He took a deep breath and exhaled before continuing. "The bad news is that the bones below the knee in both legs have been shattered into splinters. The anterior tibial arteries have both been severed. When your son arrived, one of his legs was already cut all the way through and the other one was barely hanging on."

It was not something that anyone would notice, but everyone in the group was holding their breath as the doctor spoke. Maxine was holding her hysterics in, but no one knew how long that would last.

The doctor added, "In short, Mrs. Peck, his legs are gone. There is nothing we can do to save them. I'm sorry."

Maxine gasped. Mrs. Dunbar and Kathy both felt the strength from her interlocking fingers in the hands they both held.

Speaking for everyone there, Diane asked, "Other than his legs, will he be okay?"

"We are convinced that he will pull through. He seems to be very strong. The nurses are busy prepping him for surgery now. At this point, he is sleeping comfortably. We are keeping him from feeling the pain. And the good news is, we believe that we can save both of his knees."

Maxine's emotions got the best of her and she broke down again. She was living a parent's nightmare. *Will my baby be okay?* she wondered.

The doctor stood back up. "I'm going to have to go now. They are waiting on me. We will do our very best to help your son, Mrs. Peck. Please excuse me."

Maxine was too choked up to say anything to the doctor, so she looked over at Kathy.

Kathy understood and looked up at the doctor and thanked him as she put an arm around Maxine. "Clay is in the best of hands here," she said, turning back to Maxine.

Diane agreed. "That's right. Everything is going to be fine." She looked over at William and caught his expression. She gave him a subtle nod. He nodded back knowingly. This exchange of nods was so discreet that no one noticed. … almost no one.

Billy had seen them. He knew his parents well enough to know that they had just sent a message to each other. They had something secret going on. What could it be? But he also knew that they did not want anyone to know. He decided not to ask, but to keep his eyes open.

Diane walked around and knelt in front of Maxine, speaking straight into her face. "Max, I know that you aren't going home tonight; I couldn't either if I were in your shoes. And I don't think that you should be alone, so I'm going to stay with you."

"Diane, that's very …"

"Now don't try to talk me out of it. I'm going to run home real quickly and grab a few things and I'm going to stay up here with you tonight."

"But …"

"I've made up my mind. I'm also going to grab a few things for you too. Plus, you are going to need to eat something and I'm going to make sure that you do."

Maxine smiled back at her. She gave a barely audible, "Okay."

Their pastor and his wife had not yet arrived, but Kathy had an idea. "Clay is going into surgery right now. I think that this would be a good time to pray. Coach Holton, would you start for us?"

Everyone stood up except for Maxine. They all gathered around her - - everyone that is except for William and Diane. Billy eyed over at his parents and noticed that same quiet nod between them. Curious.

As Coach began to pray, Billy opened an eye and looked up again. He noticed that his mom had grabbed her purse and was walking away in the direction of her car. It was clear that she was headed back home for a few minutes. But then Billy's open eye looked back at his dad. He was not there. He looked around quietly and finally saw him walking away in the opposite direction and disappearing behind a corner. What were his parents up to?

Billy decided to check it out. He silently removed himself from the group and crept over to the corner where William had gone. He saw his dad marching down another hall acting like he knew right where he was going. He was proceeding away from the area with all the patients.

As Billy followed his dad, the floor changed to carpet. The number of nurses and custodial staff became fewer. William walked right by a wall featuring portraits of the hospital's department heads and other prominent staff members. It was easy to see that this was where the hospital offices were located.

From around a corner, Billy spied as his dad walked up to an office window. William knocked on it, grabbing the attention of a chubby man in a tight shirt sitting at a desk. The man looked up and gave him a cheerful wave inviting William in. He said something to a lady sitting behind the desk. On the wall behind her hung a large watercolor-style painting of some purple flowers - - maybe some kind of orchids. A fake tree stood next to a table that was covered in old magazines. She gestured that he could proceed. Two ladies and the overweight man greeted William and brought him into the office.

Billy noticed the sign on the door. It read *Financial Services*. For a good half-minute, Billy stared unconsciously at the wall across the hall from him. He was lost in thought trying to figure out what his parents were up to. This was very mysterious behavior - - even for his weird parents.

The next few hours were a nightmare. They waited and waited. But the surgeons did their job with skill and precision and Clay was finally going to be okay - - as okay as possible considering his current state of affairs. But the boys were not allowed to see him.

Everyone other than Maxine and Diane had gone home. William and his son stopped somewhere and had some tacos. Billy ended up playing a few video games while William was busy making some phone calls. Eventually, he climbed into bed and opened his boring old book for school. But the world of pre-Victorian England was not enough to keep him awake. As keyed up as Billy was earlier, he fell asleep surprisingly soon and drifted into a dream.

In this dream, Billy was sitting on a hardwood floor next to a large oriental rug and an oversized wooden desk. On his other side, an enormous globe of the earth rested in the corner of a sizeable residential library. He was leaning with his back against the bookshelf that housed hardback books of every kind. He was doing nothing in particular with the baseball and the glove that were in his hands.

He realized that this was obviously the inside of the ritzy house that he had been dreaming about before. He figured that he was probably asleep and this was all just a dream. He did not even care anymore. That know-it-all butler was probably going to walk in and bug him any minute.

Right on time, James strolled in. Dressed to the nines as usual, he also carried a small silver tray. Something was on the tray, but it was covered with a fancy napkin. "So this is where you are. Everyone has been asking about you. Would you care to join your guests on the south lawn?"

"Not really." Billy's voice was soft and low. "I just feel like being alone right now." There was a moment of silence. Billy then looked in James' direction and muttered, "I guess I'm asleep now. And this is all part of some stupid dream?"

"Yes, milord. You had spent about fifteen minutes playing a video game and became bored with that. You even took a crack at reading your novel for English class, but you feel asleep. In fact, your lamp is still on."

Billy said nothing.

"Is there anything you want, Master Billy?"

Billy scoffed. "Is there anything I want? I can think of a number of things I want. But we don't always get what we want, do we, James?" He began to sound a little hostile.

James could be difficult at times, but not this time. A concerned look appeared on his face. "Your thoughts are on your friend, the track runner."

"Yep. And on other things." Billy sat there while James stood nearby waiting in his therapeutic way for Billy to keep talking. "How could God allow something horrible like this to happen to Clay? It kinda seems that God has it out for him. It wasn't too long ago that God took the life of his father."

James had to point something out. "I do not mean to correct you, sir, but you must understand, God is not the *taker* of life. He is the *Giver* of life. And He determines how long that life is going to be. It can be ninety years. It can be ninety minutes. That is *God's* call to make; not ours. We have to do what we can in the time that He has given us."

"But again, why Clay? That's what doesn't make any sense. The four of us have been the best of friends ever since we were little. We have all had our good points and our bad points, I suppose. But out of the four of us, Clay has always been the *best* of us." Billy punctuated the word *best* by looking up and meeting James' eyes. "Whenever we are busy talking about things, he is always the one who points out what is *right*. That's just how he thinks - - always positive. And running track was his world. What's gonna happen now that he lost his legs? It's just not fair!"

James let out a big sigh. His eyes showed worry that was not typical of your average butler. "No, it isn't fair. Or it certainly doesn't *seem* fair from our limited perspective."

"Huh? 'Limited perspective'?"

In an act that was completely out of character, James stepped forward and placed one hand on the back of a chair. "Forgive me for saying this, but we cannot see this situation from all angles. Only God can do that."

"But why would God allow something horrible like this to happen? Especially to Clay of all people?"

"I honestly don't know. I don't have the answers to that. All I can tell you is that He has His reasons. He is also under no obligation to share His plan with us. All we can do is proceed on faith."

On one level, Billy knew this already. Otherwise, why would this butler be telling him this in his own dream? But he was still in no mood to hear it. Nevertheless, Billy proceeded to go his angry way through this conversation. "Faith? Faith in what?"

"Faith that God knows exactly what He is doing. And peace with the knowledge that He loves us and wants the best for us."

"What?! That's crazy! How can *this* be the best thing for Clay?"

"Again, that isn't my place to say. God's plans are a great mystery." James tilted his head a few degrees and looked further into Billy. "But that isn't all that troubles you, is it? You would also like to know what your parents did at the hospital."

Billy turned his head away from James. "I don't want to talk about my parents right now," he said in a dismissive tone.

James took the hint and made a step backwards toward the door. "Forgive me. You wanted to be left alone. I shall rejoin the others." James began to leave the room.

Billy's eyes widened. "Wait a minute! What is that?" He was pointing at the tray in James' hand.

"What is what, sir?"

"That." Billy continued to point as he sprang to his feet.

James remembered the tray. "This? Oh, it's nothing. Just an idea I had. I'll be leaving now." He again turned to go.

"Wait! Let me see this." Billy marched over to James, who was looking uncomfortable, and uncovered the item. It was a copy of *Pride and Prejudice*.

James instantly went into his apologetic routine. "I was just thinking with the quiz coming up that you might want to get ahead."

Billy did not pull any punches. He was going to love cornering James like this. And this time, logic was on his side. "Look, James. This is a dream. How am I supposed to be able to read a book in the real world while I'm dreaming? Huh? Everything that I would be reading would be stuff that I was making up in my head. This does me absolutely no good."

It was time for James to clear out. "You're quite right, sir. I'll remove it right away." Again he tried to leave the room.

"Wait a minute!" A weird look appeared on Billy's face. He reached over and picked it up. "Since this is only a dream, I can do whatever I want to." He held the book as if he were going to rip it in half. "I have been wanting to do this for a long time ..."

"Sir, I really don't think that this is the best idea ..."

Billy ripped the book in half along the spine. He then ripped the two halves again in the same manner. He found himself being fueled by his own fury. All of his frustration from recent events came to a head. He thought of his parents' unyielding position and he ripped the book more. He thought of all that Clay had been through that evening. More ripping. He even began to rip the individual pages in half. This may not have been the wisest course of action; but it seemed that once he started, it was nearly impossible to stop. This was not therapeutic activity for him; it was more like feeding the savage beast within. The monster had been given free reign.

A bit uneasy with the spectacle before him, James kept backing up further and further until he was pinned against the wall. The butler was unable to do a thing. This situation was out of his control.

At this point, Billy shook himself awake. Confused, he sat up in his bed while his mind made an attempt at gaining a fix on his whereabouts. "Huh? Oh, that's right. It was just a dream." While he was regaining his bearings, he glanced down at his bed and discovered that he had been ripping up his latest copy of *Pride and Prejudice*. Bits of the novel were scattered all over his bed and some on the floor. With bitter sarcasm, he said to himself, "Well, that's just great. I'm starting to lose count of these things."

The young man thought about what had just transpired and admitted that James the butler was right about one thing anyway. Billy *had* indeed left his lamp on.

CHAPTER 22

THE ASSEMBLY

The rain started to come down sometime before Billy woke up that morning and it was still coming down as hooded students scrambled down the halls. The occasional thunder would rumble over the surrounding hills, but nothing to alarm even the more timid of his classmates. As the auditorium filled up, a few umbrellas were collecting in the corner, but more students simply shook the rain out of their hair and moved on.

Both Billy and Curtis had a rough idea why the students were all entering the school auditorium. It probably had something to do with Clay's accident. They were told just after the first period bell that they would get out of class early for some sort of announcement. Most announcements were done over the speakers, but not this time. Principal Dunbar wanted to see everyone. The students were all too happy to comply; this meant less time to do work in their homeroom class.

Earlier, Curtis and Billy had seen Mike from a distance, but the guy disappeared into thin air. He did not even report to English class. This whole thing was weird and mysterious. Curtis did not say anything to Billy about it, but he was worried. They were both worried about Clay naturally, but Mike is Clay's best friend. As Billy and Curtis entered the school auditorium, they both looked around for Mike. They half-expected to see a boisterous Mike running toward them, cracking wise as usual, with Clay laughing and following along somewhere behind him. Evidently, this was not going to be happening today.

Billy assumed that word had gotten around about Clay, but he was wrong. And no one was going to hear about it from Billy. He was in no mood to discuss it. The truth is that he actually *did* want to talk about it. But this was not the time or the place - - and certainly not with these people. He wanted to talk to someone who would listen and not try to interrupt or give advice. He simply wanted to vent.

The row that Billy and Curtis chose was nearly full already. They took the two closest seats to the aisle, about halfway down to the stage. *If all this is about Clay*, Billy thought, *then let's just get this over with and go back to class already. Or better yet, build a time machine and prevent this from happening.* Since Mrs. Dunbar had seen them at the hospital, he had no reason to believe that this was not going to be about the accident.

Just when you least expect him, there was Justin – probably with his girlfriend watching him like a hawk from somewhere close. He was carrying an envelope with Billy's name on it. "Hey, Billy!"

"What?"

"Here. Take this. Chloe Chastain asked me if I would give this to you."

That was a shock for Billy, but he expertly kept his emotions to himself. Secretly, he was thrilled to get something from her and rather surprised that she would even acknowledge him again; but under the circumstances, he felt that it was a little insensitive and grotesque to show any excitement in light of recent events. He was so embarrassed about her coming over to their really small and really old house. *Whatever could this be?* Billy stood there staring at the envelope.

"Well?" Justin was sticking around wondering what the envelope was all about.

"Well what?"

"Well? Aren't you going to open it?" Justin appeared impatient.

"Maybe. Why?"

Justin looked rather irked. "Dude. Come on and open it."

"What for?"

This whole time, Curtis was listening in on this exchange. It was all he could do to keep from laughing. He knew that this entire line of questioning was annoying to Billy, but he also knew that Billy was capable of messing with Justin. And at this point, it was good to find something funny.

Justin gritted his teeth. His voice was really low and weird-sounding.

"Come on, man. My girlfriend is dying to know what is inside of it. Help out a guy."

A puzzled look appeared on Billy's face. This look was not wholly genuine - - but it served its purpose. "If she wants to know so badly, why doesn't she just come over here and ask me herself?"

Frustration was getting the best of him. "I don't know. I just do whatever she tells me." He dropped his arms to his side and stood there.

Billy stared back.

"You're not going to open it in my presence, are you?"

"No. I'm not. You'll have to go back to 'Little Miss Nosey' all emptyhanded. If you don't like it, you could always make up something. Tell her that it's a recipe for key lime pie."

Justin stomped off with a loud sigh.

When the coast was clear, Billy opened the envelope. It was an invitation to a party at Chloe's house. He noticed that the party was scheduled for a couple of weeks away, so he quickly shoved it back in the envelope before Curtis had a chance to read it.

"So what was in the envelope?"

Billy seriously doubted if Curtis was invited - - in fact, he was just surprised that *he* was invited. He reasoned that it would be best for Curtis not to know the contents. "Oh, nothing. Just some generic greeting card."

Curtis was dismissive. "That was random."

"Yeah. Weird, huh?"

Mike looked up from wiping his face with his hands. He saw an American flag standing behind the large red curtains that bordered the stage. Behind him, he could hear the approach of high heeled shoes stepping on the wooden planks that made up the floor. Mike was already nervous – but his determination outweighed his fear. No one asked him to do this; it was all *his* idea. But this was his way of helping out his friend.

"Are you sure you want to do this?" Mrs. Dunbar walked clear around Mike and faced him directly. Her eye contact displayed both her kindness and her concern.

He nodded. "I'm sure," Mike replied in a voice that was far from confident.

Another large patch of rain began hitting the metal roof above the stage, serving as a reminder of current events outside. Mike began to wonder if it was raining over at County Hospital as well. Was Clay even aware of the rain?

"Well, if you should change your mind, just walk back right over here. It'll be fine."

A few short seconds later, Mike found himself following Mrs. Dunbar out on the auditorium stage. The students began to clap when they saw her. She was very popular with all the students. She was able to remember everyone's name and little details about them - - even years later. She seemed to know everyone in town personally. Mrs. Dunbar was in her early fifties and did not mind sharing her age – although people were generally surprised to discover how old she actually was. She always wore bright colors that complimented her African-American features. She had a love for the students - - and they returned her love.

She walked across the stage to the podium with a spirit of professionalism. Mike trailed along humbly behind. Rather than touching the microphone to see if it was turned on, she simply spoke. She knew all too well that the AV students were taking care of her – even when it came to her voice being heard above this noisy shower of rain.

The room hushed as she began. "Good morning, students. I asked your homeroom teachers to let you out of class a few minutes early so that we can make this short announcement. I'm sure that many of you have already heard about what happened to Clayton Peck, but here are the facts. Clay was run over yesterday by a car. This caused severe damage to his legs ..." She paused to inhale. " ...and they were both amputated." At this point, several students around the room gasped. Others made concerned mumbling noises to their neighbors. In the distance, more thunder announced its gentle presence. "I know that this is a shock for some of you. Many of you may be feeling frustrated or angry. Maybe you feel sadness. If any of you need someone to talk to today, feel free to come to the office. I am obligated to inform you that there are people there who are able to listen and that anything said is completely confidential." At this point, she turned to Mike with a concerned smile. Perhaps the smile was her way of giving him strength. "In the meantime, Michael Hairston has asked me if he can address the student body. Michael?" She stepped out of his way but maintained an encouraging closeness.

As Mike approached the podium, he could hear the echo of someone softly coughing twice. The sharp pinging of the rain died down a smidgen. He became well aware of the large number of students who were all looking at him. The word *uncomfortable* does not begin to describe the way that he felt at that moment. *Here I go*, he thought to himself.

"Thank you, ma'am." He looked across the crowded room. "A couple of you have asked me about Clay's condition and I thank you for your concern. Medically speaking, Clay is doing fairly well considering what all has happened to him. The doctors are saying that he should be going home in about a week. Many of you know that Clay comes from a home that ..." Mike stopped. This was not what he was supposed to say; he was now veering off his mental script. The sentence that he started was none of their business. It was not his place to speak to everyone about other people's finances. He had to be vague. "Well, let's just say that they don't have a lot. The good news is that a financial miracle has happened. The nearest that I can tell, some generous person or persons have taken care of all his medical expenses. This is a real blessing. And if I knew who it was, I would want to thank them on behalf of the Peck family."

There were a handful of people around the room that made reactive sounds - - some relief, some surprise, some approval. But Mike ignored them all and stuck to the business at hand.

"But his mom is having to take time from work to stay with him and it is going to be hard. Fortunately, their church is helping with getting them food and stuff. If you want to do something like that, just see me later and I can point you in the right direction. I have some phone numbers."

Mike stopped again. He looked back at Mrs. Dunbar who nodded back at him. He felt her hand on his shoulder. The lights on the stage were preventing him from seeing very far out into the crowd, but it did not matter. He was now paying no attention to where he eyes fell. He simply continued. "But make no mistake, this is going to be hard for him – harder than I could imagine. You all know that track was Clay's life. And he was great at it. You could almost say that he obsessed over it. It was his gift – and now that gift has been taken away from him." Mike choked on those last few words, took a breather, and cautiously started again. "Please pray for him; my friend is going to need it." Mike closed his eyes, forcing a tear to streak down the side of his face.

In the entire room, no one uttered a word. No one even noticed that the rain had stopped.

The doors had popped open and stunned students were clambering toward their second period class. Many of the students were still letting the news sink in. Bre was among them. She had inherited an exotic look from her mother's Asian eyes and her African-American father's coloring. The result was a warm skin tone, beautiful and bewitching. She pulled her black hair back behind her ear as she spoke.

"Wow! That's awful. I can scarcely believe it." Her shock was genuine. Bre did not know Clay personally, but she knew who he was. The entire student body had heard of the local, red-headed *wunderkind* who was going to run his way into track history – or so Coach Holton said.

Chloe was following her out of the room. "What's that?" Her voice betrayed her; she remained completely unaffected by the report.

Bre could easily sense Chloe's lack of concern from her tone. Although it fit her personality, Bre was still blown away. She stopped and turned toward Chloe. "I'm talking about what happened to Clay Peck."

"Oh that." Chloe kept walking. "Which one is Clay Peck?"

"The one who lost his legs. The track guy. The tall guy with red hair."

Chloe shook her head and rolled her eyes as if this whole thing was an irritant. "Okay. This conversation is getting way too sad. We're changing channels now. Guess what?"

Bre was not quite ready to drop the subject; the news was still being processed. But whatever. "What?"

Chloe's excitement level increased dramatically. "Daddy is going out of town in like three weeks and I'll have the whole place virtually to myself. Anyway I'm celebrating his absence with a little party. It will be Daylight Savings Time so we'll have an extra hour to party. Everyone who is anyone is going to be invited."

Bre's nose wrinkled up with curiosity. "A daylight saving's time party? That's a new one. Did you just make that up?"

"Yeah, girl! And it'll be so much more than that. Do you remember that little surprise I mentioned for Billy Harris?"

"Yeah."

"Well, he doesn't know it yet, but he is going to provide some special entertainment that night."

"Now you have my definite interest. I wouldn't miss it for the world. You are always cooking up something scandalous, aren't you?"

"HA! You don't know the tenth of it." At that moment, Chloe noticed Wesley walking by, just past Bre. "Oh! Hang on, will you? There is someone I must invite."

Nearly in the same breath, Chloe raced over to Wesley and began talking to him. "Wesley Porterfield! There you are. Stop avoiding me and come here."

"Hey Chloe. What's up?" Wesley sounded bored at the prospect of talking to Chloe - - or rather *her* talking to *him*.

"Oh nothing. Actually, plenty. I was just looking at my calendar and I couldn't help but notice that we have an extra hour coming up, that isn't *this* weekend or the *next* weekend, but the one after that. It's that Daylight Savings Time thing. I'm sure you've heard of it. So I was wondering if you had any plans for that extra hour."

"Why? Are you trying to tell me that you have something in mind?"

"Oh yes. You would be absolutely right. I am planning a little get-together at my house for some friends and was wondering if you would like to come. There will be some music, food, drinks, and some surprise entertainment. Strictly no parents allowed."

"You can be pretty scary sometimes."

"Does that mean you'll come?"

Wesley did not really want to go. But he was unable to come up with a quick excuse not to. Besides, he really did not have any plans for that night – too far in the future honestly. He would probably just end up all alone in that big house of his anyway. "I'm not making any promises, but I'll see what I'm doing that night."

Chloe gently touched the collar of his shirt with her right hand. She stepped in closer and looked up at his face with large expressive eyes. "Oh, I'm not worried. You'll be there. My party would be a flop without you." Her fingers danced down Wesley's shoulder. She then turned and ran back to Bre. The two of them continued their girl-talk all the way to the next class.

Wesley was uncomfortable. He obviously knew that Chloe liked him.

A bat could see that plainly – with or without its echo location. The question was: Did she actually like *him*? Or did she like the idea of him, him with all his family's money? He was pretty sure that she was not his type though. Some guys may be attracted to drama, but he was not.

He turned to go to his next class - - but in mid-turn, he noticed something. *What's this?* he asked himself. It only took a second to walk over to the bulletin board where he saw a small stack of fliers tacked up. They stated that there would be a reading of the latest chapters of *Pride and Prejudice* over at Billy Harris' house. This would be a great way to be ready for the upcoming quiz and get out of the house for an evening. It gave the date and time as well as the address. It was something to do. He pulled off the top copy and shoved it down in his backpack.

CHAPTER 23

PSYCHO GIRL LETTER

If you, the reader, would indulge us once again, we need to go back in time just a few minutes so that we may gain another perspective from recent events. Just *before* the assembly began, Berly and Maggie met up in the hallway, neither of them especially wet from the current shower. Confused-looking students from each direction were leaving their homeroom classes and filing into the school auditorium. The whole room was hoodies and earbuds. Going along with this unclear change of schedule, the girls shrugged at each other and entered through the doors.

Berly scoped the entire room in an almost involuntary search for Billy. Maggie was talking to her the whole time, but Berly gave her a series of well-practiced responses to reassure her friend that she was indeed listening – which was an inaccurate assessment. She saw Billy enter with one of his usual friends. They sat down on the far side of the crowd. Berly thought about trying to get his attention, but that Justin kid was distracting him at the time with what looked like an envelope. That was too bad. *He has no idea that I'm even here*, she thought.

"Well?"

Berly snapped out of her trance and turned back to Maggie. "Well what?"

Maggie looked straight ahead at the stage. "Oh never mind. You're not even paying attention."

"I'm sorry. What were we talking about?"

Maggie went on to explain in full detail what had transpired. Sadly,

Berly looked back over at Billy again. This time, she noticed that Justin was walking back towards his girlfriend (and she did not look happy – whatever her name was) and Billy opened the envelope, glancing inside. But he stashed it back in his pocket and quickly sat back next to his friend.

"...now tell me *that's* not weird." Maggie glanced back over at Berly and noticed that she still was not listening. Her voice stung with satire. "Oh. Were you obsessing over that Billy Harris again? Sorry to bother you."

"What? No. I was listening."

"Then what was I just talking about? Huh? I've gone though it twice now and you still have no idea what I said."

Berly turned back away from the boys. "I know. I didn't mean to ignore you. I'm just a bit distracted this morning."

"Oh? Really?" Mock surprise.

At this point, Mrs. Dunbar was walking across the stage. In spite of all those faces watching her, she always looked comfortable in front of the students. They loved her. She was cool. Trailing behind her was one of Billy's other friends. He looked decidedly unnerved. Berly and Maggie joined the students as they clapped for their principal.

The next couple of minutes were not good. Mrs. Dunbar announced that that hopeful track star Clayton Peck was in a terrible accident and that he lost both of his legs. This news knocked the air out of the girls – and pretty much everybody else.

Berly turned to look at Billy, but she could not see him well in the dark. He was just a blurry silhouette at this distance. She thought, *He must feel horrible. This is one of his best buddies from way back when. This Peck kid and Billy must be very close.*

Mrs. Dunbar then turned to Clay's best friend and introduced him as Mike. He spoke for a moment about Clay's medical expenses and about his heart for competitive track. Then he stopped. He simply ran out of words and all was silent. Mrs. Dunbar, being the wonderful woman that she was, took over for him, made some closing comments, and dismissed the students for their second period class. The lights came back up and everyone stood up from their seats.

"That explains it," Maggie said.

Berly went back to looking for Billy in the crowd, but she did her best to pretend to be engaged in conversation with Maggie. "That explains what?"

"It explains what I was talking about when we were walking in." Maggie gave Berly a glaring look. "You were really out of it, weren't you? I was explaining to you that I have P.E. during first period with Coach Pool. But since she is still on her maternity leave, we had Coach Holton again. Well today, he told us not to even bother dressing out. He must've known something about this."

"Yeah? That's no surprise since we had this big assembly."

"I know. But as far as the track team is concerned, this Clay Peck guy was the most talent this school has seen in years. But the weird part – as I explained earlier – is that Coach Holton spent the entire class in his office reading his Bible and sipping on his chamomile tea."

"Really? Chamomile tea?" This was a fake reaction. Berly was not so much interested in what happened or did not happen in P.E. earlier, or in Coach Holton's search for wisdom from the Holy Scriptures, or even what he was drinking in the process. Although disturbed about this tragic incident involving a student, she was not even thinking about Clay. She looked back in the direction of Billy. "You know what? I think I need to go see Billy. He might need me right now."

Maggie could see this coming in the dark. "Need you? What can you possibly do for him? You think that you could help him somehow?"

"I don't know, I just …" She looked back at Billy and noticed that he was getting swept up in the exiting crowd. She could not get to him even if she were on that side of the room. " …uh, you know, for support."

Maggie's voice brought her back. "Look. Right now, Billy needs you like he needs a white belt. Promise me that you won't do anything weird until we've had a chance to talk."

The sophomore grinned and rolled her eyes in comic fashion. "Okay, *mom*." A reassuring chuckle sent Maggie away.

Berly agreed, but she did not want to. All she could think about was getting closer to Billy. This was especially awkward during lunch because Maggie always ate with the Spanish club in Mr. Rodriguez' classroom a couple of days each week (a time that Maggie always described as *excellente*).

But when their school day was finally done, they both met up at Maggie's car. They stepped around the puddles and climbed on in.

"Let's see," Berly coyly began, "where were we? Oh yes. You were telling me that I should do absolutely nothing for our hurting friend Billy now that his buddy has had an accident."

"Okay, first of all, he really *isn't* our friend, not when you think about it. He is just some guy in the Chess Club who you have the misfortune of being infatuated with. And secondly, I never said that you should do nothing. In fact, there is something very important that you *could* do. But knowing you right now, you would probably try to go off and do something freaky."

"Freaky?! I wouldn't do anything 'freaky.'"

Maggie stopped and gave Berly a dirty look. "Yeah, right." She turned the key in the ignition and buckled herself in. Berly also reached up behind her and grabbed the seatbelt.

Maggie continued with her thoughts. "Look. All I know about boys is what I get from watching my brothers and I can tell you that they are just like deer." She began to speak like a theatrical storyteller as she drove. "Let's say that you are hunting. You're looking out and a great big buck walks over toward you. He is looking around the entire clearing to see if everything is safe. This time, he doesn't see you. So you get your gun ready. Careful. Try not to make a sound. Then you accidently step on a twig, it snaps, and he is outta there. Jumps right back into the woods. Deer spook easily. With boys, you start acting freaky and they're apt to disappear just as quickly."

"Where do you get off talking like that? This isn't deer hunting. I don't see why you're hatin' on me all of a sudden. You have no idea what this is like."

Silence followed for about two blocks.

Maggie posed a question. "Did you speak to Billy today?"

Berly answered like a sarcastic child talking disrespectfully to her parents. "No. I was under the impression that *you* didn't want me to."

"So you didn't make any effort to contact him at all?"

At this point, Berly started to sound a little guilty. "Uh, not really. No."

"Well? Which is it? Yes or no?"

"Technically *no*."

A sudden rush of worry appeared on Maggie's face and she gasped. "Oh no. Tell me you didn't write him a letter!"

"Whatever makes you think that I did something like that?"

She pounded lightly on the steering wheel. "Yep. You did. You wrote him a letter. When did you write it?"

Berly looked down. After a few seconds, she softly admitted, "During study hall."

"Study hall? Study hall." Maggie was thinking. "That's your last period. So you haven't had the chance to give it to him yet?"

Berly replied with that sing-song are-you-an-idiot voice. "Uhhhh. Nooooo. I haven't seen him."

Like an arrow, Maggie's bossiest voice shot out directly in Berly's direction. "Good! You must destroy it. And with urgency."

"What?!"

"Yes. Take it home and destroy it. Tear it up. Trash it. Burn it. Whatever. Just get it done – *toot sweet*, and before anyone else gets a chance to read it. Because once you give it to him, it is no longer under your control. It becomes a time bomb that will soon blow you up into smithereens."

Berly let out a nervous laugh. "That's nonsense. You don't even know what it says."

"Oh yeah? I think I have a pretty good idea. It probably sounds something like this ..." Maggie cleared her throat and then went into a mocking, breathy voice. "*Dearest Billy, I am terribly sorry to hear about your friend's accident. This can't be easy on you. I can see the deep pain in your eyes. No one else can see it, but I alone know that it is there. And I want you to know that I understand you. I can feel your hurt. And I wanted you to know that you can talk to me any time about anything because I understand you in ways that no one else can. Love, Berly.*" Her voice returned to normal. "Puke!"

Berly said nothing. She merely looked down at the floorboard.

"So? How close was I? Isn't that pretty much what you wrote?"

Berly's voice was timid. "There were some differences."

"Well, don't kick yourself. It just so happens that all my brothers have received at least two similar letters each, and my good-looking brother has received at least three. Those brothers of mine have a name for notes like these."

"What? They have a name for them? And what would that be?"

Maggie glanced over at her friend cautiously and answered. "Um ... They call them 'Psycho Girl Letters.'"

"'Psycho Girl Letters'?" Berly did not know what to make of that comment. What exactly were Maggie's brothers saying? From her perspective, Berly was only doing what she thought would help. Now she felt exposed in some way, as if she were indirectly the topic of many conversations among Maggie's brothers – even though she had nothing to do with those. "Why do they call them 'Psycho Girl Letters'?"

"Well, don't take this personally, but it is because they were letters, they were from girls, and the girls were acting 'psycho' - - *their* words, not mine. These sweet girls were nothing more than victims of their own crushes and that's all. They just thought that the best way to express their feelings was through some unintentionally weird letters."

Berly felt slightly defensive at this point. "Weird, huh? What's so weird about them?"

Maggie really did not want to go into specifics – besides they tend to vary from letter to letter. "Look. These girls try to make it sound like there is some weird mystical connection that they have with the guy. Sometimes they act like they are the cure for whatever deep depression that they think my brothers may be going through. Or rather, they are gambling on the idea that they are going through some depression and need this girl to help them work it out. That's called 'getting attention.'"

Berly wondered if her letter was just a quick attention grab.

Maggie continued. "Sometimes, the letters contain some weird imagery – like the guy rides up to her on a horse and her favorite song is playing in the background. This image is sometimes in front of a castle or by a beautiful lake. More details, but I digress. In every case concerning my brothers however, they did not respond at all the way the girls thought they were supposed to. Fast forward a couple of days and the girls who wrote the letters are then too ashamed or embarrassed to be around them. It makes everything weird between them and she realizes all too late that she was better off not writing it. And that is the tragedy of the whole Psycho Girl Letter thing."

Berly got a firmer hold on her backpack as if it suddenly contained something dangerous, as if it were the President's nuclear 'football.'

Maggie gave some thought as to how to proceed next. "Actually, boys react to these letters differently. Most of the time, they will ignore them (or *try* to ignore them) – and that is actually the best thing. But let's say that the boy has a mean streak. He could easily show the letter to his friends for a cheap laugh; and they won't care if she knows about it – and then the teasing begins. But there are some nice boys out there too. If that's the case, he will try to be polite and sympathetic. But there is still this weirdness between the two of them; so after a while, even he will begin to avoid her. In any case, don't be surprised if the boy doesn't show up, carry you away on a horse with him, and together you magically ride off into a beautiful oil painting. Because life isn't like that. Besides, to you, he may look like a handsome knight on a horse – but in the eyes of adults, he is still just a child. I doubt that Billy is even sixteen yet."

Berly looked out the window at the passing streets.

"Don't get me wrong," Maggie added. "My mom writes love notes to my dad all the time – but that's totally different. That's the way that she expresses herself. And hers are of genuine love from a wife to her husband. That's love, not infatuation."

That stung. "Infatuation?" Berly asked. "Is that what this is? Are you saying that I just got a bad case of the boy-crazies?"

Maggie sighed. "I guess what I am trying to tell you is that boys are just boys, part jerks and part sweethearts. You can't expect them to act the way you want them to. God just wired them differently than us. When we aren't idolizing them, we look at boys as if they are a bunch of crude ignorant cavemen, dragging their knuckles across the ground as they walk. On the other hand, many of them probably look at us as if we were taking a constant ride on an emotional roller coaster. Some days we're happy and everything is cool. And other days? No." She turned to glance at her friend. "Neither of these views are true or fair. Forgive me for stereotyping, but hey – my point."

Maggie pulled onto Berly's street. Both girls were quiet for a half-minute.

Almost weak from embarrassment, Berly asked, "Why do you think that is?"

"What do you mean? Why did God wire us differently?" She shrugged. "I don't know. Maybe it was for our own protection. Maybe all this confusion is to keep us from getting into too much trouble at a young age. Or maybe it gives a married couple something to work on, to find some sort of common ground. I like to think that the Creator just made us different to complement each other – two sides of the same coin – and that together women and men have the ability to approach life from two different angles. If that's the case, then we are stronger together than we are apart." Maggie stopped for a few moments, lost in thought. Then she added, "But perhaps the devil wants to exploit and distort these differences for his purposes, to tear folks apart. I can see that. We may have to focus more on God to keep that from happening. I don't know. Maybe someday I'll find out." She turned back to her friend briefly and smiled. "Ask me again in about fifty years."

Maggie brought the car to a stop in the driveway, but it was understood that they would continue to sit there for just a few more minutes. She struggled in her mind to remember something that she was going to say before she interrupted herself. Luckily, her friend reminded her by asking a question.

Berly's eyes narrowed. "Back there, you mentioned that there was something very important that I *could* do for Billy. What were you talking about?"

Maggie snapped back to attention. "That's right. You should not forget about the most powerful weapon in a Christian's arsenal: prayer. I think it was James from the Bible who wrote, 'Confess your faults one to another, and pray one for another, that ye may be healed. The effectual fervent prayer of a righteous man availeth much.'" That quote was actually from James 5:16.

"Yeah, but I'm not a man." Berly raised an eyebrow and grinned.

Maggie shot a comical glance back at Berly. "Girl, that doesn't matter and you know it. Our prayers are just as powerful as any man's. You can go off and do this, that, and the other thing whenever you see an opportunity to help people out – and so you should – but you really mean business when you shut yourself away in a quiet place and talk to God. It's kinda like this …" Maggie made a fist with her left hand and brought it up to eye-level. "Let's say that *this* is a person who you are burdened about, all their troubles, drama, hardships. And *this* …" She did the same thing with her right hand. " …is our all-powerful God with all the resources and answers at His disposal." She then brought up her fingers and connected both hands with them in a straight line. "When we pray for someone, we are building a bridge between their needs and the One Who can fulfill those needs."

She grinned again. Berly thought about being responsible for building that bridge between Billy's needs and God. "That is an interesting illustration," she replied. "I like that."

Maggie rested her hands and continued. "I know that I may be over-simplifying it a bit, but consider something else. If you are – as you say – making an appeal to God, then your thoughts are on someone else's needs, and not on yourself. That pleases Him. Selfish thoughts need to take a hike." Maggie's face suddenly became quite serious and she gestured down at Berly's backpack. "Uh, don't tell me your answer. Just be honest with yourself. But when you wrote that letter, were your thoughts really on Billy's well-being? Or were you really only thinking about yourself and your own desires?"

Berly had much to think about. What was her motivation in writing the letter? Did she do it in the best spirit of Christian charity? Or was this just another subconscious way of parading in front of him and getting his attention? And would the letter ultimately make her situation worse? At this point, she paused to open the car door and stepped out.

"Hey! One last thing to think about!" Maggie put her hands back on the steering wheel. "You can pray up a blue streak for Billy – that's fine. But don't forget about his running friend, Peck. After all, *he* is the one who is going to have a rough way. You have the ability to pray for folks you've never even met – you know, like behind their backs. Prayer is a powerful thing and there's no rule against praying for folks you don't know."

That's true, she thought.

The girls made their farewells and the car door closed. Maggie stuck around until her friend was safely inside the house.

Once inside, Berly put her backpack on the dining room table. Her cat meowed at her and got out of the way by jumping down to the floor. Berly thought about the letter. She unzipped her bag and took the letter out. She thought about all the time and energy that she spent composing it. She thought about the awesome effect that it would have on Billy. Addressing the cat, she began to wave the letter in the air and said defensively, "What does *she* know anyway? Normally, Mag is loaded with sound advice; but this time, she is wrong. All wrong. One-hundred and twenty-five percent wrong. This isn't just another one of those *psycho girl letters*. It is a sensitive and tasteful offer to help out a friend. Nothing more, nothing less. And first thing tomorrow, I am going to hand this letter over to Billy. By Chess Club, he will have read it and that'll be that. And if Maggie doesn't like, well that's just too bad for her."

The cat was not convinced and walked out of the room.

But just to prove Maggie wrong, Berly decided to revisit her beautifully constructed note. Her eyes poured over the words. This time however, it read differently. She began to see it through the eyes of someone else. Rather than a thoughtful offer to assist a friend in a time of crisis, it started to sound more and more like an immature and desperate cry for intimacy. *What happened?* she asked herself. *This was so much better earlier today.*

She sighed. Maybe Maggie was right. At this point, Berly's hands merely acted on her behalf as they ripped the letter in two. She then witnessed her hands tossing the remains into the kitchen trashcan. Operation Psycho Girl Letter had officially been aborted. Part of her felt relieved. But the other part?

She discovered that she had no more control over her emotions than she had over her hands. And here it came, the tidal wave. She raced down the hall and back to her bed – which for the next few minutes, seemed to be her designated crying place.

In the morning, she might feel like thanking Maggie for the talk. But for now, we should just end this chapter, back off a bit, and give the girl some privacy.

CHAPTER 24

BOUGHT WITH A PRICE

Both Berly and Maggie had initiated a chain reaction of support for Billy in the Chess Club. And they were not alone. The entire school showed their concern for Clay and frequently inquired about his condition. Because Mike had addressed the student body (and because he was the most vocal of the group), he had become the unelected spokesperson on this issue. Besides, Mike had stopped by to visit Clay every day since the accident.

About a week and a half went by and Clay was mending quickly. The day had finally come when he got his discharge from the hospital. The word *excited* could be used to describe how the gang felt about him coming home - - but so could the word *nervous*. What would they all talk about? How could they keep things from getting awkward?

"Why could the elephant NOT get in his car?"

Rather than a long universal moan from the others, Maggie was the one to answer Eugene. "So, *this* is the Chess Club, a quiet respite for the supposed intellectual elite." She looked around the room; the use of the term 'intellectual elite' may be questionable, but she continued to pursue her thought just the same. " ...and *you* ask why an elephant is unable to get into a car? Who let you in here anyway?"

Eugene pressed the issue of his unanswered question. "Come on, guys. This is a good one. Why could the elephant NOT get in his car?" He proudly looked around for an answer.

A sneaky grin suddenly appeared on Joey's face. "Eugene, each day you come in here and treat everyone with another joke. But let's do something different today. Let's make this fun. I propose that, if you tell us the answer, you will owe everyone in this room a dollar."

Suddenly, the students were all showing great interest in what was happening. It would seem that not all interesting plays were being done on the chess board.

This was a first. Eugene's eye squinted as if he were weighing something in his mind. "A dollar, huh? Is that a dollar to be divided up evenly between all of you?"

Joey victoriously sat back in his chair. "No. I'm talking about one dollar for each of us. So you do the math. Is this joke worth five dollars? When Berly gets here, that would make it six. It's seven, if you count Mr. H." Joey waved over at an amused Mr. Harris sitting at his desk. The teacher waved back cheerfully.

Eugene looked disappointed, but everyone else in the room was delighted. In fact, Maggie chuckled while Joey and Alejandro high-fived each other. Eugene's eyes shifted back and forth as he looked around from person to person. "What sort of sorcery is this?"

Berly entered the room. She instantly began talking as she put down her stuff and took a seat across from Quotes. "Sorry I'm late everyone. I had to find out how Rodney is doing."

"LONG LIVE RODNEY."

"He had his wisdom teeth taken out today. But his mom says he is doing well."

Billy began to laugh. "Wow! Incredible. You all go through so much trouble to maintain this fiction that Rodney is a real person."

Maggie rolled her eyes. "Oh, this again. For a second there, I thought that you were going to spare us this conversation. I suppose some things in life are just too difficult to avoid: death, taxes, Eugene's terrible jokes, and you ragging us over Rodney's absence."

Billy seemed ready to climb on his soapbox for the forty-third time. "We are already in the second quarter of school and I *still* have not seen so much as a hair from your precious club president. This Rodney, if he is real, has never shown up to Chess Club this year and each time he has some lame excuse - - which you all instantly believe. You people are both ridiculous and sad."

Joey did not even look up from the chessboard. "Nonsense. Rodney has been here."

"Not to Chess Club, he hasn't. At least, not since I've been here."

Joey continued, "I see him every day. He never misses school." He looked around the room and then back to the game in an apologetic shrug. " ...well, other than days like today."

"Yeah. How convenient. What kind of president never attends the meetings?"

Maggie, who is not one for trivial talk, spoke up. "I think we all know where this conversation is going. Billy wants to do something to promote the club." She turned to Billy with a we-are-not-amused tilt in her neck. "We *have* had this conversation before."

Alejandro moved his queen up. "And we will no doubt have it again."

Now Billy got defensive in his tone. "No, no! That's not why I brought it up." This remark brought a hush for a few seconds as they all waited for something new to be said. "But since you mentioned it ..." (Moans came from all corners of the room.) " ...isn't that something that we should seriously consider?"

Alejandro simply shook his head. His slight Latino accent shown through. "I told you earlier that I have a foolproof plan. The next time we run that signup booth, I can get new students in line. I can even get older students in line. Easily! But nobody will listen to me."

Maggie turned her head sharply toward Alejandro. "What are you going to do? Steal a bunch of orange cones and reroute traffic so everyone has to come through our Chess Club meeting?"

With an ample supply of self-confidence, Gregory Chastain adjusted his tie as he made his way down the hall toward Mr. Harris' classroom. He projected success with his fancy duds and a sharp haircut. For a guy his age, he was looking mighty dapper. The cat's meow.

As he turned the final corner that led to the English hall, he was startled by a peculiar sight. The Chess Club members were lined up and leaving the room in a single file line. One of the boys was standing by the door, handing each of the others a dollar as they walked by. And each time someone took a dollar, this young man said, "Because his keys were in the trunk." "Because his keys were in the trunk." This made no sense to Mr. Chastain, but he shrugged it off. Finally, the last kid walked by grabbing a dollar, and again the one by the door said, "Because his keys were in the trunk."

As strange, interesting, and possibly entertaining as this sight might have been to Mr. Chastain, it paled in comparison to Billy's interest when he saw Chloe's father on the approach once more. *Yikes! What could he possibly want this time?* he asked himself.

As soon as the kid passing out the bills exited, Mr. Chastain impatiently took a step inside the room. He gave a straightening tug to his silk tie. "Mr. Harris? May I have another moment of your time?" He was not exactly smiling.

William looked up at the sound of Gregory's voice. This sudden encounter was not expected, but the teacher greeted his guest as warmly as he could. "Mr. Chastain. Of course." He removed his reading glasses, placed them on his desk, and got to his feet. "But I can only spare a couple of minutes. I was just about to take my son and his friends over to Clay Peck's house for a brief visit." William gestured to an empty seat and they both sat down, William back at his desk. "Clay is the boy who had that bad accident and lost his legs. We've been good friends with him and his family since the boys were small. Chloe might have said something to you about it."

Gregory was focused on his singular purpose for coming and felt that he did not have the time nor the inclination to make polite chit-chat over the details of a student's misfortune. But he did not want to appear totally insensitive. "Uh, no. She never mentioned a word about that. Lost his legs?" His face cringed a little. "That's rough." His face returned to normal with no expression. He gave a slight pull to his jacket and it was back to business. "Mr. Harris, I do not want to come across as being pushy, but I'm going to be out of town this coming weekend and I was wondering if you have had the opportunity to reconsider my offer."

William was rather surprised. He had thought that he had been perfectly clear on the matter during their initial visit. Nonetheless, he did not let his surprise appear on his face. But the question did get him thinking. *Why is his doing this? Trying to bribe a teacher over his daughter's grades? This makes no sense? What is he up to exactly?*

He shook his head slightly. "No. Mr. Chastain, I don't play those kinds of games. Your daughter is going to have to show some effort in my class in order to make the grade. And since our last conversation, I'm afraid that she has shown no sign of improvement. In fact, to be perfectly honest, her attitude actually seems to have gotten a bit worse these last few weeks."

Gregory looked down at the edge of William's desk and released a long sigh. "I see." A couple of seconds later, he reached into his inside breast pocket and pulled out a small pad of paper and a pen and began to write something. As he wrote, he said, "Mr. Harris, I don't know how much you know about me, but I have earned a reputation for being a shrewd businessman and generally an impatient person. If I want something, I find a way to make it happen. I always get what I want. Nothing stands in my way. But, I may make a rare exception this time and sweeten the pot just a little bit. How does this suit you?" He held out the pad for William to see what he wrote.

The difference was substantial, but William remained unmoved. Even if the Harris' did not have their own fortune, he would not have taken this bribe. He and Diane had their integrity. But honestly, it was all William could do to keep from laughing. He knew that this was a lot of money; but considering how much money the Harris' were already worth, the idea seemed funny – like trying to send the Statue of Liberty in the mail using only one stamp. But the Harris' secret money was *still* a secret and he had absolutely no intentions of sharing that information with anyone - - least of all Gregory Chastain, who seemed to place a lot of his misguided faith in his combustible earthly riches.

The teacher chose to answer wisely. Rather than wanting to look like the *rich* boy with ethics, William decided to play more the *poor* boy with ethics. "I'll admit that that is a very generous offer, but I'm afraid I cannot accept it. You're asking me to compromise my integrity as a teacher and that will simply not happen if I have anything to say about it. If I *were* interested in your money – and I'm not – a guy could eventually get fired over something like that." The mood in the room was way too tense for William's comfort level, so he tried to lighten it with a short chuckle. " ... and I am certainly not wanting to get fired."

"Perhaps you don't realize just how secretive I can be. In cases like this, I promise that no one would *ever* have to know."

With direct eye contact, William replied with stern authority. "*You* would know. *I* would know. And most importantly, *God* would know. So you keep your money and I'll keep my job." That was clearly his final answer. He knew that conversationally speaking, that was the equivalent of showing Gregory Chastain to the door and slamming it shut on his backside. Naturally, this was something that he was not used to doing, but then again he was not accustomed to being put in this awkward position either.

Gregory was not surprised by his reply. He half expected it. He was really hoping that this meeting would be over soon; but now it was just going to take him a little longer. It was time to play his other card. "I was afraid that would be your answer." He stood back up, walked around his chair, and stood behind it. He was prepared for this moment and he already had it cooking in his mind. "If you'll pardon my asking, just how long have you been teaching here – here in Pecan Falls?"

This was a different direction. William did some instant math in his head and answered him without missing a beat. "Uh, here? Fifteen years. I have been teaching for twenty-two total."

Gregory's voice took on a rather sinister tone as he spoke. "Fifteen years. Hmmm. I respect your sense of ethics and I applaud you for your integrity. But I think it only fair to warn you. A few very influential members of the school board are old golfing buddies of mine. We go way back. And they listen to what I have to say."

William was about to respond, but Gregory held up a quick hand and cut him off before he had a chance to speak a word.

"I'm not a monster, Mr. Harris. And I'm certainly not talking about getting you fired; I'm not like that. But this is the time to set your ethics aside for a moment. Because rather than being fired, your contract for the next school year may simply not be renewed. I don't know how important that would be to you, but in today's economy, it is something to consider." He shifted his weight from one side to the other. "You're a family man, aren't you?"

A chord was just struck. William's eyebrows arched up toward the center and his countenance was altered. His previous eye contact was abandoned as he turned his gaze to a picture frame that sat on his desk. The photo was of Diane, Billy, and himself and was taken down at the falls. His voice was softened and cautious. "Yes, sir. My wife and I have a son. We always wanted to have more children but …" He gave a tender sigh. " …but it didn't work out that way. It wasn't anyone's fault – just not meant to be. We had even thought about adopting some kids, but we have a … well, it's a unique situation."

Gregory looked around at William's desk and the room that they were in. "Well, it seems to me that for the sake of you and your family, you can't really afford to lose this job. That would put them in a bad way." He started making his intentions toward the door. "For everyone's good, think about what I have just said." Before exiting the room, he stopped in the doorway and turned around. "*William Harris*. Hmmmm. *William Harris*. That name doesn't really flow, does it?"

William shrugged. "I suppose not. I'm quite used to it. My friends just call me *Bill*."

"I hope to hear from you soon, … William Harris." He left the room. For a while, his egotistical footsteps could easily be heard as he disappeared down the hall.

As the sound grew more faint, William sat motionless at his desk, staring at the framed family photo. He reached over and picked it up. He peered into his son's face. His focus ultimately rested onto the smiling eyes of his wife. He smiled back at the picture in response. Becoming a teacher was never about the money; it was all about the students. He had a wonderful time teaching. And these were good kids. But in the end, he knew that he had made the only decision possible. He returned the photo to its place on the desk and rose from his seat.

After a few seconds, Billy popped up from behind one of the desks close to the other door. "Well, that was nuts! You would think that a guy like that would be cool, but no. Not this guy. What are you going to do?"

William looked up and glared at him. "Were you back there again? You need to stop eavesdropping on conversations that aren't yours. Someday, you're going to get caught and another party may decide that they don't like it. Your mother and I have spent way too much money on those pretty teeth of yours just to see some strong guy come along and knock them out of your mouth."

Dismissing his dad's warning, Billy asked, "Well? Aren't you worried about what he said?"

"Of course not." He spoke while straightening the items on his desk.

Billy showed signs of surprise. "Was he being for real about his golfing buddies? And getting you out of here?"

"Probably. But I seriously doubt that he has that much clout with the school board. They wouldn't let it go that far. Since he has a daughter, he might say that I acted inappropriately toward her or some sort of ridiculous, made-up story. It would be a classic case of *he said/she said*. These things are such a long ordeal and everyone gets damaged in the process. And then once that was cleared up, the school might be scared that I would take legal action of my own or something – which I don't ever see myself doing. But the odds of that ever happening are so remote. And even then, I can't see Mrs. Dunbar going along with it. It might be interesting to see Chastain try though. But even if he did, what difference does it make?"

"'What difference does it make'? What do you mean? I would think that it would make a ton of difference!"

William stood up from his desk, placed both hands on it, and leaned in toward Billy. "I simply mean that I don't belong to him." He began to pick up a few books and laid them in his briefcase as he spoke. "The Bible says, 'For he that is called in the Lord, being a servant, is the Lord's freeman: likewise also he that is called, being free, is Christ's servant. Ye are bought with a price; be not ye the servants of men.'" [I Corinthians 7:22-23] He then closed his briefcase and picked it up by the handle.

Billy had absolutely no idea what all that meant. When his dad began to quote the Bible, he more or less stopped listening closely. "What does all that stuff mean?"

"It means that people can do all kinds of bad things to me, but I belong to God. Well, let them try. Their plans will either fail miserably or these people will have to pay the price one day for how they treated one of God's children. But from where I am standing, it is God Who will take care of me and will provide for all our needs."

"Whatever." This is where they differed. Billy was a believer in God and all that. But there was his dad's way of looking at any situation and there was a more realistic approach. Billy left the room with his nerd dad, ready to give up on any hope of his father ever getting it together. They were on their way to pick up the other boys and visit Clay anyway.

At times, Billy seriously doubted if his dad really understood what was going on around him. Having all that money laying around and not spending it was weird enough. But now he virtually had his job threatened and what did he do about it? Nothing. He just stood there quoting Bible verses and acting all happy. What a hopeless nerd! In a way, Billy understood the whole God-is-in-control thing - - he had certainly heard the speech often enough. He also understood that his dad really does not rely on this lousy job either. I mean really. He grades papers, dissects sentences, and talks about *Pride and Prejudice* in the dinky little town of Pecan Falls. How exciting is that? Quite a boring little life they've made for themselves.

Billy could not help but imagine doing things a little differently. He would have punched Mr. Chastain in his glass jaw and sent him running home through that window. Then he would sell that ugly old house and get a place far away from Pecan Falls - - and one with a spanking new dryer. Anything would be cooler than this.

Billy wondered if you could get dads mixed up in a hospital the way some urban legends claim about babies. That's it. Maybe he had a real dad somewhere else in the world. Maybe there was a super cool dad who was stuck in a total nerd family and that maybe they should switch back. No chance of that happening. Billy was definitely his father's son. They woefully looked too much alike - - right down to their infuriating cowlicks.

Sitting over on the passenger's side of the truck, William's mind was somewhere else. *Why would Gregory Chastain be doing all of this? What was his agenda?*

CHAPTER 25

CHECKING IN

Billy and his dad picked up Curtis at his house, but Mike drove himself over. William Harris sat in the truck as the three boys walked up the sidewalk to Clay's house. The older man too had wanted to go inside, speak personally with Clay, and encourage him all that he could. But under the circumstances, he felt that hovering over the boys was not necessary. There would be other times, other visits. This was not his moment. So William sat parked in the driveway and offered a quick and sincere prayer.

Curtis and Billy however were quite tense about the planned visit. They felt like actors being pushed out onto a stage without a clue of what their lines were supposed to be. What would they say? How should they behave?

Mike was a bit more confident. He had dropped by to see his best friend every day since the accident. Sometimes Clay would talk; other days, not so much. Clay was the most polite and thoughtful person he had ever known – but since the accident, his friend had shown various degrees of hospitality - - or lack of. Mike just let it go. He figured that, after all Clay had endured, he was entitled to some bad days.

This had been a hard time for the Pecks. His sister had moved off and started her own family. His dad had died. And now this. Mike would much rather be that friend who would be there for Clay, even if it meant taking on the occasional ugliness. The only thing that Mike could predict was that this would be unpredictable. It was all up to whatever mood Clay was in.

A window air conditioner unit dripped water into an already-full, five gallon bucket in front of them. Weeds grew tall in the sidewalk cracks. The exterior of the house consisted of weird orange-ish bricks that must have been popular sixty years ago. The rickety wooden porch that led to the front door creaked under the weight of the three boys - - but it would hold. The doorbell was missing but they all knew how to touch the wires to trigger the bell. Somehow that did not seem right today. Mike knocked on the door and achieved the same effect.

Mrs. Peck, looking as ragged and boney as ever, came to the door. She was her talkative self. "Oh! Boys! I'm so glad to see you. We just got home from the hospital this morning, about eleven o'clock - - or was it ten? No, it was eleven. Yes. I remember looking at the clock."

Always trying to find every angle, Curtis thought that this might be too much of an inconvenience. Their presence may be unwanted. "Clay may not be settled in yet. Maybe this is a bad time."

Billy and Mike agreed and stated that they could come back another day, but Maxine would not hear of it. She brought them inside – even threatening them with brownies and sugar cookies.

The boys were greeted by that same odor. The Peck's house had a weird smell to it. It was not bad, just different; but nothing that the boys have not encountered a million times before. All the familiar stuff was there: the giant glass grapes in an oversized wooden bowl, the fish tank with two tetras and a plastic treasure chest, the lamp with a bent lampshade turned to face the wall, the beaten-down shag carpet, the paneled walls, the same stains on the ceiling. Complimenting each other were the matching framed pictures of an elderly man and woman praying gratefully before eating some pitifully small meal. Over in the corner, stood their television, video machine, and a dozen old movies stacked up. Over the fish tank was another picture; this one featured an artist's rendering of Jesus praying against a large rock on the night of His arrest, bright moonlight beaming down on His anguished face. Someone had touched the picture up by applying a thin layer of glitter to the sky.

Clay was lying across the couch. Even though they had all visited him in the hospital, the sight of him was still startling. The mysterious space where his lower legs should be drew uncontrollable attention to itself. That would look unnatural on anyone; but in his case, it was still an unbelievable scenario. It was like a piano player who had lost his hands. It was not right.

"Clay? Clay? Your friends are here to see you." Maxine rushed over, grabbed the remote, and began to turn the volume down on the TV.

An awkward chorus of the usual greetings began. Clay did not look up as he returned their *Hello's*. He just kept staring at the game show that occupied the screen.

Maxine wanted to start a conversation among them, but she resisted that urge and excused herself from the room. She went back to the kitchen where she was making some sort of casserole.

"Have a seat," Clay said. He did not sound excited, friendly, or happy. His invitation sounded like an irritated form of politeness. They all complied with his offer and sat.

Silence. The clock ticked. The fish tank made its gurgling noise. The volume on the TV was turned down to the point where no one could hear the audience cheering on the game show.

The boys looked nervously at each other. With their eyes, they were seeming to beg one another to start a conversion. Ordinarily, they would all be talking at once. Logically, the outspoken Mike would be the one. "Well, Clay, I'll bet you sure are glad to be out of that hospital. I am certainly glad to be visiting you here in your own home again. While you were in the hospital, I would have to park around back. It's so funny to walk past dozens of nurses smoking outside." He looked at Billy and Curtis hoping to get them to chime in. "I wonder what percentage of nurses smoke."

"No kidding," Curtis added.

"Seriously," Mike continued. "I would bet that the ratio between smoking nurses to nonsmoking nurses is higher than it would be in any other profession."

Curtis again tried to keep the conversation going. "That's pretty strange. Then when we go see the nurses, they tell us what to do and what not to do in order to get better and stay healthy. And yet there they are, a majority of them, outside smoking. There must be a joke in there somewhere. Is that anything like taking marital advice from someone who is cheating on their spouse? That doesn't make sense to me at all."

Billy rolled his eyes. They did not come over to Clay's house to make unflattering remarks about nurses who smoke. He began. "Dude, we've been missing you at the school. People keep asking me about you. I tell them that you are doing well. That's what your mom and Mike have been telling us."

Silence. It was a curious silence - - full of telling. The silence spoke of great pain, confusion, anger, and disappointment. But it also was full of a well-meaning desire to help.

Mike went with the change of subject. *Maybe this one will get things started and break some ice around here.* "Track certainly doesn't seem the same without you, that's for sure."

Don't talk about track, Curtis was thinking.

Mike continued. "Cameron Phillips is pushing himself more than ever. With you gone, he has some pretty big shoes to …" Mike stopped suddenly. His face turned apologetic. He thought, *Oh no! I said 'big shoes.'*

Curtis tried to save him. "Have you been keeping up with the homework assignments?"

Clay's voice was unenthusiastic. "Not really. Although there really wasn't much else to do in the hospital. Daytime TV gets old and nighttime TV isn't much better." This did not sound like his usual tone. In the past, he was always very positive and full of good spirits. Making disparaging remarks seemed against his nature.

Curtis plugged on. "Have you been keeping up with the math."

"Sorta. Mom is good at it and she's been helping me."

"How have you been doing with this *Pride and Prejudice* book?"

"I'm trying to get into it but it's hard for me. I keep falling asleep. But I have a hard enough time reading books that actually sound interesting to me, so that's no surprise. This one seems like just a bunch of girls a long time ago going to parties and talking about boys. I don't know. Maybe there is a good story in there. Maybe I'm not really giving it much of a chance."

A bright smile appeared on Mike's face. "At least, you're honest. It has put me to sleep on more than one occasion - - and that's just in class." A light laugh followed, but Mike quickly noticed that he was the only one who had laughed and stopped immediately. "We're going to Billy's house later this week to read some chapters together and talk about them. You know, like we did last year with *The Scarlet Letter* and *Animal Farm*. It is really helpful. You ought to come to the next one if you're still having troubles with the book."

He shrugged. "Yeah. Maybe."

Silence.

Billy had an idea. "Hey! Do you want to hear a joke?"

Clay shrugged again. "Sure."

Billy sat up in his seat and began to talk using his hands. (He must have acquired that gift from his mother.) "A knight left the Chess set and got a job at the circus as a tightrope walker. On the first night, he is about to step out on the tightrope and the ringmaster yells up at him, 'Watch out for that third step; it's a doozey!'" This time, it was Billy who was the singular source of laughter. He stopped quickly and felt like a partial idiot for telling the questionable joke in the first place. "Well, I guess it isn't very funny."

Clay was far from laughing. In spite of that, he actually intervened and said, "No. It's a funny joke. A knight taking that third step would take him off the tightrope. I'm sorry. I just don't ... I don't feel much like jokes today. In fact, I don't feel like talking right now at all. I'm sorry, guys."

Silence.

Curtis stood up. "Well, maybe you want us to leave you alone for now. We'll come back later when you are feeling better." The others got up to leave and made their way to the door.

"Mike?"

They all stopped and turned around. Mike answered back. "Yeah, Clay?"

"Thanks for swinging by every day to check up on me. I guess I'll see you tomorrow?"

"Sure thing, Clay."

"Guys, will you come back later too?"

Curtis cleared his throat. "If you want us to, we will."

"Yeah. That would be awesome. I'm afraid I'm not very pleasant company right now. It's just that I don't understand why this has happened to me. All my future plans just flew right out the window. Now, I have nothing good to look forward to. I am so mad right now. Why would God allow something like this to happen? I feel like I'm being punished for something. What could I have done to deserve this? What could I have possibly done to deserve this?"

Curtis was standing all the way in front of the door, but his voice was clear and direct as though he were standing over Clay. "I don't know much, but I *do* know that God has a plan and it is usually something that we don't understand. ... at least at first."

"How can God expect anything good to come out of this? Did I do something wrong? Did I do something to make Him mad?"

Mike replied, "I don't think so. I can't see God being that way – not His style."

Curtis added, "What would Mr. Harris say right now? He would quote that verse from, I think, Isaiah 55:8-9 – the one that says something about God's ways being higher than our ways and His thoughts being higher than our thoughts, something like that."

Mike took over again. "Try to have faith. God knows exactly what He's doing. He knows much more about this than we do."

"Faith?! Humph. Is that what you came over to say?"

Billy shook his head. "No. We just came over to check up on you and see how you're doing. That's all."

Clay seemed to be getting mad. "Well, you've checked up on me. I guess you can all go."

That was weird. Clay was not in the habit of speaking to anyone that way. He usually brought warmth to the table. But the boys were hardly in the position to argue with him. If he wanted to be left alone, they were going to leave him alone. Whatever it was that was tearing at him would not go away easily. They quietly exited the room and went back to Mr. Harris' truck.

After a few seconds, Maxine returned to the den confused, sensing something was wrong. "Where did your friends go?"

"They had to leave." Clay choked a little on his words, picked up the remote, and went back to his game show.

Maxine's face reflected her confusion and her concern. "Well, that was nice of them to stop by. Don't you think so?"

Clay grunted instead of giving his mom a proper acknowledgement.

CHAPTER 26

MUSTANGS VS. CHEVETTES

Later that evening, Billy found himself sitting on the floor of his room. He had in his hand his copy of *Pride and Prejudice*. In the story, the mother of the girls was going on and on about how one of the visiting men was so incredibly wealthy - - in fact, that seemed to be the only thing this lady ever had on her mind. Without him realizing it, all this talking about marrying into wealth turned Billy's mind back to his own situation.

To him, this entire set-up was stupid. His parents were sitting on more wealth than he could have earlier imagined; and so far, the only piece of this wealth that he had seen was nothing. He could search the house up and down and never find any kind of clue that they were anything but middle-class, and probably lower middle-class at that. Being the youngest member of his grade, he was not going to drive solo to school legally at all that year; but several of his classmates were driving to school already and that looked so cool to him. With all the money his family supposedly had, he could actually get a car that would even shame Wesley Porterfield's. Getting a sweet car would certainly improve his social standing, instead of living the outcast life of the pedestrian and constantly bumming rides from others. Billy looked around. *And then what?* he asked himself. *Bring all of his popular friends to this ugly old house? One problem at a time.* Billy stood on his sleeping feet, got the blood circulating again, and cut through the house toward the carport.

William was dressed in a pair of jeans and some old t-shirt from some event he attended years ago. He was listening to a recording of a guy named

Van Cliburn banging something on a piano by Rachmaninoff, but his attention was actually focused on one of their wooden dining room chairs. It was partly propped up using a mounted set of vice grips. He was quite busy for the moment, but he smiled up at Billy as his son approached. "Hey, Sport."

"Hey. What are you doing? Fixing the chair again? Dad! Why don't we just get some new chairs for the dining room? ... and maybe a new table?" ... *and maybe a new house?* he thought. Billy's voice switched over to sarcasm. "Think we have enough money to afford that?"

William paused. "New chairs?" William thought about that proposal with some interest. "Hmmm. That isn't a bad idea." He went back to his work. "Why don't you go talk it over with your mother and see what she thinks. I'll go along with whatever she wants. I'm good either way." William hammered in another finishing nail into the upper part of a leg.

While he watched his dad work for a moment, he began to think about Chloe's party. There was absolutely no way his parents would agree to let him go. He would have a better chance at running for President. What was the big deal anyway? It was just a party? His parents were way too strict about this stuff. But how to get there? There had to be a way. Then a plan magically sprouted in his mind. It was risky and he would need some assistance – but even then, this *assistance* may not be particularly keen about the idea either. He would have to give this considerable thought. But fortunately Step One was easy. Time to engage. "Dad, I think Curtis wants me over at his house Saturday night."

Billy was not in the habit of lying to his parents. In fact, this would never occur under normal circumstances. But these unusual times desperately called for unusual methods. His dishonesty would be completely justified if it served a good purpose. ... or so he thought.

His dad stood up straight and laid his hammer on a nearby table. "That's fine with me if your mom has no objections. Let's see, that's the night that we get an extra hour." He rolled his eyes and smiled. "Yeah, you two boys will be up extra late." He stepped back from his finished product. "So what do you think? Hopefully, this chair is stronger now."

Huh? Is Billy actually getting away with this? Normally, his dad would see right through his little scheme. He must be getting better at fooling his parents – or at least, his distracted father. Just to make sure his request did not lose any of its momentum, it was time for a little compliment. Billy walked up to the chair and gently rubbed his hands over the leg that was so weak. "Thanks. Curtis will swing by around six o'clock to pick me up. And by the way, the chair looks good, good and strong."

Have you ever had one of those moments where you believed that everything would have been much better if you could just stop talking? But some people just cannot let stuff go. Billy is one of those people. In fact, there was even a brief pause in which something inside his head said, "Yeah, don't even go there." But he opened his mouth anyway and the words came out on their own. Sound familiar?

"You know, after my birthday, Curtis wouldn't have to pick me up if I had my own car?"

Physically, William appeared to be ignoring him as he went about returning his tools. But mentally, he was engaged in their conversation. "Yes. I suppose that is true."

Billy was caught off-guard again by his dad's eagerness to agree with that statement. A small feeling of hope was felt deep inside his chest. Could this be his lucky night? "Would you or mom object to me having my own car?"

"Probably not. Have you come across anything you like yet?"

Were his ears deceiving him? Was opportunity finally and unexpectedly knocking on his door? "As a matter of fact, I went down to Veazey's Auto today and …"

William stopped and turned to face Billy. "Veazey's? All their cars are new and sporty."

"Well … yeah."

"Well how are you going to afford something like that?"

Suddenly, the volume of Billy's voice sank a couple of decibel levels. "I thought that you and mom have the money to buy one."

William blatted out a quick laugh. "We have the money to buy ten. But *you* don't have the money to buy any."

Billy's shoulders lost their strength and began to slouch. "So what am I supposed to do?"

William returned to his tools as he spoke. "Easy. We will use this as a teachable moment."

That is all he had to say. Billy rolled his tired eyes in annoyance. *Here comes the speech*, he thought to himself.

William continued, "We'll check the newspapers and used car lots. We'll put together a financial plan. We'll have to figure in gas and insurance. There are lots of important things to consider. You might have to get a job, but it is hard to find a job for kids that have Sundays free. So we may not force that one. But we will definitely have to use our heads and get something practical."

Billy's little kid days were far behind him. In fact, he was nearly as tall as his father. But every once in a while, that same little boy would come out. This was one of those times. "Dad! No! You're gonna get me something ugly. Can't we please get me something that is cool?"

In stark contrast, William's voice became decidedly more stern. "You are an inexperienced driver. Why should I put you in the most expensive car we can find just so you can ding it up? In fact, your first car should probably be older than you are."

"That is so uncool!"

"Now hold on a minute." William ceased from his work and looked at his son. "What are we talking about here exactly? You looking cool? Or getting you something that you can drive?"

"Why not both?"

If Billy were not so mad, he might have actually been able to hear the hint of regret and the strong sound of reason behind his dad's next words. But no. "Look. I see this every day. Most kids who drive Mustangs end up treating them like they were Chevettes because they did nothing to earn it. They feel that they are entitled to a nice car. No sacrifice was involved. Likewise, your average teenager driving a Chevette will treat his or her car as if it were a Mustang – because they had to work hard for it. It increases in value to the person who struggled to get it."

Billy interrupted, "Ah! But that's not how it is *all* the time. Some of those driving Mustangs are very grateful to have them. They're not all that way."

"Of course not. Everyone is different. I quite agree."

Billy waited uncomfortably for a further comment. When one was not immediately provided, he proceeded with the thought. "I could be one of those that's different."

"Yes. You *could* be," William confessed. An unintentional moment of silence followed. William shrugged. " ...or you may not be."

Billy was fit to be tied. "What makes you think I'm not?!"

William's tone was calm - - which made Billy even more furious. "Well, for one thing, we're just simply talking about this and you are already getting mad and defensive. What may I deduce from that? And have you taken this issue to God first before you made all these plans? Remember what it says in Proverbs, 'Commit thy works unto the LORD, and thy thoughts shall be established.' [Proverbs 16:3] Have you even prayed about this?"

"Yes!"

"Uh-huh. And what did that prayer sound like?"

"'Dear God, would you please get me a really cool car?'"

William smiled in partial amusement and shook his head.

"I've got a book to read. Thanks for the help." He reentered the house sounding bitter.

Billy marched through the dining room, the living room, down the hall, and into his bedroom. "Taking the issue to God first? For crying out loud, it's just a car. I didn't ask for a lecture about Mustangs and Chevettes. Man, I don't even know what a Chevette is. Is it anything like a *Corvette*? They both end with *vette*." Grabbing his copy of *Pride and Prejudice*, he plopped himself down on the floor. *This whole thing is so stupid*, he thought to himself. *Everything weird manages to happen to me. What next?*

He opened his book and held it. He began to read. But before he came to the end of that page, he noticed something unusual. The page stuck to his thumb. "That's weird," he said out loud. He backed his thumb away from the book, but the page began to tear. "Rats! If I'm not careful, I'll have to buy yet another copy of this thing." He tried to pull the page from his thumb but discovered that his other fingers were also sticking to the cover and other pages. Before he realized what was happening, he had torn a page out of the book with his left thumb and another stuck between his right thumb and forefinger. Another was ripping between the fingers of his left hand. "No, no, no, no!!" Soon he found himself with torn pages attached to each finger and the book's cover hanging from his hands. "Oh man! What is going on?"

His dad had just returned from the carport and was washing his hands in the kitchen as Billy ran out toward him. William looked over and noticed all these pages stuck to his son's fingers in a curiously strange fashion.

Billy rushed over to his dad and held up his fingers. "What is this?"

William looked at his hands closely and smelled his son's fingers. "That's wood glue." He started to laugh.

"WHAT?! Oh man!" His voice squeaked, adding insult to injury. Billy was mad at first, but the sound of his dad laughing was too contagious. Almost instantly, he started laughing with his dad. Curious about what was going on, Diane walked in and soon all three of them were laughing. Yep, this one was definitely going in William's journal.

The same old bookstore was about to close when Billy raced in. His presence there at closing time was starting to be predictable. He frantically grabbed the last copy of *Pride and Prejudice* that was on shelf and rushed over to the checkout line. Again, he was in Midge's line – who else would be there? *Does this lady ever go home?* he asked himself.

Midge, appearing the same as ever in her poly-blend pants, looked at him and then glanced down at the book he was buying. "You know, we're running out of copies of that particular book. If I may make a suggestion, you might try buying up copies of something else. We've got about six copies of *The Call of the Wild* in stock."

Billy tried to come up with something funny to say. His mind was a complete blank however, so he stayed silent.

Midge's nose wrinkled up. Her eyes got inquisitive. She frowned. "Do you smell that?" She started sniffing. "It smells like gasoline." She leaned forward and realized that it was coming from Billy. "Young man, why do you smell like gasoline?"

"It was the only way that I could get the pages off of my hands."

That was all she needed to know. Midge was having a long day and needed to go home.

CHAPTER 27

A REGULAR PERSON

"I would like to state now, and for the record, that this is one of the lamest ideas ever. I've got a good mind to go home and do something that *normal* people do." Mike sat in the Harris' living room as a few more students were trickling in. Aside from Billy, Curtis, and Mike, there were about four more students in attendance so far. "I could be at home right now shooting zombies on my computer."

Billy looked over at him. "But you'd be missing all this fun," he said sarcastically through clenched teeth. "Besides, no one is forcing you to be here, ya know. If I didn't live here, I'd go home too." Billy was of two minds concerning the plans for that evening. Opening their home up to a few students to read and discuss two chapters of their book was actually his brainchild and he had promoted it. But that did not mean that he had to like it.

Curtis was fairly supportive. He enjoyed himself no matter where he was - - as long as it was with the gang. In addition, Mrs. Harris made brownies, so what would it hurt? "Yeah," he replied. "I suppose you *could* go home and read chapters 18 and 19 of *Pride and Prejudice* all by your lonesome. But I think we all know that that's not gonna happen. Besides, this is really the logical place."

"The logical place? What is that supposed to mean?" Billy asked.

"Well, I was just thinking that since your dad ..."

"I know. I know. ' ... the English teacher.'" Billy let out a defeated sigh. "This great big world is chopped full of interesting professions – and yet my dad deliberately chose to teach high school English. Why couldn't my dad be something cool? Why couldn't my dad be like a football coach or something?"

Mike laughed. "That may not be a cool as you think, Billy Boy. Sometimes the coach's son is expected to really deliver - - and I'm not talking about just making the team. I mean being the *captain* of the team. And anything less than a state title is a letdown. *But no pressure.* As the English teacher's son, you are expected to do what exactly? Defend the merits of the Oxford comma?"

Billy knew what a comma was, of course; but he was a little fuzzy on the *Oxford comma.* Was it a fancier comma than the others? Did it wear glasses, a bowtie, and a pair of leather wingtip shoes? He ignored the comment and introduced a new topic. "Is Clay coming tonight?"

Mike had been trying to persuade Clay to get out of the house for a while, but it was no use. "Nope. He said he didn't want to come. He doesn't want to do anything except watch TV and complain about having nothing to do but watch TV."

Curtis shook his head and looked at the floor. "I sure wish he would do something - - get out of the house and meet people. Maybe we could figure out a way to kidnap him - - just for an hour or so."

As the boys spoke, the doorbell rang again and Diane rushed over to let in the next student.

Mike spoke up as if he wanted to add one more comment before the next person entered. "Well, I go see him every day and he isn't listening to me. He just sits there feeling sorry for himself. I really can't blame him for that. He's having to cross some really long bridges that none of us have ever had to cross. But none of this sounds like him. Maybe you guys could try talking to him." He glanced over at Billy's mom and saw who she was letting in. Instant irritation was read on Mike's face and biting sarcasm could be heard in his voice. "Well, that's great. Sensational. Look who just strolled in here – like having to read this book isn't bad enough."

Curtis turned his head to see what Mike saw. "What are you talking about now?"

"Rich boy – eleven o'clock. This party's in the tank."

Diane was called back to the kitchen, leaving Wesley standing awkwardly next to the door. He looked uncomfortable and peered around the room for someone to talk to. As always, he was the best-dressed person there. Hair, complexion, body mass, it was all too perfect as far as the other teens were concerned. And yet, there was an emptiness in his eyes, a desperate sadness which most of the others never saw; they only saw his money and his seeming perfections.

Curtis looked over at Wesley and then returned his gaze to Mike. "Oh, come on. We all know that you don't like the guy. Why don't you give him a chance? He might be cool."

Billy agreed. "This reading is open to anybody. I'm going over there to welcome him here."

"Yeah. Me too." Curtis got up to follow Billy over to where Wesley was standing, but he stopped and turned toward Mike. "Hey. Try to behave tonight." Curtis left Mike and caught up with Billy.

"No promises," he said quietly to himself.

Curtis was the first to speak. In a loud voice, he approached Wesley. "Well, well, well. As I live and breathe, look who's here." They shook hands.

As Curtis spoke, Wesley's countenance changed to gladness. The difference was night and day. The boys had no idea just what a little camaraderie meant to their guest.

Billy echoed Curtis' sentiments with a normal inside voice. "Wesley, it is good to have you here tonight. I can't promise that this won't be dull, but at least there's food."

"Thanks for having me over, guys. I hope you fellows don't mind my crashing your little soiree. There are parts of this book that I'm not getting, so here I am. ... that is, if I am welcome here. This was open for anyone, right?"

Curtis beat Billy to the answer. "Of course you are welcome here. Did you bring your copy of the book with you?"

While they spoke, the doorbell rang again and Diane let in a couple more students. At this rate, they were going to have a nice crowd, assuming that the food would hold out.

"Right here." Wesley held up his phone. Apparently, he had already uploaded a digital copy of the book. There was something slightly funny about reading a book two centuries old on something as new and trendy as the latest phone.

Curtis approved. "Good. That means that everyone has a copy. Well, almost everyone." He theatrically turned his head to face Billy.

Billy's back stiffened uncomfortably. "Curtis …" He spoke with an *I'm-warning-you* tone. But, none of the inflections of Billy's voice were going to stop Curtis from giving his buddy a hard time. He had him right where he wanted him.

"It would seem that Billy doesn't have one – a copy of the book, I mean. Last night, he managed to glue the book to his hands." Curtis playfully smiled at Billy and rested his hand on his buddy's shoulder as he spoke. "Now, our friend here can honestly say that he couldn't put the book down."

Wesley gave a light laugh. "That's hilarious."

Billy was less amused. "Hardy-har-har."

"Oh! But that isn't even the funny part. He actually purchased another copy earlier today so he would have one for tonight; but as of forty minutes ago, *that* book was also destroyed."

"Huh? How? What happened?"

Billy tilted his head forward and glared at Curtis under his eyebrows. Again, a word of caution could be detected in his voice. "Easy …"

Curtis took the hint - - and yet proceeded anyway. "I am not exactly at liberty to say what happened to his copy. But let's just say that a toilet was involved." Curtis suddenly broke out in hysterics. "Use your imagination."

Billy interjected. "Do *not* use your imagination. It wasn't as bad as it sounds."

Wesley was trying hard not to laugh. "Is all this true?"

"Certainly not!" Billy defended himself. "That last book was actually bought late last night after the incident with the wood glue – and NOT this morning. That much of this story was false." He elbowed Curtis playfully. "But I don't see why we should go into all of that."

Curtis shrugged. "I don't know what you're worried about. I didn't tell Wesley about the fish fry last year."

Wesley was all-ears, a truly captured audience. He had been without anyone to talk to for so long that this was an awesome treat. "Why? What about the fish fry?"

Curtis was seriously cracking-up at the question. "Funny you should ask. Mr. Harris was frying up some fish for everyone last fall and it attracted every cat from here all the way to Mountain View."

Billy nearly put Curtis in a spirited headlock. "Excuse my simple-minded friend here. He is prone to flights of exaggeration. You would do well to believe only half of what this character says."

Still laughing, Curtis began to give Wesley an abbreviated version of Billy's one-man war against Jane Austen's most celebrated novel. Billy seemed to have serious issues concerning the safety of these books. Wesley began to laugh a little – a nice thing for Wesley. It broke the ice and he was able to relax a little bit. Could he actually be in the company of friends?

But then Wesley peered across the room and noticed that Mike was glaring straight at him with burning eyes. This immediately affected his mood. All of this lighthearted fun was exchanged for a chilling sense of dread. Wesley could actually feel all the hairs on his arms stand at attention. Mike's gaze was right out of a horror movie. Adding to the weirdness, in the brief time that they locked eyes, there was a loud ZAP and suddenly the lights went out - - *all* the lights. Wesley's whole body tensed up. He briefly imagined Mike coming over to kill him.

A few of the guests let out a little scream. The only light in the room came from the door and windows, and of course from those kids who were on their phones. Everything went from warm and friendly to dark and creepy in half-a-second. The effect was enough to force Wesley to wonder if Mike had some menacing form of telekinesis. Maybe he should make a run for his car.

The other guests all made alarmed noises betraying their surprise. But raising above them all was Billy's voice. "Oh, not again." He faced the group in order to address them. "Okay, folks. Don't panic. The lights will come right back on as soon as my dad reaches the breaker."

Curtis stepped toward Billy and in a low tone said, "Dude, what's up with that? Forgot to pay the light bill?"

"No. It's our stupid dryer. It must be at least as old as my parents and half the age of this broken-down house. And naturally my dad picks *this* moment as the perfect time to dry some clothes. I swear. This is so embarrassing."

Everyone could hear Mr. Harris scrambling around and saying something like an apology from elsewhere in the house. Almost immediately, the lights returned and everyone went back to their previous conversations – but with considerably more caution.

Out of his own mounting nervousness, Wesley looked back toward Mike, but found that he was suddenly gone. When the lights came back on, he had disappeared. Wesley started to freak out a little. *This guy may not be human. No wait. He merely went over to the kitchen to put another head on his soft drink. Well, that's a relief,* Wesley thought.

"Behold, the lights return, and right on cue." Curtis turned to Wesley and, in a pathetically fake British accent, said, "Come, Sir Wesley! Jane Austen awaits our good pleasure."

Avoiding a tempting glance in Mike's direction, Wesley smiled and remained focused on Curtis and Billy. He was actually around people who were treating him like just another guy, money or no money. He returned the tone with his own horrible British accent. "Please. After you, my good man." He bowed slightly forward and made a grand gesture toward the living room.

"Thank you, good sir. You are too kind."

Billy rolled his eyes as if that was the corniest thing ever to be said at a place where people were ironically reading Jane Austen. Maybe it was, but inwardly he was glad that Wesley arrived and that Curtis was trying to make him feel comfortable. Might as well; this entire thing was weird from the beginning.

The car rounded the corner onto the Harris' street. They did not need the exact address; with all the cars in the driveway and parked out on the curb, their house was easy to spot. Berly had talked Maggie into coming with her to the Harris' reading party. Maggie was less than thrilled. She brought her car to a stop.

"Okay. Just so we can get our story straight, what is the ridiculous reason why I'm here?"

Berly grinned slightly. "The same as me: to read chapters eighteen and nineteen of *Pride and Prejudice.*"

"I *have* read it. ... twice. Don't you think that a junior might stand out in a room full of sophomores? If anything, I should be at home right now reading *To Kill a Mockingbird* for my own class. Look, I should just march in there and tell them all the truth. I'll tell them that you twisted my arm to come tonight because you are too chicken to come over here on your own like a big girl."

Berly got a little defensive. "I asked you to come over to keep us going in the right direction since you've already read it."

"That's funny. I thought my job – as I understand it – is to make sure that you don't embarrass yourself too much when you start drooling over Mr. Harris' goofy son." Maggie stopped herself short as she did the math in her head. "Wait a minute. Or is that the whole point of this?" She looked back up at Berly. "Are you here just to get noticed?"

"Ha! Certainly not." Berly was not convincing.

"Whatever."

Both girls got out of the car and made their way up to the house.

Upon ringing the doorbell, Billy answered. Absent-minded as always, he told the ladies to come in and grab a seat anywhere one could be found. They ended up going one direction while his mind went another.

Wesley returned to the living room after a couple of brownies and a small cup of milk (that is the best thing with brownies after all). He began to look for a seat. There was one available next to a lovely young girl. Wesley did not know her personally, but he *did* recognize her as another sophomore. He decided to approach her. "Hi there. I don't think that I know you. My name is Wesley."

"Well, hello Wesley. I'm Lauren. It's nice to meet you." Her voice was bright, intelligent, and had a touch of humor behind it.

"May I sit here?"

"Sure. Be my guest."

He sat in the seat next to her and offered her a brownie. She took half. "So Lauren. That's a pretty name."

"Yeah. There's a kind of story behind it. My dad loves classic movies and I was named after a famous movie star. All three of us girls were. I have an older sister named Greta and a younger sister named Audrey. Dad calls us his little starlets."

"So did your dad make star-shaped signs with your names on them and hang them on your bedroom doors? That would make them look like real dressing rooms."

"Ha! No. But that's funny. I can see him making signs for us all: Audrey, Lauren, and Greta."

Wesley made a face. "Greta? Your poor sister."

Lauren laughed. "Oh no. I think it's a pretty name. But I like mine better."

Wesley knew nothing about these movie stars, but he was enjoying talking to this girl. So he decided to keep this going. "So this *Lauren* who you were named after, have you ever seen any of her movies?"

"Well, I've seen one of them one night with my dad – and it was pretty good. She was being held up in this hotel in the Florida Keys by a bunch of gangsters. Then this hurricane came down on the hotel. All the gangsters got scared and were freaking out …"

Wesley found himself genuinely interested in what she was saying. While she was going on about this old movie, he was busy studying her face and familiarizing himself with her voice. She was actually interesting to him. And the best part was that she was not treating him like a stack of hundred dollar bills. Come to think of it, neither did Curtis or Billy. Wow. That was refreshing. He may have come to the right place that night. Here, he felt like just a regular person, one of the crowd.

Diane was busy making grilled cheese sandwiches when William entered the kitchen. "These are almost ready and the cheese dip is over there." She pointed.

"I'm on it," William replied. "'Blessed are they who do hunger and thirst after righteousness for they shall be filled.'" He lifted the bowl.

"Honey, I think you are taking that verse a little out of context."

"Fair enough." He left the room with the cheese dip and set it out for the kids. Within seconds, he was back for the chips and put them out as well. The drinks were already in place. He returned to the kitchen and leaned against the countertop next to Diane.

In a joking get-out-of-here voice, Diane turned to William and said, "Uh … shouldn't you be in there to monitor this thing?"

"Can't. Billy said, and I quote, 'Dad! You're not seriously going to be in there, are you? Thanks to *you*, I'm going to be a social outcast.'" The quote portion of William's sentence was naturally done in a 'Valley-Girl' voice - - which Billy does not have.

"Oh, go on. What if an argument gets started? They may need someone in there to referee."

"What argument? They're talking about a book that is over two centuries old. This is Jane Austen we are talking about. What could possibly go wrong?"

CHAPTER 28

THE BRICK TISSUE BOX

Surrounded by fellow students in the middle of his own living room, Billy shook his head in frustration. "I am not understanding this at all." It was clear that others in the group were agreeing with him.

Immediately, Mike's eyes went wild with anger. "Oh? I understand. I understand completely. Allow me to explain it to you. Apparently this *Mr. Darcy*, or whatever he is, is way too good to talk to Mr. Collins. He is just another rich snob. He probably sees Mr. Collins as being so far beneath him that he isn't even worth his contempt." That sentence may have been worded strangely, but he managed to get his point across.

The dozen or so students around the room were momentarily startled by Mike's outburst. It stood in contrast with the indulgent voices that had been reading the book out loud. First, the power outage caused by a cantankerous dryer caught everyone off guard; now an explosive reaction from Mike. What next? A herd of spooked bison?

Wesley shifted unnervingly in his chair. He might have been having fun earlier talking to Billy, Curtis, and this interesting girl Lauren, but not so much now. He knew that Mike's comment may have been made in general, but he still felt that it was directed at him.

Fortunately, Maggie was there to save the day. She had read the book twice before (including once last year in Mr. Harris' class) and had seen one of the many movie versions. She was not exactly playing hostess or a leader of the group, but she was able to speak up and help them out. She brushed her hair to the side and said, "That's not it at all. It's all a question of propriety."

Billy's face was already rather blank. But somewhere down in there, he spoke up. "*Propriety*? What do you mean?"

She clarified. "It's all about what is socially appropriate or inappropriate."

Mike acted as if this were personal. Sometimes, people are deliberately trying to be offended no matter what. This was one of those times. "So it is inappropriate for this Mr. Collins to even speak to Mr. Darcy? Why? Just because he's rich?"

Curtis had been silently thinking about what had been said. "No. I don't think that is what they are saying at all. I think it is because they have not been formally introduced by a common friend." He turned his eyes to Maggie. "At least, that's how it sounds. Is that it?"

Maggie pulled one of her legs up in the chair. "That is it exactly. In this culture that we are reading about, that is simply not done. To speak to someone of his class socially, you need to have a formal introduction, and it has to be made by a common acquaintance."

Mike looked back at her. "Speaking of introductions, who are you exactly?"

Berly finally spoke up in a dismissive voice. "It's okay. This is Maggie. She's with me."

Mike wanted to ask, *And just who are you supposed to be, friend of Maggie?* But he stopped himself. Instead, he leaned back in his chair. "Well, I would have a difficult time living in that culture, I can tell you that! If I want to meet someone, I'll march right up to that person. I'm not shy. And I don't care who they are. No one is better than anyone else." Mike sat straight up in his chair and looked directly at Wesley with fiery eyes. "And if any of these rich, uppity people don't like it, they can either get over it or get out of my face."

The recipient of that comment was difficult to miss. Everyone was quiet. Billy sat in his seat stunned by his friend's obvious rudeness. This was not how tonight was supposed to be. Having all these kids over to read a couple of chapters in this classic book may have been a total mistake. He looked around the room at the other students to see if anyone else was as uncomfortable as he was. The truth was that they were all uncomfortable, but none more than Wesley. The implication was clear and unapologetic.

Like some unscripted, messed-up joke, Diane walked in with a big plate full of brownies. "Some additional brownies are ready. Why don't you all take about a ten minute break and grab some while they're warm?" The other students complied, eager to lay hands on them while they were nice and soft. Mr. Harris even marched in with plastic cups and a second gallon of cold milk - - whole milk! The students were prepared to drink it up like kittens.

Curtis rushed over to Billy. He had definite concerns about Mike's attitude toward Wesley. This was inexcusable. Other guests may have missed it, but they caught it head-on. "Can I see you for a minute? We need to talk about this." They disappeared back down the hall and into Billy's bedroom.

Mike sat there, his eyes still cruelly fixed on his target.

Likewise, Wesley sat paralyzed in his seat, completely aware of Mike's stare. Everyone else had gotten up and were walking around engaging in polite banter. He wanted to follow their lead; but as long as Mike was giving him the cold stare, that seemed impossible. After a moment, Wesley gathered the nerve to get up out of his seat and started quietly for the door. He figured that he might as well go back home. Obviously, his presence was a distraction. His noiseless departure remained unnoticed by everyone - - everyone, that is, except for Mike, who began to grin.

Students were talking. Brownies were being devoured at an alarming rate. In a few minutes, Wesley's absence would be noticed by Lauren, as well as the two boys. But he was gone with no announcement, no goodbye, nothing.

Mike spoke to no one. He kept looking up at the closed door. It had only been just a few short seconds since Wesley left, but Mike was not yet finished. He still had more to get off his chest. He sprang to his feet and exited the house, making a beeline for the departing Wesley. Perhaps he could catch him before he got to his car.

Outside, Mike yelled after Wesley with his arms extended. "Hey! Moneybags! Where are you going? Weren't you enjoying the book reading? Or was the conversation amongst us surfs not stimulating enough for you?" Without missing a beat, Mike went straight into a bitterly sarcastic tone. "Oh wait! I think I just broke some sort of protocol. We haven't been formally introduced yet."

Wesley was just reaching his car when he stopped and turned to face Mike. "I'm sorry, but is there something that I have done to offend you?"

Mike took one step forward and his voice became low and stern. "Your whole being offends me – you and your fancy car and your big house, all your pricy clothes and the snobby way that you conduct yourself. Is that why you came out here tonight? To show off in front of the bourgeois?"

Wesley opened his car door. "No. Far from it. Aside from trying to get a better grasp on this book …" He held up his phone and then tossed it onto the passenger seat. " …I guess I came out looking for some friends, people to socialize with. But it looks like I came to the wrong place for that."

"You can say that again, Wesley Porterfield the third."

Wesley looked down at the road and seriously thought about getting in his car right then. Instead, he took a deep breath and looked back up at Mike. This time, it was Wesley that was giving the piercing look. "You know what's so funny? Most people want to be my friend *because* of my family's money. You actually *dislike* me because of it. So once again, people don't see me at all; all they can see is the money. I don't know what it is about it, but it always seems to distance me from being in the loop. But I did learn something valuable tonight while I was here. When it comes right down to it, you're just as big a hypocrite as I have ever seen in my life."

That was it. From where Mike was standing, that Rubicon was crossed and that bridge was burning. "A what? A hypocrite?"

"You heard me."

"And just what is THAT supposed to mean?"

With keys in hand and his hands on the top of the car, Wesley leaned toward the car and looked over the top at Mike. "You may not know this but you and your little friends have a reputation; and it's a good one. Everyone in the school talks about how great you are, you and Clay, Billy, and Curtis. People really look up to you – and you don't even see it. You four are supposed to be these really awesome Christians. I really don't know what any of this Christian stuff is; but I can promise you one thing - - if THIS is what Christianity is all about, then I don't want any part of it. You're just another jerk - - and your friends probably are too. Just sayin'."

Touché. Mike was a rather mouthy person and has been pretty much all his life. But for the first time in perhaps ages, he was actually without words. Could Wesley be right about him? He was supposed to have been reflecting the love of God to those around him. Rather than just standing there dumbstruck or trying to defend himself, he slowly turned around and started to walk back toward the house.

"See you around the school, Christian." Hate-filled scorn stabbed its way through the night air and hit Mike right in the craw. In spite of his tough exterior, those words stung. Behind him, he heard the car door slamming shut.

For a split second, Mike had a thought.

He thought of his parents and the other '*scrollers*' at their church – or that is the moniker that the four boys secretively gave them. While their pastor was preaching the Word of God, the '*scrollers*' spent the entire time scrolling up and down on their phones. These were the folks who sometimes spent the service texting each other back and forth debating where they were going to eat after church rather than listening to the message. When the service was dismissed, Mike's parents and others were out the church doors like racehorses right out of the gate. The boys sometimes wondered how often someone unintentionally stomped on Bro. Wayne's feet as they sprinted to their cars.

This embarrassed Mike to no end because he knew that their pastor was the type of person who prayed hard over the messages and was no stranger to study. Bro. Wayne never went into a church service unprepared. He did all the work of a pastor while holding down another job, going to school one night a week, and trying to spend time with his family. Mike and the other boys considered it rude of his parents to be surfing the internet while the preacher was delivering his sermon. After all, these sermons were messages that God had put on his heart. They owed it to him to hear it out. Plus, it was only for their benefit.

Mike also knew that Bro. Wayne was not an idiot. There was no one-way mirror between the pastor and his congregation. He could easily see what all was going on. For example, there was a huge difference between someone who accessed a Bible app on their phone and those who were surfing the internet and/or playing games during the message. He also knew who was using that time as a quick power nap. Some of the kids were writing notes to each other and laughing amongst themselves. Impatient people were constantly looking at their watches. And just because these people were sitting in pews, it did not mean that they were invisible to someone at the pulpit. Mike felt that this behavior was a pointed insult to the pastor – and yet, Bro. Wayne never said a word of complaint.

Afterwards, his family would go out to eat and that was a nightmare all its own. If someone who sat down after them got served before they were, or if the food was not done just right, or they added up the amount incorrectly, Mike's mom was ready to do battle with the manager. But Mike was told by friends who worked in the restaurant business that that was typical. The Sunday lunch crowd was the worst. Mike often wondered if his mom understood that their server might not know Christ. They may be the only Jesus that this person would ever see – and their family had been setting a terrible example.

And now Mike was becoming the very thing that he disliked in his parents: prideful, arrogant, essentially all the things he accused Wesley of being. This was not cool. In addition, it was one thing for Wesley to think that way about Mike, but now Mike's attitude was being connected to Billy, Curtis, Clay, and all other Christians. *And who would ever think that way about Clay?*

In that frozen moment in time, a revelation came to Mike. He was being judgmental when he himself had issues to iron out with God. Just because he was not scrolling on his phone during church, who was to say that he was listening the message? His mind was often on other things during that time as well – and he would be lying to say otherwise. And even though some people were on their phones, how was he to know if they were hearing the sermon or not? Some folks can to two things at once – even though it might look rude. It was certainly not his place to pass judgment on these others.

But instead of looking at all the faults of other people, he realized that he needed to address the faults within himself. He and God had a lot of work to do; he needed to roll up his sleeves and start cleaning his own house. This was called humility, something he had lost contact with over time. The others may need to have that long talk as well; but that was entirely between them and God.

In that moment, Mike was determined to be different, to be genuine, to be more Christ-like. He needed to reacquaint himself to what Scripture called his "first love."

As that split second ended, Wesley started his engine.

No. This cannot be the way God intended it to be. Mike had failed God and he could not just let the conversation end this way. He turned and started back toward Wesley's car.

Wesley glanced over and saw Mike approaching. He cursed. "I don't have time for this," he said to himself. He threw the car in drive and stepped on the gas. The tires on his sporty new car squealed as he sped away from the Harris' house. In the back windshield, he could see Mike running after him and waving his arms. "What is that fool doing now? Is he trying to hit my car? Does he want a fight?" Fortunately, it was too late; Wesley was headed home.

In the meantime, Mike stopped running. After a couple of deep breaths, he turned back.

Other than half of a brownie, Wesley had not eaten anything over at the Harris' house and was feeling a little hungry. He ran in at that little place next to the bookstore and grabbed one of their popular ghost-pepper cheeseburgers and some fries to go. He planned to eat in the solitary atmosphere of his own home. At least there, he was welcome. He himself wondered how he was feeling. Furious or sad? Maybe it was a tossup. He had really hoped to be making friends, real friends - - not the vain, superficial friends that he was used to. Instead, all he found were fake Christians. The last thing the world needed was a bunch of people who were all too willing to talk about the love they have for everyone, but say the opposite with their actions. Those could be found in abundance.

But even he had to admit that Billy and Curtis were very friendly to him that evening. And as far as he knew, Clay had always treated him nicely. He was also curious about this girl he had just met. She seemed cool. But Mike was awful. The good news is that this evening was done. He had spoken his mind and was about to shut himself up in that huge fortress he called *home*.

His handsome sports car quietly rolled up into the driveway and came to a stop along the side of the house. Wesley turned off the engine and sat there quietly for the next ten seconds or so. Deep depression began to overwhelm him. The sun had gone down a while ago and his surroundings were finally showing signs of the darkening night. He reached in the bag and ate a small pinch of fries.

Climbing out of the car, he heard another car on the approach. He dismissed the sound at first, but this other car stopped right in front of his house. This sounded suspicious enough. Interested, Wesley turned and found Mike making a deliberate leap out of his car.

"Wesley! Hold up!" Mike began running up to him.

Wesley suddenly found himself in defense posture. He realized that he had no weapon with him. Maybe he could knock his assailant out with the cheeseburger. If he had to, he could thrust it in Mike's mouth and let the ghost pepper work its magic. "Mike, I'm in no mood to ..."

"Whoa, whoa, whoa! I didn't come over to fight." Mike thought under the circumstances to stop and maintain a safe distance; he realized that he had adequately ticked off Wesley and did not want to make matters any worse. He had done enough damage for one night. Now he wondered if he could fix something for a change. "I actually came over to apologize."

"Apologize? You? Yeah, right."

There was quite a lot that Mike needed to say and he was not sure how this was going to come out. But it was time to jump in with both feet. "Look. I just wanted to say that you were absolutely right, right about me, right about almost everything. And I just wanted you to know that I'm sorry. The truth is that I have not been a very good Christian lately. I freely admit that I am extremely imperfect. But please don't let my poor attitude and my obvious imperfections taint your views on God. Fortunately, the God I worship *is* perfect. He's perfect and loving and forgiving. And trust me, if He can forgive someone as imperfect as me, then He is indeed a mighty powerful God. Our churches are filled with imperfect people; but that's who God wants. He has seen value in me – value that I don't even see in myself. And I know for a fact that He sees value in you. So if you are on your own quest for God, I truly want for you to find Him. And please don't let someone like me – with all my flaws – stand in your way." That was about it, but he did not really know how to end his little speech. So he simply added, "I guess the bottom line is I'm sorry for the way I have acted." He looked down and noticed the bag of fast food in Wesley's hand and took a step back to leave. "I'll, uh … I'll just leave you now to whatever you were doing." He turned and started to walk back to his car.

Wesley honestly did not know how to react. This was the first time that he had ever seen Mike acting in a way that was not full of bottled-up hate. Searching for something to say, he looked up at Mike's car sitting in front of his house. "Dude, did you follow me all the way to my house in order to apologize? How did you do that? I made a stop on the way."

Mike turned back and grinned. He was a little embarrassed by the question. It did seem that he went out of the way - - but that was not all of the truth. "*Follow* would not be the most accurate word. I would've come out here at some point anyway." He pointed to a large white-bricked house with Doric columns surrounding the entry way. "I live just right over there in that oversized dog house, the brick tissue box."

"Huh? You live over there? Are you talking about that house with the gazebo on the side? The one with the outlandish fountain in the front? The house with the practically naked statues around a pool in the back? I make fun of that house all the time!"

Mike was laughing. "Yeah. It's a little gaudy, isn't it?"

"Well, it certainly has a style of its own."

Now both boys were laughing.

"Well, that's a diplomatic way of putting it. My parents aren't like independently wealthy or anything. But they *do* make more money than most people in this town and feel like they have to have the biggest and best thing out there. But I don't like being there. It's always, 'Take those shoes off. Don't touch this. Don't smudge that.' They even have a game room that I am not allowed in unless my dad is home. Sometimes I think they love their stuff more than they love me. Once I had my friend Clay over and …" He paused and looked up at Wesley. Just a few minutes ago, Mike hated Wesley's guts and now he was about to confide in him. Weird. Maybe he should dismiss the thought. "Actually, you don't want to hear all about that."

Wesley's mind began to work. "Uh, Mike. May I ask you a personal question?"

"Uh … I suppose so."

"Is your problem with me actually about me? Or is it more about my money and because your parents have money?"

Mike's eyes blinked and then looked toward the ground. "Well, that's a toughie. I never thought about it like that before. Maybe."

"It sounds to me like your problem is with your parents. And maybe you've been directing all of that frustration out on me. Okay. So your parents have money. Is that wrong?"

Mike felt inclined to answer even though he may not like what he had to say. "Uh, not really. I guess not. At least they earn their money. But I do sometimes wish that they didn't have so much of it. They would pay more attention to … Well, the money just makes my parents different."

"Different? How?"

Mike was hesitant at first. This was stuff that he had not told the others – especially Clay, and Clay was his best friend. It made them sound so spoiled. "Well, my folks just do weird things, and it is all because of their money. As an example, they flew down to Mexico last year for the Fall Equinox. They went down there to catch a shadow that appears that day in this place called Chichen Itza. The shadow looks like a snake on the side of a pyramid. But naturally, they got bored with it and left before this thing began. Why would they fly all the way down there just to go back to their hotel and watch it on TV? But that's how my parents roll. The month before that, they went skiing in Colorado and before that it was some beach in Florida and before that it was something else … They love to spend lots of money on nothing. And they're constantly posting pictures on social media of all this money they throw around. It's like their way of bragging to all their family and friends. It's embarrassing. And then there's the dogs …"

"The dogs? Oh yeah. I hear them barking every so often."

"Oh yes. I'm sure you do. My mom calls them her *babies*." Mike rolled his eyes at the thought. "They have like ten Pomeranians and they are so annoying. They bark all day and half the night. If one starts, they all start. Ugh."

Mike and Wesley stood there talking for the next ten to fifteen minutes. Mike had Wesley laughing at his stories about those dogs. He explained how they were all named after cities that have hosted the Olympic Games. He also said that his friends do not really come over much because he did not want them to feel poor – and this was mostly for Clay. But he used the dogs' constant racket as an excuse.

251

Mike again looked down at the bag from the restaurant and realized that he was keeping Wesley from eating. The ghost pepper cheese may be hot, but the burger itself would be cold. Mike was not doing Wesley any favors by standing there for so long. "Well, I had better be getting home. ... or maybe back to that reading party over at Billy's." He looked at the time on his phone. " ...or like I said, *home*." Mike turned to head back to his car.

"Hey, Mike!"

"Yeah?"

"We never did find out how this party ended - - not the one at Billy's house, the one in the book. You know, the dance with Mr. Darcy, Mr. Collins, and all them Bennett girls."

Mike pondered over this idea for just a moment. He smiled back and suggested, "Maybe after Mr. Darcy was insulted, a bunch of ninjas fell from the ceiling and killed Mr. Collins."

Wesley began to rub his chin and stare off into the distance. "A violent plot twist. I like."

After a quick laugh, both boys made their farewells. When Wesley went back into his house, he had determined that this night was not a total waste and that maybe he found what he was looking for after all - - a friend. The strangest part was that this new friend was the most unlikely of people, the one person who hated him the most.

Mike also felt that he had gained something interesting as he hopped back into his car. In his case, there was a renewed interest in being the best Christian that he could be. That desire had finally been restored. Perhaps for years, he had been growing more and more apathetic toward his relationship with God. But now he could see that people were watching him from afar. He did not realize it at first, but he was representing God at his school. Yes, an ambassador for Christ. It was a very flattering responsibility. And who knows? Maybe the opportunity of becoming the best Christian possible could be a fun challenge. *We will see*, he thought as he started the engine.

CHAPTER 29

OFFICER PECK

Maxine had been saving up all her sick days; but due to recent events, she had now run out. Her employer had been extremely generous, but the day came when Maxine had to go back to the dry cleaners where she worked. That left Clay at home by himself on this particular Friday. As most moms would be, she was extremely worried. She arranged for Clay to have a phone with him and a list of helpful emergency numbers in case he need it. Fortunately, she knew that Diane would swing by later that day with some lunch. She fully expected to return home to a bunch of empty Chinese food cartons, those cute little boxes, lining the end tables around the living room.

Clay was healing faster than usual, even for a kid his age. He would not have to wait much longer for his appointment with someone about getting prosthetic legs made up. But for now, he had nothing to do but recline on the couch with the TV remote in his hand, bored out of his mind. Usual daytime television had long gotten on his nerves. It consisted of shows featuring ladies bickering about politics, hammy actors on soaps, or know-it-all hosts talking about nonsense in front of audiences that would clap at anything. He drifted over to the sports channels.

Under normal conditions, Clay had no problem losing himself in the world of sports. But now, it was difficult. The baseball highlights, clips of football players, and interviews with basketball players filled the dimensions of the living room TV. During the sports news, the channels delivered the latest news on golf, tennis, hockey, bike racing, car racing, and even figure skating, strangely enough.

That poor young man had already fallen into the trap of self-pity. This would prove to cripple him more than his missing his legs. But then something new happened. Clay began to feel an incredible itch down on his lower leg. He reached over to scratch it, but there was nothing there. How could he feel an itch where his leg did not exist anymore? For a moment, the itch was unbearable. He did not know what to do. After a few frustrating minutes, the urge passed. But the experience had set his mind on an unstoppable course. He was now completely focused again on his tragic loss.

Clay looked up from the couch and saw sprinters racing on the TV. That was it. Track was his thing and now even the television was mocking him. He turned it off and tossed the remote just beyond his reach. "Well, that was not very smart," he said in a cynical tone. Maybe there was something he could do. He looked around the room and a photo on the wall grabbed his attention. It was a family portrait. The picture featured younger versions of his parents. His older sister was a teenager with braces at the time. And there was little Clayton, bright red hair, big smile, missing his two front teeth; his dad used to call that his 7-10 bowling split smile. He guessed that he was about six or seven in that picture – maybe eight. He looked at his dad. His father's hair was a darker red at the time. He had a chiseled face, a dimpled chin, and a slight smile with pride in the family God had blessed him with.

Clay's eyes next looked over at a portrait of his dad that sat in a cheap frame propped up on a table. His dad was in his full policeman's uniform and stood in front of the American flag. That same picture, surrounded with flowers, was displayed on the coffin at the funeral. Clay could still remember how he felt at the time. He closed his eyes.

Eighth grader Clayton Peck was missing school that day. He remembered feeling hot and uncomfortable in that suit. His mom sat between him and his sister on the front pew. Behind him sat his friends with their families, Mike's being directly behind him. They were there to pay their respects to a great man, but also to show love and support for their friend. In front of him sat a long gray coffin with a flag draped across it. Along the side walls, uniformed policemen filled the room.

The music died down and Brother Wayne rose to his feet. He approached the pulpit and started off by mentioning that Phillip Ward Peck was a mere forty-eight ("far too young") when he passed away and that the pastor had gotten to know him pretty well over the past twelve years or so. He listed those family members who were surviving him. He brought up the fact that he had done a tour in the Marine Corp and that he had served on the Pecan Falls Police Department with distinction for the past twenty-two years.

Brother Wayne rested his hands on the edges of the pulpit. "In preparing for funerals," he said, "I typically ask the family of the deceased if I could borrow their loved one's Bible. I like to look through the pages to see if there are any highlighted or emphasized verses. Maybe this person had a favorite passage of Scripture – something that had special meaning to him or her. These favorite passages sometimes become a springboard, an ideal cornerstone for the message. This way, we get to take a good look into their personality and walk away from this experience a little bit richer for having known this person. And so it was with preparing for Phillip's funeral." He looked down and picked up the Bible in front of him. "This one is his. In fact, I believe this one was given to him by his wife Maxine shortly after they were married."

Clay had been avoiding visual contact with the pastor. But at this point, he felt inspired to look up. He saw his dad's tattered old Bible as Brother Wayne lifted it up at eye-level.

"I must confess, my plan didn't work. I couldn't find a single passage that stood out to Phillip. But let me show you what I *did* find." He opened the Bible to a random page and held it up for everyone to see. From anywhere in the room, people could see that various verses were highlighted. Some were yellow. Others were green. Pink. Orange. There were verses that were underlined. He had drawn other lines connecting some verses to others. The margins were filled with handwritten notes in black, red, and blue ink. No one could make out what these notes said at that distance, but it was clear that he jotted down his thoughts and perhaps some cross-references to other verses found elsewhere. Whatever was on that page, he had studied it thoroughly and wholeheartedly.

"I also found this." Brother Wayne turned to the next page. What they saw there was another page featuring pretty much the same thing.

"And this …" He turned to the next page. Same thing. By this point, a handful of people had gasped. Soft spoken comments were being made throughout the room – inaudible from Clay's seat, but he could still hear them whispering. "And this …" The pastor held up another colorful page. "In fact, let's just do this …" The pastor then fanned the pages, held the Bible up sideways, and allowed the pages to fall displaying what Phillip Peck had done to his Bible. Those in attendance marveled at the flashes of bright colors and scribble marks everywhere. It was evident that this Bible had been gone through many times. "I have to be careful how I do this. These maps in the back are all lose." Some people sneakered at that last revelation.

One of the men in the back corner was so overcome, he started clapping. This led others to do the same. In just seconds, the entire room was filled with applause. *Is this even allowed at a funeral?* Clay wondered. *This is like illegal or something.* But he looked around. Policemen everywhere stood and were clapping. The pastor grinned and nodded. Billy's sister and her husband looked down at their infant twin girls tucked neatly in their carriers. In spite of the loudness, the babies slept soundly behind pink pacifiers. Clay relaxed and thought that this pleasant display of approval must be okay – even though funerals were a somber event.

He felt his mother's hand reach over for his. She gripped it tightly.

"That's right, ladies and gentlemen. Our friend here lived by God's Word." Brother Wayne stepped down from the pulpit and walked directly to Clay. Chills shot up Clay's back as soon as he realized that the pastor was breaking that comfortable distance. But the pastor lovingly and reverently placed the Bible into Clay's small hands. Clay looked up at the smiling face of Brother Wayne. In that instant, the pastor resumed talking and returned to the pulpit.

"Matthew 5:6 records these words from Jesus' Sermon on the Mount, 'Blessed are they which do hunger and thirst after righteousness: for they shall be filled.' Friends and loved ones, I submit to you that Phillip had that same hunger and that God had indeed filled him as He said He would. There is an old saying, 'You can't take it with you.' But something tells me that there are certain things that you *can* take with you when you die. The knowledge that you get from reading the Word of God is one of those things. And I will argue that when God called Phillip home last Monday, he died a wealthy man."

A chorus of *Amens* echoed across the room; one of the loudest came from Curtis Baker's dad.

The pastor continued on with his message. After a while, it was over. Clay remembered the long parade of police cars in escort to the cemetery. Blue lights were everywhere. Cars pulled over to the side of the road; some drivers even stepped out of their cars and offered a sympathetic salute. At the gravesite, there were more words of comfort followed by a twenty-one gun salute. Policemen dressed in their finest folded the flag and the chief himself brought it over to Clay's mom. He recalled that the chief's gloves were the whitest gloves he had ever seen. Some guy in a kilt played *Amazing Grace* on the bagpipes. The whole thing seemed extremely formal - - and yet loving and personal. Everyone was so kind. People greeted the family as they were sitting: the Hairston's, the Baker's, the Harris', folks from the church, city officials, the mayor, others. The police department's German shepherd even came over and licked Clay's hand.

Clay opened his eyes and peered across the living room at his dad's portrait once again. The son missed his father as much now as he did nearly two years ago. His father had the kind of gray hair that betrayed his earlier red. What Clay wanted right now was for his dad to walk right in the room and embrace him with those strong, freckled arms. His mother was always there for him, but it was his dad who was the most affectionate with Clay and his older sister.

It was a quick illness. His dad barely had time to discover that he was sick. And then just like that, he was gone. Unwelcome tears swelled up in Clay's eyes. Before he could stop it, he found himself crying. He must have wept for a full exhausting minute. One thing that surprised him was the semi-loud wailing that he did. He had not cried like that in a long, long time. He was actually glad that his mom was not there after all.

As the feeling passed, he noticed his dad's wore-out Bible sitting in front of his picture. He reached next him to get the wheelchair that they were borrowing from the church. It was awkward, but Clay somehow managed to shift his weight around and prop himself up in the chair. He wheeled himself over to the far side of the room and picked it up. In his hand was his daddy's Bible. He opened it and looked at the familiar handwriting all over the pages. Just holding his dad's Bible and seeing the notes that he wrote brought him a sense of closeness and comfort. It was as if his dad were there with him, directing his attention to various passages, and inviting him to continue this spiritual journey where he had left off.

There were a number of wealthy people in town with some pretty cool and expensive toys, but Clay could not help feeling that the single most valuable treasure in all of the Pecan Falls township was right there in his hands. The first verse of Psalm 77 caught his eye with its bright yellow highlighting. Clay began to read aloud. "I cried unto God with my voice, even unto God with my voice; and he gave ear unto me."

INTERMISSION

Sunday went well. Church services were great. The boys went back to visit Clay. People took afternoon naps during a televised car race. ... all the usual stuff. But the following week was full of activity.

Mr. Harris got Alejandro's attention during Monday afternoon's Chess Club meeting. He directed the student to a boy shyly watching them from around the corner. Alejandro did his best to lure him in and make him feel at home. His name was Chris and he wanted to play Chess. He was slightly older than Billy, but smaller. He claimed to already know how to play, but this was not truly the case. But that did not slow them down; Mr. Harris simply took him to the side and showed him the fundamentals of the game. He introduced Chris to the rules, how each piece moved, the final objective, and so on. He then played a game with him with constant narration as he talked throughout the entire process. Chris began to understand how a game is supposed to go. Soon he was playing against the others ... and, sadly to say, losing very badly.

Somehow, Billy had gotten his sticky fingers on a few of those new car brochures that you can get at all the big dealerships. The photos of the new cars looked awesome. He tried to imagine how sophisticated he would look sitting in one of those sporty new automobiles - - or even better, a shiny new truck. When he finally worked up the courage, he took his two favorite ones to his parents for a 'simple discussion.' He might as well have been trying to buy a Saturn V rocket. His folks began to talk about a budget, including gas and insurance and blah, blah, blah. The conversation concluded with Billy darting back to his lonesome bedroom even more angry and frustrated than before. He wanted to punctuate his exit with a slam of his 60-year-old door – but he had more sense than that. Such an act would naturally be interpreted as a surefire invitation for both mom and dad to have some sort of attitude-adjustment lecture right there in his bedroom. He decided to pass on that for now. They could always fight about that tomorrow.

Wesley Porterfield the Third made his way from class to class already out of habit. A fairly good student, quizzes and tests came and went, all of which he took in his stride. Much of his time was unsuccessfully spent trying to avoid Chloe. She had been doing her utmost best to win his attention. What she did not realize was that Wesley was used to that from his old school. At first, he was flattered by the flirting, but then he realized that they were flirting with his money as much as they were with him. At this point, he had a difficult time determining the difference - - so he handled it by not returning any attention at all.

He was rather looking for this Laura who he had met at Billy's house. Here was someone who was interesting. But for whatever reason, he kept missing her. He was hoping to find her at some point, to be sure.

But if there was something that was different about that week and gave the few people who cared something to talk about, it was that Wesley and Mike had started being civil to each other and were apparently becoming okay friends. They were not hanging out or anything, but they would see each other, smile, and crack the occasional joke. The first people to notice were naturally Billy and Curtis. At first, they freaked out a little and wondered what was going on. But they were very impressed and proud of Mike's new behavior. This was precisely the Mike that they have known all their lives and it was nice to finally have him back. All they needed was Clay and the picture would be complete.

Tuesday night at nearly nine o'clock, Wesley sat in his dark house alone and lost himself deep in his thoughts. His troubled life had seemed to come to a crossroads. Mike and some of the others had given him some things to be thinking about and now he was confused. There was something about Mike and his friends that could not be put into words. Was it confidence? Was it peace? Whatever it was, they seemed to glow with it. It followed them around and could be almost felt as they walked by. They certainly looked comfortable in their own skins. Wesley was jealous of this undefinable quality and wanted to know if there was enough of it for him.

At some point earlier that day, Mike and Wesley had exchanged phone numbers. So Wesley picked up his phone and called. Mike invited him to walk over to his place and talk about it. While Wesley made his way over there, Mike managed to confine all those Pomeranians to another room where they barked for a while. Mrs. Hairston opened up a big bag of chips and brought them some dip as they sat in the dining room. There, Mike opened up the Bible and explained a few verses to him.

All of this was completely new to Wesley. Naturally, he had heard of Jesus before and had vague ideas of what He had done, but no one had ever explained to him who He was or why He had come. At first, it was difficult to understand, but the more Mike spoke the more it began to make sense. Then Mike turned his attention to our sinful state and our need for redemption.

It was already getting late, but that was okay. No one there would have done anything differently. And the cool part was that Wesley entered Mike's home as a tortured and confused young man, but he left that night as an accepted part of a loving family. He took that step and had been redeemed from his sins. Wesley now belonged to God.

Everything was right on course. Chloe sat at her computer, building what she thought would be the most hilarious piece of entertainment for her big party coming up that weekend. She could not ask for better material. She clicked on SAVE. "There," she said to herself. "It's all done." At this point, all she really needed was for her dad to split and for her guests to arrive.

Chloe was originally going to avoid mentioning the party to her father. She knew that he would just say 'No' anyway. Well, she ended up asking him just the same and he predictably told her that she could not have the party – there or anywhere. He began to provide her with an unrequested list of reasons why that was not a good idea. She reciprocated with statements about unfair treatment. Soon, they were yelling at each other. ... again. What followed was the same drama that had been performed a hundred times before in their home. It was like following the steps to a familiar dance. She left the room. He followed her. Yelling at each other the entire way, she ran up the stairs. He yelled up the stairs and she yelled down the stairs. He informed her that on no uncertain terms was she to have the party. She retreated to her room slamming a door that was very much used to slamming. Rinse and repeat. This time was different because he was leaving at that moment on his business trip. So Gregory furiously grabbed his briefcase and a suitcase of clothes that were waiting by the door. He tossed them into his car and slammed the trunk lid shut. Red-faced with anger, he plopped himself down into the driver's seat. He was just about to start the car, but he stopped himself. He was confused and worried about his daughter. His other two children hated him and were living with his ex-wife. All he had was Chloe. How did his life get to this point? He leaned slightly forward and rubbed his hands through his hair. He had something to tell his daughter, but she was not in a listening mood. She was never in a listening mood. He had already told her about what was laying heavily on his mind, but she did not care. He calmed down a bit and started the car. He needed to have that talk with Chloe, but the airport was about an hour away. Gregory looked down at his watch. He had to scram lickety-split. Their lovely father-daughter chat would have to wait another day.

Chloe continued with her plans for the party in spite of what her father had said. Besides, she had put so much detailed work into her little surprise. She had realized that mentioning the party to her dad was an enormous mistake on her part. But she would be fine as long as she had the house cleaned up upon his return.

Thursday night, students gathered again at the Harris house for a little more *Pride and Prejudice* (or *'that book'* as Billy called it). These events started off merely as a way to stay a few steps ahead of the novel, but now they were becoming quite the social event. More students showed up this time. Billy had hoped that Chloe would come; but so far, she had not.

Kids were bringing soft drinks and desserts, while William manned the grill. Hot dogs and hamburgers were being eaten by the scores. Diane provided milk and cookies. No sooner did she have the chocolate chip cookies out of the oven that a flock of teenagers would descend upon them while the cookies were nice and gooey soft.

These events also allowed Berly and Maggie to get to know Curtis and Mike a little better. Mike started off by apologizing for his rotten behavior the other night. He tried to offer an explanation, but Maggie stopped him. Everything was cool. Actually, Maggie felt a little like apologizing for even being there; this was below her grade level. But she had fun and the others profited from her attendance.

Wesley came and enjoyed himself. But he was a bit disappointed because Lauren was not there.

At one point, Billy, Curtis, and Mike were all standing around the grill next to Mr. Harris - - all of them with their books in hand. One of the guests bumped into Billy at just the wrong time. His copy of the book fell from his hands and right on the grill next to the hot dogs. Curtis reached down to pick it up, but suddenly the book began to burn. Billy stopped him. He sighed loudly and grabbed some starter fluid squirting some on the book. It made a fairly impressive flame for about half-a-minute. In an attempt at being funny, Mr. Harris took a spatula and flipped the book over; he said that the first few chapters were done. The horrible fate that awaited any book in his possession became the source of many a joke that evening. In fact, the jokes rained down on him like balloons during a Presidential primary election.

Friday afternoon saw Chris' third appearance at the PFHS Chess Club, but he still had yet to win a single game. He was completely new to the experience and was up against some fairly seasoned players. But then Mr. Harris volunteered to play him. It is true that he had a little coaching now and again; but he came out now having won his first game. He was electrified. He could not wait to go home and tell his parents that he had won — and against a teacher. The others in the group congratulated him. Quotes even gave him a thumbs up.

Billy was puzzled. How could this kid beat his dad?

Immediately following the meeting, William and Billy made their way over to the truck to go home. With a loud squealing sound, Billy drove it out of the parking lot and onto Pecan Falls' main drag.

William turned to his son, "Don't we have someplace to go on the way home? Shouldn't we go by the bookstore and try to replace yesterday's copy of *Pride and Prejudice*?"

Billy rolled his eyes. "That isn't very funny. … but yes." A few moments went by before Billy mentioned something that was gnawing on him. "Uh, dad. I noticed this new kid, Chris, beat you at Chess today. I don't understand how that happened. You must've lost on purpose. He's terrible."

"Oh, he's not terrible. He's just new and inexperienced, that's all."

"Still, you didn't win."

"Oh? That all depends on what your definition of 'win' is. If winning is meeting your objective, then I won."

Billy was getting ready to pull into the bookstore parking lot. "Let me get this straight. Your objective was *not* to win the game?"

"Now come on, Billy. What would I be proving if I won? That I can beat some kid who barely knows how to play? I have been playing this game for over thirty-five years now. What do I care about winning? And I can't go home and brag about destroying some young kid in chess, now can I?"

"But you can't just throw every game just because your opponent is younger than you."

"I know. But what if he lost? I could tell that he was getting discouraged. When that happens, sometimes a kid will quit trying altogether. Is that what I want? Or do I want him to stick with it? My purpose behind that game was to encourage him. So I think I won. What do you think?"

Billy did not know what to think. He simply brought the truck to a stop.

William turned to look at him in the eyes. "Don't get me wrong. Winning is important. We should always strive to do our best at everything we do. But beating that kid at chess was not my goal; my goal was for him to win. This may sound like nonsense to you now, but I hope someday you will learn that we sometimes win by losing. Don't ever be afraid to lose. It can be more valuable than winning."

This made no sense to Billy, but he was at the bookstore now. It was time to try something new. From behind the seat, Billy grabbed a coat and a cowboy hat. He put them on and looked at his face in the mirror as he applied a fake mustache. One pair of sunglasses later and he was good to go.

William stared blankly at his son as he closed the truck door to go inside. *I may have to include this one in my journal,* he thought to himself.

Midge was at her usual post at the register at the bookstore. The next costumer in line passed over a copy of *Pride and Prejudice*. She thought that there was something rather peculiar about the gentleman buying it. He was wearing dark sunglasses and kept a large cowboy hat low over his forehead. But the real kicker was the obvious fake mustache.

When she hesitated, he looked up at her and saw that she was staring at his face. He struggled to work up a more cowboy accent – an octave or so lower than his normal voice. His speech came across just as fake as his unnatural, ten-cent mustache.

She was not fooled for a second. With curious eyes, she reached over and lifted his hat on his head and pulled the sunglasses to the end of his nose. Then she gently pulled half of his mustache off so that it hung over his mouth. The people in line behind him were laughing as she took the time to plainly explain that there was no age restriction on purchasing a copy of a Jane Austen novel.

Billy had only dressed up like this because he was embarrassed about buying yet another copy of this accursed book. But as a result, he was more embarrassed than ever before. He gave her the money, grabbed the book, and did not even wait for the change.

"Hey! Where are you going? I had to order a dozen more copies of *Pride and Prejudice* thanks to you, young man." The other folks in line laughed again, but harder this time.

Billy retreated back to the old truck where his dad was sitting in the passenger's seat. He climbed in and started the truck again. "I have got to learn how to *not* destroy these books. This is making me mad." He looked over at his dad who was giving him a disapproving look. Billy briefly thought about what he said. "I just totally split an infinitive, didn't I?"

CHAPTER 30

THE BENEFIT OF THE DOUBT

The fall colors were beautiful in the Ozarks. Every direction you faced gave way to God's amazing pallet of flaming reds, cheery yellows, and warm oranges. The change of color along with the cooler weather seemed to be a generous reward for the humid summertime that everyone endured.

Saturday, the day of the big party, finally arrived and Billy was about to explode with anticipation. But that afternoon found the Harris' all working in the front yard, armed with jackets and cotton gloves. Diane and William were working with the rakes while Billy was busy loading garbage bags with leaves. A radio on the front porch was keeping them abreast of the college football game. They only stopped occasionally for a quick drink or whenever one of the neighbors came by for a friendly chat.

Billy secretly enjoyed the time that he spent with his parents doing things like this; but today, he was not going to let it show. He was busy being mad at them over this car issue. Honestly, he was not truly angry, but now his attitude was more of a matter of principle than anything emotional.

After tying up a bag and walking it to the curb, Billy pulled off his gloves and headed to the house. Even without seeing him, William and Diane could keep up with where he was due to the sound of leaves being kicked as he walked.

"Where are you headed off to?" his dad hollered out. "We're wanting to finish this job before it gets too dark to see."

"I'm just grabbing a quick drink and I'll be right back." Billy disappeared through the door and his parents continued with their work.

Billy marched into the kitchen, leaving the light off. He grabbed a glass out of the cabinet and filled it halfway with orange juice. After one sip, he heard the distinct sound of a phone buzzing. The noise came from the kitchen table. His dad's phone lit up with the name and number of *Fletcher, Louis*. The area code did not even look familiar.

Thoughts began to roll over and over in his mind. *Who is this? Louis? Do we even know anyone named 'Louis'? Wait a minute! Louis? Wasn't that the name of the accountant guy from New York or something? I'd bet this is the guy who handles mom and dad's big money. Of course, it is.*

The phone buzzed again. This was the third time it buzzed. Billy picked up the phone, looked at the display, and then peeked out the window at his parents. He was about to run the phone out to his dad – but then he started thinking, the kind of thinking that usually gets people in trouble. He pressed the green button and brought the phone up to his ear. "Hello?"

"Hello? William?" It was the same voice as the man who was visiting their home that day, the dude with the ugly comb over.

"No. This is his son Billy."

"Oh. Are either of your parents there?"

Billy was not usually a dishonest person – but here came the lie. If one lie makes a person a liar, then infer what you will. "No sir. My mom is out running errands right now and dad is inexposed." *Inexposed*? Where did that word come from? He meant to say *Indisposed* but it came out wrong. Now it sounded like he was in the shower or something.

There was a brief and awkward pause. "Uh, when you see your parents, would you do me a big favor and tell them that Louis called?"

Now here is an interesting situation. Should Billy just politely agree to pass on the message and hang up? Or should he shoot for something higher at the risk of getting in trouble? All this big money that he has yet to see was indirectly his anyway. And talk about tempting! Why was he even hesitating? He decided to go for it.

"Mr. Louis. I think maybe you should know that I know all about it."

A momentary silence followed. "'All about it'? I'm not sure what you mean." Louis sounded a little confused - - well, maybe it was an intentional confusion.

"What do you mean *I'm not sure what you mean*? I mean that I know what you know. But you don't know that I know, you know? But you need to know that I know, you know what I mean?"

"You lost me. Come again?"

"You know what I mean. You know exactly what I mean. About the money."

"Uh, young man, would you just deliver the message for me please? I would appreciate it."

"Mr. Louis, I'm talking about all the money. The big money. The money that you manage for my parents. All about Crowe Athletic Equipment."

The mention of Crowe's must have thrown Louis for a loop. There was a deep breath. The voice on the other end of the phone changed its tone. "Oh. You do, huh?"

"Yes sir. And since I am now an active part of what goes on in terms of this money, I was going to ask you to do me a small favor actually. My parents and I were wondering if you could send me a small amount of money, something so small that it wouldn't even be missed. Something like … five hundred dollars?"

"Five hundred? I see. I suppose that is something that wouldn't be missed. In fact, that is something so small, I wouldn't even have to bother your folks with that on our regular reports. Does that sound good to you?"

Billy was beaming. "That would be perfect."

"But are you quite sure that five hundred would be enough? If you are talking about something that would slide by unnoticed, why not make it a cool thousand? Or five thousand, for that matter?"

Billy's hands began to shake with nervousness. It was all that he could do to keep from dropping the phone. "Fi … fi … five thou … thousand?" He was acting so cool about the whole thing before; now he was struggling to keep it together. *Calm. Remain calm*, he begged himself.

Louis' reaction certainly was not one of surprise. He even laughed a little. "Why not? With a major corporation like Crowe's, five thousand dollars is nothing."

Billy was raptured with excitement. He truly wanted to shout out as loud as he could, but he kept his control well. "Why not? That would be wonderful. How soon can I get the money?"

"Well ordinarily, I would say tomorrow. But since tomorrow is Sunday, it would have to be Monday. ... unless it is an emergency."

He blinked a couple of times. "Uhhh, Monday would be fine."

"Excellent. I'll email your parents the proper forms. They can sign the necessary paperwork and scan them back to me at their leisure."

Billy's smile disappeared and was replaced with confusion and worry. "Uh, paperwork?"

Louis' voice remained very professional as if he had done this twenty times a day. "Naturally. But you already knew this since you 'know all about it' - - in your own words - - and since you are now an active part of what goes on."

Billy said nothing. And yet he said quite a bit with his silence.

Louis now had the upper hand. "Young man, your parents know nothing about this money that you are requesting. Do they?"

Billy was busted. Perhaps he was always busted. "Uhh, no." *Those two shysters?* he thought to himself. *No way!*

"Yeah, that is what I thought. You see, your parents had already informed me that you discovered their little secret. They also told me that I am not to just hand over money to you should you ask. Although they *did* say that it was highly unlikely that you would do something that low. They did not think that you were capable of such deception. It looks like there *is* a greedy side to you that they didn't know was there."

Billy suddenly had a wave of fear sweep over him. Where were his parents anyway? He had been inside far too long for a quick drink. He went over to the window to look out. Good. They were laughing out by the curb with Mr. Baker. That will keep them occupied for more than a few minutes. But he still felt guilty about Louis' comments. His parents gave him the benefit of the doubt. And he just proved them wrong. But at the same time, he was angry with his parents because they were going way over the top on shielding him from this dream come true. Think about it: they have all this money. Billy could have anything he ever wanted if his parents were not standing in the way. How irritating.

"You don't have to tell my folks about this, do you?"

"Let me make something clear to you: I do not keep secrets from my clients. If they ask, I need to tell them. You may not have a problem with keeping information from them, but I do. However, if you were to *volunteer* this information to your parents yourself, you may escape whatever punishment they give. Just a thought ... Nevertheless, this is a big secret. Your parents do not want anyone to know about the money. You haven't told anyone, have you?"

How was Billy supposed to answer that? He really cannot tell the truth here. Trouble would crush him like a hydraulic press. He told his three friends, but none of those losers would believe him. He also told Chloe (Yay! Tonight's party!). She seemed to be the only one who would even listen to him. After all, she did invite him over to her big party with all those rich friends of hers. But Billy lied once again. "No. No sir. I haven't told anyone. Phhhfft! I can keep a secret."

"Good. It is vitally important that no one knows about your family's wealth. Whenever they do great things for other people, they like to keep it on the down-low. Bill and Diane are good people. I wish I had more clients like them."

"Good people? How are they good people? They're hording all this money and not sharing it with their own son." It occurred to him that he was getting loud, so he backed off about halfway through that sentence. Fortunately, his parents clearly did not hear him.

"You said earlier that you *know all about it*. Did your parents tell you how I fit into all of this?"

"Uh, I don't think so."

"Well, let me tell you something ..."

Oh no, thought Billy. *All I need is another long-winded speech.*

"I used to be a very religious man; but in my case, money was god. And I faithfully worshiped her. I really knew how to play the game too. I had a Manhattan apartment, but I also owned places in Florida and Maine. But my marriage was falling apart and my children rarely ever saw me. I was always working and telling myself that it was all for them. Then Crowe's Athletic fell into your parents' hands. They brought ideas of their own to the table, ideas that I was against. They wanted to begin ministerial programs to those who wanted it into their factories and stores. They closed on Sundays so their employees could have that time off. Then they began to give large amounts of money away. To me, I thought giving away ten percent of their profits to various faith-based charities was financial suicide. But I was wrong. They began to make more money than ever before. More money rolled in – so more money rolled out. They kept raising their contributions to more than ten percent - - a lot more. I saw these financial miracles taking place and I was completely at a loss. I finally asked them about their secret and that is when they spoke to me about their faith. Later that day, I accept Christ and I haven't looked back since. In the weeks that followed, my wife noticed my behavior and decided to accept Christ as well. My wife and I still have our various homes, but our approach to money is changed. My kids are grown now, but they too have seen a change in me and have all turned to Jesus."

There was the Jesus reference that Billy was waiting for. If there was ever a common denominator in his life, it was Jesus. It always boiled down to that. He could not wait to get off this phone. Fortunately, it sounded like Louis was getting to the end of his story.

"So your parents changed lives all over the world with their generous nature. They are always helping people. And with that help, comes the gospel message. Many people have made eternal decisions as a result of your parents' money. And you can add my family and me to that list of people who have benefitted from knowing them. Working with them is one of the greatest pleasures of my professional and personal life."

Louis said a few more things. So did Billy. Eventually, they managed to come to end of their talk and Billy ran the phone out to his dad so Louis could speak to him. It was nice that Louis respected his parents quite a bit. But Louis did not have to live with them the way Billy had. How could a son get his parents to listen to reason?

He was still a bit irked that his so-called friends would not believe that the Harris' had all this dough. He had to admit that it was near impossible to convince *anyone* so as long as Mr. Harris was driving that squealing truck and drying clothes in that torture device. But that really did not matter at this moment. Billy was about to launch his little party-bound scheme.

CHAPTER 31

PLAN SET IN MOTION

There are times in our lives when action is required: times of national crisis, people we know and love are having an emergency, opportunities to further the Kingdom of Heaven, et cetera. Times of deceit, moments of fleeting pleasure, episodes defined by a self-centered agenda – these are not. That is when it is best to stop, think about what you are doing, and then pursue a different course of action.

How nice it would be to rub some of that off on Billy right now – but no such luck. He has abandoned his wisdom and has decided to follow a dangerous trail. And it was not so much the idea of the party that was so wrong, for we will all find ourselves outnumbered from time to time in a place where people do not have the basic foundation. The crime here is that he was lying to his parents and to his friend Curtis. So now the night of Chloe's big party had finally arrived and Billy's plan was being put in motion. It was not a very good plan – but it was full speed ahead for this young man.

William and Diane's impatient son was wearing out the carpet by pacing back and forth in front of the living room window waiting for Curtis to arrive. Curtis was going to be taking Billy to Chloe's big party - - the only problem was that Curtis did not know it yet. Neither did Mr. or Mrs. Harris for that matter. They were all led to believe that Billy was going to be spending that evening chilling out over at Curtis' house like he often did on Saturday nights – eating the usual junk and warming themselves over the latest video games. Tonight, they were supposed to be parachuting into an enemy base courtesy of a new download.

While Billy was watching the clock, William sat at the computer looking at some numbers. Now that Billy knew about their fortune, they did not have to be as sneaky about these things. In some ways, that was a relief. His focus now was on something entirely different, something that weighed heavily on his heart.

He already knew the passage, but he wanted to see it with his eyes this time. He grabbed his Bible and flipped the pages over to James 1:5-8 and read it out loud. "'If any of you lack wisdom, let him ask of God, that giveth to all men liberally, and upbraideth not; and it shall be given him. But let him ask in faith, nothing wavering. For he that wavereth is like a wave of the sea driven with the wind and tossed. For let not that man think that he shall receive any thing of the Lord. A double minded man is unstable in all his ways.' Is that what you are telling me?" He closed his Bible and his eyes. "Almighty God, I formally request that you give me this wisdom. This is a delicate issue and it is too much for me. I am way over my head here. But it isn't too much for You. If You are indeed calling me to this task, please arm me with the skills required. And may You get the glory." William sat now in silence.

Supportively, Diane appeared behind her husband and laid her hands on his shoulders. "Do you really feel led to do this?" She had just approached him and yet her words sounded like they were engaged in the middle of a conversation. She actually was. It was part of a discussion that they had started earlier.

"I do. I really do. I've been praying over this and I can't get it out of my mind. I believe God can use this in His amazing way."

Diane agreed. "Then go ahead. And the sooner the better."

William said, "I'll go make the call." He got up from the computer and clicked off of the site. Privacy was needed for this call. This usually meant that he went back to their bedroom. He could talk there without being distracted. As he walked by, he looked over at Billy. His son seemed aggravated over his friend's delay. When William got to the bedroom, he closed the door and began to punch the numbers on his phone.

"Louis? Hey, man. This is William. Doing well? That's fine. Say, I've got a little project for you. You know those pieces that that museum approached us about buying? Yeah. I want you to sell them. Absolutely. I really think that this is the right time. But only under specific conditions. In fact, I have something special planned. Yeah. Well, this is a unique situation and I need your help. Someone here desperately needs some assistance and this way we can help them and still keep the money a secret. I was thinking that ..."

William reemerged from the bedroom and was walking past Billy's duffle bag. It contained Billy's church clothes for the next day as well as some odds and ends – par for the course when staying over at Curtis' on a Saturday night. Friends like the Baker's were a godsend, people that they could always count on.

Billy had about as much patience as he usually did, none. "Good grief! He just lives a few houses down. What is keeping him? I probably could've walked there and back ten times already," he fumed.

William sat down on the couch next to Diane. "Watched pots never boil."

After looking outside again, Billy turned to his dad. "What is that? Is that from Proverbs?"

"Nope. Just a popular old saying."

Billy turned his angry face again out the window. Still, there was no sign of Curtis. "Well I'm not trying to boil anything. I'm just ready to get out of here."

Diane turned around to look at him. "You look like you are about to boil." Her voice was only partly making a joke; it also hinted of concern.

Another opportunity to whip that dead horse arrived. *Don't go there*, Billy thought. He went there anyway. "You know, after my next birthday, I wouldn't have to wait like this if I had my own car."

William answered the challenge. "Yep. And we are willing to help you with that. But we aren't buying you a new sports car for you to wreck on the first day."

Whatever.

Diane continued the thought by delivering the second half of the same sentence. "Besides, your father and I love you too much to give you everything you want. We all have the tendency to want things that are not in our best interest."

Great, Billy thought sarcastically to himself. *What did they do? Rehearse this? My parents have clearly united against me. I'm not going to get very far with them. Why do my parents have to be so stupid?*

Billy looked again through the front window. The town was still enjoying this daylight. This time tomorrow, it would be much darker due to the time-change later that evening. Suddenly, Curtis' car inched into their driveway. Billy noticed it and did not wait for his friend to finish parking before he headed toward the door.

Diane asked the question again. "Where all are you going?" She knew that she had asked that question before, but she repeated herself just the same. Parents do that sometimes.

Billy's stride came to a screeching halt. With an overly theatrical sigh, Billy answered her with all the subtlety of an axe. "We're gonna grab some pizzas and then head back to Curtis' house." He was out the door and closed it behind him before his parents could say anything more.

Curtis had just turned off the engine to his car and was getting out when he noticed Billy marching toward him. He noted that Billy looked royally upset. *What now?* he thought.

Billy immediately started barking at Curtis. "What are you doing getting out of the car? We've got a schedule to keep. And by the way, could you be any more late? Let's scram already." He was moving directly to the passenger door.

Curtis was taken aback for a moment. He looked at his watch and then held it up as if Billy could see it from there. "What? It's only 6:01. Are we on a strict timetable that I wasn't aware of?"

"Just get inside and start this machine." Billy climbed in.

Curtis looked across the top of his car over to where Billy had just stood. He sighed and quietly said, "Oh, wow. You're certainly in a mood tonight." He then opened the door and got in. He started the car and gently pulled away from the curb.

Neither boy said a word. The car traveled one whole block before Billy started. "Come on, man. Is this as fast as this one-cylinder toaster will go?"

Billy's bitterness had officially spread to Curtis now. "Uh, maybe you haven't noticed, but this is a residential. Thirty-five miles an hour is what the sign said and that is how fast this car is gonna go. The pizza place isn't going anywhere."

"Dude, show a little initiative. The cops won't care. They won't stop you unless you're doing like ten or fifteen miles above the speed limit."

"That's a big gamble there. You don't know that. Look, I just got this thing and I don't think my parents want me to bring home a speeding ticket this early into my driving career."

"You're sixteen. Speeding is what sixteen-year-olds do." Billy sat there and thought to himself, *Maybe I ought to get out and walk.*

"This night is going to be epic!" Bre shouted at Chloe as they descended the staircase at the Chastain home.

"WHAT?" Chloe could not hear Bre due to the incredibly loud music. But it was not just the music that was loud. The house was full of young people - - mostly college age students.

Bre took a deep breath and repeated her statement, this time directly into Chloe's ear. Chloe's earrings dangled so low that Bre wanted to make a joke about them picking up any waves and using them for receivers. But any joke spoken under these conditions would have been a complete waste of time. With the music blasting this loud, she could tell that this would be a night of saying everything two or three times.

Chloe responded to Bre's statement. "Yes, it is. There is nothing like a great party to take your mind off of meaningless junk like school." Even as she spoke, she made a quick visual scan of the room.

Bre had a rough idea of what Chloe had just said and pretended to have heard every word. She noticed that her friend had been looking around the room which drew her focus to the people there. "I see a few kids here from school – quite a few actually. But some of these guys I don't know. So who are all these people? Friends of yours?"

"Phffff! I wish! No! Tyler's older brother – the cool one, not the dorky one – is in college and he invited these guys down. Since we were having this party, I told Tyler that they were all welcome to hang out here and that they could bring their girlfriends. But only on one condition: they have to furnish the drinks."

Bre's smile grew wide across her beautiful dark face. "Excellent."

All the boys at the party were dressed comfortably, the majority in knee-length shorts and t-shirts with either their university represented or a trio of Greek letters. A small handful mixed in wearing clothes that used to be described as 'grungy.' Most of the girls were dressed in very short shorts and a top that matched, dressed for comfort. Those who were still in high school did their best to blend in with those in college. Only Bre and Chloe were dressed to kill, both in soft silky short dresses – Bre in red and Chloe in white. Chloe may have gone a little too far with the makeup though.

"It's a win-win. They get to hang out at my house and lift this party to a higher level and we get all the drinks with none of the stupid sneaking around or trying to replace dad's stash. I hate having to depend on other people to replace stuff like that."

Bre agreed. "This is much easier. Good for you."

Chloe continued to look around the room. All over the place, there were well-built college boys and random girlfriends. Chloe thought the girls had cute figures and might normally feel threatened by them. But she was too busy looking for someone in particular.

Some of their guests were playing beer pong. A number of them found their way into Gregory's game room and were shooting pool or playing darts. Loud laughing gave the music its only competition. Some had started the latest slasher flick over in the 'media room' on a projection TV. Nearly everyone was going in and out of the kitchen at regular intervals. None of these interested Chloe. She kept on her search.

"What are you looking for?" Bre asked.

Chloe turned to her and waved her hand. "Nothing. There are just a couple of crucial elements missing, that's all. As awesome as this party is, it would be an utter failure without our special guest. Well, actually *two* special guests." She interrupted herself. "You!" She grabbed some dude by the collar. Smoke was swirling about his head as he exhaled. Chloe was mad. Never letting go of his collar, she vocally escorted him toward the front of the house. "Look, we just went over the ground rules. Where were you? I don't care what that is – no smoking period! My dad quit two years ago, which means that he is now super-sensitive to the smell. If he even remotely senses it on the furniture, the curtains, anything, it means my neck. So take that junk outside." She opened the door and sent him out to finish his smoke on the porch. The young man in question silently complied. Chloe turned back to Bre. "And that one even goes to our

277

school, the big dummy. Whatever that was, it didn't smell like tobacco. I don't know and I don't care. They just better not be bring that in *my* house. Now where were we?"

Bre smirked and fixated on Chloe's face. "Two special guests. Well, I know who one of them is. You're watching for Wesley."

Chloe gave a fake surprised look. "Why, Bre! How did you figure that one out? He is only one of the finest guys in the entire school."

"But who else are you missing?"

"Oh, no one special ..." Chloe said behind a mischievous grin. "Only tonight's entertainment. But don't worry. I'm sure he'll be here. Besides, I don't think that I could honestly scare him off. Maybe tonight will help with that."

Bre increased her focus. "That *does* sound intriguing. I can scarcely wait."

"Well, then. I'll make sure that you get a front row seat. It will be quite a show – and that's a Chloe Chastain guarantee."

Wesley turned off the lights and set the alarm to the house as he exited. He descended the front steps to his car and climbed in. The debate on whether he should go or not had been going back and forth in his head all day like an endless tennis game. In many ways, he had no desire to attend Chloe's stupid Daylight Savings Time party. *Just what is that anyway? That's not even a thing. No one has a party for that.* It did seem rather meaningless. But it was something to do. Sitting around in this cold mausoleum while his parents were out-of-town again did not appeal to him that night. So he just found himself going - - even with all of Chloe's not-so-subtle advances inevitably on the horizon.

CHAPTER 32

A RED FLAG

This was not right. It was starting to feel more like a long, unbearable road trip rather than a quick pizza run. The silence was unbearable. Curtis continued to stare at the road ahead as he drove. Billy preferred to watch the houses and trees as they seemed to pass, secretly keeping up with their whereabouts on a mental map. In the meantime, the sun had just disappeared behind one of the many surrounding hills. Curtis reached down and turned on his headlights.

It was quite obvious to Curtis that Billy was angry about something. He replayed their earlier conversation over and over in his head and could not imagine what this was all about. In retrospect, Billy did seem rather detached when they spoke on the phone. Curtis considered the notion that Billy may have had it out with his folks just before he arrived and this may have put him in a bad humor. These things happen. He decided to be the one to engage his buddy in friendly conversation. "So what's up with you, tonight? It's been like fifteen minutes and you haven't said two words since we left your house." (The truth is that it had been nowhere near fifteen minutes, but it certainly felt that way.)

"Two words." Billy's reply had been a cold way of saying that he was in no frame of mind to talk.

I guess I walked smack into that one, Curtis thought to himself. Whatever rotten mood Billy was in started its successful transfer over to Curtis. "Are you going to be this nasty all night? Because if you don't want to come over, I can always turn this bucket around and take you back home. I'll call Mike and maybe we'll go over to see how Clay ..."

"Alright. Pull over right here."

"Do what?"

"Dude! Right here! Stop the car!"

"For what purpose?"

"Just stop."

"Alright already." Curtis pulled over and abruptly stopped the car. They were currently sitting in a very nice residential area, the more aristocratic side of town. Curtis was confused. He noticed that Billy's attitude that night had been weird, but why would he want to stop here? But before he could ask the question, Billy opened the car door and got out. "Hey! What is all this about?"

Billy turned around and looked back at Curtis without making eye contact. "Thanks, man. You're a real pal. I'll find someone to give me a lift back to your house later tonight. See you in a few hours. Save me some pizza."

"Huh? Just what do you think you are doing? Get back in the car."

"No way. Chloe invited me to a big party at her house tonight and this is the only way I could get there. Thanks buddy. I owe you one." He then closed the car door and began walking away.

Curtis was on the edge of being furious. This was not at all what he had expected. He undid his seatbelt and popped out of the car too. "Huh-uh! Wait a minute! Do you mean to tell me that you just used me tonight to get over to some stupid party over at Chloe's?"

"Oh, good grief. Don't sound so hurt," Billy said as he continued to walk away. "You know it isn't like that."

"Well then, how is it like? Do tell."

Billy stopped, turned around, and sighed. "Everyone *cool* is going to be at Chloe's tonight – no offense. And she has invited me to hang out. So I'm going to this party."

"I don't like this, Billy. This is NOT cool on so many different levels. For instance, what do I say if your folks call?"

Billy started walking away at the posing of this question. "You're a smart guy. You'll think of something." Billy had a considerable distance from Curtis by this time.

Curtis was dumbstruck. He stood there staring at Billy's silhouetted outline as he walked down one of the residential roads leading away from where the car was. "I'm not lying for you!" Curtis yelled. He could barely make out Billy waving back at him.

This entire situation left Curtis flabbergasted and ticked. He took a few steps away from his car in the opposite direction from Billy. "I can't believe this. I *cannot* believe this. This is bad." He looked up, over the posh houses, over the trees that stood like guardians over the houses, further up at the darkening sky. He knew precisely Who to talk to. "God, what am I supposed to do now?" He waited for an answer quietly. In the distance, he could now hear the frogs and crickets just beginning their nightly concert. A change of expression took over his face as he looked back toward Billy's direction. "I know exactly what to do." His voice sounded with decided resolve.

With a quickened pace, he began his way back to the car while he hit a speed dial button on his phone. He was pulling it up to his ear as he was getting back in his car. "Hey! Mike? Yeah, it's me. Billy needs some strong help right now. How soon can you get to Clay's? Good. Let him know that I'm on my way too. There's a bit of a crisis happening and we need to get a higher authority on this job right now. I'll see you there." He hung up his phone and started his car.

Billy had a general idea which house was Chloe's, but it was quite obvious when he got close. Cars were lined up around the front of her house. All the lights were kicked on. But he could have found it blindfolded because he could hear the pulse of the music long before you could see her house. The house itself was a knock out in every way. It may have had some slight age on it, but it was still magnificent. The house might even be described as 'outrageous' by Pecan Falls standards.

As the sophomore approached the front porch, he noticed about four guys blocking the door. They were all smoking and had cups in their hands. With slurred speech, one of them with long dark curly hair said, "Hark! Who goes there?" The others laughed and elbowed each other playfully. "What's the secret password?" They laughed harder this time. All four started to repeat the question. "Yeah. What's the secret password?"

Billy was caught a little off-guard. He should have expected this, but he was not really thinking about what he would find. How do you deal with tipsy people? He decided to play it as cool as he knew how. "I don't know. What *is* the password?"

If these guys were in the mood, things could have gotten ugly depending on how agitated they were. But they were amused and began to snicker at his reaction. What followed was a failed attempt at speech accompanied by drunken, sputtering laughter. In seconds, they were all playfully debating over what would make a suitable password – each with their own convictions. Fortunately for Billy, Chloe came to the door and saved the day.

"Alright guys. Step to the side. This is a special guest of mine."

They reacted with a touch of sarcasm as if he was royalty but without anything special about him. But Chloe grabbed Billy by the wrist and pulled him through the group of self-appointed sentry guards. As Billy passed through them, he detected their reeky smell and it reminded him of minor league baseball games.

As soon as they entered the house, Chloe said, "Thank goodness you're here."

Wow. That was so nice to hear. Billy was now feeling accepted at this cool party - - a party that his stuffy parents would never approve of. "Are you kidding? I wouldn't miss this party for the world. Thanks for inviting ..." Billy stopped in midsentence when he saw the interior of the house. There was a lot to take in. The house itself looked pretty old, but not a bad-old - - more of a classic old. But all the things in the room looked new, like the showroom of a furniture store. He had often wondered if anyone actually lived like this. *We could live just like this*, he thought, *if my closefisted parents would pay out for once.* The second thing he noticed was the people who populated the room. Some of them were people that he went to school with, but the majority of them were older, college-age people. This party was going to be way cool. The third thing that he noticed was the ever present music that was blaring.

"Hey! This place is great!" Billy had to shout.

Chloe struggled to hear him over the music. "What?"

Billy leaned closer to her ear. "I said that I think your house is awesome!" He noticed Chloe's dangling earrings and caught a whiff of her perfume as he spoke.

"Thanks! It's not much - - but it's home."

Billy thought her joke was a bit funny, but he kept playing it cool (or at least, he *thought* he was playing it cool). "Yeah. I like a house this size. We're currently looking for a new one. The place we're in is just way too small. You understand."

She could not quite hear that comment thanks to the music. She asked him to repeat it. He did.

Chloe was doing her best not to laugh at him. "Oh yes. I quite agree." She looked up and saw Bre. Bre looked back at her and gave her a knowing wink. Chloe grinned.

Bre figured out in no time that Billy was the surprise guest. Otherwise, why would he even be there? He was so far out of his social class at that moment, he should be crying.

Billy inhaled deeply and tried to look like he was built in. "It's so nice to be here tonight; to just chill with other kids like me - - without having to put up with the riffraff in this seedy little town."

Chloe looked around the room. "Well, you've come to the right place."

"What?" In spite of them shouting in each other's ears, they still struggled to hear each other.

Chloe held up a finger signaling him to wait right there while she walked off. She raced over to the stereo and turned it down a bit. It was still loud, but at least they could hear each other. She did not know why the music was so loud to begin with; half the people there had earbuds and their own tunes on anyway.

"I said that you certainly came to the right place tonight."

"I'm trying to remember what you said earlier this week. Something about your dad being out-of-town this weekend?" he asked.

"Uh-huh. He went on a business trip to San Antonio. ... or maybe it was San Diego. It was 'San something'. They're both the same."

"Well, which one was it? San Antonio or San Diego?"

"I don't know. Whichever one is close to Mexico."

Billy looked a little confused. The wisest course of action would be to let it go; but as stated earlier, he had abandoned all his wisdom tonight. If he had a lick of sense to begin with, he would not have even come to that party for starters. "I think San Diego is right on the border - - but I'm pretty sure that San Antonio is kinda close to Mexico too. That was where that big battle was fought against the Mexican army."

(In reality, Mr. Chastain's business trip had taken him to Lansing, Michigan – nowhere near Mexico.)

"Well, what difference does it make anyway?" Chloe just asked the question; she was far from interested in hearing a legitimate answer. In fact, she would not even be talking to him if she did not have something special up her sleeve - - which she just remembered about incidentally.

"One is in California and the other is in Texas. That's quite a long ..."

"I'm sorry but I can't possibly think about that right now because ..." She raised her voice considerably to finish her sentence. " ...the music is too loud!" The music was still pretty loud even though she had turned it down some. "But enough of that noise. Come here. I want you to do something for me. Let's go somewhere quiet – somewhere where we can be alone."

She grabbed his hand and led him toward another room. Something inside Billy began to freak out a little. Chloe was actually holding him by the hand. This was delightfully unexpected. Her hand was small and warm. He felt something like electrical shock waves running up the length of his arm and across his shoulders. His feet felt lighter. He just got there and the party was already looking monumental.

After zigzagging their way through the crowd, the two of them found themselves in Mr. Chastain's study. There were some books on shelf. On the far side of the room sat a large desk with a computer, a desk calendar, and one of those funny Newton's cradle things. Chloe rushed over behind Billy and closed the doors. They were sliding doors, hidden in the walls. In full view of Billy, she reached down and locked the doors.

This action set off a red flag in Billy's brain. He really should not be in there alone with her. His parents would totally flip out right now. As far as he knew, Chloe could use this opportunity to throw herself at him. With the music booming in the background, he felt like he was playing out a scene in a movie. This could get naughty real quickly. No one was seducing anyone - - but it certainly felt that way. There was no denying that this looked bad.

Honestly, Chloe was only interested in Wesley - - but Billy did not know that. At times like this, it is easy to forget about the consequences of our actions. Luckily, none of that would be happening in this story; no permanent damage resulted.

Nevertheless, Chloe got really close to Billy - - in a very flirty way. The concept of personal space was irrelevant. He let her lead him over to the computer. She reached down and took his hand in hers again. Standing directly in front of the computer, she placed his hand on the mouse and gently used his hand to influence the curser on the computer monitor. There was a function all set up ready to begin and the arrow slowly moved toward a button that said *Upload*. Her finger came down on his and together they clicked down on the mouse. The function began.

Billy was a little bewildered by this whole event. "What is this? What did we just do?" He narrowed his vision and his eyebrows got very serious. "What is going on here? Are you trying to upload some kind of file or something?"

She shrugged playfully. "Nothing much. I just edited a video and I wanted *you* to be the one to upload it on the internet for me. Don't worry; it's cool."

A slight smile appeared on Billy's face as he turned to face her. "You got me interested. Do I get to see it?"

"Oh yes. But not quite yet. You'll be able to see it soon. We'll have our own premiere here at the party. In the meantime, there are guests that I am neglecting. If you'll excuse me ..." She again motioned him out of the room.

In a few short seconds, he found himself outside the office, once again in the company of the other guests with the doors of the office closed and Chloe running off to find Bre. "What was *that* all about?" he asked. That little episode was weird and mysterious. Questions filled his eager head. The answers though eluded him.

... for now.

CHAPTER 33

BLENDING IN

One of the greatest gifts from God that is often taken for granted is the company of good friends. Billy did not yet understand that. What he certainly did not know is that his friends were standing in the gap for him even though he may have acted poorly toward them. Good friends will do battle on their behalf, even when help is not requested.

Maxine let Curtis into the house and sent him down the hall into Clay's room. He found Clay sitting on his bed while Mike took a chair next to him. After a rough explanation of the circumstances, Curtis got down on his knees in front of them both. They held hands as a united praying force.

Clay began. "Almighty God: The evil one is working on Billy. We pray for Your protection on him. Please deliver him from the traps that are set before him tonight …"

Matthew 18:20 says, "For where two or three are gathered together in my name, there am I in the midst of them." Clay's prayer was not the kind that you would expect to hear from some seasoned minister. It was just the words of a regular teenage boy. But you better believe that God was all ears that night.

Their friend was busy looking about the house. He floated from room to room looking at the other guests. Many of them were completely unknown to him; those he may have recognized, he still did not know. Chloe was his single connection there. And for now, he wondered where she had gone. Starting any kind of conversation at a party such as this was going to prove difficult for him. Marching right up to strangers and starting deep conversations was not really his forte – that was more Mike's specialty. But he somehow managed to find his courage buried deep within and had decided to make a go of it.

He quickly found the first target for this social experiment. Billy sat uneasily in a seat next to an unknown, college-age type. "Hi. I'm Billy." The other guy turned to look at him but did not say anything. Billy waited for a polite response, but none came. So he tried again. "Are you a friend of Chloe's?" The other dude did not even change his expression. In fact, he really did not have any expression at all. Nothing. A complete blank. Perhaps he had trouble hearing. Billy repeated the question. This time, the other guy grinned but still said nothing. Clearly this was pointless. So, Billy felt that it was time to move on.

He made his way into another room and approached two girls who were laughing hysterically. The laughter was somewhat contagious and Billy had this same urge to laugh as well. After a few seconds of mutual laughing, Billy was curious enough to ask, "So, what are we laughing at?" The ladies began to laugh even more. "No really. What is so funny?" The laughing raised up another notch. "Uh … was something that I said funny?" Now the girls were laughing so hard, they could scarcely stand. As their bodies got limp, they began to rely on each other for physical support. Now they were howling with laughter. "I don't get it. Is there something wrong with me? Is it my hair?" While he was growing more self-conscience, they kept laughing harder and harder. The more Billy spoke, the harder they laughed. *I'm not having any success with these people*, he thought.

Wesley got out of his car and walked up the path to Chloe's front door. The boys previously standing at the door had long since gone inside since one of them had thrown-up in the bushes. So Wesley approached the door unhampered by any half-drunken, would-be bouncers. He rang the bell and waited, folding his arms behind him. After about ten seconds, he reached over and rang the bell again. Nothing. All he could hear was the thumping from some muffled loud music. *Why am I trying so hard to attend this horrible party? I don't even want to be here at all.* Wesley was mentally preparing himself to leave. He decided to split and go back to his car and drive back. His lonely abode was calling. But before he had the opportunity to turn on his pivot foot, Chloe opened the door excitedly.

"Wesley! You're here. I was beginning to wonder if you would ever show up."

Wesley avoided making eye contact. "Hello, Chloe." That lonesome house of his was now looking cozier in his mind.

She stepped outside and linked arms with a hesitant Wesley. She escorted him over the threshold. "Now that you are here, we can get this party started. This is your first time here, isn't it?"

"Yep."

"Well, I'm going to have to give you the extra special VIP tour later tonight. Are you thirsty?"

"No. Not right now. Who are all these people?"

Chloe began to laugh nervously. "Actually, I don't know. It's like I just opened the door and they all fell into the house. But don't worry; now that you are here, this party won't be so lame."

Wesley gave a crooked smile. "You are giving me way too much credit." Chloe thought his crooked smile was cute - - but being cute was far from Wesley's intention.

Chloe let go of Wesley's arm and twirled to face him. "Well, you just wait. This evening will certainly be one for the history books." Her eyes narrowed, which told him that something sneaky was going on.

Wesley had been avoiding eye contact but now he looked in her eyes as if he were studying her face. "*One for the history books*? Why? Just what sort of things do you have planned?"

Suddenly, Chloe's voice was changed from *flirty* to *very flirty*. "What indeed?" She lowered her chin and looked at him through suspicious eyes. She grinned. "Stick around and find out. This is gonna be fun." She turned and walked away in an alluring fashion.

Wesley certainly noticed. Physically, she was very attractive. But there was something about her personality that he did not trust. He thought, *I wonder what she meant by that.*

Billy missed all of that. He was wandering around throughout the house. He had noticed a while earlier someone either going in or coming out of a nearby door. Out of curiosity, he approached the door and opened it slowly. He instantly regretted that decision. A girl screamed from inside as he slammed the door shut again. Quickly, he raced away from the door to the other side of the room and pretended clumsily that nothing happened. But seconds later, the door opened again and an embarrassed young woman stormed out, purse in hand, and making a break toward the front door. She was followed by the guy that she was with. He looked furiously around the room to see who it was that interrupted them. Fortunately for Billy, the guy gave up and chased after his date.

The eight people or so that were in the room with Billy saw the whole thing and burst out with laughter. Billy was not really in a laughing mood, but he forced himself so that he could blend in. But if it were not for Chloe, he would have left at that moment. This was not really his idea of fun. He decided to quietly make his way into the room where some guests were watching a movie on a projection TV. Until he could spend more time with Chloe, maybe he could pass the time with whatever they were watching.

We all know what you are thinking. This boy is just going from one boring scenario to another. But worry not. The plot is about to thicken …

Diane had just finished putting the rest of dinner in the fridge as William put the last of the dishes in the dishwasher. They both adjourned from the kitchen/dining room to maybe find some old movie on TV. But on the way, Diane spotted Billy's blue duffle bag by the front door.

"Well, lookie here," she pointed it out to William. "Someone was in quite a hurry when he left. All his church clothes he planned to wear tomorrow are right here." She crossed over to the front of the couch and plopped herself down. "Why am I not surprised?"

"Maybe he'll want us to bring them with us in the morning. He can change there."

Diane looked over her shoulder at her husband. "Well, there may be other things in there that he may need before then. You probably need to call him just to make sure."

"That's not a problem. It would only take me a minute to run over to the Baker's." William pulled his phone out of his pocket and began to dial as he replied. "I'm on it."

Billy's phone rang okay, but he never heard it. He shut off the ringer.

After enough time, William lowered the phone from his ear and looked at the screen. "Hmmmm. That's weird. He didn't pick up. It kicked me into voice mail."

"They are probably too busy playing video games or something. Try calling Curtis. Do you have his number?"

"Yeah. It's in here." The phone rested in William's right palm and he scrolled down to the correct number with his right thumb.

The boys were all taking turns. Mike's prayer had followed Clay's and now Curtis' was winding down. "Heavenly Father, I don't know what has gotten into Billy tonight. Whatever it is, would you please knock some sense into him before he does something that he might regret? Please help him to find the right path. Please watch him and take care of him. All this we pray in Your Precious Son's Name ..."

In sincere unison, all three boys said, "Amen."

They sat looking at each other for a couple of seconds. Curtis then began to stand. He put his hand on Clay's shoulder with a firm and brotherly grip. "Alright, guys. Thanks. I'd better be getting home. I'm supposed to be picking up some pizza and my kid brother is probably going into full berserk mode right about now."

Clay looked back up at Curtis. "Hey, dude. Call us back when you hear something." He did not say it, but this was the first interaction he has had since the accident that was not totally focused on his missing legs. It felt nice. These were truly his lifelong friends.

Mike's facial expression suddenly changed. He viewed Curtis with questioning eyes. "Hey. What did you mean just then?" His words were laced in authentic interest.

Curtis did not know what he meant. "Huh? Do what?"

"You know - - during that prayer just now. What was that? You asked God to knock some sense into Billy before it was too late. That's a strong prayer, a heavy prayer, full of meaning. What if God actually did just as you asked?"

Right on cue, Curtis' phone began to ring. All three boys were startled slightly (although these tough guys would never admit it). Something about that ringing seemed scary and supernatural. Instantly, their blood ran ice cold.

Curtis pulled his phone out of his pocket in order to see who this call was from. It was the one person in the world that he did not want to talk to: William Harris. His friends looked to him with apprehension. Curtis returned their gaze with a pained look on his face. He reluctantly turned his phone outward to show his friends. Their jaws dropped.

Curtis Baker clearly did not want to pick up, but there was precious little choice in the matter. In that instant, he weighed the situation over in his head. Something deep inside was forcing him to do what he did next. He answered the call and brought the phone up to his head. "Hello?" This was going to be super awkward. He did not know how he was going to be able to hear Mr. Harris' voice over the sound of his own heart beating.

If Billy's dad knew anything, he covered it well. Mr. Harris' voice betrayed no suspicions. "Hey. I'm sorry for bothering you, but Billy isn't answering his phone. Could I speak to him, please?"

"Uh ..." How was he going to get out of this one? Here come the half-truths - - and he was going to have to pour it on thick. "I don't think he can come to the phone right at this moment."

"Oh? Why not? Is he in the bathroom?"

Now is his chance to lie. The bathroom is the perfect alibi - - at least, for however long it would take for someone to come out. And for all Curtis knew, Billy really could be in the bathroom at that exact moment. If he could convince Mr. Harris that his son would call him back later, Curtis could try to get Billy on the phone and tell him to call his dad right away. If he played his cards carefully, that would make it right.

No. That would be dishonest. He may be able to muddle through the call without technically lying – but the core of his statements would not be the truth. Falsehoods would be at the heart of his meaning. And lying would not truly solve anything; in fact, it would make the situation worse. In addition, Mr. Harris would eventually find out the truth. Once that happens, Mr. and Mrs. Harris would never be able to truly trust Curtis again. And what about the example of his friends? What about God? Curtis just got finished praying to God, and now he is thinking about lying. How pathetic is that?

Curtis closed his eyes and began to speak. "I cannot get Billy to my phone right now because I'm not with him at this moment. That is to say, he is not with me."

"Oh? And just where is he?" came the voice over the phone.

Curtis took a deep breath. *Here it goes.* "I'm assuming that he is at Chloe Chastain's house."

"Chloe Chastain's house? I thought he was with you. What is he doing over at the Chastain's house?"

"Well, she is throwing some big party tonight. She invited Billy and so he went."

There was a long pause.

"He didn't say anything to us about any party."

Curtis could hear Mrs. Harris in the background. "Party?"

Mr. Harris continued. "What kind of party is this? Is it very …?"

"Very."

"Did you know anything about this when you picked him up tonight?"

"No, Mr. Harris. I swear. I was surprised by it myself."

"I see." Mr. Harris gave another thoughtful pause. "Well, I'm just going to invite myself over to this party. I'm sure there is nothing like a concerned father to liven things up."

"Do you know where it is?"

"In this small town? Everyone knows where the Chastain's live. Curtis, thank you for your honesty. You've done us a service tonight."

Curtis' face said, *What have I just done?* He ended the conversation. "You're welcome, Mr. Harris. Bye." He sat down stunned.

Clay and Mike said nothing. They simply stared at Curtis in disbelief. They understood that Curtis only said what he needed to say. Had they just witnessed strange forces at work?

Curtis was still shocked from the entire conversation. He made sure that the call was done and then he quietly put his phone down. He cleared his throat uncomfortably. "Uh, guys? We may need to pray for Billy all over again. His parents are going to kill him."

William quickly slid his arms through his jacket and grabbed his keys. "I need to get Billy. He has decided *not* to go to Curtis' house and has gone to some wild party over at Chloe Chastain's instead."

Diane's face was very concerned as she watched her husband. "Yes. Go get him and bring him home. But please be careful. Don't do or say anything dumb."

"Don't worry. I won't. I may not win any *cool daddy* awards tonight in the eyes of our boy, but I won't do anything weird. Trust me."

She tried to lighten his mood. "Is this one for your journals?"

He replied with an amused grunt. With that, he was out the door and gone. The truck made its usual loud squeal as it backed out of the driveway.

Diane prayed.

CHAPTER 34

TONIGHT'S ENTERTAINMENT

Billy stood in the back of a room watching an enormous projection TV. Seated there were a half a dozen guys and a couple of girls. They were watching one of the many movies in the *Axe-Head* series (do not ask which one; they are all pretty much interchangeable). Billy had heard of them and was mildly curious. Joining the movie-watching crowd seemed like a good way to 'lay-low' until he could talk to Chloe again. He looked up at the screen and was instantly drawn into the action.

Some movies have to be seen from the very beginning. This was not one of those. As expected, Billy already knew that he did not have to be bothered with 'plotlines'. The plot was simply this: a group of beautiful and sexually-charged young adults retreat back into the woods for some unsupervised immoral activity and are then killed off in a variety of gory techniques by some big brute with an appreciation for axes, large knives, and other pointy objects.

At this particular point in the movie, a lovely young woman was wearing her boyfriend's shirt (pretty much all she was wearing as far as Billy could tell). She was looking all over the farm house for her friends and was having no luck.

Some of the guys in the room with Billy sat up in their chairs and became very excited. In spite of the boys' enthusiasm, the two girls in the room started talking about something unrelated, trying their best to rise above the noise. Billy overheard what the boys were saying. "Is this the part where …" "Yeah, yeah." "Quiet, you two. This is the good part."

Billy would have preferred to have someplace else to go – especially if that involved talking to Chloe. But fueled by his own curiosity, Billy decided to stick around as the movie played itself out.

The girl in the movie walked outside into the rural nighttime scene, still calling out for her suspiciously absent boyfriend. (Billy may logically presume that her boyfriend had already met his untimely demise in the film.) Everything was lit up with blue moonlight. Somewhere behind a wall of fog, the sound of a motorcycle began to get louder. The girl fearfully turned to see where this noise was coming from. Suddenly breaking through the eerie fog, the silhouetted form of a man riding a motorcycle was headed toward her. He was swinging what looked like a lawnmower blade on the end of a chain. But rather than seeking shelter, the young woman took off running down the road away from her pursuer and screaming like an idiot.

Several of the boys in the room offered commentary in regard to her lack of intelligent thought and offered her an alternative course of action, which was hopelessly ignored since viewers are incapable of communicating with movie characters. It was clear to assume that this actress' part in the movie was just about finished, unless her body made a brief and frightening cameo in the last reel.

Something down inside Billy strongly urged him to consider leaving the room. He kept telling his head, *this is just a movie, this is just a movie.* But apparently his legs did not get the message. As curious as he was, he did not want to see what was about to occur next. He made his way to the door doing his best to leave the room without drawing attention to himself; this was not an issue considering how focused the others were on the film. Perhaps he could find Chloe. As he made his way into the hallway, he could hear those watching the video. They formed a loud choir reporting the kill with their yells and moans. The first of these sounds started low and crescendoed into an inescapable declarative chord. "OHHHHHH!!" "OHHHHH!!" Billy's curiosity was satisfied. The celebration of violence with no purpose would have to continue without him.

Billy came to this party really hoping to blend in. His little experiment was not working at all. The longer he stayed, the more uncomfortable he became. He imagined Curtis catching up with the others, his arms busy carrying pizzas and soft drinks. That was the kind of fun that he understood.

But alas, he finally saw Chloe again. He managed to get her attention. She responded with a bright cheery smile and a comforting wave. Both Chloe and Bre began to make their way over to him. Just before they reached him, two of her more inebriated guests bumped into each other in full view of their hostess. The result was a spilled beer on the carpet and some cursing on the part of Chloe. She then quickly ran off to get something to clean up the mess.

Her choice of words certainly gave Billy pause. What she said was not particularly strange. People may not speak that way at *his* house, but this was language that he heard many times a day from other students. Plus, you cannot turn on the TV without hearing it as well (maybe it was a television rule somewhere). But he always pictured Chloe as some kind of perfect girl, an angel among us. Somehow hearing her swear tainted the vision he had of her, made her appear earthy and soiled in terms of her character and personality.

Oddly, it was not the idea of her cussing that bothered him as much as it was her casual attitude toward the word *hell*. When she bawled at her drunken guests, she asked what they thought they were doing and did so emphasizing the word *hell* in her sentence, perhaps to add weight and passion to her outrage. It suddenly occurred to Billy that people who use the word *hell* so easily as an expression must not take the reality of Hell very seriously. But previous conversations with his parents, listening to his pastor, and reading his Bible had given him a disturbing mental image, one that cannot be taken lightly.

Side note: This culture has, in fact, stopped using a capital letter *H* when writing out the word *hell*; and yet, the rules of English make it clear that we capitalize the names of proper places. Maybe the English language no longer sees Hell as a real place.

Cartoons and movies always poke humor at the concept of Hell, primarily falling in one of two possible categories. The first one is of people getting up in Hell's version of morning, punching a timeclock, and working under hot, subterranean conditions with demons tormenting them with their little pitchforks. This shows Hell as a bummer. The second category presents Hell as a bunch of drinking buddies gathering in a dark cave for a screaming heavy metal concert featuring pentagrams and goats' heads. Everyone is partying it up with the devil for eternity. Little goodie-two-shoes are not allowed, but it looks like a blast. This is usually accompanied with images of heaven filled with a bunch of bored people sitting on clouds strumming on little harps. This idea depicts Hell as an awesome treat and Heaven as a dull and unexpected punishment. But these notions are manmade misconceptions and lead to false ideas.

The Bible says that Hell was not made for man. Someday the devil and his army will be cast into Hell where the wrath of God will be poured out onto them. Mankind was tricked into sin and thereby suffer the torture and agony that was meant for the devil. The heat is beyond our understanding. The Scriptures also speak of worms that torment and painfully gnaw on their victims without any kind of relief. Those who are there are thought to be gagging and drowning in the toxic fumes. The claustrophobic darkness, loneliness, hopelessness, despair are all on a level that cannot be measured by earthly standards. There is no relief, no day and night cycle, and no hope; only eternal pain and eternal regret. But one thing that is often overlooked is that God's presence is not felt there. People have no appreciation for God's ever presence until it is taken away. And simply put, that is what makes Hell unbearable.

The other idea that always seemed to short-circuit Billy's brain is that of eternity. All songs, movies, books, even video games have an ending point. Eternity does not. If Billy took the longest amount of time he could wrap his head around and multiply that by a million, it still would not even come close since there is no end. Then a thought overtook Billy's mind. *At any given point in eternity, you can still say, "This is only the beginning."*

So how can people use the word *hell* in such a glib fashion? How can someone trivialize something as serious as that?

Billy began to look around the room. Now all he saw were the hollow eyes of people who were headed to Hell. They were busy having their own version of fun and not facing the reality of their spiritual peril. He knew that he was supposed to warn them somehow, but he was afraid. How could a person witness to a bunch of people who were fairly intoxicated anyway? Suddenly, a wave of fear struck him in the gut. He knew that he had to leave the house. A voice inside said, *Do it now. Don't even wait.*

He remembered how to get to the outside door and quickly made his way through to the main hallway. He seemed to float over to the door. He did not even think about Chloe and how rude this may appear to be. The only thing on his mind was exiting this house of spiritual death. His hand reached out and turned the knob. He gave the door and gentle pull, but to his surprise the door closed again. A severe chill leaped up his spine. *Did demonic forces just close this door? This is like a scary movie.* He looked over and Chloe had closed the door by leaning on it.

"You're not leaving yet are you?" Her voice was rather flirty and friendly.

"Well, I was … uh …"

"The cool part is just starting." Chloe grabbed him by the arm. Her touch did not exactly affect him the same way that it did before, but she still managed to lead him into the room with the big TV. "Everyone, it is time for tonight's entertainment. I've already asked Bre to bring everyone into the media room." She leaned him up against the wall as she began to address the others. "Hey! Everyone! Come in here." About two dozen people or so were already filing into the room. "Come in and find a place to sit." With the remote, she paused the movie that was on. Those watching it began to moan a little. "Don't worry. This will only take a few minutes and then you can get back to your stupid movie."

The last of the guests walked in. Wesley himself was standing in the rear of the room, always within Chloe's peripheral vision.

"Alright. Is everyone in here? Good." Chloe made her way up to the front of the room just in front of the enormous lit-up image. "Folks, I have made a video for tonight's entertainment and I think you are going to love it. I have a copy of it right here." She held up a disc and quickly replaced the one already in the player. "But just so you know, with the aid of Billy here …" She gestured toward Billy and motioned him to come up to the front where she was. " …I put it on the internet so anyone could see it." She again turned to Billy. "Billy? Why don't you come up here and be one of the first to watch it? Right here in the front?"

Billy was reluctant and even a little shy, but he walked over to Chloe. Something in the back of his mind was telling him that he should not have even come, but he thought that he would go ahead and do this thing – whatever it was – and then make a gracious exit. He sat front row center, exactly where Chloe indicated.

In the meantime, the other guests were wanting to clap. But they did not exactly know what they would be clapping for, so they refrained themselves.

Chloe started the video, quickly spun toward the audience, and gave an excited little clap. "Showtime!" With that, she was out of their way and running to the back of the room where she could observe those in attendance.

A video selfie of Chloe filled the screen. The picture featured her sitting in the driver's seat of her car. "Hi, everyone! Chloe Chastain here and I am coming to you from the home of Billy Harris." The camera panned to the side to reveal the front of Billy's house.

Billy felt the heat on his face from blushing. He tried to smile a little, but he was quite ashamed of his house. And there it was, being projected on this big wall in all of its ugliness before everyone's eyes. Sitting there in Chloe's house, his house looked even smaller and more unattractive than ever.

The image moved back to Chloe's face. "But the question that you may be asking yourself is 'Why am I here?' The truth is that I'm wondering that myself." She gave a hint of a laugh and continued. "I happen to know that Billy has a bit of a crush on me."

Billy had a full straight-up blush going on now. The crowd gave out a loud collective, "Awwww ..." A couple of the guys sitting around him even gave him a gentle nudge.

With that reaction, it was difficult to make out the next thing that the video said. But the video continued to play, not waiting for the crowd to get quiet. " ...plus, he is a hopeless nerd." She rolled her eyes and dropped her smile. The tone of her voice altered. "His dad is a jerk of a teacher. I'm guessing that his mom is some scary hag too. And their house looks a bit run down in this creepy neighborhood." A few in the crowd chuckled.

Billy was no longer smiling. A sense of extreme hurt and discomfort swept over him.

"Well? Shall we go see just what kind of a dump this is?" The camera followed her as she got out of her car. The image swung back and forth a bit when she was walking. The image was taken from about waist high. It seemed to look like one of those undercover detective news shows, as if a hidden camera was part of her purse.

Everyone in the room was busy trying to make out the image that they were seeing. Billy had no trouble; it was clearly his front door. He saw the image of himself opening the door. His awkwardness led to more snickers from the group of guests. As the Billy on video kept trying to convince Chloe that they had another house, a pricier house, the few chuckles grew into louder, uproarious laughter. Billy faced the floor and began to wish that he could vanish. When he finally looked up again, he saw the image of him lifting his underwear off the floor and trying to tuck it into his pants. The room roared.

While nearly everyone was enjoying the video, Chloe had acknowledged that her phone was vibrating in her pocket. She pulled it out and noticed that it was her father calling. She pressed the *ignore* button and slid it back into her pocket.

Praying while driving was an old habit of William's. Even with the noisy fan belt, he considered it a quiet place and a solitary place when he was driving alone. He prayed for his son. But his prayer seemed incomplete until he had prayed for himself, prayed that God would bless him with wisdom in this situation - - a prayer that he was used to praying as a godly parent.

Billy had no idea that so many people were praying for him that night. His mom was on the couch at home having prayed. And his three friends had also just finished praying. This would never occur to him because his thoughts were only on his own schemes and his own pleasure. Now, his thoughts focused only on his own misery.

The Billy on the video grabbed a paper towel and spin the entire roll. It kept unrolling and unrolling. The more it unrolled, the more everyone laughed - - everyone except Billy. Surrounded in close quarters on all sides and yet he felt such loneliness. This was actually worse than just loneliness, because all the attention was on him looking like an idiot.

Billy had had enough. Without even giving it any thought, he rose to his feet and began the slow, shameful walk toward the front door. Everyone remained laughing at the video which was still not over. People pointed at him as he walked.

He heard Chloe speaking to him in a loud voice. "What's wrong, rich boy? I thought this is what you wanted: to be more popular." She followed him to the front. As he walked out, she stood in the doorway yelling. "Check it out! You're the life of the party! THANKS FOR COMING!" She slammed the door behind him. By this time, the video was winding down. Chloe ran in front of everyone and was casting her shadow on the screen. "He tries to pass himself off as being filthy rich, but you should see his house." Everyone was still laughing so Chloe spoke as loudly as she could. "I promise you, if his house were to burn down - - and I mean to the ground, it would be a service to the community!"

This last sentence had everyone in hysterics ... almost. Two people were not laughing. Bre did not know what to make of this. Maybe it was because she had not been drinking as much as the others. The other guests had been sufficiently loosened up. But Bre stood in the doorway watching everyone with a sense of horror. In her heart, she did not approve of how far Chloe had taken this little gag of hers.

The other non-smiling face in the room belonged to Wesley. He observed Chloe as she walked Billy to the door and as she returned back to the front of the room. At the sound of her making that crack about the Harris' house burning down, Wesley was furious. He also began a deliberate march toward the door.

Chloe noticed him as he exited the media room. Her smile fell from her face as she gave chase. She caught up with him at the door. "Wait! Wait! Wesley!" She ran past Bre, who was not enjoying any of this. "Wait a minute, Wesley. Where are you going? The party is just getting good. So what did you think of my hilarious video?"

He was thoroughly disgusted with her and did not care if she knew. "Do you want my honest opinion? Or would you like me to tell you what you really want to hear?"

Chloe was shocked. "You didn't like it?"

"Chloe, sometimes I am convinced that you are the most vicious person that I know."

Bre looked away. She was well in listening range, but she just could not face either of them at that moment.

Chloe forced a smile. "Come on, Wesley. Snap out of this. It's a party. We're supposed to be having fun." Her voice reverted back into a more sultry tone. "And I still owe you that VIP tour of the house."

She began to put her arms around Wesley's neck in an attempt to reel him back in. Wesley had other ideas however as he pushed her arms away.

"You just pulled this guy apart in front of all these people. You would've destroyed him if you had the chance, and all because his family is somewhat poor. Why don't you save your little tour for someone who isn't as squeamish as I am?" He looked past her at the door and started walking. He did not look at her as he passed. "I'm going home." The door closed behind Wesley.

"Wesley?" Not all of her guests had seen this little drama unfold, but there were just enough to make her realize that she had made a fool of herself over Wesley. She felt an immense cry coming on. There was no preventing it at this point. She quickly ran upstairs to get away from everyone and be alone. Even Bre kept her distance.

Wesley angrily stepped away from Chloe's house and stomped his way over to his car. Within a few seconds, he turned on the ignition and sped off. He did not notice that he was being watched the entire time.

Billy had no way home, so he had been standing from around the corner of Chloe's house. The sun had gone down, but there was still plenty of light to see. Now what was he supposed to do? He could spend the better part of that evening walking home. Instead, Billy pulled his phone out of his pocket and called the first person he thought of …

CHAPTER 35

WHEN I WAS YOUR AGE

Billy's distinctive ringtone sounded from the phone in William's shirt pocket. As he drove, he reached in and answered using the speaker phone option, placing it in the passenger's seat. "Billy? Is that you?"

For Billy, his father's familiar voice was enough. He felt much better hearing William's strong baritone. It communicated a dozen auditory images at once: *home, security, family.* This time, the sound of his dad's voice did not communicate the word *nerd* at all. Since his dad had been there from the beginning, there was no sense in Billy pretending to be something he was not. He decided that honesty was certainly the best policy now more than ever – perhaps the most intelligent thing that he did all night.

"Yes sir, it's me," he answered. "Dad? I've … uh. I've done something terrible."

There was a momentary pause. In a patient and understanding voice, William said, "I'm listening."

Wow. This is going to be tough, he thought to himself. Daylight savings time had not yet kicked in, but the sun had already gone down and it was getting darker. With it, the temperature too was dropping. Billy had only been standing outside of Chloe's house for a few short minutes, but he was already feeling chilly. He returned to the corner of Chloe's house where he could get an okay view along the front and across the spacious yard. No one was coming or going at present. It was now time to come clean with his dad.

303

"Well, Chloe Chastain invited me over to this big party at her house. I really didn't know what to expect actually, but I knew that you and mom probably wouldn't agree to let me go." Deep breath. "So I didn't tell you about it. That way, at least you never told me that I *couldn't* go. In fact, I didn't even tell Curtis about it. I kinda tricked him into bringing me. What I did tonight was completely wrong; I know that now. I allowed you and mom to think that I was going to Curtis'. I am so incredibly sorry. Anyway, she only invited me so that ..."

Billy's voice began to choke up as he attempted to speak. Once it started, he could not make it stop. His eyes were swelling with tears. A huge tsunami of emotion crashed right into him and he was helpless in its path.

William was on the phone deeply concerned. "Billy? What did they do to you?" He listened and for a moment all he heard was the sound of weeping. "Billy? Did they hurt you physically?"

Billy was finally able to get some words out. "No. It wasn't like that."

William took a deep breath and tried again very slowly. "Billy? What happened tonight?"

Somewhere inside, Billy found the strength to talk. "Dad, she only invited me over so that she and all the others could laugh at me. I wanted to be so popular with these kids. I wanted them to accept me and to want me to be a part of their crowd. But they're horrible people, dad." He turned his back again to the front of the house and gazed at nothing in particular along the right side of Chloe's house. "I wish that I had never come here tonight."

The tone of his dad's voice changed on the other end of the phone. "I have a question for you. Why did you call me?"

"What do you mean?" Billy perked up.

"Well, you could've called Curtis and *he* could've picked you up."

Billy's jaw dropped. His brain wasted no time putting his two's and two's together. If this were a 1940's cartoon, his head would have turned into a donkey's and then back again. "OH MAN!! I didn't even think about that!"

"Well, I'm certainly glad that you didn't."

"Dad?"

"Yeah, Billy?"

"I've learned something very valuable tonight."

"And what is that?"

Billy's tone suddenly got very serious. "I've learned that all rich kids are horrible and I hate them."

William was rather surprised by his son's rather superlative statement. "Well, that doesn't make any sense. That would be like saying that all poor kids are nice and that isn't true either. Besides, I can pretty much guarantee that we have more money than any of them – and you're a good kid – when you aren't trying to deceive your parents."

Billy had a nice chuckle at that comment. "Dad, would you please do me a favor?"

"Sure. What is it?"

"Would you come pick me up? I'm at the Chastains' house. And I want you to come as soon as you can."

William eyed the truck he was in and grinned. "Okay. I'll see what I can do. But let me ask you something first. When is the last time you sincerely talked to God?"

Billy was not expecting that question. For the most part, all he could think about was going home. He answered, "I don't know. It's been a while, I guess."

William's voice was difficult to describe. It was part *wise old sage* and part *loving friend.* "Well, while I'm making my way over there, why don't you give it a try?"

"Alright. And dad?"

"Yeah?"

"I'm very glad I called *you* instead of Curtis. Right now, I want to be at home with you and mom."

Back in William's truck, a slight smile appeared on this father's face. "And I'm all too happy to come get you, squirt. I'll see you as soon as I can get there."

"Bye, dad."

"Bye."

They hung up their phones.

Billy still stood at the corner of the house to the right of the front door facing away from the house. He took a deep breath and began to talk to God. He was being real and sincere. Because he was facing away, he failed to notice the set of headlights approaching the house from the other side. "Heavenly Father. I know it has been a while since I have honestly talked to you like this. I'm sorry."

William parked his truck on the far side of the house, turned off his headlights, and climbed out. By some miracle, the fan belt did not make a peep. He began to take the long walk across the yard to the front door of Chloe's house.

"I'm sorry for so many things actually. Coming here tonight was not at all smart on my part."

At this point, William looked across and saw Billy's back. He altered his course to intersect with his son.

"And I learned that some people just don't want to be my friend. Please help me to get over that. And I imagine that I've hurt those who love me. Right now, I just hate being here. I want to leave this awful place so bad. I know it'll take dad like fifteen minutes to get here, but I can't wait. Can you please get my dad over here sooner than that? Over here in record time?"

William was within a few feet behind Billy when he spoke. "Alright! Are you ready to go?"

The sound startled Billy. He turned around. There was his dad. "Dude! How did you …?" He instinctively ran up to him and gave him a hug. For a moment, it looked like he was about to knock his dad over. He buried his face into William's chest. "Thank You! Thank You!"

"Huh?" He laughed a little. "Here. What's all this about?"

"Oh. Sorry, dad. I was talking to someone else."

William gave another slight laugh. "That's fine. I understand." He appeared to be thinking about something for a moment – like a memory – and gave another brief chuckle.

Billy looked up at his father. "Did I just say something funny?"

"No. Not at all. I was just thinking about the things that I put my own parents through …" He reached up and shook Billy's hair around with one hand. " …when I was your age."

They disconnected and started the long walk back to his truck. William noticed his son was starting to shiver a bit and offered his jacket to his son.

"No thanks. I'll be fine."

"Are you sure? I have another one in the truck."

"Well, in that case," he nodded and laughed a little bit as his dad took off his jacket. Billy promptly put it on. It was toasty warm from his dad's body heat and felt wonderfully nice.

After a few quiet moments, Billy began to speak. "Dad, this has been the worst night of my life."

"Well, you know what Scripture says …"

"Dad, right now I don't really want to hear another Bible quote."

A slightly surprised and disappointed expression came across William's face. This was different. He did not know what to say. So they kept walking in a strange sort of silence.

After about six more steps, Billy finally said, "Alright. What does the Bible say?"

William began talking as if those quiet seconds never occurred (which amused Billy). "'And fear not them which kill the body, but are not able to kill the soul: but rather fear him which is able to destroy both soul and body in hell.'" [Matthew 10:28]

By this time, they had both returned to the age-old truck. Billy began to make his way over to the driver's side, a habit that he quickly developed after getting his learner's permit.

"No, sir." William signaled him over to the passenger's side. "Kids who lie to their parents don't drive in this family."

Billy easily relinquished control with no fuss. Under normal circumstances, he may have objected rather loudly. Not tonight. Pitching a fit never even entered his mind.

Before getting in, William grabbed another jacket and put his arms through the sleeves. A quick zip later and they both sat in the truck; but rather than starting it, William was having an idea. He turned to his son with inquisitive eyes. "The 'worst night of your life,' huh?" He was definitely thinking. "Well, what if we tried to change all that? We *fall back* tonight so we gain an extra hour. Are you hungry?"

Billy considered the knots in his stomach following that horrible ordeal at Chloe's. "I'm not exactly starving, no."

"Could you eat in about an hour?"

"Uh, yeah. I guess so."

William's face lit up as he spoke. "Good, because I've got a great idea. Let's go down to Little Rock."

"Little Rock?"

"Yeah. Just you and me. It's only an hour away. We've got time." William gestured over to Chloe's house. "You thought *those kids* were important. Let's go see if we can have dinner tonight with some truly important people. It'll be fun."

"WHAT? Important people? We're not dressed for that. Don't you have to wear something fancy?"

"Oh, that doesn't matter. Trust me." William pulled his phone out of his shirt pocket and began to make a call. "But first, I've got to call your mom."

As William spoke with Diane on the phone, Billy had pulled his own phone out and began to text messages to Curtis. He had just remembered what he had done to his best friend and it sat on him like an elephant. If you subtracted the amount of time that it took to type out the messages and get them back and forth, and cleaned up the texts for any spelling and punctuation errors, than their conversation went like this ...

Billy: "Hey man. Tonight was horrible and it is all my fault. I'm sorry."

Curtis: "Dude! That's all you had to say."

Billy: "Thanks."

Curtis: "Thanks? For what?"

Billy: "For being you. For being my friend through the good and the not-so-good. I guess folks like me need to be taken down a notch or two every once in a while."

Curtis: "Hey! Do you want to go down to the Falls after church tomorrow?"

Billy: "That would be great. We need to go again before the weather gets too chilly. Good call."

Curtis: "See you at church."

Billy: "Okay. Bye."

Billy was completely ignoring the phone conversation that his parents were having. If he had been listening, he would have heard the following ...

"Diane? Yeah. He's a little shook up now, but he'll be fine. Say, I've had a flash of inspiration. I think I'll take Billy down to Little Rock for dinner. <pause> That's right. Would you do me a favor and call Officer Thomas and let him know that we are coming. <pause> Oh yeah. It'll be fine. I'm with him. Plus I honestly think that it'll do him a world of good. <pause>

That's right. Then he can see for himself. You know, first-hand. Do you want us to swing by and pick you up? <pause> Okay. Suit yourself. Right. Exactly. Yeah, if you would. Just call Officer Thomas and when he gives you the address, just text it to Billy. <pause> Well, you know if it doesn't pan out, we'll just grab a bite somewhere and come home and that'll be that. <pause> Alright. We'll see you when we get home. Love ya. Bye."

William turned back to Billy. "Well, we're set." He turned the key to the ignition and they were off. "Let's go meet some truly important people."

Important people, Billy thought. *What sort of hoity-toity place would take us in dressed like this?* He looked down at his plaid shorts, his superhero shirt, and a jacket a couple of sizes too big for him. *Who are we planning on meeting down there?*

CHAPTER 36

IMPORTANT PEOPLE

The hills were darkened. Father and son followed the headlights through town after tiny town. Their pace quickened once they hit the interstate. They drove past a number of larger towns, an Air Force base, restaurants, car dealerships, malls. Their route bent toward the right onto Interstate 40 briefly and they veered to the left going into Little Rock.

Many U. S. cities were built on rivers, cities such as St. Louis, Memphis, Louisville, Cincinnati, New Orleans, the list goes on. They can be rather beautiful at night. If you live near one, then you know. That is how Little Rock is. By far, the best way to come into Little Rock is from the north and crossing the bridge. The dramatic movement of the mean Arkansas River is calmed by the reflection of the city's bright lights. In the foreground is an ensemble of other bridges, most notably an old train bridge with its web-like structural beams. Bright colors race up and down all the bridges with new fanciful lights. Tall buildings presided high over the city. One of these buildings had lights streaking down the sides like a bright multicolored waterfall. Another had many interior lights on and resembled a large, vertical crossword puzzle lit up from within. Far in the background stood the capital building with its brightly lit marble dome looking like a giant Faberge egg at rest on a box shaped carton.

From the passenger side (best for observation), Billy gazed out the window. Being from a small town, it was strange to Billy, to think that people actually work in some of these beautiful monuments of metal and glass.

"What was that address that your mom sent?"

Billy snapped his attention back to his dad and looked down at his phone. "Uh, Broadway and Capital."

"Okay. Broadway and Capital. That's easy enough." William maneuvered their truck off the interstate and began to zigzag it through a maze of one-way streets downtown.

It was fascinating to see these streets at night. They were so busy during the day; but at this time, they were strangely empty and abandoned. Most of the activity on a Saturday night was occurring down by the river. Random cars were parked at the parking meters since they are not enforced during non-business hours. The two of them pulled into one such spot situated directly behind a parked police car.

William turned off the engine and all was silent in the cab of the truck. The father was releasing his seatbelt as he spoke. "Okay. This is it. That good man there is Officer Thomas. I'm going to go talk to him; you can stay here in the truck or you can come with me."

Billy nearly interrupted him with something that was weighing on his mind. "Dad, I've been meaning to ask you something – and I know this is random. Why is it that the people in Chess Club say *'Long Live Rodney'* every week?"

William was caught off guard by the timing of this question. It had nothing to do with where they were or what they were doing. A hundred times earlier would have been more appropriate. Nevertheless, he stopped what he was doing and turned to his son. "That? Oh, that's just a silly tradition. After everyone comes in, they mention who is absent. After that point, the first time someone brings up their name in conversation, they all say *LONG LIVE Whoever*. The club started that tradition long before any of the current members have been there. The students don't even know why they do it, but they do."

A hint of frustration was felt in Billy's voice. "I've been in there for weeks and weeks and never knew that."

A crooked smile appeared on William's face. Gently, he said, "Billy, all you had to do was ask." With that, he opened the door to the truck and got out.

Billy was left alone thinking that he should have asked for the truth behind the enigmatic president, Rodney. He thought he would remember to ask his dad in a few minutes. But no, he forgot all about it.

The police officer stayed in the patrol car as William walked up. They spoke briefly. Obviously they had known each other for a while. The policeman pointed over at a courtyard in front of one of the buildings and William turned to see where he was being directed. Shortly after, William was back at the truck opening the passenger door for Billy. "This is it. Let's go."

Billy climbed out of the truck and looked around. They were currently parked between the two tallest buildings in the state. *Do important people eat here?* he asked himself. The teenage boy tilted his head back to see the top of both buildings. "Where are we going?"

"Right over there." William gestured across the street to the courtyard just below the tallest building. There were a few benches strategically placed. William led his son across the street. "That's him. Right there." He pointed briefly. Billy's dad was pointing at a rough-looking, poorly dressed old man sitting on one of the benches. He was obviously some raggedy, homeless guy. He just sat there, doing nothing.

In a loud whisper, Billy protested. "Dad! What is this? I thought we were going to have dinner tonight with someone important."

He looked at Billy with no small amount of curiosity. "Did I say that?" In a brief moment, he realized that his son was right. But then a beaming smile reappeared on his face and he looked over at the homeless man. "Well, maybe there is a new definition of *'important'* waiting for us to discover sitting right over there. Come on. Let's go check it out."

Armed with his charming grin, William charged forward while Billy followed, always keeping at a safe distance. His dad rounded the bushes and sat on the bench right next to the old man. "Hey there, old-timer. My name is William and this is my son Billy." He gestured at his son, who hesitantly waved back. "Can I ask you what your name is?"

The old man had on a tattered old coat, a pair of wore out pants, and what appeared to be several layers of shirts. His lace-up boots had also seen better days. His scalp was covered with an old knit cap which also contained some holes. He was missing most of the fingertips on his gloves. The man had crazy, untrimmed eyebrows, some stubble on his thin and baggy face, and not a tooth in his head as it would seem. In a low mumbling voice and avoiding making eye-contact, the old man softly said, "Bill." His speech was weird; it was as if he was trying too hard to speak. Perhaps he did not talk as often as most people and it sometimes caught his mouth off-guard when the occasion called for it.

"Bill? That's funny. All three of us have the same name. My son and I were just wondering how long it has been since you've had something to eat." In contrast to the homeless man, William's voice was strong and energetic. In fact, this may not make any sense, but his voice had a luster to it - - that is to say that it lit up the scene. He was able to pull answers out of this old man with his magnetic personality. They began to have a light conversation of sorts.

Young Billy took a step closer. That was when he detected the smell. This guy totally reeked. He smelled as if someone took a pile of dirty clothes from the gym at school, covered them with cream corn, and then dumped them out in some barn somewhere for a pig to sit on. Somehow the teenager managed to control his gagging reflex and soon learned how to breathe around this old man. After a while, he failed to even notice it anymore - - well, not so much anyway.

Billy was not quite sure how it all happened, but he soon found himself helping his dad escort this tired old man to a nearby diner with a 1950's theme - - not unlike the pizza place up in Pecan Falls, except this was primarily a burger place. He noticed that his dad was in absolute control of the conversation, but not in an overbearing sort of way. He was strongly encouraging this man to contribute. Oddly, the conversation itself seemed to generate the power that the old man needed to physically get to the diner. His dad was like a battery pack for other people. Cool.

The three of them sat at a table – as opposed to a booth. The waitress came around and took their drink orders. The waitress automatically knew who William was and asked about Diane's whereabouts. After a quick answer, William introduced his son to her. Apparently, his parents had gone through this scenario a number of times before and were regular customers. Officer Thomas also entered the diner and took a seat close to the door, watching the proceedings from a comfortable distance. Soon, they were all perusing the menu.

As the food arrived, the old man removed a small fancy box out of his coat pocket. This red box was made from wood and was beautifully hand carved with intricate designs. He drew a fair amount of attention to it as he gently handled it. Billy was instantly intrigued. He thought, *What is so wonderfully important to this old man? Whatever could it be? Something priceless?* He glanced down to see what was in it. The oldster turned the latch on the small box and slowly lifted the lid. The anticipated surprise turned out to be the man's false teeth, which he excitedly inserted into his mouth with an accompanying clicking sound. Billy was partially grossed out at the sight, but he also wanted to bust out laughing. Fortunately, William gained his attention first and signaled Billy not to react, thereby causing the man to become uncomfortable or embarrassed. Billy tried to ignore it - - and was successful. His dad had always taught him that having class had nothing to do with how others treat you, but how you treat others.

While the old man ate, William pulled a small Bible out of his pocket and began to show him a few things. The old man listened intently. He was not the only one. Billy too had been observing his dad - - but not quite the same way. He was fascinated. Who was this man? Was this really his dad? He had always been such a nerd before. Not only did they keep the knowledge of their money a big secret from Billy, but now it appeared that there is this entire secret life that his folks have been living. Now some of the things he had seen began to make sense, especially the entire Clay incident. This was becoming a bit weird. ... but a good kind of weird.

After a while, they were all eating their own deserts. Between bites, the old man turned to Billy and asked if he could show him something. From another pocket, he produced a smaller case and opened it. It was a genuine Purple Heart. He was awarded it for injuries sustained in war. He told Billy the story of how it happened and it occurred to the teenager that he was sitting across from a living piece of history. This forgotten old man who Billy ordinarily would try to avoid on the streets had a fantastic and dramatic story to tell, his ups and his downs, the people who he had known and loved, his travels, his experiences, the events he had seen.

Billy did not have to do a thing. His dad was there and knew exactly what to do. The three of them and Officer Thomas walked down a few blocks to a homeless shelter where Bill could sleep on a cozy cot. But before he went in, William gave him the small Bible with his card inside. He also happened to have a gift card for a store to be used only for food. The folks at the shelter came out and acted like they had apparently seen William many times before - - perhaps he and Diane were financial supporters of this establishment. At this point, a discovery like that would not surprise young Billy.

But just before old man Bill turned to go inside, he went up to Billy and offered his hand. Billy was not too thrilled about shaking the dirty hand of a homeless old geezer, but something compelled him to do so – if nothing else, just to keep things from getting awkward. And as the war vet thanked the teenager, Billy caught himself locking eyes with this man. Under those bushy eyebrows were some glassy gray eyes. They were grateful eyes, intelligent eyes, eyes that had seen many changes to the world around him. Billy did not know what to say. Fortunately, nothing needed to be said at all. The old man turned toward the shelter's entrance and tottered his way inside with the aid from an orderly.

They walked back to their vehicles and William made his farewells to Officer Thomas. The ride back to Pecan Falls seemed long to Billy. He and his dad laughed, told funny stories, and even sang some of the silly songs that Billy liked when he was little. Billy shared with his dad about his brief history with Chloe and went into more details about that night. But somewhere along the way, Billy must have fallen asleep. When they got home, his dad pushed him over and told him to get in the house – or that is how it seemed.

The son was grateful to be back home. This long night had seen him act ugly toward his best friend, made him the target of ridicule to the very people he idolized, and found him in awe of his nerd/hero father. He managed to get a small drink, brush his teeth, take care of any bathroom business he had, and striped down to his boxer shorts and a tee-shirt. In record time, Billy was collapsing into his bed. It felt like a warm, cozy cloud. Having just met a man who had no bed, Billy appreciated his that much more.

William came to the door to say 'good night.' "So Squirt, do you think we were able to salvage something nice from this terrible evening?"

Billy stretched across the entire length of his bed, lightly punching the headboard with his fists. "Oh yeah. It was really great. Those rich kids really ticked me off earlier. But after our trip to Little Rock, I guess having lots of money has its advantages after all."

William's eyebrows shot up in surprise. "Uh, I don't think you understand. It doesn't take a lot of money to do what we did tonight. It only takes a thoughtful heart that is sensitive and willing to follow the Father's direction. That is something that anybody can do – no matter how much income they have at their disposal."

"Is that what we are called to do? Feed the hungry?"

"Honestly, were it not for the grace of God, we could be just as homeless in two seconds flat. So feeding and meeting the needs of the poor is certainly one way that we can show our gratitude to God for all He has done for us. But I wouldn't say that it's all about feeding people who are hungry; it's about looking for ways that we can serve God. And His plan is unique for everyone. What we did tonight is just one thing that your mother and I do. We try to be open to whatever work God has for us at that particular time."

"That's cool actually." Billy gave a sleepy smile.

William agreed, "Yes, it is. It's really cool." He walked across the room to Billy's bed, lifted his bangs up, and kissed him on the forehead the same way that he used to when Billy was little. "Look, it has been a very long day and an even longer night. After all, we did gain an hour. You look exhausted."

"I am," he said under a yawn.

William had just thought of something to share with his son. "You know, the recipe for a nice, peaceful sleep comes from taking the time to get to know God better. The formula is right there in Matthew 11:28-30, 'Come unto me, all ye that labour and are heavy laden, and I will give you rest. Take my yoke upon you, and learn of me; for I am meek and lowly in heart: and ye shall find rest unto your souls. For my yoke is easy, and my burden is light.' Now try to get some shuteye." Then he turned around and began to leave the room at last.

"Dad?"

William turned in the doorway to see his son. "Yes?"

"Thanks for coming to get me tonight. I love you. And tell mom that I love her too."

A warm, but slightly surprised, grin appeared on William's tired face. "And I love you, big guy. Now get some sleep." William turned off the light and closed the door behind him.

Everything in the house was silent. The only thing that could be heard was the familiar banging sound coming from that awful dryer. The doors were all locked. The lights were all out. And so it was with Billy. He could feel all of his energy seeping into the mattress. His bed had never felt so good in his life. Sleep overcame him starting down in his feet and working its way up to his head. He felt as if he were in a motionless freefall.

Billy slept.

CHAPTER 37

JOURNALS

So Billy had worn himself plum out over the course of the evening. This comes as no surprise whatsoever. In fact, all you readers out there may be tuckered out just from reading about his big night. But let us not neglect his ol' buddy Curtis. What was he doing (besides praying) the night of Chloe's big party? For the moment, we will rewind a few hours and pick up the action where we left him, over at Clay's house.

Curtis had prayed with his small band of prayer warriors, spoke on the phone with Mr. Harris, and then prayed all over again. Shortly after that, Curtis left – but he left feeling terrible. He had found himself in the uncomfortable position of having to inform Mr. Harris of what had happened. But he could not lie – and telling half-truths is the same thing as lying. To be perfectly frank, it was his best friend that put him in that dangerous circumstance in the first place; if anyone was to blame, it would be Billy Harris Jr. But we digress. Pointing fingers is a waste of time when we could be sharing their interesting tale.

Curtis stopped to pick up the pizzas (which were getting cold) and took them all home. After informing his parents that Billy was not coming after all, he ate and retreated back to the den.

Less than an hour later, his phone buzzed. Sure enough, it was Billy. The message read (making corrections in spelling, grammar, and punctuation), "Hey man. Tonight was horrible and it is all my fault. I'm sorry." Curtis smiled. Apparently, everything would be okay. Curtis knew that Billy would come around sooner or later – he always has. God truly answers prayer. Curtis began to reply back.

"Dude! That's all you had to say."

"Thanks."

Curtis looked down at his phone with curiosity. Was Billy thanking him for forgiving him so quickly? He texted back. "Thanks? For what?"

Billy's reply came quickly. "For being you. For being my friend through the good and the not-so-good. I guess folks like me need to be taken down a notch or two every once in a while."

The boys then made plans to see the Falls the next day after the morning service and texted their goodbyes. But something about this string of texts struck Curtis as strange. He scrolled back up and re-read the conversation. *"Folks like me? What was that supposed to mean?"* he asked himself. Curtis went back in his mind over the past few weeks. *Billy was talking about his family as if they were wealthy. Was that what he meant? Was Billy taking this gag too far or has he actually convinced himself of this nonsense? Wait a minute. Was it nonsense?* Curtis strode over to the computer and logged on. *If nothing else, I can prove him wrong with just a little research.* He grinned at the thought.

He looked up the stellar history of Crowe Athletic Equipment from its humble origins to its meteoric rise as a powerhouse corporation. Over the next twenty minutes or so, he familiarized himself with products, stores, merchandizing, and the like. Finally, he found an article that might be what he was looking for. Crowe did indeed have a board of directors. Their job was to keep the place swimming in the right direction. But the whole time, the founder was always at the head. He read on. Upon the founder's death, that position fell to his niece Diane Harris and her husband, William.

"DO WHAT?" Curtis did a double take. "Picture. Where's a picture?" He did some clicking around with no luck. Finally, he found a group shot of the board of directors that included a couple standing in the back. They *could* be the Harris'. He zoomed in. About fourteen years had gone by since the photo was shot. Their hair was slightly darker. They were both thinner in those days. And the man was holding a one-year-old baby boy. The baby was cheesing it up for the camera, proud of those two little baby teeth on the bottom row. Could that be Billy as a baby? Yeah, it was them. "Uh ... wow! So Billy was telling the truth. How cool is that?!"

He began to laugh at himself. The truth was right in front of his face and yet no one, not even Billy's best friend, would believe him. This was hilarious! One of the biggest enterprises in the world was being controlled by his buddy's family - - and they just lived in an average home just five houses down. This was too much. He sat at the computer for another ten minutes or so, reading some more, and then he logged off and laid down on his bed.

He lost himself in thought. He was thinking back to his friend Clay and his mom's modest finances. *I'll tell you one thing*, he said to himself. *If I had that kind of money, the Peck's would never have to worry about another medical bill ever again.* He stopped and considered that thought. *Wait a minute.* He sat up. *Clay's bills were paid by some mysterious stranger. Some generous person or persons took care of that. I wonder if ... Oh man! It has to be. Wow! This reminds me of the time when someone anonymously helped Mr. Piper replace his diesel rig when ...* Curtis may have stumbled upon something. *... when he lost it in that big fire. Oh wow! Come to think of it, someone quietly gave money to the Brown's when they were adopting those twin girls from Haiti. What's going on around here?* He was so excited about his discovery that Curtis got up and grabbed a pencil and some paper. He began to make a list of times that he had heard about local people being assisted by a silent benefactor. This little mystery was getting rather interesting.

It had been a long night. Let us review what we had witnessed for a matter of public record. Billy deceived his parents, felt out-of-place at a party, was publicly humiliated by the girl he was stuck on, was rescued by his dad, and had dinner with a homeless man down in the capital. Crazy night with a wild finish.

From William's point of view, the drive back to Pecan Falls from Little Rock seemed all too short. Father and son filled the time sharing funny stories and singing campy old songs. After a while, Billy started to slow down. They were still a few miles outside of Pecan Falls when William looked over and noticed that Billy's eyes were getting heavy. The truck may have had a half-tank of gas, but Billy himself was running on empty. Soon, he was out all-together. He had had a big night anyway so William did not mess with him. His son had earned this sleepy moment.

Soon, William pulled into their quiet driveway and turned off the engine. One of his greatest pleasures since bringing Billy home from the hospital as a baby had been watching him sleep. It was one of the most beautiful sights in the world to both William and Diane. Their son might be a teenager, but that much had not changed. The dad was still overwhelmed by the great gift God had given them. It was now time to get his son in the house, but William kept looking at him. Two minutes lapsed and he finally gave his son a gentle nudge. "Billy? Billy? Wake up. We're home. You need to go inside and get in your bed."

Billy moved slowly and had a big stretch. He then tried to open the door to the truck with his weak eyes barely open. William walked around the truck to be of assistance and directed his son toward the house. This sort of scenario had played itself out many times over the past fifteen years with slight variations in detail – the most popular of which involved William simply carrying Billy inside with his sleeping head firmly resting on William's shoulder, legs dangling in unresponsive slumber. Now that Billy was nearing man-size, that was *not* going to work; his days of being carried were long gone. Billy got up and stumbled his way to the house like something from a zombie movie.

While Billy was getting ready for bed, William had gone into the kitchen and poured himself a small glass of milk (whole milk – not 'diet milk' as he called it). After a few sips, he took the wet clothes from the washing machine and loaded them up in that demon-possessed dryer of theirs. He started the noisy appliance and finished his milk. On his way to bed, he stopped by Billy's room and had a small talk with him. The talk was wonderful. He informed his son that feeding the poor was not just a game for the rich – but that people from any social strata could exercise generosity. From there, he kissed his boy on the forehead, turned off the light, and crossed the darkened hall into their room.

Diane was in bed and had been for the past hour. William tried not to wake her, but she was already awake. Naturally, she was concerned about her baby. "So how's Billy?" she asked as she tilted her head upright. "Will he survive?"

"Oh, I think so. I just needed to get him out of that place." He untucked his shirt and pulled his socks off.

Though sleepy, Diane was articulate in what she said. She had given her little speech a great deal of thought. "Well, I don't like where this has been going lately. He used our debit card without permission. Tonight, he deliberately withheld from us where he was going. It sounds like he has been ditching his good friends for a different crowd – and we don't even know these people. Do you suppose it is merely his age or do you think his discovery of the money had affected him somehow?"

William was unbuttoning his shirt. "I don't know. Perhaps a combination of the two. Growing up is difficult enough. And let's be honest: The little guy just found out that his parents possess a lot more money than he had ever believed. At least, you and I have been around the idea long enough to show a little discipline or just blow it off. For us, it really didn't change anything – except we can be a lot more generous than we were before. For him though, this changes everything. Just think of all the potential ways that big money can alter the life of a teenager."

"Did tonight help any?"

"I don't know. It certainly wasn't anything like he expected." That last concession forced a little chuckle from William.

Diane laid her head back down. "I wish that we could show him that the money doesn't mean that we are entitled to any special treatment. People don't serve us. On the contrary, the money gives us a greater opportunity to wait on *others*, to meet *other* people's needs."

"He'll get it," William said as he stood up. "It may take some time, but he'll get it. You should've seen him tonight. I could tell by his eyes that he was soaking it all in."

She added, "That's good. And don't forget about this party he attended. I don't know what all happened, but he probably got to see how the other side of money lives."

William pulled his belt clear of the belt loops. "Well, he didn't go into any huge detail, but it sounds like he wasn't invited to be accepted. He was made fun of."

Diane made a sad face at the sound of this news. "Aww. Poor Billy."

"Yep." William walked over to the restroom. When he reemerged, he was wearing some pajama pants and a fairly recent college shirt. He opened the drawer on his night table and pulled out a journal. He began to write.

"What are you doing? Are you recording all of this?"

"Yeah. I want to get it down while it was still fresh in my mind."

"How many of those do you have now?"

"I am finishing up my tenth one."

"I love reading them. It is so nice to be able to revisit those memories."

Ever since Billy was a baby, William had written down various episodes of his son's life, important milestones, and little cutesy things that he would say. But William now found himself recording other important events, times when he himself had to struggle and learn as a father.

Side note: This may sound silly, but William was not born a father. When Billy came around, he had no previous experience as a parent, neither him nor Diane. They both had to learn everything on the way. Sometimes it was a real struggle. And sometimes they messed up. They discovered that parenting was not an easy job. The hardest part was learning how to be resented at times by the one you loved most. On occasion, it would seem that the pain was not worth the effort. But it was totally worth it. So please be patient with your parents; and hopefully someday, your children will be patient with you.

After a minute or so, Diane rolled over toward her husband. "Wow. It is hard to image. He's already a sophomore. In less than three short years, he'll be graduating. I don't think that I'm quite ready for that. He's just growing up way too fast."

"Tell me about it," William said while still writing. "What I don't understand is how it took me years and years and years to get to the age he is now, and Billy seems to have gotten there overnight." He finished writing and returned the journal to the drawer where it sat before. He turned off his lamp and crawled into bed. "I was thinking about something Mrs. Dunbar told me years ago. I remember when Billy was about five or six, I made the comment that I was really going to miss him being a two-year-old. Then she said something very wise to me. She said that her kids were grown and that she *still* enjoys them, even in their adult years. She told me to enjoy our son at whatever age he was at that time. And she was right. It would be a shame to spend the entire year he was fifteen wishing he were still twelve; and then wishing he were still fifteen two years from now." He started laughing to himself. "I don't think I'm making any sense."

"You're not. You should stop talking and get some sleep."

"You mean that I should stop talking so that *you* could get some sleep."

She rolled back over. "That thought never entered by mind."

As his body began to relax, he added, "I don't know if we have disciplined our son properly tonight, but I am reminded of Proverbs 29:17. 'Correct thy son, and he shall give thee rest; yea, he shall give delight unto thy soul.'"

Mentioning 'rest' seemed like the logical place to fall asleep, so they both responded obediently to the call. Moonlight broke through the blinds and lit up the floor in carefully measured geometric bars. All was quiet in the house.

… well, except for the clamor coming from their horrid dryer.

CHAPTER 38

NOBLESSE OBLIGE

(pronounced: noh-BLES oh-BLEEZH; It's French.)

Billy slept.

After a good while, he found himself in a dream. It seemed to take a few seconds for everything to come into focus. As the details became clearer, he noticed that he was standing in a sort of dining room, but completely unlike any that he had seen before. The rectangular room was made mostly of handsome rough-cut stone, possibly slate. Although the walls were made of dark gray stone, the room itself was unusually bright. He noticed that the room was strangely lit from above. The weird sunlight gave a shimmering watery effect over the entire room. He looked up and noticed that the ceiling was glass with a pool of rippling water above. This explained why the light was refracting in a relaxingly nice way. Strange, but pricey-looking, paintings of nothing definable adorned the walls. A merry tune by Mozart was playing in the background. Angular windows revealed a rocky coastline.

This was all too peculiar. But far stranger was when he caught a glimpse of himself in a large wall mirror. *He* was the one dressed like a butler this time, right down to his white gloves. He then looked over and noticed that it was James sitting in the master's seat somehow and just finishing up a meal. James was impeccably dressed and was reading the financial section of the newspaper as he ate. The scene gave Billy the impression that it was sometime in the mid-afternoon.

The dining table and matching chairs were perfect geometrically – but also uncommonly ugly in his down-to-earth opinion. Still, they left the impression of being expensive. The same could be said of the utensils, dishes, and even the nearby vase. At least, the flowers were pretty.

James had just laid down his utensils and wiped his mouth on a cloth napkin which also matched the color of the room. "Now *that* was truly a superb meal. Excellent. Billy, would you please offer my gratitude to Francois? And tell him that the salmon fillet was a poem – a culinary sonnet."

A poem? he thought. *All I see is fish.* Billy was confused. James was supposed to be the butler and Billy was the master. A switcheroo? He had to get to the bottom of this. "What is going on here? Shouldn't *you* be waiting over *me* while I eat?"

James turned in slight anger toward Billy. "That is a rather cheeky statement for a butler to make."

"Butler?! Who dreamed this up?"

James casually dropped his napkin onto the table next to his gold leafed plate. "Apparently, you did. In this house, *I* am the master and *you* are the butler - - and a rather bold one at that. Don't forget your place, young man."

"This isn't how my dreams are supposed to be." Billy looked around the room and then once again at his reflection.

"Well, I am the master of the house in *this* dream. And by the way, I want to thank you for giving *my* house a more cosmopolitan sense of style than those traps that you dreamt yourself in." James made a grand sweeping gesture to this strange-looking domicile. It was very modern in a Mediterranean way. "Do you not agree?"

Billy thought the room was weird, but he wanted to say something nice. "I do like the watery light effect."

James sneered and seemed dismissive toward that particular comment. "Visually stunning perhaps – but dreadful for reading. But alas, we are not here to read. We need to relocate anyway. Come with me, Billy." James rose up from the table to face his new manservant. "But before we go any further, I would like to congratulate you on *your* recent promotion."

This confused young Billy. He had no idea to what James was referring.

"What are you talking about? What promotion? Going from a rich dude to some lowly butler?"

"Of course," James said with a celebratory smile. He began to talk and lead Billy into the next room. "Billy, my boy, there are many things that you need to learn. I speak of the merits and rewards that accompany a servant's heart ..."

Billy followed James like a student receiving instruction.

"From an immature point of view, becoming wealthy and having people do all your work for you is a desirable thing. But in the end, a person can become lazy and mentally soft. Understand that I am speaking in generalities; this is not always the case. But more often than not, that is what occurs. Recall your Scripture ..."

At this point, Billy had to interrupt James with a lightly sarcastic comment. "That's just great. Now even my former dream butler is going to be telling me about what the Bible says."

James spoke with excited energy. "And why not? The Bible gives us the perfect example. Upon meeting God's Son, we should all rightfully get down on the floor and worship. But in an unexpected twist, he declared in the gospels that one of His purposes in arriving was *not* to be served, but to serve. What a tremendous pattern for us all. He healed the sick. He fed the multitudes. He even washed the feet of His disciples. This does not sound like the actions of a king as we know it – and yet, He is the greatest King of all."

By this time, the two of them had walked down a long hall and entered what Billy instantly recognized as a large personal library, right out of the old movies. Hardback volumes filled the shelves with visual harmony. The overhead chandelier was unneeded at this time thanks largely to the enormous amount of natural light pouring through the bay windows on the far side of the room. These windows had stained glass portions which featured many colorful artistic designs. In front of the bay window sat a small table with two chairs sitting opposite each other. Something was resting on the table under a large handkerchief. Billy stepped past a large globe which he gave a gentle turn.

James crossed over a large Oriental rug and hardwood floor toward the table and expected Billy to do the same. "Jesus served his disciples and now you will perform a service for me." He lifted the handkerchief up in the air revealing an exquisite chess set. The board itself was part of the table and consisted of black granite and Mother of Pearl inlay. One player's pieces were made of gold and the other out of jade. He noticed that they possessed strategically placed gems. Diamonds adorned the crowns of both the kings and queens. The rooks had rings of amethysts swirling around their tops. Sapphires were attached to the bishops. Even the pawns had emeralds on their heads. Billy picked up a knight and noticed that small rubies burned in their eyes. Beautiful. He marveled at how handsome this set was. This could be the most expensive chess set on earth - - well, certainly the most expensive in his dream world.

Billy smiled. "Wow! That's dope!"

"Oh, I know that it is a little humble looking for your fastidious tastes, but the same rules of the game apply. I am guessing that you still know your way around the board. Please have a seat and brace yourself for a great game."

The lad tenderly returned the knight to its rightful place on 1B. "I'm really not so sure that I want …"

"SIT DOWN!" James cried.

Intimidated and a little startled by James' booming voice, Billy instinctively obeyed and looked up at him.

Towering over his young opponent, James had a wild look in his eyes as he brought his hands up. "Young man, do not treat me like one of your little high school chums. I am challenging you to perhaps the greatest game of all time. Do you even know the history that you are now ostracizing? This exercise dates back fifteen centuries from ancient India where it was known as *Chaturanga*. It was then transported through Persia and into medieval Europe, and finally brought to the Americas by the Spanish. All that history, all that tradition, generations of chess masters, it has all led us up to this climactic moment. Mankind itself is hinging on what we are about to do. Today, we play Chess! Not only that, but we shall play precisely the way they did it in the days of yore. That means none of this *parley* business! We play *TO THE DEATH!!!*"

"WHAT?!"

James laughed as he sat. His voice resumed its friendlier tone. "Good grief, child. People don't play Chess to the death. Where is your sense of humor?" At the sight of a somewhat comforted Billy, James waved toward him. "Gold over jade. You have the opening move."

Billy was still unsure about this whole thing. He hesitated, but then looked down at the board and moved a pawn. James stared down at the pieces in silence and made the same opening move. After a few seconds of quiet chess-playing, Billy broke the hush. "Would you like to know where I've been all night?" He moved another pawn.

James did not react. His eyes continued to look intently down at the chess board. Without any sign of caring, James answered, "I already know. But if it makes you happy, we can talk about tonight's events." He moved his bishop forward. "You decided to mislead your parents so that you could attend a party that you mistakenly *thought* would be fun. After an episode in which you were openly disgraced, your father came to pick you up. Then you ventured off into the big city to do a little charitable work and enjoy a delightful dinner of cheeseburgers and fries to punctuate the evening. Your dad shared the gospel while you shared a vanilla milkshake." He finally looked up at Billy. "So just what did you *learn* from the experience?"

Billy answered the question without hesitation. "I learned that the friends that I already have are awesome." Billy reached down and took James' pawn with his pawn. "I also discovered that I dislike rich kids with a purple passion."

James replied without missing a beat. "*You're* a rich kid."

"Yeah, but my parents were smart enough to ..." Billy's sentence stopped in a screeching halt. What was he about to say? After getting so horribly ticked at his parents for not allowing him to have free-reign with their money, their actions suddenly made a little sense to him. Maybe he was not as mature as he thought he was. Perhaps his parents were right in trying to guard him from himself. Maybe he was now having to face his own weaknesses.

James moved yet another pawn forward and looked back over at Billy, nodding in a sympathetic fashion. "That's right. Your parents decided to raise you in a common middle-class home. They were unsure of how you might turn out if you were reared among the rich." He looked back down at his pieces with a shrug. "In fairness, they were unsure about how you would end up being brought up under more normal conditions, but let's give your parents come credit for trying." James went back to being quiet again to give his young opponent some time to let that reality soak in a bit. Then he sat up straight in his seat and raised his voice back up to its usual aggressive level. "May I pose a personal question?"

"Sure. Why not? I mean you *are* in my subconscious mind anyway." Billy had lost the pawn in front of his king, so he moved a bishop in front of it as a defensive measure. *What would happen if I lost this game of chess to my subconscious? Either way I win.* "Knock yourself out."

James moved his knight over and spoke slowly, crafting his question with care. "If someone came along and decided to make a movie of your life, who do you suppose would be the hero? You?"

"Certainly not me – I can promise you that." He gave a light laugh and then thought about his answer. "I reckon after tonight, I would say that my dad was the real hero – the way he comes to my rescue time and again." He brought one of his rooks up out of its hidey hole.

James merely nodded, but in a way that Billy could not tell if that was the approvable answer that he was looking for or not. James' face and body language were not so easy to read. He apparently brought his poker face to a chess game. When Billy was around him, he felt that there was so much more that James was not sharing.

James continued. "You're on the right path; but that's not quite right. This does bring up another interesting question however. So what about the villain? If your life were being turned into a movie, who would be the bad guy?"

Billy scarcely had to think about his answer. "Oh, that's easy. Obviously Chloe. It took me way too long to understand that, but I totally get it now. She has hated me from the beginning. Wow, do I ever feel like an idiot?!"

James' face looked doubtful. "Think so? You honestly think *she* is the bad guy?"

Billy was certain about his answer at first, but he could be wrong. "Uh … her dad maybe? Mr. Chastain? He was threatening dad's job the other day."

James shook his head. "Now you are getting colder, as the expression goes."

Billy was not sure of anything anymore. "Could it be those rich kids at the party?"

Clearly that was also a wrong answer. James silently shook his head.

Billy thought hard. He finally snapped his fingers and pointed right at James. "I know! It's the devil – the ultimate bad guy!"

James laughed slightly. "Well, I'll have to give you credit for that. That's not the answer I was looking for; but First Peter 5:8 does describe him as a roaring lion, seeking whom he may devour. He wants to totally destroy you and any kind of work that you could do to further God's Kingdom. But I was thinking about the 'hidden villain' – the one that you would never suspect. The bad guy in your movie would be much closer to home." James moved on and said, "Don't worry. You'll get it sorted out before it's too late. Of course as your dad brought out earlier tonight, you cannot simply dismiss all rich kids as being bad, just like you cannot assume that all middle-class or lower-class kids are good."

James moved his other knight across to the vacant square in front of his king while he carefully considered his next words. There was a line of reasoning that he wanted Billy to consider. "Here is something else that I would like you to think about. There are far too many simple minds in this world that are focused only on the *differences* between people: rich, poor, black, white, tall, short, left, right. And so it goes. People are always trying to divide us up. An untrained observer would think that everyone should belong in some demographic someplace and stay there. We should sit still with our little label that was imposed on us, pointing at people who are different. But the truth is that we are far stronger when we are united." James shifted his weight and cleared his throat before continuing. "I believe that it would be a more profitable use of our time to focus our attention on what all these people have in common."

Billy looked up at James' face in curiosity.

James continued his inquiry. "So young man, what quality do rich people have in common with poor people? What do all these classes share?" He sat back in his seat and patiently waited for Billy's response.

Billy sat motionless as the wheels in his head began turning. After a few thought-filled moments, Billy looked back at James with an answer. "What do all classes have in common? They all have sinned. They are separated from God and need to be restored to Him. They need someone to tell them about Christ."

James nodded. "Very good."

Billy thought for a quiet moment. In a soft voice, he added, "My dad does that."

"Correction: *Both* your parents do that."

"It's crazy. This entire time, I looked at my dad as if he were the biggest geek in the world. Everything he said would embarrass the fool out of me." He chuckled for a moment. "But now ..."

The chess game was momentarily suspended during this time of reflection and repose. There were some important matters to discuss in the company of all these surrounding books in that beautiful library.

James was waiting for Billy to finish his sentence. "*But now* ...? You were saying?"

"Now ..." Billy took in a deep breath. He was about to say something that he never thought he would say in a million years. "Now I think dad is kinda cool."

"You have it in you to 'be cool' as much as he does. Even back in Pecan Falls, the pecan doesn't fall too far from the tree. You share your parents' generous spirit."

"Pffff! I wish." He looked away toward the trees just outside the bay windows. Pecan trees.

"It's true. For years, you and your associates have been making sure that your friend Clay had something to eat during lunch at school. The four of you have developed quite a little support system. You found a creative way to work through literature books and have even made the deliberate decision to open it up to others outside your little network. And there are other examples. I could go on, but I don't want to fill you with pride."

Billy ignored the flattering words and put a question to his chess opponent. "But what I don't understand is why my parents don't do more with their money. If they are sitting on this much dough, why don't they just start doing big things with it?"

James stood up from the table and walked over to one of the book shelves. "They do. Big things come from small things. The mighty oak comes from little acorns. But they do not want their wealth or their generous spirit to be made public." James had picked up a Bible and was walking back with it.

This sounded strange to Billy. "Why not? That's silly."

"It isn't silly; it's scriptural. Child, revisit the words of Jesus." He opened the Bible and began to read from Matthew 6:2-4. "'Therefore when thou doest thine alms, do not sound a trumpet before thee, as the hypocrites do in the synagogues and in the streets, that they may have glory of men. Verily I say unto you, They have their reward. But when thou doest alms, let not thy left hand know what thy right hand doeth: That thine alms may be in secret and thy Father which seeth in secret himself shall reward thee openly.'"

He may not have known what the Bible meant by *alms*; but for the first time, Billy had heard that passage and it began to make sense to him. "So God rewards the things done in secret? Why is that?"

James searched his mind for a good way to explain it. Then he looked down at the chess board and had a flash of inspiration. The two of them had already exchanged both pawns in the king's column. At present, James' knight was sitting directly in front of his king. Likewise, Billy had moved a bishop in front of his king so they now faced each other from a distance. He smiled and glanced back up at his opponent. "Young man, look down at your bishop? If you were small enough and could stand precisely where your bishop is right now, what would you see directly in front of you?"

This was an odd way of making a point, but Billy went along with it. "Ummm …" He looked down at his bishop and followed the column with his eyes to the far end of the board. "I would see your knight."

"Okay. Good. Now here is my next move." James picked up the knight and moved it two squares forward.

Billy caught on to James' incorrect move. "Uh, that isn't legal. Knights move two spaces one direction and another space to the side."

James complied and moved his knight one square to the right, then returned sitting upright in his chair. "*Now*, what does your bishop see directly ahead?" James looked at Billy's face and grinned.

Billy shrugged. Starting from the bishop, he followed his eyes down the column again and reported, "The king."

James leaned forward and looked right into Billy's eyes. "Your mother and father are good knights for God. Like the knights on a chess board, they boldly advance forward and then take a step to the side so that others too can see the King."

Billy was silent. He was not used to hearing anyone talking about his parents in such a positive way, but this compliment was a difficult one to grasp. What precisely was James trying to say?

James continued. "When people give to the needy in a very public fashion, the attention falls on themselves. They get to spend their time in the spotlight, and that spotlight is all the reward they will get. But your parents do not crave the spotlight. When people give in secret, the focus is taken off of them and put on God. God gets the credit and the glory - - which is where it truly belongs. And God will one day reward them with a reward incorruptible."

Billy had no idea what to say. He was left silenced by the whole thing.

James explained further. "Look. Your parents recognize that all this wealth is simply a huge gift from God. And like all of His great gifts, it is best used for furthering His kingdom. So with all the needs of people around the world today, this is simply a classic case of *noblesse oblige*."

"No bless ... huh? What is that? It sounds familiar. It's French, isn't it?"

"Oi, monsieur. It was mentioned in one of your classes a couple of years ago. Your subconscious mind knows precisely what it means."

Billy gave James a comical look. "Why don't you pretend that I have never heard of it before and tell me what it means?"

"*Noblesse oblige* is an expression meaning that it is the obligation of members of nobility to use their wealth and their influence to aid people of a lower status. In the case of your parents, God has placed them in a unique position in which they can help others less fortunate than themselves. Not only do they answer God's call, but they actually have fun doing it. I think that you would find it much more enjoyable than spending large amounts of money on yourself. Any idiot with tons of money could do that, but it won't make them *happy*."

Billy looked down at the knight and thought about his parents. He thought about the evening that they had just spent feeding that old homeless man. He thought about all the money that was going to those various charities in their accountant's report. He thought about the mysterious way his dad disappeared at the hospital on that horrible afternoon of Clay's accident. His eyes moved from the knight to the king. "So, my parents are knights working for God's kingdom." He looked back up at James. "That sounds like quite a responsibility." He reached up and rubbed his chin. " ...and a rather fun hobby." He smiled at last.

The older man looked back. He nodded. "Have you given any more thought to my questions?"

"Which ones?"

"You have forgotten already? If your life were made into a movie, who would be the hero and who would be the bad guy?"

Without warning, an irritating, high-pitched noise filled their ears and interrupted James' line of questioning. The sound itself was piercing and electronic in nature.

"What is that awful noise?" yelled Billy.

James looked up at the ceiling. "If that noise is what I think it is, you need to wake up right now. You can think about answering my questions later. You've got to go wake up."

"Wake up? But I just got here. Besides, it has been a long night already – and we didn't finish our game."

"The game can wait! Go wake up!"

"But who is the bad guy in my movie?"

James spoke with a sense of urgency and alarm. "There's no time for that. You need to wake up now. I believe you are in considerable danger." James stood up and began to collect the chess pieces. "We will have to postpone that game. Now go on. Now! Don't worry about the chess board; I'll put all this away. You worry about getting out of your house. Go!"

CHAPTER 39

THAT EXTRA HOUR

Billy's dream faded away. In its place was a blurry vision of his dad trying to lift him up with both arms. Billy could barely make out what his dad was saying over that loud noise. His mom also seemed to be in the room pulling on his arms and desperately calling out his name. The bedroom lights had been turned on.

His dad sounded anxious through all the confusion. "Billy! Billy! We need to get up now!"

Billy's body was feeling incredibly weak. He had no energy. He struggled to speak, but even that required a huge amount of labor. He tried to concentrate, but it was no use. "Can't. Too tired." He sincerely wanted to be left alone; whatever this crisis was, it could wait until later. He felt himself heavily slipping out of his dad's arms and collapsing back onto his bed. His own exhaustion was fighting against his parents. The sight of his dad's face retreated back again into a thick cloud of blurriness. And then all was dark again.

Voices. He heard the frantic voices of his parents. They were both yelling his name and telling him to get up. Someone said something about a fire. *Was the house on fire? Could that loud noise be the smoke detector? Wait! It all makes sense now. The house is on fire. I have to get up. UP!*

With all the power he had, he fought to sit up in the bed. His dad was there to help him. His mom was on his other side and helping to push him up out of the bed. There it was. There was that boost of power that he needed. His adrenaline gland must have kicked in. He was wide awake now; but it was a scary, frantic kind of awake. Everything seemed to be moving faster than usual. He could not focus on anything due to the frenzy around him. His heart was racing. Hands shaking.

He ran to the bedroom door, but was scared to touch the doorknob. Plus, that side of the room was decidedly hotter than where the bed was.

"We can't go that way, Billy," his mom said. "There is too much smoke in the hallway. I'm afraid that your window is going to be our best option."

"- - like our ONLY option," William added.

William was already at the window, unlocking it and struggling to open it. For some reason, the window was refusing to cooperate. "What is wrong with this thing? The window is being stubborn." He turned to look at Billy. "When is the last time this window was opened?"

Billy thought, but thought quickly. "Uh, it was since before we painted the house."

William's eyes narrowed. "When you painted the wall outside your room, didn't you bother to ... Never mind that. There's no time."

Smoke was now billowing into the room just above the door. The three of them all knew that standing straight and breathing that stuff in would be dangerous and fatal. They all bent over closer to the floor to inhale breathable air.

A rush of sudden panic swept over Billy. "Now what are we going to do?"

William grabbed a baseball bat and headed for the window. "I'll tell you exactly what we're gonna do. We're gonna get out of here."

"Quick! Billy! Let's get over here behind the bed!" Diane was pulling on Billy's shirt. He followed her to the farthest corner from the window. They both got low to protect themselves from flying glass and so they could breathe easier.

"Atta-girl. Good thinking." William grabbed a fistful of the Venetian blinds and yanked them away from Billy's window, ripping them from the wall. In a smooth continuous motion, he also managed to get low and inhale more smoke-free air. He then stood straight and got into position.

Billy was watching him in complete awe. The geeky English teacher was gone. Instead, he saw the same strong father he had known when he was little. It then occurred to him in a flashing moment of clarity that his dad was *not* the one that had changed; he had always been who he was. Maybe it was Billy's own perception that had altered over the years.

"We're ready." Diane hollered back to her husband.

Well, whether you're ready or not, here it goes, William thought to himself. "Alright. Play ball." William began smashing the window pane. Whatever resistance the window offered, it was no contest against William's determination. He did not holding anything back as he attacked that window with full force. That bat was flying. The majority of the glass was gone in a second and the screen merely popped out. The central framework was the challenge. Billy's dad gave it a fierce pounding. One blow after another after another. As soon as the bat made contact, here came another hit. And another. Billy had no idea that his dad was capable of delivering such blows. When that was cleared, he used the bat to knock out all glass that may be lurking along the edges.

Diane was way ahead of him on that end. She had already grabbed the thickest blanket in the room. When she could tell that her husband had finished his part, she rushed over and tossed the blanket over the windowsill. "Here! I'm putting this here so we don't cut ourselves on the way out." This idea was met with tremendous approval by the others. "Go, go, go!!" she yelled at Billy. "Go on! Get out! And don't cut yourself on any of that glass on the ground."

Billy certainly did not argue. He knew that going first could make him look cowardly, but he also realized that his mother was not going anywhere until her son was safe on the other side of that window. By that reasoning, the fastest way to get his mom to budge was to go and be quick about it. So he pretty much flew out of the house with no trouble at all. Diane came next. She was a little slower than Billy; but hey, she made it. Lastly, William squeezed out of Billy's bedroom window.

In a physical sense, they were now safe. The three of them ran around the darkened side of the house to the front yard. The dewy grass felt wet on their bare feet. Diane was dressed in a nightgown and William was still in his pair of pajama pants and a Red Wolves shirt. Poor Billy was only in a pair of boxer shorts and a white tee-shirt. He was quickly getting cold now that they were out of that burning house and scrambling around in the night air.

As they were rushing through the yard, Diane asked, "Did you manage to hit the fire button on the alarm system?"

"Yes, I got it," William answered. "I guess we are about to see if it works. We never tested it before," he mused. "I also managed to grab my phone since it was by the bed."

All that adrenalin in Billy's blood stream was beginning to fade already. This meant that Billy was quickly descending into a weird, yucky feeling. "OH! I swear! This is the longest night of my life!" he said.

Diane gave a small smirk. "Well, we did gain an extra hour."

Billy scoffed and added, "Well, next year, tell the Daylight Saving Time people that they can just keep that extra hour. This night is way way too long."

William chimed in with a quick laugh. "Well, maybe we should just move to a place that doesn't observe Daylight Saving Time."

"Oh yeah. Where is that?"

William was quick with an answer. "Uh, I think Arizona and Hawaii as well as a couple of towns in Indiana."

"Hawaii?" Billy got excited. "Now you're talking."

Diane added, "But I seriously doubt that we could blame Daylight Savings Time for our house catching fire." By this point, the three had made it to the front of their yard by the road. Diane had other things on her mind than Daylight Savings Time. "Is everyone okay? I've got to make sure."

"I'm okay, mom."

"Are you sure about that?" Diane began to check her son out and made sure that he was not bleeding anywhere.

"Mom, I'm fine."

"Just humor me. This is what moms do." She turned to look at William. With a look, she asked the same question and he also replied without spoken words. Everyone was okay physically.

Billy was fine, but now he had some time to do a quick inventory. Horrified, he looked back at the house and his eyes widened. "WHAT?! Oh no! You've got to be kidding me!" Billy began to shout down towards the burning house for some unknown reason.

Filled with motherly concern, Diane suddenly ran over to him to find out what was wrong. "What's the matter?"

In a half-angry voice, Billy answered, "I left my copy of *Pride and Prejudice* on the kitchen table!"

All three of them stopped and silently looked at the house. The side of the house from the car port to the living room was completely ablaze. Naturally, the kitchen and dining room were between the two. The fire provided warmth and a brilliant, dancing, orange light in contrast to the cold moonlight. If the book were on the table, it was doubtlessly gone now.

William gave a thoughtful frown. "I don't know. It might come out of this. Let's be optimistic."

Diane and Billy both chuckled at this comment.

Fire trucks could be heard on the approach. "Good. Here they come now," William had said. He left the two of them momentarily to greet the firemen when they arrived. But while this was going on, Billy began to feel an irrational sense of anxiety.

"Uh, mom? What are we going to do?"

"What do you mean?"

"I mean what are we going to do about our stuff? Wha- What about the house?" Billy was beginning to get excited to the point of shouting.

"The house?"

"And our stuff? The house? What about our money?"

Diane gave counterpoint to Billy's loud and frightened tone by answering him in a calm voice. "Baby, our money is in a bank. We don't keep our money in the house. But even if it were in the house, what's the big deal?" She stood directly in front of Billy and gently placed both of her hands on his shoulders.

"But what about all our things?"

"What things?"

"The other things?"

Enough of this. A few of their neighbors had seen the fire and were approaching the Harris', so mommies have to do what mommies have to do. She gently placed her hands on either side of Billy's face and spoke to him in a tender, loving voice. "Let it burn, baby. Just let it burn. We don't care about those things."

"But mom ...!"

"Look, baby. Your father and I came out of the house with our most valuable possession: *you*. Everything else can be replaced. When we have you, we *are* the richest people in the world. And as long as the three of us are together and God is with us, we can get through anything."

All this drama in one day was too much for him to take. Feeling completely overwhelmed by recent events, Billy collapsed to his knees and began to openly weep.

Diane put her arms around her son. "*Now* what's the matter?"

Still crying, Billy choked out his sentence. "Mom, people are coming over here and I'm outside in my underwear."

She brought his face under her chin in a firm hug. "I know, baby. It's okay. I promise." She ran her fingers through his soft hair.

While Diane was consoling her son, two fire trucks had arrived and the firemen had gone straight into action. Shortly after, one of the firemen approached the family. He was a man in his late twenties and had a low voice. "Mr. Harris?"

William's eyes lit up. "Rodrigo!"

"Is everyone out of the house?"

"Yes. This is all of us."

The fireman continued his questioning. "Is everyone okay? Do we need to call an ambulance?"

"We're just fine, Rodrigo. Thanks."

Most of the dozen or so firemen present were working hard to put out the flames. While that was happening, another fireman walked over. But this time, it was William who recognized him first. "Eddie!"

This man was a little younger and had a higher pitched voice and a thick country accent. "Hey, Mr. Harris." He finished walking over. "Is this everyone?"

Rodrigo answered. "Yeah. This is it." He looked over and saw Diane and Billy sitting there. "Hey! Wait a minute. Is this little Billy?"

Eddie had the same reaction. "Little Billy? Wow! He's not so little anymore." He walked over to talk to him. "You might not remember me. You were really little when I went through your daddy's class."

"You had to be this tall the last time I'd seen you." Rodrigo leveled his hand down below his waist to indicate how tall Billy was.

William spoke up. "He's actually in my class *this* year. He's a tenth grader."

Rodrigo looked up at his former teacher. "Which class is that? *To Kill a Mockingbird*?"

"No. That's eleventh grade. This one is *Pride and Prejudice*."

Both firemen gave a sound of recognition and made positive comments on having to read that book in his class. This caused Billy to reflect on what he was hearing. From the sound of things, it seemed a foregone conclusion that all of Pecan Falls had risen from the ranks of his dad's classroom. What a remarkable legacy. Perhaps his dad was more important in this town than he had estimated. He must have had an influence on many people. But maybe it was not just this small town. Some of them may have found their way out of Pecan Falls and moved elsewhere. Maybe some have even become teachers in other towns. Is it possible that his dad had a large network of former students who are helping to mold the minds of another generation? And what about people who were not even born yet? How far could his power and leadership go? He wondered what it would take to find someone who had not been guided by his father's teaching. This was an astounding prospect.

A third fireman walked over from the blaze to the Harris' to see if they were okay. It was soon clear that they were. This fireman was as big and as buff as the others. He had dark smudges on his face already and he sported a reddish handlebar moustache. Billy summoned up the courage to speak to this man. "So when did *you* go through my dad's class?"

The fireman looked down at Billy and smiled. "Son, I'm forty-nine years old. I'm probably older than your daddy. But thanks for the compliment, kid."

Open mouth, insert foot. Billy was embarrassed enough standing outside in his underwear. Now this. It was all just icing on the cake after his public shaming at Chloe's and the apparent posting of that video on the internet. Maybe he was testing the limits of his own humiliation. They say that whatever does not kill you makes you stronger. If that were true, he should be juggling cannonballs right about now.

The older fireman looked over at Billy again. "Hey kid. You in the boxers. I was just going to ask you if you were cold. But it looks like someone is already taking care of that."

"Huh? What do you mean?" Billy was indeed cold; but now, he noticed a pair of strong hands placing a thick blanket on his shoulders. He turned and found himself looking into the kind face of Curtis' dad. "Oh?! Thank you so much, Mr. Baker." He wrapped himself up. It was nice to get the nighttime chill off of his legs and arms.

That same fireman looked around. "Well, it looks like you've got lots of company coming so we'll just back off now and let you talk to them. If you need anything else, just let me know. We'll be here for a while." He walked back toward the house rejoining the others.

A greater number of their neighbors had come out of their houses and were slowly walking toward them. Between the moonlight and the light from their blazing house, the neighbors could be seen fairly well – minus their faces.

Billy looked very nervous. "Uh, mom? Dad? This looks kinda creepy."

Diane added, "Yeah. *Night of the Living Neighbors.*"

Over the next few seconds, they found themselves surrounded with people who they had grown to know and a few that they did not yet know. Someone gave Diane a warm cup of coffee. Another person gave Billy a plastic bottle of water. Cookies and peanut butter crackers somehow arrived. People were talking to them and asking questions. The Harris' found themselves telling the story more than once about how they got out of the house.

Before long, Billy noticed that one of the neighbors had made herself busy, rushing around from person to person. She was passing around an old coffee tin and people were putting money in it as she went by. Considering their unique financial status, Billy was mortified. So now people were collecting money for them? This did not seem right at all. He leaned over to his mom and whispered his concerns in her ear. "Look mom. These folks are taking up a collection. We can't take their money. These people need it far worse than we do. How do we refuse their help without giving away our secret?"

Diane whispered back to him. "Oh no. We have to take it. We don't want to insult them. We will use it exactly the way that they want us to - - and likewise we will be there for them when they have a need. What we tend to forget is that God sees it all. Their act of giving allows them to receive their own blessing from God."

Another thought struck Billy. *Wait a minute! How is it that all these people in their pajamas have money with them? Our neighbors are not just weird – they're a weird kind of weird.* He resigned himself to the idea that there were a great many things in his life that did not make any sense. Billy decided that he was not going to lose any sleep over it. (That's not right; that's exactly what was happening.)

A number of concerned neighbors had already crowded around the scene, but one tore her way through the crowd. Kathy Baker arrived and went into full charge mode. Curtis was trailing slightly behind. "Diane! Diane! Are you alright?"

Diane smiled up at her friend and gave her a huge hug. "Yes. We're fine. Thank you."

Curtis rolled his eyes while his mom began to talk. "That's good. You and the guys are coming over to our house when you are done here. You got me?"

Diane's eyebrows shot up. "Oh? Kathy, I really don't want …"

"Nonsense. You need a warm comfortable place to go before the sun comes up. Curtis and I will pull the bed out of the couch and Billy can crash in Curtis' room as he usually does. It'll be no trouble at all. Besides, I think we have some extra pizza from earlier tonight. You're sure everyone is alright?"

"Oh, yes. We're fine. Wait till you hear what happened." Diane repeated the story for Kathy which followed with some friendly chit-chat.

At some point, Kathy broke away from the conversation. She turned to Curtis, "You're with me. We've got work to do." With that, she began to make her way back home.

Slightly away from the crowd, William was standing off to the side in amazement. It was one of those thought-provoking moments that consumed his brain. He could scarcely believe what he was witnessing. He saw the support of his neighbors in action. He noticed the snacks and drinks that were brought. His poor son who was shivering in his underwear now was wrapped in a warm blanket. With each passing moment, he became more emotional. In a voice so soft that he could barely be heard, the words from Matthew 25: 34-40 came naturally from his lips. "'Then shall the King say unto them on his right hand, Come, ye blessed of my Father, inherit the kingdom prepared for you from the foundation of the world: For I was a hungred, and ye gave me meat: I was thirsty, and ye gave me drink: I was a stranger, and ye took me in: Naked, and ye clothed me: I was sick, and ye visited me: I was in prison, and ye came unto me. Then shall the righteous answer … '" Tears had already begun to weigh heavily on his eyes. Now it was clear that his voice was trembling. "'Then shall the righteous answer … '" His voice failed him. He just stopped. His throat was not going to let him finish. It did not really matter anyway. No one could hear him.

… almost no one. "'Then shall the righteous answer him, saying,'" The familiar sound of Mr. Baker picked up the quotation where William had left off. He had been quietly standing behind William and had been listening to what he was saying. Strangely, he was able to quote the same passage. "'Lord, when saw we thee a hungred, and fed thee? Or thirsty, and gave thee drink? When saw we thee a stranger, and took thee in? or naked, and clothed thee? Or when saw we thee sick, or in prison, and came unto thee? And the King shall answer and say unto them, Verily I say unto you, inasmuch as ye have done it unto one of the least of these my brethren, ye have done it unto me.'"

Silence. William slowly turned around. His eyes worked their way up from the ground to look at Curtis' dad in the face. They looked at each other for only a moment until William stepped forward. Their arms wrapped around each other in brotherly love.

For years, Diane and William had gotten comfortable in demonstrating their love for God by giving that love to others. Theirs was a unique ministry. They were furthering the Kingdom of Heaven by using the financial gifts that God had given to them. But this was different. Now they were the recipients of other people's love and affection. One may think that it was uncomfortable for them - - and it was; but they also felt love and a true sense of community.

Diane had been talking to some of the ladies and Billy was never far from her. But during a break in conversation, one of their neighbors, Stacey, approached her. "Diane? Can we see you for just a minute? You too, Billy."

They both looked confused but went along with her. They followed Stacey to the center of the small crowd. Stacey's husband was also standing in the center waiting for them.

In a loud voice, Stacey's husband addressed the group. "Ladies and gentlemen. Most of you know me, my name is Scott and this is my wife,

Stacey. We were thinking that it would be a great idea to pray for the Harris' right now. We would invite everyone who wishes to pray along with us."

No one in the crowd objected. Billy, Diane, and William were all directed to the middle of the crowded circle. Several of them put their hands on the Harris' shoulders. Those who could not reach them placed their hands on those who could. Even a couple of the firemen joined in. Billy did not really like the attention, but even he could sense the serge of power by having people praying for them. His final verdict was that it was cool. Diane and William's attitude was one of obedience and thankfulness. They gladly welcomed the blessing.

Scott began to pray. "Almighty God and Heavenly Father, we gather here in the wee-hours of the morning to thank You for delivering the Harris' from their burning house. You have given them safety in what could've been a horrible tragedy. For that, we offer our gratitude. We also lift them up in prayer as they face the challenge of salvaging what they can and as they begin the process of finding a new home. We pray that You already have the solution to their financial troubles on the way. In addition, God, we pray for some reassurance for this family. May they soon feel Your awesome presence and your inexhaustible love. All this we pray in Your Wonderful Son's name, Amen."

A chorus of croaking *Amens* rose from the crowd and spontaneous hugging began.

Billy slid down into a sleeping bag in Curtis' room. *At last*, he thought as he once again prepared to get some shuteye – like a whole two-and-a-half hours or so. They were careful not to wake Curtis' younger brother – which was practically impossible anyway. "We better get to sleep quickly," Billy said. "Extra hour or no extra hour, that sun will be coming up soon."

Curtis' mind had been at work all night. He had to spill the beans or he might explode. And since it was essentially just the two of them now, this was the perfect moment. "By the way, I need to apologize to you."

"Huh? For what?" Billy sat up slightly confused. After all, it was Billy who had been a jerk that night.

"For not believing you. I did a little digging around the internet tonight. And guess what I found …" Curtis was obviously excited.

His friend leaned toward him from across the room. "What?" He had no idea what to expect.

With a great deal of satisfaction, Curtis continued. "I discovered that your family is indeed running Crowe Athletic Gear. Also I learned that your family has so much money, it would be an insult to call it a fortune." He was so proud of himself for finding that out.

"Oh that." Billy rolled over, not sounding especially excited.

"*OH THAT?* Dude! Instead of buying your dream car, you can buy the entire lot. What's up with that?!"

"Well, now that you know the truth, you might as well forget about it."

"*Forg ... Forget about it?* Wha ...? Weren't you the one trying to convince us earlier? What about all your big plans in case you ever landed on some real money?"

Billy laughed. "Well, guess what? I was wrong. It isn't *our* money. It's God's. And we need to use it the way *He* would want it used. It's all His anyway." He laid his head down again and a thought popped into his mind. "You remember the Parable of the Talents?"

Even though this looked like a random question, Curtis answered, "Sure. The three employees who were given the talents. One had five, another had two, and finally the guy with only the one. The dude with the one just buried it in a hole and eventually gave it back like a fool."

"That's right. Even though these guys were given those talents to invest and make grow, all that money still technically belonged to the boss man. That's how it is with us. Our money, our time, our talents, even us – we completely belong to him. And my parents believe that this money can be best used for God if no one knows that it is even there. So until further notice, this dough is a secret – totally invisible."

"Do you really believe that?"

It took a few seconds for Billy to answer. "I'm starting to."

Mercifully, the sun finally came up and that horribly long night at last came to an end. At church, people gathered around to pray for the Harris'. After a stirring message, the two families went back to the Baker's house for Sunday lunch and a long, well-deserved nap before evening service. The boys agreed that the trip down to the Falls would wait for another day. But while Mrs. Baker was busy working on lunch, the Harris' and Curtis took a few minutes to return to the burned-out home. Was there much to salvage? They wanted to find out.

While they were there, they came across the fire marshal and the insurance investigators who were occupied with paperwork detail. They escorted William over to what they believed to be the source of the blaze. The two of them pointed to the charred remains of their vintage dryer, burned to a crisp and yet hauntingly recognizable. This spiteful thing almost seemed to make fun of them with its arrogant pose – practically saying, *For countless ages, I have dried clothes in my rotating belly, from bell-bottoms and parachute pants to polyester blouses and skinny jeans. I defy you all to count the sum of socks and underwear that have crossed my threshold! Mu-ha-ha-ha-ha-ha!!!*

William looked directly at the scorched appliance and assessed the situation as thus, "I guess there is no excuse not to get a new dryer now." William was trying to be funny. "Perhaps this was what Shakespeare would call the 'rude mechanical.'" Like most dads, he laughed at his own corny joke. His son, on the other hand, did not get the vague reference to *A Midsummer Night's Dream*.

Speaking of dreams, Billy thought back to his, the one in which he was playing Chess against James. He quietly said to himself, "Well, if someone were to actually make my life into a movie, I now understand who the villain would be. It would be that scary old dryer."

From the far side of the house, Diane gasped so loudly that William, Curtis, and Billy were all startled by the sound. They rushed over and found her crying in front of a burned trunk. The large wooden trunk had been in their family for years and had now suffered extensive damage from the fire. Inside were all the Harris' loose photographs. Expecting the worst, she was too afraid to open the trunk. William took the liberty. Miraculously, they were completely undamaged. Diane held up a small portrait of her and William taken at their wedding, her in her long white wedding dress and big hair, him with a skinny face and a pathetic little moustache. William was amazed. He picked up a photo of little Billy smashing a cake on his first birthday.

Diane had already made digital copies that she emailed to herself and discs that were kept in a safety deposit box – but these were the originals. These were the ones she cared about. After Diane stopped crying, her and her husband had a nice, sweet prayer of thanksgiving for their pictures being spared.

But the blessings did not stop there. William managed to find all of his journals miraculously undamaged as well.

Billy found his trombone slide.

CHAPTER 40

A RAPID DESCENT

Monday morning arrived right on time and the students were having to report to the school auditorium for yet another surprise announcement. Scarcely anyone actually knew what was going on. Noisily, they sat in roughly the same seats in which they were growing accustomed. In the case of Chloe and Bre, they could always be found in the back row towards the center. Wesley was typically on the right side about three-quarters of the way back. But this time, Mike and Curtis were sitting with Wesley.

The lights on the stage were on their full brightness and indirectly lit up the entire room; nevertheless, someone had pulled the house lights up to about half of their capacity. This gathering was a last minute idea, so a couple of the A/V guys were rushing to get off the stage after quickly pushing out the podium and plugging in the microphone. A few in the crowd gave sarcastic applause which were received with embarrassed smiles and a quick wave.

Mrs. Dunbar, being as professionally dressed as ever, made her way onto the stage. She waited for a half-minute or so in order for the late-comers to settle. When it appeared that everyone was there, she began her brief announcement. "Students, may I have your attention please? This will only take a few minutes and then you can get back to your classes."

Some students continued to talk, but a little strategic shushing from their classmates brought the room into silence. Their love and respect for Mrs. Dunbar outweighed their desire to be humorous.

Mrs. Dunbar continued. "Thank you. Many of you already know what happened over the weekend ..."

Chloe looked around. A slight wave of panic tickled the back of her neck. The party may have been a bit wild at first, but she did not think it worthy of the school's attention. She barely had enough time to remove all traces of the fiesta before her dad returned late Sunday night. Could this really be about her? As far as she knew, nothing else happened that weekend – other than a little confusion over the time change. Luckily, she felt more comfortable as she listened to Mrs. Dunbar's next statement.

"But in case you haven't heard, our English teacher Mr. Harris and his wife Diane lost their home to a fire in the early hours of Sunday morning."

What a relief, Chloe thought.

A loud laugh echoed throughout the auditorium and was quickly restrained. Some turned toward the back of the room to see where the laugh was coming from. Even Mrs. Dunbar was caught off guard by this rude outburst. Looking into the spotlight, she was unable to see the source of the laugh.

"Many of you are familiar with their son Billy, a sophomore here at Pecan Falls High ..."

Another quick laugh managed to escape from Chloe. At once, she covered her hand squarely over her mouth. She was painfully trying to keep herself from laughing, but only because others around her turned to look at her in disgust. Even Bre grew uncomfortable, wondering what was going on. Chloe looked back at her apologetically.

Just a few rows down from her location, one of the senior boys whispered to his girlfriend, "That's funny. Chloe mentioned something at her party about the Harris' house burning down Saturday night. Remember? She said that it would be a service to the community or something like that. Then it actually caught fire just hours later. Weird." This comment to his girlfriend was not unique; other students began to whisper similar statements to each other. Some were even texting.

Mrs. Dunbar had to regain their attention and the whispering stopped for now. But the texting continued. "I have asked Mrs. Parker and Mrs. Abernathy to distract them while I make this announcement. From my understanding, there is very little left. Naturally Mr. Harris denies that there is a need, but if any of you wanting to donate money or clothes, you can see Mrs. Parker in the biology lab or Mrs. Abernathy in the journalism department. I have been told that the church where the Harris' attend is already helping them with food."

Chloe lost it. Another momentary outburst confirmed to the student body who it was having a laughing problem. Again, she quickly stifled the sound as much as she could. She was now feeling a bit embarrassed about it – and Bre was embarrassed to be next to her. Thanks to the miracle of texting, the few students who were at Chloe's party had managed to connect Chloe with the burning of the Harris' home. And from there, the rumor began to spread like a wild fire.

Mrs. Dunbar was furious, but never showed it. This would have to be dealt with another time. "That's all. Students, you are dismissed." Controlling her disappointment, she walked off the stage as the house lights were raised to its normal level of illumination. Students began to get up and leave at a predictable pace. Mike, Curtis, and Wesley were among the first to leave the room; they were in a hurry to find Billy.

One of the older boys sitting three rows in front of Chloe turned toward her and spoke. "Smooth work, Chloe. Real slick. Confessing your crime *before* you actually do it? That's the gutsiest thing I have ever heard of."

Chloe's enjoyment of the announcement dropped along with the smile on her face. She looked at the senior. "Huh?"

One of the girls sitting between them had another comment. "That wasn't *even* funny. Someone could have gotten seriously hurt. You could've killed someone." The girl did not stick around for a rebuttal; she simply walked off.

Chloe was aghast. "What are you talking about?!"

Everyone who had been sitting in that section was now listening to what was being said. The first boy spoke up again. "That number you just did over at the Harris place. Mighty brave. You said something about their place burning down while we were at your party. Later that night, it actually *does* burn down. That sort of math is so easy, even *I* could figure it out."

"Do what?! You think that *I* had something to do with that?!"

"If the shoe fits …"

People around her were now vocalizing in agreement.

Chloe was losing her patience. "That is completely stupid. Your imagination is getting away from you. *No one* is going to think that."

At that point, a boy way at the front of the room, way beyond earshot of their conversation, yelled at her from the entire length of the auditorium. "Hey Chloe! What do you do for an encore? Fix his brakes?" All students still in the room heard what he said.

One of the girls on the other side of Bre asked, "Are *you* a part of this? What time did *you* leave the party that night?"

Bre was now on the defense. "About 9:00 or so. The party kinda fizzled out after Billy left. Why?"

"Uh-huh," she replied doubtfully and walked away.

Chloe and Bre looked around. Everyone was getting as far away from them as possible. In fact, the room was emptying out at a breakneck pace. The two would be alone in no time at this rate.

Did I just miss something? What just happened? Chloe wondered. She was feeling rather insecure, but made up for it by getting angry. "Well, that deescalated quickly." She rolled her eyes in her usual, annoyed fashion and said, "Come on, Bre. Let's get outta here."

Bre was furious and spun her head over toward Chloe. " ...or what? Are you going to burn *my* house down too?" She stormed off getting away from Chloe. If Chloe was in any way responsible for that fire, Bre wanted nothing to do with it. She was already unhappy with the way Chloe made a complete fool out of Billy at the party. Just what was not beyond her abilities? How far would she go? What would she *not* do? This was too much - - way too much.

With a school presently full of students, Chloe was now alone in that enormous room.

About ten minutes earlier, Mrs. Dunbar was preparing to walk on stage and make the announcement about the Harris' losing their home. Students were filing into the room at normal teenage speed. Chloe and Bre had already found their way to their seats. Wesley walked in with Mike and Curtis. Billy and Mr. Harris were out of the room somewhere – probably talking with Mrs. Parker and Mrs. Abernathy about the fire.

Coach Holton had been subbing for Maggie's regular PE teacher who was still on maternity leave. He told them early on not to dress out due to an assembly. When he released the kids, Maggie caught up with Berly out in the hall next to the trophy case.

"Do you know what's going on?" she asked Berly.

"No idea. They don't run these things by me," she joked.

"Well, I guess we are about to find out."

Nearly everyone was already seated when the two of them walked into the auditorium. They quickly found seats near the aisle. Berly looked around the room but did not see Billy anywhere. She did, however, see Chloe and her friend in the back, cheerfully talking and laughing with the people around her. *I wonder what that's like*, she thought. She pushed her glasses back up her nose. *Pretty and popular. Must be nice.* The two girls engaged in their usual small talk and wisecracks until the lights dimmed.

Mrs. Dunbar's announcement knocked their breath out. Berly was especially surprised. *A fire? Poor Billy. I wonder what they are going to do,* she thought.

Someone in the back of the room let out a single uncontrolled laugh.

Berly leaned in toward Maggie. "Who was that?"

"I don't know, but that was pretty rude." They both turned around momentarily and then drew their attention back toward Mrs. Dunbar.

Another laugh.

Maggie turned. Even in this limited light, she noticed everyone looking over at Chloe, who was now covering her mouth. "Oh wow. Okay. That's that Chloe girl that Billy seems interested in. Remember the queen bee?"

"Do what?" Berly spun around to see. "Sure is."

Right then, a girl sitting on the other side of Maggie leaned forward and told someone in front of them about Chloe's fire comment at the party. Both girls overheard the remark and were shocked. But Mrs. Dunbar commanded everyone's attention once again, finished her bit, and left the stage. The lights came back up to normal prompting the students to rise out of their seats. Maggie and Berly stood up as well.

Berly's mind was spinning. "Well, this couldn't come at a worse time – right on the heels of his buddy's accident. Not cool. I wonder if there is anything that we can do."

Maggie was sympathetic. "Yeah. I have Spanish Club during lunch today so we'll have to talk about this after Chess this afternoon. Heh. When I say it like that, I sound busy."

At that point, their attention was drawn to the back of the room. Something was happening. It looked like a handful of students in the rear of the auditorium were exchanging heated words with Chloe. The bubbly demeanor she was previously wearing had changed to extreme agitation. To make matters worse, a boy in the front of the room yelled back at her at full volume. "Hey Chloe! What do you do for an encore? Fix his brakes?" It was impossible to escape the sound of his voice as it filled the room.

"What's going on here?" Berly asked.

"The plot thickens," Maggie said. "It sounds like she made a comment about the Harris' house burning down before it actually did. Now the students all think that she did it." As she was talking, the two girls got caught up in the crowd of exiting kids. At the last minute, they looked up and saw Chloe surrounded by others in full-debate fashion. Chloe looked mad. Even her friend Bre looked unhappy with her. Then that was it; they both found themselves in the hall standing next to that same trophy case.

Berly pulled her hair back behind her ears and readjusted her glasses. "Sheesh. That got bad. Tell me, is this always how high school is?"

Maggie shrugged. "Pretty much." Her face became distant. The wheels in her mind were turning. "You know what I think? I think this isn't right."

"I know. Who would do that sort of thing?"

"No, no. That's not what I mean. I mean this is too easy."

"Too easy? What is?"

"Well, look around. What do you see?"

Berly looked. Everyone was walking to their lockers or to their next class. But they were all talking about Chloe – and it was not nice talk. She said, "They all look like a battle is about to break out and everyone is getting on the same side."

"Exactly," Maggie added. "And on the other side, there sits Chloe. Something about this is plain wrong." She looked down the hall in the other direction. "Yeah. If there is something that I don't like about high school, it would be this playground mentality. You would think that we would've grown out of it by now. An argument breaks out and suddenly everyone is taking sides – preparing to fight in a war that isn't theirs. People are always looking for ways to get involved in stuff that isn't their business. It's childish."

That reminded Berly of something. "What was it that we heard the other night at church? It was something Paul said about childish things. *When I was a child …*"

"That's right. 'When I was a child, I spake as a child, I understood as a child, I thought as a child: but when I became a man, I put away childish things.' Sadly, I picture a lot of our classmates dragging these same childish attitudes with them into the adult world. This is too much drama for me. Whatever happened to 'Blessed are the peacemakers'?"

They noticed that Bre stormed out of the auditorium using the other door. She came out looking as angry as a wet hen. And she was noticeably alone. Turning both ways, she regained her bearings and stormed over to her next class. Chloe was probably still inside the auditorium.

"So what do you think is going on here?"

Maggie considered the question. "Judging from how childish everyone is acting, I can't see them possibly being right – the crowd, I mean. The bandwagon is loaded with misinformed people who aren't thinking clearly. I don't know." She paused in thought. "Maybe Chloe *didn't* do it." More confidently now, "Yeah. In fact, I would be very much surprised if she had anything to do with this at all. And as usual, people are turning on her as if they needed to find someone to blame."

"Popularity is a fickle game."

"True dat."

Chloe popped out of the door next to the girls. They instinctively looked up at her. But they were caught off-guard by this sudden action and did their best to 'look natural.' Chloe was not fooled.

"You. Yeah, you." Chloe took a few steps closer to them. "I'll bet you two were just talking about me, weren't you?"

Busted. The truth is that they were, but not in the way that Chloe assumed. Being put on the spot like that, Berly tried to speak. "Umm. We uh …"

Chloe's face turned red with fury. Before Berly could say anything else, Chloe stomped off and disappeared around a corner.

About a minute later, the two girls finally exhaled.

CHAPTER 41

MUNICH AND MEX

That assembly was the launching point of a very strange day. Chloe maneuvered her way from class to class in silence. As a whole, the student body may have been keeping clear of her, but it was painfully obvious that she was still the subject of conversations everywhere. Even in the ladies' restroom, they would see her and suddenly have to walk away giggling about something - - as if she did not know. She had considered pretending to be sick just to go home.

Billy was having an equally strange day. At first, he was avoiding people. He naturally assumed that people were going to tease him for that video that Chloe set up on the internet. She sure did make a fool out of him. And now with their house gone, he was in no mood to be messed with. But he was surprised at the reception he received. People were greeting him and asking how he was doing. Even seniors were giving him high fives. This behavior was beyond his comprehension. He had heard that they were the subject of that morning's announcement, but no one had said anything to him about Chloe's apparent guilt. He honestly did not understand it, but he did not question it either. He was too busy enjoying his skyrocketing notoriety.

Billy's sudden rise in popularity certainly did not escape Chloe. She saw everything and it was making her furious. His swift acceptance seemed to be at her expense. She had been the trend-setting force of the sophomore class. Perhaps she overestimated her importance in the minds of the juniors and seniors; but as they moved on, she would naturally move up. It was the natural order of things as time had proved in the past. But what was

357

all this? Why was she being treated this way? And why was Billy suddenly Mr. Popular? He was just the hopeless son of a nerd teacher. Pathetic really.

At lunchtime, she sat alone facing the wall. She was not in any mental condition to look at anyone while she ate. Billy, on the other hand, had invitations to sit with every table in the room. The whole thing was surreal. He had arrived at last. This was great. Now all he needed was a sweet car, some spending money,

… and of course, Clay.

On this particular Monday, Wesley had opted to get the lunch offered in the lunchroom: square pizzas, corn, green beans, lemon cake, sweet tea. He lifted his tray and was about to go sit with Mike and the guys until he saw Lauren. He rushed over to where she was and asked if he could sit down. She agreed.

"Well, well, well. Lauren, it's cool to see you again. I haven't seen you around at all lately. In fact, I don't think I have seen you since the night of the reading over at Billy's house."

She smiled. "Yes. I have been out of town. You're Wesley?"

"That's right. Did you and your family go on a vacation?" Wesley asked as he took a bite of his pizza.

She shrugged. "No. My great-grandmother was sick so we went over to be with her. She lived over in Chattanooga, Tennessee. She died while we were there and so we stayed to take care of the details."

Wesley regretted prying so much. "Oh, I'm sorry."

She smiled back at him. "Don't be. She lived a long, happy life. She knew the Lord, so I know that I will see her again one day. The service was beautiful. After her funeral, she wanted us to go to the top of Lookout Mountain and have a singing service. It was awesome. So peaceful and cool. And all those fall colors were perfect."

Wesley picked up his fork and stabbed at his green beans. "Well, I've got some news myself."

"And what's that?"

"I accepted Jesus while you were gone."

Lauren's face lit up. "You did? That's the best news ever. Welcome to the family."

"Thanks. The funny part is that it was actually Mike that led me to the Lord." He ate some green beans from his fork.

"Mike? You mean that guy that was so mean to you that night?"

"The very same."

"HA! God arranges funny things. Well, that's awesome. That is so cool."

"Yeah. We've become pretty good friends since then."

"That's excellent. It is too bad about the Harris' house though. I guess we won't be having more of those reading parties – if you can call it a *party*." She took a bite of her chicken wrap.

"Actually Mike is going to take care of that too. Today, he said that the next one will be at *his* house. The only problem is that his folks have like a dozen Pomeranians and they bark constantly. At times, I can even hear them from my house."

"Oh no! Pomeranians hate me." She laughed.

"Well, let me correct myself. One of them doesn't bark. Lillehammer will just lick you to death. She's the only sweet one."

"*Lilly Hammer*? What sort of name is that?"

"Yeah, Lillehammer. All these dogs were named after cities that have hosted the Olympic Games. Isn't that funny? Mike says that it all started with Munich and Mex."

"Mex?"

"Yeah. His name is Mexico City, but they shortened it to Mex. They also have two Angora cats: Sochi and Nagano."

Lauren laughed. "That's so weird."

"Yeah. I thought so too. Anyway, they have a detached garage and Mike says that he is putting all those dogs in there until after the party. I don't know what his parents are going to say about it though. This should get pretty interesting." The both of them began to laugh.

Lauren was still laughing when she added, "They could name one Salt Lake City and call it Salt for short."

"Salt-For-Short? That's a funny name." He began laughing a bit harder.

Instead of laughing, Lauren's face dropped and became rather serious. Admittedly, the joke was not especially funny. Wesley noticed that she stopped laughing, so he looked up. He noticed that she was staring at someone or something standing over his head. She silently pointed directly behind him and he turned to see who it was.

Like something right out of a horror movie, he leaped back when he saw Chloe – no more than twenty inches behind him. His tray and silverware made a loud noise as he jumped. His drink nearly tumped over (that's a Southern term). This action drew the attention of everyone in the room.

Chloe's eyes were wild and pained. "So. *This* is your type." She pointed at Lauren and started to look her over. "How cute. You seem to have simple tastes. I'm very happy for you both." She took two steps back and turned. As she walked by where she was sitting, she shoved her food tray off the table, against the wall, and onto the floor. She cared nothing about the mess she made. Her pace increased. Walking turned into running. She grabbed her things and made a dash for her car and sped off. She did not even swing by the office to check herself out; she just left and did not return for the rest of the day. To her, it must have felt like diving off of a tall cliff – once you commit yourself to the idea and jump, you could not stop. She certainly did not try to reschedule her Geometry test - - she was probably not ready for it anyway.

The rest of the students in the lunchroom were stunned. They instantly threw themselves back into full gossip mode. Justin's girlfriend was totally in her element. Billy, for one, was very glad not to be romantically attached to her; she generated way too much drama for his liking.

Wesley apologized to Lauren for the awkwardness of this episode. He made it clear to her that Chloe's objectives have never been especially discreet. And he certainly had no intention of dragging everyone's focus into what was supposed to be a nice private conversation between two people. Lauren was most understanding and cool about the whole thing. After a few minutes, they were back to laughs. Who knew that two people would enjoy a lunch over their mutual disdain for some demonic-eyed Pomeranians and their ear-splitting bark?

Justin quietly began to make his way over to Billy. But Billy saw his advance, held up a stopping hand, and said, "Not today, Justin." The floppy-haired boy did a silent U-turn back to his girlfriend and was probably in trouble deep with her for his lack of information. Her icy look would be his companion for the remainder of the day. Things were not looking good for Justin.

You, the reader, may begin to feel a bit sorry for the lad in question.

... or not.

CHAPTER 42

SOMETHING EVEN GREATER

While all that drama was going on at the school, Clay sat at home. Expectedly, he had some good days and he had some bad days. His bad days outnumbered the good and he was in the middle of one of the bad. Fortunately for him, this was Mrs. Peck's day off. After watching a few game shows, Clay turned off the TV and his mom helped him back to his bedroom. He just rested on top of his bed facing the wall. Once again, he lost himself over to his periodic depression.

His mom went about doing her thing in the kitchen and then went into the living room to fold the clothes. Her work was interrupted by a knock on the front door. Curious, she went over to the door and opened it. There, she saw a man and a woman both dressed in military uniforms. This was quite an unanticipated diversion. "Can I help you?" she asked.

The man spoke first. "Greetings ma'am. My name is Master Sergeant McClure and this is Staff Sergeant Andrews. We were asked by …" He looked down at a card. " …Mike Hairston to visit with Clay Peck. Is this the correct address?"

A few minutes later, Maxine came to Clay's bedroom door followed by McClure and Andrews. She tapped on the open door as she came in. "Clay? Clay, Mike sent these servicemen to speak to you. This is McClure and this one is Andrews."

Clay remained on his bed facing the wall and not turning around to even see them. His voice was bitter and sounded rude. "I don't really feel like speaking to anyone right now." He sighed loudly. "But I guess the courteous thing to do would be to welcome you in."

"Thank you," McClure said. They entered and stood at ease. The thin bedroom carpet muffled the sound of their shoes.

"I'll just leave you three to talk. Would either of you like some sweet tea?"

"None for me, ma'am."

"Thank you, but no."

"Alright. I'll just be in the living room if you need anything." At that, Maxine left them in the room with Clay.

Clay remained facing the wall. It was rather ill-mannered, but he chose not to face them. Just the same, McClure and Andrews were totally professional as they stood next to the bed.

McClure spoke. "Your friend Mike had explained to us that you were a skilled runner and that you had planned to attend college on a track scholarship. But that you were recently the victim of an accident."

"Yeah. That's right."

Andrews added, "And he had told us that, if that didn't pan out, you were planning on going into the service. And that at some point, you would apply for college as a member of the United States military – possibly with security detail, like your father."

"That's true."

McClure picked up the conversation. "I hope that you don't mind, but we got a little nosey and spoke with your doctor. We understand that your recuperative powers are doing you credit and your strength is returning. Your teachers have reported to us that you are generally caught up on your school work and that you would be welcome to return to your classes at any time."

"So let me get this straight," Clay said. "So far, you two have spoken to the doctors, my teachers, and Mike. Well, it seems that you two certainly know a lot about me."

McClure and Andrews looked at each other. Was this some sort of hostility they were sensing?

Clay continued, "So while you were doing your homework, you probably had a nice long chat with Coach Holton about the sunny future that I was supposed to have - - that is *before* the accident. The teachers probably all described me as a nice kid. Someone probably filled you all in about my dad's death a couple of years ago. Probably Mike. Why did Mike send you over here anyway?"

Andrews answered cautiously. The situation appeared to be getting more delicate than anticipated. "Well, Mike asked us to come over and talk to you about your future plans. That's all."

Clay's bitterness was beginning to transform into light rage at this point. "What?! What future plans? What possible future can I have? My track career was finished before it really even had a chance to begin. There is no way that I can run anymore. I can't even get around without someone else's help. And to be perfectly honest with you, I think that it is more than a little insensitive, cruel, and very stupid for Mike to send over a couple of *recruiters* to my door."

This accusation completely surprised his two guests.

"...in fact, I did not expect this from Mike at all. He probably thinks that I could just rub a little dirt on it and I'll be okay. What a jerk. Even he should know that this is not something that I can just walk off, because I literally cannot walk! Obviously, I'm not going into the military, so why don't the two of you split? You're wasting the taxpayers' money by coming here to begin with."

"Excuse me for interrupting, but did you say *recruiters*?" McClure inquired. "I think there is some kind of misunderstanding."

Andrews clarified, "Clay, we're not here as recruiters."

"Then why are ...?" Clay stopped. He suddenly felt his heart sink. What was he missing? Using his strong arms, he turned himself over to see them. He looked at their faces and then lowered his gaze. Both McClure and Andrews were standing on skinny metallic prosthetic legs. "Oh no. What have I done?" He began to have a long overdue cry. "I'm so sorry. I'm sorry. I didn't kn ... Did I say something wrong?"

They both moved toward him as he kept apologizing. McClure placed a firm and kindhearted hand on Clay's shoulder. "No, no. Not at all. You're fine. You're a young man who is going through a lot right now. Teenage years come with enough strangeness built in, but now you have to work your way through this as well. It's tough."

Andrews continued the sentiment. "Your friends love you. At present, they are trying their best to understand what this is like for you. But they realize that they can't. That is why your friend Mike called us. We know exactly what you are going through. *We* know what it is like to have big plans and watch them suddenly disappear."

"We also know what kind of struggle you have before you. And we know about the awkwardness that your friends and family are going through. And if you want someone to talk to, we are here to listen."

Clay was still crying. "But I don't know what I am supposed to do. What am I supposed to do now? Will someone please tell me?"

McClure's voice sounded strong as he answered his question. "You do what you're doing. You can take a little break. But when that bell rings, you need to get back in that ring and fight. And fight hard. You cannot just sit and do nothing." At the sound of this, Clay's sobbing let up some. McClure continued, "Look! You had your eye on the prize. You had dreams of greatness. Now you have been denied that greatness. So what do you do? You stop, reassess, and then pursue something even greater."

Andrews picked up from there. "Your friend Mike told us that you believe what is written in the Bible. Well, what does it say in Philippians 4:13? 'I can do all things through Christ which strengtheneth me.' Bad things happen to everyone, but it is through God's power that you will be able to overcome."

"That's right," McClure said. "And whatever plans you may have had, God sometimes trumps our plans with even bigger plans of His own. We need to learn how to let Him work in our lives. And he has put the potential for these better plans within your grasp. You can take any kind of tragedy and turn it into triumph."

Andrews' face suddenly brightened. Her voice rang like a bell. "You know what? You are perfectly named. It fits you completely. Your name is *Clay.* For years, the Potter has been molding you into something beautiful. After a while, you actually feel that beauty. Your life has purpose and meaning and you are well on your way to that place where you want to be, where you feel you should be. But then without warning and without explanation, the Potter destroys the work that He has done in you because He knows that He can do better than that. And that is exactly where you are today. So be comforted. You are literally the clay in His hands."

Clay was considering these words.

Clay spent the rest of the afternoon becoming more acquainted with his new friends. They made plans to be with him as he went into the next phase of his adjustment. This was not something that Clay would have to do alone. These bridges were easier to cross with those who have been there.

Classes were over for the day. The Chess Club was busy playing their games as William sat behind his desk. He had just received a text message from Diane. She found a house that they could move into immediately. What a blessing! They could be spending the first night (with limited furniture) as soon as tomorrow evening. William was quite thrilled, but something else was on his mind at that moment. He began to text Diane: *Please pray for me. I believe this is the time.*

A moment later, her reply came across the screen: *You got it.*

He looked up at the clock in his classroom. It was shortly after 4:00 in the afternoon. He stepped out into the hall to make a phone call.

Across town at the Chastain house, Gregory also looked up at the clock. His mind was busy on his work, but suddenly he heard the front door being thrown open and slammed shut. It would seem that Chloe was home and that she was furious. She had driven down to the Falls to calm down, but that did not work. She was still fuming.

"Chloe? Is that you?" Gregory asked. "You were already in bed when I got home last night."

Chloe stomped her way into his office. She was visibly upset and violently threw her backpack in a nearby chair.

Gregory asked, "What's wrong? What happened?"

Chloe began shouting, "All the students were called into the auditorium to talk about what happened to the Harris' this weekend ..."

Gregory interrupted, "Wait a minute. Mr. Harris? Your English teacher?"

"Yeah." She spoke as if that was a minor point. "And everyone there seemed to think that I ..."

"Whoa! Back up. What happened to the Harris' this weekend?"

She waved her hand to signify that it was insignificant. "Oh. Their house burned down or something."

"Wait a minute. Their house burned down?"

"Yeah. To the ground."

Gregory's eye narrowed. "Are you sure?"

"Well, that is what they were saying at school today. How would I know?"

Gregory's face turned very hopeful and he brought his hand up to stroke his chin. "Well, well, well. That *is* very interesting news."

Chloe threw her hands up in the air in frustration. "But that isn't the point!" If she was not so angry, her voice would have been funny considering its high register.

Gregory's phone began to buzz at him. He looked down at it in surprised satisfaction. "And *there* is Mr. Harris now. Right - - on - - cue." Ignoring Chloe's crisis, he picked up the phone and answered it. "Hello? This is Gregory Chastain. Mr. Harris, it is nice to hear from you."

Chloe's voice was piercing. "I'm not finished yet! Why won't you listen to me?"

Gregory placed his hand over the mouthpiece of his phone. "Honey, I'm on the phone. Could we continue this another time?"

She squealed and bolted out of the room, grabbing her backpack on the way out.

"Well, I think I can." He checked the clock again. "That's fine. It is no trouble at all. I'll see you then. Bye." With a tap of his finger, he ended the call and set his phone on his desk. Looking down at it, he laughed and whispered, "Houston, we are go." He then heard Chloe running up the stairs and slamming the door to her bedroom. It shook a few picture frames.

She began to yell. "Dad! You're driving me crazy! I hate you! *I hate you!*" She threw her backpack on her bed and unzipped it. She then began to pull out the contents of her bag one at a time. "And I hate Mr. Harris! I hate English! I hate *Pride and Prejudice*! I hate Chemistry! And Geometry! And World history!" With each subject she named, she threw the book onto the floor with a loud thud. When she was done with that, she went over to the mirror, picked up some lipstick, and began to write on the glass. "And I really HATE BILLY HARRIS!" She then shoved everything off of her vanity table and her desk. She slung a jacket across the room and knocked a hundred stuffed animals off of her large pink bed. Then she let out an ear-piercing scream.

The birds outside her window took to their wings.

Gregory grabbed his car keys as he heard all of the commotion. He shook his head. "Typical day." Right now, there was no time to argue with his headstrong daughter. He had an appointment to keep with his little girl's homeless English teacher.

After a few minutes, Chloe picked herself up off the floor and looked around the room. *What a mess*, she thought. *Well, I'm not sticking around here.* She noticed that her dad's car was gone and that he was nowhere to be found. This was the best news she heard all day. Still, she figured that she did not want to be hanging around the house either. She also took to her car and sped off faster than the legal limit.

CHAPTER 43

NO STRINGS ATTACHED

"Smoke?"

Berly answered Billy's question. "Check."

The Chess Club members were all sitting in a circle. They had finished playing and were making their final preparations for a special presentation at lunch the next day. They were acting on an idea that Billy had in order to promote the club to the rest of the student body. Billy was going over his check list and the others were responding.

"Signs?"

Eugene replied, "Check."

"Masks?"

"Check," Alejandro and Eugene answered back in unison. Quotes gave a thumbs-up.

"Clothes?"

Maggie answered, "Check."

Berly called out the last thing on the list. "And you have the music?"

Billy held up an audio cd. "Check. And Berly, Maggie, and Joey will open and close the doors. Excellent." He turned to the new guy. "And Chris, you're with me." He looked around from person to person. "That should be everyone."

Chris, the newest member, was all excited to be a part of the club's antics. This should be fun.

Eugene could barely contain his excitement. "This is so incredibly cool! No one else in the whole school knows anything about this, just us and Mr. Harris."

Maggie looked across at him and said, "Uh, that isn't exactly true. Apparently Rodney knows about this as well."

Eugene was surprised and slightly irritated. "What?! Rodney? How?"

Maggie tilted her head over toward the culprit. "Quotes told him."

Eugene spun his head over toward Quotes and yelled, "Quotes?! YOU AND YOUR BIG MOUTH!"

Quotes lowered his head.

William had only been hearing half of what was going on. While the students were going over their check-off list, he had made his way over to the window and kept his eyes on the parking lot. Mentally, he was in prayer. Something had been weighing heavily on his heart and he was taking it to the Almighty.

Billy began talking. "Again with this mythical Rodney. When are you guys ever going to give it up?"

"This entire thing sounds really risky," Alejandro added. "I already told you, I know exactly how to make the Chess Club grow. Why will no one listen to me?"

Berly patted him gently on the shoulder almost in a condescending way. "Thanks, Alejandro, but I really believe that Billy's plan is going to work just fine."

William saw Gregory pull into the parking lot, park, and get out of his car. He turned again to the students as if he were trying to get rid of them without making them aware of it, one of at least two delicate maneuvers that he would have to operate in the next hour. "I'm sure it'll be terrific. But it is now time for all of you to go." He walked around the room and watched them get up and arrange the seats in their proper place. "Get a good night's sleep and we'll see you tomorrow. I should be in here a half-hour early in the morning in case any of you need a place to stash your stuff."

The chess sets were already put away. All the students had to do was grab their belongings and walk out the door. Each was saying 'good-bye' in their way as they exited.

William had other plans. He discreetly made his way over to Billy and spoke to him. "I'm going to be here for a few more minutes. But I'll be out there in a little bit. Go on." He softly patted his son on the arm.

"Alright, dad." Billy obediently followed the others out of the room. But as soon as he entered the hall, he passed Gregory Chastain who in turn greeted William standing in the doorway. Mr. Chastain was sporting a nice black suit. His shirt was clean and white, but the top button was unbuttoned and he had no tie.

"Mr. Chastain, thank you so much for coming." They shook hands. "I hope that this doesn't take up too much of your time."

"Not at all, Mr. Harris. Not at all. Glad to do it." The friendliness of his voice was a complete one-eighty from their last encounter.

"Come in and have a seat." They stepped into the room leaving Billy to linger in the school corridor, desperately curious of what they were going to talk about.

Inside the classroom, William began talking as they both sat. "I know this is unusual, my asking you to come out. No doubt you are probably wondering what this is in regard to."

"It's not that much of a mystery. I think I understand. Chloe told me that you lost your home this weekend in a fire. So now you've had some time to think about my little proposal and this may be the perfect moment to take me up on my generosity. It's the only thing that makes sense, a fortunate offer given the unfortunate circumstances." He began to reach for his checkbook nestled warmly in the inside pocket of his jacket.

William gave a silent laugh and stopped him. "No. That isn't it."

Gregory's eye narrowed in confusion. "Oh? This is not about the offer?"

"No. And I thought that I made it clear that I cannot take your money. That hasn't change at all."

There was an impatient undertone deep in Gregory's voice. "And I thought that *I* made it clear that you cannot afford NOT to take it. Let's be honest here. No one gets rich by being a teacher, not in this town. Everyone knows that. Your benefits probably aren't especially good either. I'll venture to say that your medical and dental isn't the greatest. You have a family to provide for and I'll bet anything that your retirement fund is nothing to brag about."

"Sorry, but it is still not enough to entice me to accept your offer."

Gregory's head shot back and his eyes momentarily looked around before zeroing back on William's face. "But in addition to all that, you were told last time that your contract for next year may not be renewed. And this is a really lousy time to try to find work. *Now* I've discovered that you lost everything in a fire. And yet you *still* refuse to take my money?"

William's voice became unexpectedly stern. "I will not take your money." There was a finality to the sound.

Gregory's eyebrows lowered and his eyes were reduced to a squint as he tilted his head. "Do you hate my daughter that much?"

"Hate your daughter?! I don't hate your daughter."

"So you still foolishly and stubbornly hold on to your precious integrity?"

Both their voices were now being raised toward each other.

"Of course. God has called me to a higher standard."

Gregory laughed. "God has called you to a higher standard. Humph! Is that the only reason why you won't accept my offer?"

"It is certainly reason enough, but that isn't the only reason!"

"Not the only reason? Well, enlighten me if you please!"

"Alright! I refuse to take your money because you cannot afford it!" William punctuated his sentence by standing up.

Gregory backed down and leaned forward in his seat. "What did you say?" he asked in a much softer tone.

William walked over to the window as he explained. "That's right. You cannot afford it. Oh sure, this check of yours may clear, that's true; you're not worried about that. But it doesn't take a lot of digging around on the internet and a little simple math to see what is happening to your company. Chastain Enterprises is currently in distress."

Gregory said nothing. He just breathed heavily and his eyes turned to the floor. He wrung out his hands and planted them on his knees as he listened to William.

William walked back over to his desk. "For years, your company has been digging a hole in the ground and now it can't get out. From what I can tell, it may be time to trade your precious golden golf clubs in for a used bowling ball."

Again, Gregory tilted his head to one side and looked at William. "A bowling ball? What are you saying?"

"Simply this ..." He reached into a drawer and pulled out some papers and passed them on to Gregory. "The economy is bad and your sales have gone way way down. Income for your company has dropped tremendously. Losses at seventy percent last year, forty percent the year before. They're projecting even worse for this coming year." He pointed these numbers out on the forms, but he did not have to; Gregory behaved as though he was all too familiar with them. William continued, "I also read where your company has been sued on two different occasions and that has stung you pretty badly."

Gregory was embarrassed. "I can see that the teacher has been doing his homework."

William sat down. His voice became more sensitive. "And I'm sorry to report that that isn't all that I know." He decided to proceed cautiously here; this is precisely where his wife's prayers would come in handy. "Four years ago, I understand that you went through a very bitter divorce."

Gregory tried not to react but it was too late. A nerve was triggered.

William went on. "Now, I know that this sort of thing affects people on every possible level. I didn't see any numbers attached to this, but may I also assume that the process has affected you financially?"

Gregory was silent for a moment. It was obvious that this was indeed a painful subject for him. "She ended up with her share, if that's what you mean. And our other two kids live with her. They get their piece each month. The only reason why I have Chloe in the first place is that she hates her mother more than she hates me."

William felt bad. This was too much like *prying* for his comfort. He knew before he went into this conversation that it would be painful. He had no intention of destroying someone with his words. As a high school teacher, he saw that from time to time. Kids can be mean. But there was a purpose in this, so he needed to continue. "I'm sorry. Look, I know that this is none of my business. And I'm not some financial wizard, but from where I am sitting it looks like your company is going to go bankrupt if this trend doesn't change - - and soon. How much does Chloe know?"

Gregory shrugged helplessly. "I've tried to explain the situation to her without too many details. But she won't listen to me. Everything she has ever wanted was hers for the taking. Actual work is a concept that she is totally unfamiliar with. And she has no concept that her world is crashing down around her."

William ventured a thought. "I'm guessing that she wants to go to college, but probably for all the wrong reasons. And considering your current situation, you can no longer bank on the idea that you can simply pay her way through."

Gregory nodded. "She seems to be lacking the work ethic needed to succeed in the world today. And I'm hoping that she will soon develop a passion for gaining good grades."

William added, " ...and until that happy day arrives, you are doing what you think will keep her GPA afloat. Is that the plan?"

Gregory shrugged. "Well, a good parent wants their children to succeed."

William placed his hands on the top of the desk and leaned slightly forward. "But she has got to earn it on her own. As a parent, you need to encourage her all you can. But sadly, some people have to get their schooling the hard way. In the meantime, what exactly do you plan to do about your company?"

Changing gears – you could see it on Gregory's face. "The company? I don't know." His face became pensive as his thoughts drifted back to his family. "My grandfather started this company over sixty years ago. My father built it up to something massive. And as the company became bigger, so did Pecan Falls. In fact, our dear town as become nearly synonymous with Chastain Enterprises." Now his voice got noticeably sadder. "I am the third generation Chastain to hold the reins. Now I will be connected with its demise - - and possibly with the demise of this town. Some legacy, huh?" He turned and meet eyes with William. "Do you know how many families in this community are dependent on the success of our company?"

William sat with one hand on the desk. "So what is your next step? What do you propose?"

He took a deep breath. "I've been looking into that. There has been some mismanagement. And I freely admit that it is partially on me. I would like to change that. I'm looking into hiring this young married couple – true visionaries – who say that they can turn things around without letting people go or decreasing anyone's salaries. They have been very successful with other companies. Their track record speaks for itself.

And the truly wonderful part is that they are willing to come on board with us here in Pecan Falls."

William smiled momentarily. "Sounds fantastic. So what's the problem?"

"The problem is that I cannot afford to hire them, nor can I afford to implement their ideas should they come."

In an ironic twist of fate, William reached for a steno pad and a pen. He wrote something on it. "How much would it take to get this project started? Something like this?" He scooted the pad toward Gregory.

His breath was taken away. He never even saw it coming. "Uh, yeah! Something like that would do nicely. In fact, that is exactly what it would take. You must be some kind of mind reader, Mr. Harris." Gregory drifted in thought for a moment, snapped out of it, and laughed. "But that kind of money doesn't exist - - not in this dinky, little hillbilly town," he said while shaking his head.

William reached into his desk drawer and pulled out an envelope. He held it up at eye level for Gregory to see. "See this?"

Gregory looked up, slightly bewildered. "What is that?"

"This is a personal check from me to you for the exact amount of money that I just showed you."

He paused and then gave another little laugh. "You're joking."

William's expression was serious. "No, I'm not. I'm very genuine."

A confused expression seized Gregory's face. "Would you mind explaining to me just how you are able to write a check for that amount?"

"It's rather complicated. But to put it simply, I have some heirlooms. A few items of some historical value were passed down to me. A high-profile museum wanted them very badly and has been hounding me for years to sell. So I finally agreed. Besides, they can be appreciated in a museum more than in some secured location anyway. But none of that is important. The point is I now have the money that you need to save your company."

Gregory could not believe what he was hearing. This did not sound right. "You mean you don't want that money for yourself?"

The answer came without a thought. "No."

Mr. Chastain was speechless. For the first time in a long time, he did not know what to say. A tiny wave of emotion peeked through. Something new happened. The shrewd, heartless businessman seemed to show authentic concern for Mr. Harris' well-being. A moment went by with no sound. With cracking voice, Gregory finally spoke. "Now wait a minute. What is going on here? Sir, you just lost your house. You and your family don't have a home to go to. What about your wife? What about your boy? Where can they go?"

William showed no emotion at all. He was steady as a rock as he kept holding the envelope in the air. "I know. Don't worry about my family. We have insurance. We're taken care of. It'll be okay. I promise you, my family and I will be okay. The important thing at this moment is to make sure that *you* don't lose *your* house - - and that all those people in your employ don't lose theirs as well. You see, I *do* know what it's like to lose your home. And I want to make certain that that does not happen to you. Not today."

Gregory swallowed. He was not sure what to do. "I don't understand."

William began to speak slowly. "Then let me clearly explain what is happening here." He held up the envelope slightly higher. "This is not a bribe. I do not want anything in return. I will not hold this over your head. And people do not need to know where this is coming from. I do not want any credit for anything. This will be our little secret. I simply want you to take this money and use it to resurrect your company. I will not ask for any part of this money back. I will not use this episode as some way to exercise power over you. I simply want to give it to you. And when it's yours, it's yours. Who knows? You might even have enough left over to buy that bowling ball I mentioned. If you want, I can even teach you how to throw it." A slight pause followed. "And once you leave this room, it will be as though it never happened. I will not miss it nor will I talk to you about it ever again. It is a free gift."

"No strings attached?"

"No strings attached."

For a brief moment, no one said anything. William was quietly waiting for Gregory to make the next logical move. Gregory was hesitant because this sort of generosity was not normal. In fact, he began to question Mr. Harris' mental capacity.

William's voice became quite informal. He sounded less like a teacher and more like a trusted friend. "Look. Greg, all you have to do is take it. Please. Save your company." William held the envelope out slightly.

CHAPTER 44

TREASURES IN HEAVEN

There was no sound. Gregory looked at the envelope. His initial thoughts were about his daughter, true; but he was also thinking about all those people who worked for him - - and all the other daughters and sons out there. If what William was saying was true, he would be a fool not to accept it. He reached out and touched the envelope gently with his fingers. Soon they tightened enough to hold. He could feel William's grip begin to loosen. The teacher's hand eventually pulled away. The envelope was now in Gregory's possession. He opened it and peered inside. Everything was exactly the way William said it would be, right down to the last decimal point. Gregory released a soft chuckle. This was a dream come true. With this simple check, he was finally able to secure his company and save so many jobs in their sweet little community of Pecan Falls. He could finally get that ball rolling. What a blessing.

William closed his eyes slowly and opened them again. "There. That wasn't so hard, was it? By simply reaching out and accepting the check, you have taken the first step to saving the company that your family has built. How do you feel?"

Gregory choked on his words. He looked up at William's eyes and smiled. "I'm not precisely sure." He looked back down at the envelope again. "I feel a little confusion … a tremendous amount of relief … um, gratitude …?"

"Anything else?"

He hung his head down. "Well, I guess I do. I feel … humbled."

William got up from his desk and walked around to one of the seats directly in front of Gregory and sat. "Believe it or not, that's a good thing."

"Yeah? What's so good about it?"

"Right now, you are approachable. People who lack humility have a difficult time listening to what other people have to say."

"Well, I certainly thank you for this check. But with all that you are going through, I still don't understand how you could let all this money go so easily."

"Oh, it's not as bad as you think. It's very easy actually - - and for two main reasons. The first is that it seems awfully silly to jealously hold onto something that is so temporary. I'll admit that money is handy to have; but it can bring as much bad as it does good. Secondly, I can let go of it because ..." William stopped, looked both ways, leaned forward with a humorous grin, and whispered, " ...it really isn't my money."

Gregory was immediately scared. "Huh? Is this stolen? Are you trying to get me in trouble?"

William was laughing. "Don't worry. Everything is legit. What I mean to say is that this is my money to use. I can save it, spend it, sit on it, burn it, throw eggs at it, or simply give it to whomever I wish - - or better yet, whomever *He* wishes."

"Who is *he*?"

"The One Who owns everything, all of heaven and earth, the Creator. And He allows us to abuse it or use it wisely."

Gregory had absolutely no idea what William was talking about. He became even more confused than before. "What is all this anyway?"

William stood up from his seat and naturally gravitated toward the front of the classroom as if he were teaching a group of students. "I don't really know much in the financial world, but I do know something about the human soul. So bear with me while I try to explain."

Gregory was now totally focused on William, with his mental pencils sharpened as it were.

"Spiritually speaking, you may have convinced yourself in the past that you are perfectly comfortable sitting on a sizeable nest egg. You congratulate yourself on your strong portfolio. But in reality, you are facing spiritual bankruptcy and ruin. You don't realize that you actually owe more for your mistakes than you are capable of paying. And we're not talking about jail time - - this is something far far worse. In fact, we cannot fathom how great the punishment is. Part of our inability to understand the punishment is that this punishment was never meant for us. The devil and his angels are the real targets of God's wrath. But sadly, because of our sins, we're headed there just the same. And yes, it is something that we all deserve."

"What are you talking about? You mean hell?"

"Oh yes."

"Look, I have a church. It's true that I don't go very often. But I've never heard the pastor talk about any of this. He doesn't ever talk about hell – not that I know of."

"Well, I can't answer to that. I don't know anything about your pastor or your church, but I can say that the good news of the Gospel is just as real. They both need to be told. And just because your church may never talk about it, that doesn't mean that you can ignore it. In fact, this issue is unavoidable – no matter what they say or don't say at your church."

Gregory got momentarily defensive. "But I'm a good person."

"No, you're not. And neither am I. We aren't fooling anyone - - except maybe ourselves. No one is. Romans 3:23 says that 'all have sinned and come short of the glory of God.' But even if you commit only one sin in your entire life, you are still guilty. There's no way to escape it."

"Well, that's awfully strict."

"To you and me, yes. But God is still a God of wrath and cannot tolerate sin. But here's the cool part. He is also a God of love and mercy. And *that* is why He would like to give you a gift."

"A gift? What gift?"

"Eternal life. The opportunity to spend eternity with Him. The only means of escaping eternal punishment otherwise."

Gregory shook his head and looked at the floor. He was thinking about the person he had become, all the mistakes he had made, the way that he had done business, the things no one knew about. Mr. Harris was describing something great, but Gregory knew that God should not be wasting his time on an old sinner like him. "That sounds nice, but He doesn't want me."

"Oh yes, He does. He made you. He loves you. He has bent over backwards to show His great love for you. He gave up His Son to die for you."

"You're talking about Jesus on the cross."

"Yep. Just imagine: the Son of God left His throne in Heaven to become human. Jesus lived a perfect life and still died an excruciating death taking the punishment for all your sins. And after being dead for three days, He came back to life, conquering death. And now he offers that new life to you."

"But I'm not good enough for that?" He looked down at his sweaty palms and then back up to William. In a gloomy voice, he added, "I've done too much that's ... I just don't deserve it; that's all."

"No one is good enough for that. He doesn't care about how bad your sins are or what you have done. In fact, it is because of our sin that He wants to clean you up."

"Clean, huh?" Gregory looked down at his white shirt and thought a little about this. "Clean sounds really good." He looked back up at William. "Well, let's say that I *am* interested. What do I have to do to get this new life?"

William pointed down at the envelope in his hand. "Well, what did you have to do to get that check? You simply reached out and took it. Look, if you want this gift of salvation, you simply accept it. There is no paperwork to sign or membership fees. No trial basis. No hoops to jump through. No stunts. It just takes a simple prayer. Talk to God. Just you and Him. Confess to Him that you are a sinner and request His free offer of salvation."

"It can't be that easy. Nothing is that easy."

"Getting that check was easy. Someone just had to make it available." He again pointed at the envelope. "In this case, God deliberately made it that easy so that no one would have an excuse NOT to believe."

Gregory was speechless again. He looked down at the envelope. This was given to him to save his company and he simply accepted it. Now he was being offered the opportunity to be forgiven of all his sins. He looked back up at William. "You make a convincing argument, good sir."

William leaned back on his desk and folded his arms. "It wasn't me. It was all God."

Gregory's voice sounded a little weaker. On some level, he sounded like a man who was spiritually drowning and was crying for help. "Okay. Let's say that I was wanting to be free of my sin, who do I need to talk to?"

"Just God. Man cannot save you. You don't have to find some holy man and ask for permission. You don't have to perform this, that, or the other thing until so-and-so thinks that you've earned it. Simply put, you *cannot* earn it. It *has* to be a gift. God did all the work."

"Talk to God?" He laughed and shook his head. "I wouldn't even know what to say."

William pulled a Bible out of a drawer and flipped it open. "Well, it just so happens that King David gave us a pretty close example of what to say right here in Psalm 51 – uh, the first three verses." William quickly found the passage he needed. "This needs to be in your own words, but it might sound something like this: 'Have mercy upon me, O God, according to thy lovingkindness: according unto the multitude of thy tender mercies blot out my transgressions. Wash me thoroughly from mine iniquity, and cleanse me from my sin. For I acknowledge my transgressions: and my sin is ever before me.' Just go to God, ask for forgiveness of your sins, and accept the salvation He wants you to have."

Something was burning in Gregory's mind. He looked back down at the envelope. All he needed to do was to reach out and accept it. And whether he did or did not, this simple act would mean all the difference in the world. He had a request, but he did not know how to phrase it. "Uh …"

William hopped to his feet. "Oh. I imagine that you have some unfinished business with God that you'll want to tend to. Would you like for me to stay or leave you alone with Him for a minute or two?"

"Yeah. If you don't mind …"

Somehow, William knew what he meant. He smiled from ear to ear and made his way to the door. "I'll be just down the hall if you need me."

"Thank you."

William exited the room quietly.

Gregory sat there in silence for a solid minute. … maybe two. He was rolling this information around in his head. Looking down at the envelope, emotion was creeping up on him; but this time, he did not fear it. He did not know how to pray, so He just closed his eyes and assumed that this would be alright with God. As far as the actual words were concerned, he did not know where to begin, but somehow it came out. Making it up as he went, he simply spoke to God. "God, I don't think that I can fool You. I have done so many things that I am not proud of. In fact, I've always hoped that my good would outweigh my bad somehow. Now I know that just one bad outweighs all my good. That makes it impossible for me. I know that none of us would have a chance without your Son's sacrifice. Now it all makes sense. God, I am such a sinner. I cannot hide my sin from you, so I freely admit my guilt. Please, save me from my sin. Save me from myself. Make me one of Yours. I believe that You did what had to be done for me to be free from my sins. Please grant me that freedom from sin that Mr. Harris was talking about. And I thank You with all that is within me."

When he was done, he felt free. There was a load lifted off of him. Gregory had never felt this sensation before. He had become a changed man. He sat there and soaked it all in. He was free.

Before Gregory's prayer a minute earlier, William hopped to his feet. "Oh. I imagine that you have some unfinished business with God that you'll want to tend to. Would you like for me to stay or leave you alone with Him for a minute or two?"

Billy sat on the floor in the back of the classroom listening in on this entire exchange. As was becoming a bad habit for him, he had snuck in the other door and crawled in as Mr. Chastain and his dad sat down earlier. Billy was thoughtfully reflecting on everything that was said over the past fifteen minutes or so.

"Yeah. If you don't mind ..."

William smiled from ear to ear and made his way to the door. "I'll be down the hall if you need me."

"Thank you."

William exited the room quietly.

In a few seconds, Billy looked over and saw his dad crawling over toward him. Once there, William assumed a position right next to his son – right there on the floor. Together, they listened as Mr. Chastain began to pray. The whole thing seemed like God at work.

Billy had a small notebook in his hand and began to write something. He passed it over to William. It read, *No rust. No moths. No thieves. Well played, sir.*

William read it and gave him a smirk. His son had just reminded him of a passage of Scripture [Matthew 6:19] that read, "But lay up for yourselves treasures in heaven, where neither moth nor rust doth corrupt, and where thieves do not break through nor steal." Left-handed William gestured toward Billy's pen, received it, and wrote a message of his own. *I didn't do anything. Jesus did. I was only the messenger.*

They exchanged a silent fist bump and a smile.

CHAPTER 45

WOUNDED

We really do not appreciate its full weight, but the prayer that Gregory Chastain expressed just changed his eternal destiny. This was the single most important decision of his life and everything about him was hinging on how he would respond.

But let us take a short rewind back to moments before his conversation with William. The Chess Club dismissed and Gregory Chastain was joining Mr. Harris for a nice long talk. As that was commencing, Berly was sinking down into the passenger's side of Maggie's preowned car. It was not a pretty car, but it got the job done. Both girls sat in comfortable silence as Maggie pulled out of the student parking lot and past the flagpole.

Maggie's parents were attending an employee appreciation dinner that evening and Berly's folks were on a date night, so dinner was on their own. It was still early yet; but because of the time-change, they were both fooled into thinking that it was later than what the clocks said.

"Anthony's?" Maggie asked. It was a single-worded question, but she undoubtedly got her point across.

Berly answered back, "Sure. Why not? A pizza sounds good to me." She thought for a while, not about food, but about the sight of that well-dressed, middle-aged man in the hall. "That's the third time we have seen that guy visit Mr. Harris after Chess Club. I wonder what his story is."

"Well, you know who that is, don't you? That's Gregory Chastain, as in Chastain Enterprises – one of the pillars of this community. Yes, that Chastain. And *that* makes him the father of none other than ..."

"…Chloe Chastain," Berly finished her friend's sentence. Her face dropped as she said, "That totally figures. I wonder if he was there because everyone was talking about his daughter earlier. After all, it was Mr. Harris' house that she's accused of burning." She paused a moment in thought. "I have to confess to you, Maggie, I never liked her. Of course, I have only known *of* her since the beginning of school."

Maggie agreed. "I guess the only time that we've even met her was this morning after the assembly. And even then, we really didn't talk. She just gave us a sound chewing-out. But just seeing her up and down the halls and how she presents herself, she always struck me as being way too much of whatever she is."

Berly stared out the window. "Yeah. I guess there is plenty to dislike about her and not enough to like. I mean I could probably pay her a compliment if I really thought about it." She paused for a second. "She has nice hair," she said flatly.

"Yep. It would be so easy to fall into that trap, isn't it? We've got to be very careful."

"Amen to that," Berly automatically replied. But that was like a preprogrammed response. About ten seconds floated by. A confused look took over Berly. She turned to her buddy and said, "What a minute. What was that?"

"I said that it would be easy for us to fall into that trap."

"What trap?"

"You know, the same ol' trap we all fall into. From Matthew 7:1? 'Judge not, that ye be not judged.' Besides, remember what we were talking about earlier? Nothing's changed. I still don't think that she had anything to do with the fire. I could be wrong. But if everyone in the school is climbing onboard some bandwagon against her, it makes me stop and reconsider. Seriously, when is the last time that an unruly mob has been right about anything? And if everyone in the school can be wrong about that, then I think there is room for me to be wrong about my first impressions of her." She shrugged. "I've been known to be wrong before."

"What if your first impression was right on the money?"

By this time, Maggie was pulling her car up into the parking lot at Anthony's. "It's still not my place to judge." She pulled into a spot and killed the engine. "Okay, let's assume for a moment that my first impression of her was that she was totally rotten. And let's also say that I was completely right – that Chloe Chastain has absolutely no redeemable qualities and is by far the worst person to ever cast a shadow at Pecan Falls High. In fact, let's just go ahead and say that she actually *did* burn down the Harris' place. Then what? What do we do about it?" She looked at Berly and paused.

Her friend sat there anxiously. "Ummm …"

Maggie relieved her friend of having to answer. "Exactly. What do we do? One thing we cannot do – that's burn *her* house down. That would only start a horribly tragic trend around this otherwise quiet little town." Her face lit up as an idea came to her. She reached into the back seat and grabbed her Bible. "When in doubt, ask the Authority." She began to flip through some pages. "Ah-ha! Here it is. Matthew 5:43-47: 'Ye have heard that it hath been said, Thou shalt love thy neighbor, and hate thine enemy. But I say unto you, Love your enemies, bless them that curse you, do good to them that hate you, and pray for them which despitefully use you, and persecute you; That ye may be the children of your Father which is in heaven: for he maketh his sun to rise on the evil and on the good, and sendeth rain on the just and on the unjust.'"

Berly interrupted, "Okay. So we need to keep these people in prayer. Is that what you are saying?"

"It isn't what *I* am saying; this is what *God* is saying. But there's more. 'For if ye love them which love you, what reward have ye? do not even the publicans the same? And if ye salute your brethren only, what do ye more than others? do not even the publicans so?'" She closed her Bible. "So if I am interpreting this correctly, *anyone* can be nice to people who treat them well and nasty to people who treat them ugly. Yet we are called to go the extra mile. We need to be nice to everyone, even when they are not nice to us. And it really doesn't matter who they are."

Berly added, "I guess it is difficult to hold a grudge against people when you are busy praying for them – and I mean really praying for them." She paused for a moment. A rather obvious example of this flew into her head. "Christ did that. Even from the cross, He was praying for the forgiveness of those who nailed Him there. I couldn't do that." She opened the car door to get out; Maggie followed her lead. Berly looked up at the sky. "Wow.

Only one day into the time change and I can already tell that it's getting darker earlier."

"Yeah. By the way, I don't think that Chloe is the enemy here. She is just flesh and blood. The Bible says that we wrestle not after flesh and blood, but against principalities, powers, and all the rest. I would have to look it up. Paul knew what he was talking about – or I think it was Paul. People are just people," she said in a dismissive tone as they made their way to the door. "It is the ideologies that we are fighting against, not people." It was actually Ephesians 6:12 that she was struggling to recall.

"Let's be honest," Berly added as she opened the door to Anthony's. "The *real* enemy is Satan." As they stepped in, the first thing that saw was Chloe sitting alone and eating an extra small pizza. Berly quietly turned to an equally surprised Maggie and whispered to her, "I would say *Speak of the devil*, but that would be grossly out of context."

Maggie urged her friend to keep moving. "Let's see if we can do this without making a scene."

The two of them successfully made their way over to a table completely unnoticed by Chloe. This might have been a small victory since no other customers were in the room. The waitress signaled that she would be over to get their drink orders in a minute. The only other sounds in the room were of the kitchen staff preparing a takeout order and Don McLean finishing up his musical lament over the early death of an anguished painter. Since Chloe was situated directly under the speakers, the two girls could be quiet without necessarily being quiet.

The waitress came along and took care of them by finding out what they wanted. On the way back through, she stopped by Chloe's table to see if everything was fine. She then went on to place the girls' order.

The songs changed. Now Lonnie Donegan was barking at full volume about his experiences on the Rock Island Line. Chloe looked highly annoyed at the sound coming from overhead. *What is this?* she wondered. *Did people actually listen to this back in the day?* On the upswing, there was no way she could hear Maggie and Berly talking over this skiffle, rockabilly, or whatever this stuff was.

What were they doing there anyway? This situation made no sense. Maggie wondered what force brought them to Anthony's at the same time that Chloe was there. Maybe it was just the pizza. But then again, what possessed them to have a seat and stay? She turned back to Berly and asked, "So, what are you thinking about?"

"The same thing that you're thinking about. I am thinking about her." With a flick of the wrist, she gestured toward Chloe.

"Oh? You think that I was thinking about Chloe?"

"I don't have to think; I know," Berly answered back. "I was just replaying the scene in my head over and over – earlier today when the students all gathered around her in the auditorium and gave her what-for. Then she was standing there in the hall angry and alone. One minute, I myself was wondering what it would be like to be in her shoes, little Miss Popular and all. Now, I am still wondering what it would be like to be her – but this time, sitting there alone and friendless, despised by just about everyone. And then that scene during lunch today – I forgot to tell you about that. That Wesley kid was sitting with sweet Lauren today at lunch. I guess Chloe didn't like it and raised a ruckus. Food everywhere. Not cool."

Maggie raised an eyebrow. Usually, she found herself asking all the deep questions. This time, however, Berly seemed to be driving the conversation forward. "So what are you saying? Are you telling me that this is her comeuppance? Is all this some kind of payback for the way she may have been treating people? The "Golden Rule" lives well into our century, I agree; and that maybe this is a modern happening of *Do unto others as you would have them do unto you.*"

"Actually, Scripture says, 'And as ye would that men should do to you, do ye also to them likewise.'" [Luke 6:31] She pulled out her phone and started scrolling around looking for something.

Both of Maggie's eyebrows shot up upon hearing Berly's correction. *Step to the side, folks. Here comes Berly,* Maggie thought. "Well, tell me this if you're so smart. What do you think should be our next move?"

"I'm way ahead of you." Berly had been on her Bible app and already had an answer to Maggie's inquiry. "It says here in Ephesians 4:31-32, 'Let all bitterness, and wrath, and anger, and clamour, and evil speaking, be put away from you, with all malice: And be ye kind one to another, tenderhearted, forgiving one another, even as God for Christ's sake hath forgiven you.' BOOM! Word from Paul. And he writes like a boss."

Maggie backed up and took a hard look at her friend. "Girl. You're too much. So, what specifically are our orders from above?"

Berly looked over at Chloe and sighed. "Make friends with her, I guess."

"Do what?"

"Oh please, I don't mean all buddy-buddy. But I think that we should go over there and at least introduce ourselves – make some kind of an effort. We can certainly do that without getting all kissy-faced with her. Maybe God can use this in ways that we would never expect."

"That is the most sensible and mature thing that you have said in years," Maggie added. "Remind me to tell Sir Lancelot; he would be proud."

"Why thank you, Magpie." Berly looked at her friend all sly. " ...I think."

By now, the speakers were playing a song by Spanky and Our Gang. Over and over, they sang, "I'd like to get to know you." *How corny and appropriate*, Berly thought as she slid out of her seat. "Here goes nothing," she whispered.

Maggie added, "'Once more unto the breach, dear friends.' ... or *friend*, in this case." They both stood tall and began walking.

"Yeah. What you said."

Chloe had already finished up her pizza and was daydreaming. She had finally cooled off in a manner of speaking, but she was still hurt. She was hurt by the students, by Wesley, by Bre, and by her dad. She had never felt so wounded. Perhaps the entire world was filled with people who hated her – she just never realized it until that day. If all of the people who hated her were to be called out and made to line up, just how long would that line be? It would probably go all the way around Pecan Falls about a dozen times. Maybe she could take a number and get in line too.

Her life was not perfect by any means, but it was certainly a lot better before she had met this brat Billy Harris and his egghead father. She did not want to live with her mom and those two siblings of hers; they were always trying to run her life. At least her dad was gone half the time and she had relative freedom to do what she wanted. And she had a nice car. But what was it that she wanted? None of this stuff was making her happy. Just what would make her happy anyway? She had no idea. Perhaps she was always meant to ... She looked up. Two smiling girls were standing there.

The one with stylish glasses spoke first. "Hi. Aren't you Chloe Chastain?"

Half of Chloe's mind thought, *Those glasses look cute on her.* The other half of her brain was somewhat outraged. She repaid the polite question with a blank stare.

The older one started talking. "We're sorry to bother you and we can see that you have just finished with ..."

"Excuse me. Who are you?" She sounded like someone who was squeaky clean and trying not to get dirty.

Berly was swiftly reminded of Mr. Darcy's retort to Mr. Collin's cheeky approach in *Pride and Prejudice*. *Oh well, no stopping now,* she thought. "Oh! I'm sorry. I'm Berly – that's short for Kimberly. And this is Maggie – and she's just short in general." She laughed at her own joke, while Maggie gave her a gentle nudge. "We were wondering if we could join you for a few minutes."

"Why?"

Berly's face dropped just a few millimeters. "Uh, just to talk. That's all."

Chloe was incensed. "*Just to talk*, huh? Do you two think I'm *that* stupid? I know exactly what you're doing. You want to get me to talk about what happened today at school so you can both run along and have something to report to all your nosey little friends. I'm probably quite the talk right now on social media. I know what they are all saying about me."

Maggie shook her head. "No, no. That's not ..."

"Wait just a minute!" Chloe interrupted. "Haven't I seen the two of you before?" She opened her mouth wide. It was all coming back to her. "You two! You were the ones over by the trophy case this morning! The two that were busy talking about me!" She grabbed her purse and started to get up from her seat. "You certainly have a lot of nerve to come over here. Well, I have had enough of this!"

Berly was desperately trying to reason with Chloe. "Wait! That's not what was happening. We were only ..."

"Don't bother trying to explain anything. I know precisely what was happening." She rushed over to the register where the waitress was nervously standing. "Here! Keep the change." Chloe threw more than enough money down on the countertop. In no time at all, she had made her way to the door with both Maggie and Berly trying to talk her down. Everyone was making noise at once. Chloe tossed the door open in an overly theatrical display of fury and stopped halfway out. "And for the record, *girls*, I had NOTHING to do with the Harris' house burning down!" With that, she disappeared out the door. In about a second, she had thrown her purse in the front seat of her car, started up her machine, and recklessly sped out into the unsuspecting traffic. She was gone.

Berly was standing in the doorway. All was quiet. Even the music did not play. With a defeated expression, she turned around to face Maggie. "Perhaps we should've prayed about this first," she confessed.

Maggie nodded silently.

CHAPTER 46

LUNCHROOM HORRORS

The energy level was sky-high for the members of the Chess Club the next day. This lunch period was going to put them on the Pecan Falls High School activities map. In fact, their little club was going to rule the place after their performance was over. Total social domination. The road before them was paved with stars. Quotes had no trouble keep his mouth shut, but it was all the others could do to hold their tongues until it was over.

Tuesday was chicken strips day at PFHS and most of the sophomores were in the lunchroom. Only a handful ate their lunch outside. Some of the juniors and seniors had off-campus privileges for lunch, but there were plenty of them represented in the room - - that was certain. Chloe, the high profile outcast, was eating her lunch by herself with her back turned toward everyone; no one would be messing with her. Wesley was eating with Lauren. Mike and Curtis sat together and were waiting for Billy. Mr. Harris did not have lunch duty that day, but he was there in full support of the club and he clued the other duty teachers and Mrs. Dunbar as to what the Chess Club had planned – so everything was cool. It was now zero hour.

Billy, with an enthusiastic Chris in tow, set up a CD player in the back of the room and put in an old CD of something called *Semper Fidelis* by a hilarious-dressed fellow named John Philip Sousa, the March King himself. The sound was cranked way up. As soon as the music began, Maggie turned off the lights in the lunchroom. At the sudden blindness, a few of the students screamed at this unexpected turn of events. Other students laughed at the ones who screamed. Joey turned on some bright blue lights that they had managed to borrow from the theater department. These lights were strategically placed near the entrances of the room. Berly and Maggie opened the doors. Fake smoke (also on loan from the theater department) poured into the room. Everything was trotting along as planned. Students all over the dark room turned curiously to see what was going on.

A shadowy Eugene walked through the smoke. He was dressed in a formfitting body suit with a cone-shaped, cardboard vest and a sort of strange helmet that was supposed to resemble the top of a rook. All eyes were focused on this chess-inspired demon. He did an awkward dance for a few measures of the song. The choreography itself was in horrible contrast with the military march that was playing. Some people were amused because it was desperately awful. They did not realize that this was merely the beginning of the sad presentation.

A second pair of doors now sprang open with more fake smoke and red lights rather than blue. The students threw their attention now to Alejandro, who entered dressed the same way except he had a head that looked like a horse – obviously portraying the knight. The fake knight was supposed to rush out beyond the smoke and to begin his unique dance; but instead of doing a dance the way they rehearsed it, he simply walked forward with his arms outstretched, urgently looking for something to hold onto. "I cannot see a thing," he mumbled with a voice that came from a bucket. Lunging forward, he came right at a couple of students and knocked over the napkin dispenser onto the tile floor quite by accident. One of the students screamed and just about fell to the floor as well.

Few noticed, because by then a bright yellow light illuminated the final set of doors. They opened revealing more smoke and Quotes dressed as a chess king. Again, all three were wearing unflattering formfitting suits, cardboard vests, and homemade masks. Fortunately, Quotes' mask allowed his face to be seen, leaving the students with a disturbing mental image. He already had the unfortunate habit of terrifying students with his appearance.

With much 'dancing,' the three actually met up and did a terribly choreographed fight scene. It may have been fairly well rehearsed considering the talent involved; but perhaps the gift of dance was not necessarily given to these three well-meaning lads. Their talents were more suited for the game of chess rather than theatrics.

Many of the students were laughing at the painful spectacle. Others were screaming any time the participants got anywhere close to their proximity. Whether their exhibition was to eventually promote the dignity of the Chess Club or provide the student body with comic fuel was now up for debate.

About halfway through the song, a drum solo boomed through the speakers. Tuh-da-da-da-da. At this sound, all three pretended to be playing invisible drums and gathered to stand in formation. They played these phantom drums with all their heart. Then the other two stood perfectly still as the "rook" Eugene stepped forward and pretended to play a lone trumpet. When this 'solo' came to an end, Alejandro the Knight joined him playing some kind of air-clarinet (although the students clearly heard a gaggle of flutes joining the trumpet and the curious absence of any clarinet). A few measures later, here came the trombones. Quotes played a mock trombone with much more gusto than his two companions had displayed. The whole thing was an unlikely pairing of *inspiration* and *horror*. But even though Alejandro was unable to see much, they all looked like they were having fun doing it. And that is what made it fun to watch. It was fun. What else mattered?

For the remainder of the song, the three were supposed to march around the lunchroom, up one aisle and back down another. But this was when things went awry. One of the juniors deliberately stuck out his foot in front of Quotes. The giant king went crashing to the floor. Humiliated, he stood back up, faced the guy who tripped him, and picked up his lunch tray. In a tremendous display of physical strength, he snapped the lunch tray in two. Green beans were everywhere. At the sight of this, the guy who tripped him was experiencing genuine dread. What sort of unholy strength was that?

Quite unexpectedly, a weird sort of roar came from deep within Quotes' chest cavity and escaped through his mouth. It seemed to be a voice so unnatural (almost profane) that it caused fear into the hearts of all who heard it. He bellowed, "YOU MESSED UP MY DANCE!" It appeared to be language. … from Quotes?!

Alejandro quaked from fright. "¡Que milagro!"

Eugene swallowed his gum and turned to Alejandro. "Well, whadduyah know?! IT TALKS!"

This was the first time either of them had ever heard Quotes speak and the sound made their blood run cold. It startled Eugene so bad that he fell over backward for a moment. As he went down, he heard something rip behind him. "Oh no. That can't be good." He did not know what to fear more: the sound of Quotes' voice or the uncertainty of his wardrobe malfunction.

At the conclusion of the number, Berly and Joey rushed over some homemade signs for the performers to show. Eugene held up a big sign that said *PFHS CHESS CLUB*. This was followed by Alejandro holding up his sign. It read *MONDAY, WEDNESDAY, AND FRIDAY AT 3:30-4:15*. And finally Quotes held up his sign (which was sideways at first, but he soon corrected it), *MR. HARRIS' ROOM*.

They finished their embarrassing routine and exited the room at the end of the song. Berly and Joey closed the doors behind them and Maggie turned on the regular overhead lights. All of the students in attendance stared blankly at the doors. Everyone was silent – the proverbial cricket sounds. After a few seconds, the students turned their attention back to their previous conversations. There was no clapping. They reacted as if nothing at all happened. Well, a handful of them were a little traumatized by the experience and were being comforted by some other students. At times like this, it was perhaps a good thing that a school had counselors.

Billy turned off the music, grabbed the CD player, and set it in front of his dad who took it and left for his classroom. Then Maggie, Berly, Joey, Chris, and Billy ran out into the hall to help out the others.

Eugene was growing more conscience of the ripping sound that his tights had made. He speedily got the attention of Joey and Alejandro. "I think I just ripped something back there. How bad is it?"

The other two guys checked it out and quickly stood back up, looking back and forth at each other, hesitant to say anything.

Eugene was growing impatient. "Well?"

Joey put a hand on Eugene's shoulder and said in a mirthful voice, "Well Eugene, I guess this means that we're family now."

Eugene's eyes grew wide with fear. "Is it that bad?"

Alejandro was not as amused. He slapped Eugene on the arm. "Dude! What is wrong with you? Why weren't you wearing any underwear?"

"Because these tights were too tight and I couldn't get them on otherwise." Embarrassed, Eugene retreated to the restroom where his clothes were.

Excited with news, Berly ran up to the others. "Hey everyone! Check it out. Rodney is here and he caught the entire thing. He thought it was awesome." Surrounding students cheered.

Billy rolled his eyes and sounded beaten. Yes, the entire thing was Billy's idea – but he was a bit disenchanted by the lack of applause following their exhibition. He had hoped that people would be inspired to join the club after the show, but now he was prepared to lament over its poor reception.

This was different. He had changed recently. After enjoying the sudden popularity for a day, he was already feeling less passionate about assisting the Chess Club – and even reevaluating his presence there. "Y'all are terrible. Rodney? I am almost embarrassed to be associating with people who believe in the Phantom of the Chess Club. But even if this Rodney supposedly thought it was awesome, he must be much nerdier than originally thought possible. Sad."

"Well, he is on his way back here now." Berly brushed the hair away from her face and turned around to look. "That is, I *thought* he was."

Joey smiled and gave Billy a light nudge with his elbow. "Hey, Billy. You've always wanted to meet Rodney. Here's your chance. Opportunity knocks."

"You all must think that I'm an idiot. If this Rodney were even a real person, then he would be hands-down the King of the Nerds, one of those incredibly smart guys who gets his left and right shoes mixed up. No thank you. Right now, there isn't exactly a shortage of weird people in my life. Why would I want to make room for one more?" He stomped off in search of his other friends.

"Suit yourself," Joey hollered back just as Rodney was coming around the corner behind them.

Rodney was a slightly-taller-than-average senior. Well dressed, handsome, friendly, he looked like he could have a promising future as a weather man. The girls considered him 'gorgeous.' He greeted them all with a warm and congenial accent. "Hey, guys!"

The others gathered around him with a familiar series of high-fives and fist bumps.

Rodney was full of enthusiastic praise. "That was terrific! Alejandro and Quotes, you two dudes and Eugene totally killed it out there. Great job! These costumes are the best. And I especially loved the lights and the smoke. That was really cool. It was the best thing to happen to our lunchroom since Mrs. Knox brought out the strawberry shortcake two years ago."

Alejandro folded his arms in a sulky manner. "My idea would've been better."

Rodney looked around the group as if he were looking for someone. "So whose idea was this anyway?"

Maggie shrugged her shoulders and smiled up at Rodney. "It was mostly Billy's."

"Right. You mean the new kid, Mr. Harris' son. Where is he anyway? I'd like to meet him."

Berly answered, "Pffff! Gone. He has some old friends that he was going to catch up with."

"Yeah. You just missed him," Maggie added. "He's a real piece of work, that Billy."

Rodney was abruptly inquisitive. "What does that mean? So, what is this kid like anyway?"

Joey stepped forward. "Well, I don't want to sound judgmental or anything, but he *is* pretty much the biggest nerd I've ever seen. I'm surprised that he is in the Chess Club honestly."

The others sounded off in agreement.

Eugene came out of the restroom and joined the others in his usual street clothes. Fishing for a big-fat compliment, he lifted his hand and got Rodney's attention. "Yo, Rodney! Check it out! You caught the show? So did you see me out there?"

Rodney looked over at Eugene and his smile fell. "Oh yes. I certainly did. And I hope to never see that side of you again."

CHAPTER 47

THE VILLAIN APPEARS

Mike exploded as Billy sat next to him at their usual table in the lunchroom. "Dude! And just where have you been this entire time?"

"What are you talking about? I was doing the music for that plug, the one for the Chess Club."

Curtis turned back to his juice box. "Oh. Is that what that was supposed to be? We were waiting for the police to arrive and haul those scary costumed people away. I don't know what's creepier – that dancing thing we just witnessed or that stuff over there." He pointed at a nearby student's lunch tray. "I think that supposed to be jalapeño cornbread."

Even though the initial lack of response bothered him, Billy was now looking for some positive vibes concerning the club's routine. "No really. What did you think, guys? Was it cool or what?"

Mike spoke up. "Billy, Billy, Billy. Are you still talking about that train wreck? We've moved on since then. Important stuff is going down and you're talking about that lame whatever-that-was."

Curtis had to agree. "Yeah. That ship sailed."

Billy was taken aback. Slowly and forcefully, he said, "Guys. It just happened." He emphasized each word that he uttered.

Mike was sounding a little desperate. "We get that. Now get over it. You've got bigger things to worry about here in the present tense."

"Huh? Like what?"

"Like *her*." Mike pointed over at Chloe, still sitting alone with her back to the entire room. She was watching the wall as though it were a giant television.

Curtis picked up his bag of chips. "She came over here just a few minutes ago and asked for you. She wants to talk to you. Apparently now – she says."

"She wants to talk to me?"

Curtis popped a chip in his mouth and said, "That's right. She says that *you* owe *her* an apology. Isn't that hilarious?"

"*I* OWE *HER* AN APOLOGY?! Is she out of her twenty-four karat head?"

Mike leaned forward, keeping it inside the huddle; but he could not help getting a little bit excited as he spoke. "Can you believe her gall? First, she pretty much obliterated you at a party. Then, there is this video on the internet of you acting all weird at your house - - which is rather funny by the way, no offense. And finally, the rumor mill is reporting all over campus that she is actually responsible for your house going up in flames. And honestly, I kinda believe it, even though I *did* hear it from one of the journalism students (and that automatically makes it questionable). And on top of everything, she now expects you to publicly apologize. I think she has issues to reconcile – like BIG issues – like 'call in the professionals'."

Billy was getting a little steamed at Chloe, but he had to clarify that about the house fire. "Well, I can tell you guys that she absolutely did *not* burn the house down. That much we know for certain. The fire started because our deranged clothes dryer finally decided to dramatically retire."

Curtis posed the question. "Okay. So what are you going to do?"

Billy started to strip off his jacket and pull up his sleeves. "I'll tell you what I'm going to do. I'm gonna go over there and I'm gonna talk to her." There was a hint of ruthlessness in his voice - - one that the others rarely ever heard.

Mike spread out his fingers in an attempt to stop him. "No, no, no, no. You must not leave this table. I suggest that you totally avoid her. If you like weird girls, we can find all sorts of them around here without crawling over to Chloe."

"Not only am I going to talk to her, but I'm going to give her a big piece of my mind. It's about time that someone around here told her off."

Curtis objected. "Don't do it, man. This is a major league mistake."

Mike was squarely behind Curtis' statement. "Dude, steer clear of this. Just let her stew in her own drama. This is not your circus and these are not your monkeys."

Billy looked back at Mike square in the eyes. "But this *is* my circus." He then turned to Curtis. "And these *are* my monkeys." What he was actually saying sounded ridiculous out of context, but he was deadly serious. Billy's mind was made up. He stood and said, "No way. After all that junk that she has put me through, I'm about to go and have the last word. Someone needs to go teach her a lesson."

As he began to walk, nearby students had overheard his comment and started whispering to each other. Within seconds, it seemed as if the entire room was watching. They all figured that a fight was about to bust out - - not just a fight, an epic struggle to the death. Even though the majority of lunch period was over, it was high noon at Pecan Falls. These students would all remember the fateful day that Billy Harris Jr. took down the high and mighty Chloe Chastain. The days of her social reign were coming to a pathetic end and a revolution was about to begin.

From his manner of walking, everyone in the room could plainly see that he was filled with equal amounts of angst and confidence. But Billy's march over to Chloe's table slowed down once he glanced over at the back of her head. Something in his attitude changed. In his mind, he saw the face of her father and how desperately concerned he was for his little girl. Billy then thought about his dad talking to that old homeless man down in the city a couple of nights ago and how grateful he was for the meal. He imagined all those neighbors laying warm hands on him and his parents in fervent prayer later that chilly morning. Physically, the Harris' were standing in the glow of their burning house; but their hearts were standing in the glow of their neighbor's love.

What is this? he questioned in his head. *Just what do I think I'm doing? Everyone here is watching me. Am I so sure that this is the right thing? I could so easily destroy her right now and become the most popular guy in school. But is that truly what I want?* Billy remembered that his dad was telling him something important a few nights ago. *Wait. What did dad say the other night? What did he say after he lost that chess game to that new kid? Oh, I gotta remember. Um, 'sometimes we win whenever we lose' – something like that.*

Billy's walk came to a complete stop. He slowly turned his head and saw all those faces looking at him. He then turned to see the faces of his disappointed friends back at the table. Curtis and Mike were shaking their heads and looking down. The rest of the room seemed to be cheering him on – but did the consensus of the room make things right? What would Clay think of all this? What would his dad see if he were to walk in the room? What was God seeing right now? He then turned back around to see the back of Chloe's head. Was she really so different than anyone else in the room?

At that point, he remembered James' all-too-relevant question: If his life were turned into a movie, who would be the villain? This time, the answer came crashing down on him. *Oh wow!* he thought. *The villain isn't Chloe or her dad. And it isn't the rich kids either. It's not even that inferno of a clothes dryer. It's me. I'm the villain. I'm the villain in my own story. I'm the bad guy. I have treated everyone so badly. I've only thought of myself this entire time. Ha! When it comes to being selfish, I've got Chloe beat. I should be the one to know better. I've been angry at my parents, and they were just trying to protect me from myself. I've been short tempered with my friends. At this point, I wouldn't even be surprised if my concern for Clay was more about how his accident has affected me. Oh, man. I'm such a jerk.*

He now found himself standing over Chloe. He had zombie-walked the rest of the way to her table. He had no idea what he was going to say, so an automated series of words fell out of his mouth. "I understand that you wanted to speak to me. Would you like me to sit?"

Chloe gestured to the seat opposite from her. He walked around her and sat, positioned with his back against the wall. He looked up at her. Other than whatever emotions she was supposed to have on a worldly basis, Billy now saw someone who had never been introduced to God's love. And just past her head, he noticed that every eye in the room was turned to face him.

An awkward silence ruled the room for only a few seconds. Then Chloe inhaled deeply and began what was obviously a well-rehearsed speech. "Ever since ..."

"Stop right there." Billy held up one hand. The entire room froze. He mentally acknowledged that he needed help. Now that he knew who the *villain* was, he realized that he could not proceed any further until he has had a talk with the *HERO* of his story.

Chloe's eye widened as she stared at him. Billy interrupting her messed up the momentum of her prepared speech and was certainly not a part of her plan.

"Hold that thought," he added. He leaped up out of his seat and left the room to the complete surprise of everyone there.

As Billy exited one door, Berly and Maggie entered through another. Their laughing and talking halted when they looked around. Everyone in the room was quiet, like they were under some hypnotic spell. An eerie sense of dread seized the two girls as they peered across the crowd. They walked carefully over to their usual seats as though the floor were covered with tiny alligators. Afraid to even breathe, they sat in cautionary silence.

Berly finally leaned over to Maggie and whispered, "Do you think our little song and dance did this to them?"

Maggie replied, "I wonder if there is any way to reverse the process." She got her Psychology book out of her backpack and started leafing through the index.

CHAPTER 48

CHECKMATE

Billy shot out the lunchroom door, frantically looking around. *Where can I go?* he asked himself. *Where can I go?* He found a janitorial closet, opened the door, and squeezed in as best as he could considering all the supplies and stuff that were in there. He managed to pull the door closed behind him, which really was an impressive feat.

With the only light coming in under the door, he looked upward into the surrounding darkness. In reality, mops, bottles of cleaning agents, and the walls were almost directly in his face; but in the darkness, he felt as though he were standing in a huge void, a section of space with no stars. Perfect.

At this point, he began to pray. "Almighty God, I know that you are an immense God and that it is a bit cramped in here. But I really needed a prayer closet right now and this will just have to do. I want to start off by saying that I'm sorry for all the trouble that I've caused everyone. I need to live the kind of life that directs people to You - - and I haven't done that at all. I've been craving the material things of this world and giving temporary things greater importance in my life than You. This is clearly a form of idolatry. But I also want to confess my anger and leave it with You. I certainly don't mind confessing to You that a huge part of me wants to tear into her and let her have it. But I also know that I sometimes win when I allow myself to lose. I may be taking this out of context but somewhere in the Bible we are told not to worry about what we will say. [Matthew 10:19] So I formally request that You will be glorified by whatever I say

402

out there - - because she doesn't know You at all. And she needs You. In Your wonderful Son's name I pray, Amen."

Right before the very first day of school, Billy had a dream in which he had to diffuse a bomb. Now he wanted to see if he could do that again.

At this point, he pulled the latch on the door and it practically burst open. The janitor had just come around the corner and was about to open the door actually when Billy popped out. The sophomore looked at him and remarked, "Uh, excuse me, sir." The janitor had seen nearly everything in the over the three decades that he had been working there. He did not think a thing of it.

Chloe was confused and irritated as Billy resumed the seat in front of her. It would seem that no one in the room made a sound during those few peculiar minutes that Billy stepped out.

He looked across the table at her. All of his anger was gone, washed away. He smiled back at her. "Uh, sorry about that. Now what were you saying?"

"I have been waiting for you since lunch started and now it's almost over."

"I understand that and I'm sorry. Now what did you want to see me about?"

"I want you to apologize."

He tilted his head slightly and looked at her. "Uh, I just did."

She leaned forward. Her voice was getting angry. "I'm not talking about that. I'm talking about what you've done to me."

Clearly, he had no idea what she was talking about. His mind had been somewhere else for the past five minutes.

Chloe turned her head to the side and began to talk to herself. "Good grief! He is both poor *and* stupid." She turned back toward Billy. "Let me spell it out for you, Mr. Moneybags. My life is now miserable thanks to you. You seemed to like me and muscled your unwelcome way into my life. I like someone else; but guess what! You somehow completely destroyed my chances with him. Now everyone at this school is against me because they think that I burned down your ugly, old house - - which I assure you, I did NOT do. And don't even get me started on your dad and his stupid class."

Billy did something really strange. He reached over and picked up

Chloe's water bottle, unscrewed the cap, and started to pour it on the floor beside her – or that's how it looked. But actually they heard it splashing down on someone's head.

Justin was crawling on the floor next to them and hollered, "Hey!"

Billy's voice was not one of surprise; he had seen Justin approach them on his hands and knees. "Oh. Hi, Justin."

Justin made his way back to his feet and was rubbing some of the water out of his hair. "Uh, I was just …"

"Eves-dripping?"

"Gemme a break, Billy. I only do what my girlfriend tells me to do."

"I'll tell you what. If it'll make it easier for you, how about if I write out a full report on what we say and get that to you later?"

"I don't know about that. What if …"

"Dude. Trust me. Have I ever lied to you before?"

Justin thought about the question and was at a loss.

"Now go tell your girlfriend and be the big hero."

A big campy smile stretched across Justin's face. *Great day*, he thought. *Billy is going to give me a full report. Tight.* He walked back to his girlfriend as if he were all that. Little did he know just how much trouble he was about to have.

Chloe, however, was furious. She had been ignored way too long.

For once, Billy was able to accurately assess her mood. So he decided to give her what she wanted. "I believe that you are still waiting for that apology. So I'm offering it now. I'm sorry."

That was not near enough for her. "Ha! That didn't sound very sincere. Is that the best you've got?"

She was right. That did not sound very sincere at all. What was so strange about it was that Billy really was sincere. A thousand things came to his mind, a thousand things that he wanted to say. Perhaps this would be the best time and perhaps God would direct his words. This was not anyone's business but theirs, so he brought the volume of this voice really low so that only she could hear him. He brought his hands up to the top of the table and began to speak. He spoke slowly and clearly.

"You want sincere? Alright." He took a deep breath, exhaled, and met her eyes with his. "I'm sorry for a lot of stuff. I'm sorry that I ever even bothered you. I honestly thought that I could get you to like me and I was

404

dead wrong. I'm sorry that I tried to become so popular and *now* I'm sorry that I am – or I seem to be. I'm also sorry that you are being shunned by everyone. That was *never* my intention; that was never my goal. I'm sorry that I spent so much time pursuing friendships with people who don't like me – and I did that at the risk of losing the incredible friends that I already have. I'm sorry that I put such a high priority on the temporary junk of this world. The stuff you buy doesn't last or even bring peace and contentment. I'm also sorry that I have only recently discovered just how cool my parents really are. And while I'm on the subject, your dad loves you. I don't agree with the way he shows it – but it's true. And I'm sorry that you don't see that."

This seemed to have hit a nerve with her. She could no longer look at him, so she looked down.

He continued, "I'm also sorry that everyone here is blaming you for something you didn't do. And I'm sorry that I can't change that. I'm sorry that I can't do anything to help."

She continued to look down. Her eyes began to swell.

Billy also sat in thoughtful silence. But then something changed. He tilted his head. His tone took on a more hopeful quality. "Well, maybe there *is* something that I can do about that." He got up from where he was sitting, stepped up onto his seat, and then climbed to the top of the table.

Chloe tried to stop him, but it was too late. She was altogether accustomed to being the center of attention, but that was the last thing that she wanted right now. She became scared. In addition, he had already given her some things to think about. But what was Billy doing now?

"Uh, can I have everyone's attention please?" he asked in a loud voice (a ridiculous question considering that he already *had* everyone's full attention). "I hate to bother you all and I know that lunch is almost over but I need to set the record straight. I have heard that many of you think that Chloe Chastain had something to do with my house burning down. That is completely untrue. In our house, we had this hundred-year-old dryer that caught fire. We started a load and went to bed which may have been a bad idea in retrospect. Anyway she had absolutely nothing to do with that. Also some of you may think that I am mad at her because of things that she may have done to me at a party this weekend."

At the mention of this, Chloe began to weep. Only Billy could tell that she was making a horrible face, like a weird, leaky prune. This unflattering and painful expression was accompanied by a soft squeaky whine that was barely audible. But there was nothing she could do; if she got up now, everyone would see her crying. There were way too many cell phones in the room for her to risk it.

He looked down and noticed that she was crying, but he did not draw people's attention to that fact. Instead, he demanded everyone to look at him with his actions and his tone. Any possible consideration that her fragile condition may get was diverted to him now. "Well, I can honestly say that I'm not mad. And if *I'm* not mad at her, I don't see any reason why any of *you* should be either."

Just beyond her reach, Billy noticed that there was a napkin dispenser, the chrome kind with the star on the side. With his foot, he discretely scooted it across the table and stopped it directly in front of her. She helplessly reached over and pulled some napkins out and wiped her face with them. By some miracle, this was done in such a way that no one caught on. She, on the other hand, interpreted this as another nice gesture – one that she perhaps would not have done.

Billy continued his speech. "As far as I'm concerned, we're just friends. And I urge you all to be her friend as well. High school – and life in general – is way too short to be collecting enemies." He spotted Justin sitting next to his girlfriend in the crowd. "Justin? How was that? Are you good?"

Justin held up both thumbs. "We're all good here."

Justin's girlfriend was not the only one who was 'all good.' Mike and Curtis were worried for a while, but now they looked relieved. Not just relieved, they were quite proud of how Billy handled the situation. And singlehandedly swaying public opinion back in Chloe's favor was a bonus, the perfect use of self-sacrificial power. They were not quite sure if this was a picture-perfect display of maturity on his part, but it did have the merits of being unpredictable. And yet, they were not the only ones who approved of what was said. Since all of this was practically a public statement that Chloe and Billy were not likely to be an item anytime soon, a hidden smile could be found on Berly's face as well.

"Alright. That's all I have. Now let's say we finish our lunches before the bell rings." Billy stepped down from the table and resumed his seat directly across from Chloe. He had a big smile on his face - - not mean or vindictive, but warm and friendly. He honestly hoped that this would meet with her approval. "So how was that? Did you think that might help you at all? I hope so."

Chloe had been analyzing some of the events in her head. She thought about how she had pretty much put Billy up for public ridicule just a few nights earlier and revenge was temptingly within his grasp. But he resisted. In fact, he had built her up and defended her. And she knew it. Because of his kindness, she had been bested. It was checkmate — one in which Billy lost the battle; but in doing so, he actually won the war. He had repaid evil with good. She felt another huge cry coming on. She had to get out of there … and quick. Off she went, disappearing into the ladies' room.

Billy sat there watching her go - - surprised and not surprised. So far, nothing that she had done was making any sense to him; and so in that regard, he probably should have seen this random act coming. But what was he to do next? It almost immediately occurred to him to look for the *kind* thing to do. When faced with a dilemma, go with kindness.

A nearby bulletin board had caught his eye once again — as it was designed to do. There were still a dozen or so fliers for the next *Pride and Prejudice* reading tacked together. The next of these events was scheduled for that very night at Mike's house. "Well, it's not exactly the approach that I was looking for, but it's a start," he said, sighing to himself as he got up and walked over to it.

He pulled one of the fliers free of the tack and saw Berly and Maggie sitting nearby — not knowing about their previous run-ins with her. He walked over and leaned between them, handed over the flier, and asked them to take it into the restroom. He requested that they do their best to invite Chloe. Both girls got up and entered the restroom to find her.

It would not be too hard to imagine that they found her crying. But they approached her, gave her the flier, and invited her as warmly as they knew how. After all the humiliation that she had faced and the emotional doubt that she was currently going through, the last thing that she wanted to talk about was that literature book - - especially with a bunch of people she did not even know — or even like. But other than Billy's speech, it was the first kind words that she had heard in two days.

The time and address were both on the handout.

CHAPTER 49

NOT A CLUE

It will not surprise you to learn that Chloe was an emotional wreck, injured by recent events. When she got home, her dad came out of the kitchen to greet her. She completely astounded him by rushing over and giving him a huge embrace. Before then, she would just as well punch him in the face as to look at him. But they sat down and talked over a bowl of popcorn. It was one of the most difficult things that she had ever done in her life, but she tried to explain what had happened over the past few days. In doing so, she had to confess outright about having the party against his authority. To her complete amazement, her dad took it all in and did not lose his temper. His disapproval was still there; it just manifested itself in an unexpectedly civil fashion.

Then she listened to him as he tried to explain his recent encounter with Mr. Harris. She could not fully comprehend why all of this had happened. Her dad was acting completely different after having some kind of life-altering conversation with Mr. Harris. And earlier that day, Billy Harris showed her every kindness following her cruel trick on him. Maybe the Harris' really did have something that was missing from the Chastain home, something money could not buy. How was she to reason with this?

As the evening approached, she looked again at the flier. She showed it to her dad.

A fairly large gathering of Mr. Harris' students descended upon Mike Hairston's house to continue reading the final chapters of *Pride and*

Prejudice; but it was not as if these sophomores were just dying to find out how it ended. Still they were anxious to finally get this book behind them. There seemed to be a mental red tape marking the finish line of this nineteenth century novel, and these students were ready to cross it. Diane and William were both on hand as Mr. and Mrs. Hairston played kind hosts to the twenty or so students. (Truth be known, the students were enjoying the book much more than they anticipated, go figure.)

The sharp sound of an entire herd of Pomeranians barking stemmed from the detached garage. Mike had hoped in vain that they would bark themselves hoarse, but he remembered that their bark was rather hoarse to begin with because they typically barked all the time anyway. Curtis and Billy were rather pleased to know that the dogs were not to be found inside the house proper. The two cats, however, only came around when they wanted some attention – much easier on the ears.

After the meeting started, another knock came to the door. Mr. Hairston and Mr. Harris (no relation) were surprised to find Gregory Chastain standing there. William introduced them and invited him to come in. Standing behind him was Chloe, puffy-eyed from excessive crying. Gregory filled him in on the short version of what was going on and William quickly got Diane's attention. Berly happened to be walking by and immediately gathered the situation. She grabbed a Bible and escorted Diane and Chloe to an upstairs bedroom and away from the other students. There they talked.

While they were talking, we need to point out that Proverbs 22:1 says, "A good name is rather to be chosen than great riches, and loving favour rather than silver and gold." Fortunes can be gained and lost in short order and sometimes without notice. Gregory Chastain would certainly vouch for that. But how we deal with those who God puts in our path is something that cannot be reclaimed. Real treasure lies in the time that we spend growing closer to God and encouraging others in their relationship with Him as they travel down their own spiritual journey.

As the kids were preparing to read their Jane Austen, Mike was grinning from ear to ear, but it was not because of the book. Sitting just to his side was Clay. His buddy had gotten out of the house and decided to circulate with the others. Obviously, he was enjoying a little more celebrity that night than usual. The only time people noticed him before was whenever he crossed the finish line somewhere. But being popular was never one of his goals, so he just endured it. It did not take long before people were just treating him as they always had, like ordinary folk.

Jane Austen went largely ignored that night, but she will get over it. Having Clay back with them was amazing. But after a while, Chloe and Berly came back downstairs in locked arms. Diane was following them. They were all smiles. Word got out quickly that Berly had led Chloe to a saving knowledge of Christ. Mr. Chastain wasted no time rushing over and giving his daughter another huge hug.

Billy walked over to his mom and asked, "So Berly talked to Chloe?"

Diane smiled back at him. "She sure did. You should've seen her. She was right on target and knew just what to say. She shared her own testimony and then explained what Jesus did on the cross. After a while, Chloe began praying on her own. The whole thing was exactly the way it was supposed to be."

Billy had no idea what to say. "Really? That is so cool. Huh. Berly did that. Wow."

For the next few minutes, people were gathering around Chloe and giving her hugs. This was a completely new feeling for her. For the first time in her life, she felt free from sin and all the things that she disliked about herself. A tremendous weight had been lifted. She felt closer to her father than ever before. And now she seemed to have a family she never knew she had. She was experiencing acceptance. Even the students there who had not made that decision noticed an irrefutable change in her and made a mental note of it. Chloe was so excited she wanted to tell the world - - starting with Bre. She excused herself to step outside for a few minutes where she pulled out her phone.

Back inside, the focus once again fell on Clay (and further away from poor ol' Jane Austen). Wesley was just now getting to know him better and asked him when he was going to return to school.

He shrugged. "Any time, I guess. Probably tomorrow. I'm gonna need some help getting around for a while, but my friends have assured me that there are plenty of people on hand to see to that." He chuckled at the thought. The group also gave a light spontaneous laugh.

Curtis smiled back at him with that contagious smile of his and said,

"Poor Coach Holton. He's going to have to manage track without you. He'll be sorry not to have you."

An impish little grin appeared on Clay. "Well, I'm not so sure that I'm done with track to be perfectly honest. I don't know yet what is going to happen whenever I get my prosthetics, but mom has done some research into track events for amputees. After looking over this material, I have to admit that I'm getting pretty excited. Who knows? I may be coming back to Coach Holton soon. I haven't told him yet, but I'm hoping to see him tomorrow."

Mike smiled back at him. "He'll be very excited to see you back."

Maggie yelled out, "He'll be excited already. Mrs. Pool comes back from her maternity leave in the morning. He won't have to cover her classes anymore. The bad news is that now he has to replace all of her chamomile tea that he drank."

"Right," Clay agreed laughingly.

Lauren did not know Clay until that night, but she felt comfortable enough to speak up. "So Clay, why now? Why did it take you so long to come back to school – if you don't mind my asking?"

He smiled and sighed. "Oh. I don't know. My head was in a fog, I guess. I mean this is pretty serious drama. I did a lot of crying and soul searching during that time. But I got some really good advice from a couple of soldiers who had lost their legs in service for our country." He looked over at Mike. "*Someone* gave them my address. I guess this was Mike's way of knocking some sense into my head. Anyway, thanks man. I really needed something and you came through in a big way."

Mike smiled back at him. "Any time, bud."

A few of the students made those sickening *Awwww* sounds. But rather than puking, Clay and Mike just went with it. Besides, it momentarily helped to drowned out the sound of those Pomeranians way over in the garage.

"Wait just a second," Curtis interrupted. "I almost hate to bring this up, but you had plans. You had your future all mapped out. So what's on the agenda now?" The entire group was quiet and respectful as Curtis posed the question.

Clay thought about it. "Hmmm. What's on the agenda now? It is true that I had a plan. That plan was to become a track star and a sensation, getting noticed in all the papers, riding on a college scholarship, and on and on and on. That's true. But now I can see that my plan was way too small, you know. I would've been just another track star. I would've had my day in the sun, but it would service no lasting purpose. It would've been all about me. But *now* if I get noticed, I would have a voice, a *real* voice. God might have allowed this to happen to me so that I *would* have a voice. Maybe I can reach people, people who would've never heard me otherwise, people who need to hear what I have to say. Maybe when kids who are in worse shape than me take a look at what I have done, it will give them enough hope to do things too. I could be like an inspiration or something. I have never thought about my potential in that way. I guess whatever God has planned." Nearly choking up, he stopped and looked down for a moment. When he raised his head again, he looked right at Curtis. "You asked me what I'm going to do next. I have no idea. Not a clue. Plans are fine, but I know that I can face an uncertain future as long as the Almighty has my hand, leading the way." He looked over toward Billy's dad. "Mr. Harris! I'm trying to say something, and I don't know how. What do the Scriptures say?"

Mr. Harris looked back at Clay, busting with pride and smiling. He then quoted Jeremiah 29:11. "For I know the thoughts that I think toward you, saith the LORD, thoughts of peace, and not of evil, to give you an expected end."

What an awesome experience, Billy thought as he slid for the first time into the new sheets on his new bed in his new home later that night. *We didn't even come close to finishing that book for English class, but I feel so much better about being the guy that God made me to be. I am actually looking forward to tomorrow, now that I have my act together at last. It is such a nice feeling to have finally arrived. I am no longer doing stupid stuff. Hello, Maturity. It is nice to meet you.*

He reached over to turn off his new lamp on his new night table. Instead, he accidentally knocked it over and it broke on the floor.

"Rats!"

CHAPTER 50

PLEASE DO

So we have now come to the end of our long journey and are now preparing to bid farewell to the good people of Pecan Falls. Billy, a kid with nothing, wanted much. Along the way, he discovered that he actually had something – but that something was worth nothing if he kept it to himself. Then he learned that he already had everything, and now it was his job to give it away. This is a valuable trait no matter what a person's financial status – and an attractive quality. Nothing is uglier than a selfish hoarder.

Is this a lesson that Billy had learned thoroughly? No. But he was on his way. Many of life's lessons take years and years to perfect. You too will make mistakes, learn from them, and then go back to making the same mistakes on occasion. This may make no sense but life is an enormous classroom; go into it ready to listen to God and discover what you are to learn each day.

Clay's nervousness would normally be going through the roof. He had absolutely no idea how this would feel. But God was giving him the courage that he needed to see this project through. Some of that courage was being hand-delivered in the form of Master Sergeant McClure and Staff Sergeant Andrews. Clay had requested that they be present during this consultation. His mom made double sure that they were there, but she only had to mention it to them one time.

Maxine stood in the corner of the room, finally confidant that they were going to receive some good news. But since losing her husband, facing the absence of her daughter's young family, and enduring this horrific crisis with Clay, she had learned that every single day is a day to be cherished. She did not get angry with God or blame Him for any of their troubles. Instead, she was learning to lean on God as the One that would help her through life's tough times – which is how it should be.

But she had her son. By definition, that made it a good day.

The prosthetic specialists came in and spoke with Clay. They explained what was going to happen. The process was not as long as he had thought it would be. In a short few days, he found himself walking on treadmills and performing other forms of physical exercise. It was hard work, unbelievably hard, but McClure and Andrews were there every step of the way and he fully appreciated their support.

Late one night, Officer Thomas found himself sitting across the table from Diane and William. They were laughing and having a nice conversation over some cheeseburgers and fries. Because it was late, there were not many people at this Little Rock diner at the time. They had finished their food and remained for a while, free to chat. Eventually, William got up and paid for their dinner as well as the bill for the entire party a few tables down from them where Billy was sitting.

William returned to his table and sat next to his wife. He leaned in toward Diane and Officer Thomas and confessed, "I wonder how much longer he intends to be." He gestured over at the other table. The three of them looked over at Billy and observed the teenager as he was eating and sharing the gospel with three homeless people at once.

Diane took the final sips from her soft drink and set her glass back down. "Well, this is the last time we do this on a school night," she mused.

In a last ditch effort to recruit more people into the Chess Club, Joey and Maggie had set up a booth in the lunchroom one afternoon. After scaring the students half to death with their disturbing presentation, they decided to go with a more traditional route - - and finally prove to the more timid students that they really were not that frightening after all. No therapy needed this time. So they sat there at their booth with a blank sign-up sheet on a clip board. The students walking back and forth provided plenty of high traffic, but no one came. Joey and Maggie were beginning to think that they were wasting their time.

To their astonishment however, a relatively normal-looking student actually approached them and asked where he could sign up. Stunned, they handed him the clipboard and proceeded to give him information about meeting times and location. Other students quickly came up behind the first guy with questions about the club as well. From that moment, things got weird. In just an Ozark minute, there was a long line stretching from the booth out into the hall and towards the front door of the building. In fact, it seemed that nearly the entire school was signing up for the Chess Club. It looked like a genuine Pecan Falls miracle, right off of some cheesy television movie.

Joey and Maggie were flabbergasted by this overwhelming and immediate response to their boring old booth. What they failed to realize is that Alejandro was outside the building manning one of those sandwich board signs that read CHESS CLUB – SIGN UP TODAY AND GET FREE TOAST!!! Alejandro folded his arms and leaned up against the building beaming with a look of victorious satisfaction on his face.

"I told them I knew how to get students to attend the meetings," he said to himself. "But they wouldn't listen to me." Now all he had to do was figure out a way to produce a hundred loaves of bread and a dozen toasters or so.

Proudly decked out in rented bowling shoes, William turned back at Gregory and showed him which fingers went in which holes. He supported the bowling ball with his left hand. Although he was left-handed, he bowled with his right.

Gregory was captivated and listened with raptured fascination.

Observing the proceedings from a comfortable distance, Billy and Curtis elbowed each other in mild amusement as they both dug into a paper plate of nachos. Even more amusing to them was the idea that the Gregory Chastain, owner and CEO of Chastain Enterprises, was now taking bowling lessons from Billy's dad. How did they get to this point? Obviously, the Almighty had an unmatched sense of irony and humor.

William narrated while he took position. He showed Gregory the dots on the floor and how they were all arranged. He positioned his heel accordingly and gave a few mock swings to illustrate how to throw the ball. Then came the dramatic release. The ball seemed to glide effortlessly across the slick wooden lane. It delivered its characteristically soft roar followed by the crash of pins making contact. Nine pins were down. William waited for the returning ball and picked up an easy spare. The teacher turned around to give a triumphant bow. "And that is how it's done. You'll find that this is a lot different than golf. See how beautiful it is in its simplicity? Now it's your turn. Don't be scared."

Gregory had a rather nervous look on his face. He got up looking completely lost. Golf was a no-brainer for him, but this? With bowling ball in hand, he asked William a couple of quick questions about how to hold it again.

William helped him to get his stance just right. The teacher also pantomimed again how to swing the ball. He was trying to be as encouraging as he could; after all, Gregory was going to help him with his golf swing next week.

Gregory let go of the ball like a pro. William, Curtis, and Billy watched the ball skate down the alley. It was a beautiful strike. Gregory turned back toward William to see his teacher's jaw drop. Curtis and Billy were busting a gut laughing. It would seem to all that Gregory knew a lot more about bowling than they were led to believe. William was partly embarrassed and greatly amused by the whole thing.

Gregory sat back in his seat looking smug and ready to teach the teacher a thing or two.

Later that month, a town nearly eighty miles away was hit by a devastating flood. No one was killed, but the loss of property was crippling. The Knights of Pecan Falls answered the call. Clay, Mike, Curtis, Billy, and now Wesley organized an enormous drive. Key students who were influential in whatever cliques (for lack of a better term) were brought together for a meeting to discuss what could be done. Then they were sent out. Everyone in the school got involved. They then contacted students from other schools in several counties and got them to do the same thing. Teenagers from the whole area made a huge impact. Their entire lunchroom at PFHS seemed to be overrun with cases of bottled water and other food stuffs. The school auditorium was covered with bags of warm clothes,

---

coats, and blankets. Mrs. Dunbar was moved to tears when she saw with her own eyes what her students could do. Then the parents saw what the kids had done and followed their example by organizing assistance with the rebuilding. The response was extraordinary. The flood victims were profoundly grateful.

Billy had been giving it a lot of thought. As the boys were eating their lunch in the cafeteria, he leaned over to ask a question, "Hey guys. What do you think of her?" He pointed discreetly over at another table.

"Of who?" The three pretty much spoke in unison.

"Of her. Of Berly." He pointed over to Berly's table again.

"Is she the one who is normally sitting with that other girl?" Clay asked. "Where is *she* anyway?"

Curtis answered, "Her friend's name is Maggie. I think she eats lunch with the Spanish Club twice a week. You can bet that's where she is right now."

Mike laughed. "Do they think it helps their conversational Spanish to have a mouth full of food?" He took a huge bite from his sandwich wrap and mumbled something unintelligible about his English skills.

Curtis blew his straw paper at Mike and asked, "¿Cómo se dice 'Grow up' en español?"

Clay was back to Billy. "So what about this other girl? This Berly? You like her or something?" Everyone stopped chewing, looked over in Berly's direction, and then turned to face Billy.

Billy shrugged. "I don't know. Maybe. I just keep thinking about how she went to bat that night over at Mike's and led Chloe to the Lord. I just thought that was super impressive. Plus, she's smart and cool. And she totally rolled up her sleeves and got busy with the flood relief stuff. Her and her friend were both here late each night when we were throwing that together. They even took Chloe of all people and put her in charge of blankets."

Mike held up his drink as if he were making a toast. " ...no small task. Here here!"

Curtis picked up his bag of chips and began eating them. "Yeah. She's cool. Her and Maggie are both cool."

Mike perked up. "Yeah. Personally, I think you should go over there and talk to her. It seems a pity to have her sitting by herself. You should really do something about it, but you won't. You're too scared." He gave Billy a gentle elbow nudge.

"I am not. You're just saying that to make me go over there. I can go talk to her on my own accord."

"Oh yeah? Prove it."

Curtis agreed. "Yeah. Prove it, Billy-Boy."

"I think I will." He gathered his lunch, got up from his seat, and turned a full half-circle in Berly's direction.

After half-a-dozen steps, Justin popped out of nowhere and got in his face. "Hey, man. Where ya going?" The very act of speaking apparently dislodged his bangs from their perch. He instinctively reached up and pulled his hair up again, momentarily revealing his forehead. This would seem to be a constant and instinctive course of action.

Billy sighed. "Justin, look. If you don't get out of my way, I might be forced to hit you in the face."

Justin was horrified. "Dude! I was just asking a simple question!"

Billy laughed. "Well, I was just kidding anyway. But seriously, step to the side."

Justin could tell that Billy was quite serious. He backed off, closed his offending mouth, and returned to his seat next to his irritated girlfriend.

Billy was nervous – and yet not nervous – when he got to Berly's table. He did not know what to say. Should he try to be clever? Maybe he should consider - - whoops! She saw him. It was too late to think now. He abandoned his thoughts of saying something smart or funny. His mouth opened and the words simply rolled out. "Uh, you're sitting by yourself."

Berly looked surprised, but not upset. "Yeah. Maggie has Spanish club during lunch today."

"In that case, would you mind if I joined you?"

She smiled. "Please do."

CHAPTER 51

HIS BELOVED EYESORE

Autumn leaves eventually surrendered to the cruel and colorless winter. Like the seasons, students too adhered to the year's regimented passing. But a few months later, the warmth of spring brought with it an explosion of greens and new growth. Renewed life had returned to the wintery hills surrounding Pecan Falls. And all too soon, the school year ended and the students rejoiced at the arrival of summer.

The next school year was about to start and Billy had finally turned sixteen, again the last in his class to do so. His dad took him to a nearby town to pick out a car. In spite of all their wealth, they chose one that fit within the limits that his parents had set for him. To the outsider, it did not look like much; a previous owner had taken an old Chevette and turned it into a convertible. Visually, it was a strange choice. The car itself was way older than Billy; truth be known, it was nearly older than his dad.

Age works nicely on some cars. The word *vintage* or *classic* might come to mind. But in this case, the word *ugly* might be more appropriate. The paint job on the car was difficult to describe. It looked like how a globe might appear if it featured faint, unfamiliar continents. Fortunately, these patterns were not as bold as those on a Holstein cow. The guy who originally drove this car off the lot was probably wearing a black turtleneck with a houndstooth blazer and more than likely smoked a pipe. But Billy did not care. To him it was a car. Grotesque as it was, it was still his beloved eyesore.

The happy moment finally came. Billy tossed his unzipped backpack in the car, opened the top, allowed William to select some of his old-timey music, and was driving it off the lot with his dad riding proudly in the passenger's seat. It was a glorious day in spite of some cloud cover. The pleasant and lovely drive took them past the rolling hills of the Ozarks. The smooth guitar sounds of Ritchie Valens accompanied them as the cool breeze hit their faces. Every once in a while, William would tell Billy to speed up or slow down, whatever was appropriate. He was also telling his son the usual jokes using funny voices. They were looking forward to showing Billy's mom (and Berly) the car that they got.

As they were nearing Pecan Falls, they noticed some orange cones ahead. It would seem that earlier someone was working on a busted water pipe, but had temporarily abandoned the project to get some backup tools. The sight of the cones shot some slight tension up Billy's legs as the inexperienced driver approached, but he was determined to remain calm and simply pass by quietly without incident.

Deprived of warning, a mangy-looking dog with a happy expression stepped out onto the road right in front of the ugly car. The next second went swiftly. William said, "Watch out for the dog!" At the same instant, Billy shouted, "I see it!" Without a moment to think, he swerved to miss the rogue mutt, ran over a couple of cones, and drove straight into the dugout ditch filled with water where work was being done. The car sank down gently to the bottom of the large hole and settled. The two Harris' found themselves still seated in the submerged car with cold water up to their armpits. The only part of the car above the water was the windshield and a couple of headrests.

Speechless and sitting in cold water, William looked all around in disbelief. Billy looked back at his dad as if his driving days were over in an instant. The entire event happened so incredibly fast that both father and son had to sit there a moment to process how they got to that point.

Billy was unsure of what to do next. In the most apologetic voice he could conjure up, he said, "Uh ... that was a complete accident." Yes, his remark was quite the understatement as he reported the most obvious observation on planet Earth.

William was facing forward, still not really knowing what to say either.

An uncomfortable moment transpired. During those seconds, Billy thought about how much he had wanted a new sports car, and now he was quite comfortable in the knowledge that he did not get one. He turned hopefully to his dad and said, "You're always quoting Bible verses. This may be a good time for one."

William said nothing. He was not angry; he just had nothing. This was way too high on his weirdometer.

Billy tried again. "You have a verse for every event that happens. Surely you have one for this …"

Still nothing.

Billy thought hard for a moment. "Actually, I can think of the perfect verse for this occasion. How about, 'Blessed are the merciful … '?"

William turned and glared at Billy.

"' … for they shall obtain mercy.'" Billy's voice sounded like it was asking a question more than anything. Maybe it would be best for him to be quiet. He looked down at the muddy water that he was sitting in.

Something from the floorboard floated up to the surface of the water right in front of William. He reached over and scooped it up. It was a sopping wet copy of *Pride and Prejudice*.

Billy looked over and saw what his dad was holding. "Oh! There is it. That must've floated out of my backpack."

William peered at it in half-amusement, then handed it back over to Billy. In a sarcastic voice, he said, "Keeping a copy for old times' sake? Well, why don't you put this someplace safe before something happens to it?"

Billy took it and tossed it over his shoulder. They heard the splash that it made as it landed.

They were still both sitting silently in water when they were visited by a guest. That happy-looking dog that was crossing the road walked over and looked down at them for a few seconds. He appeared to be smiling as he panted, tongue hanging out and all. Both father and son remained mute as they looked up at the animal, half-expecting to hear it make comment or crack a joke. The dog then lost interest and decided to move on. The two of them followed the dog with their eyes. After a short time, William and Billy started laughing. The next few minutes were dominated by their helpless hysterics. When they finally recovered from this laughing fit, William asked his son about his cell phone.

"In my pocket. And yours?"

"Same. Well, that's no good."

They climbed out of the sunken car with a fair amount of struggle. William looked past Billy and down the road. "We aren't especially far from Pecan Falls. If we start walking, we'll probably be dry before we get home." His suggestion was followed by the faint rumble of distant thunder echoing off the scenic hills. It became obvious that in a few moments both father and son were about to be rained on.

Billy shrugged. "Sometimes I think our lives would make a good reality show. It seems to be one unfortunate episode after another."

His dad laughed. "Whatever you say. Personally, I feel very blessed. I'm in my mid-forties and still have all the cowlicks I had when I was ten." He shook his hair with his left hand to illustrate.

The two began the long hike, each step accompanied by a squishing sound.

Billy started laughing again. "I wonder what mom is going to say about all this."

William smiled. "Well, whatever it is, it's going to be hilarious. Your mom is the queen of the one-liners. No one can craft a zinger quite like your momma. And you can expect her to hang this over your head from now until rapture."

Billy thought about the book floating in what, spatially speaking, would be the backseat of his submerged car. "So how do you feel about that book back there anyway?"

"I think it's far too wet to read. You need a dryer copy, one that is relatively free of water."

"No. I meant your impressions of the book."

"*Pride and Prejudice*?" William answered with a great deal of assuredness. "It is easily one of the best books from that period of English literature. It has withstood the test of time with good reason ..."

Billy interrupted him. "No, dad. Really. Off the record, what do you honestly think about it?"

"Honestly?" He looked over at his son with a sideways smile. "As good as it is, I think that there are way too many chapters in which the two oldest sisters try to overanalyze everything that men say. If they continue to do that into their married lives, they will ultimately drive their husbands to distraction ..."

Father and son continued to talk as they started the long, wet walk home. Shortly after they started, it began to drizzle. And the drizzle became rain. Strangely, it was not a cold, unwelcome downpour, but rather a warm, gentle rain. Their situation never gave them the impression of being the victims of some meteorological misfortune, but rather the recipients of love from above. God's blessings were descending on the two, in their hair, in their clothes, on their faces. This rain was something to be enjoyed and embraced.

After about ten minutes of walking and talking together, a car approached them and slowed down. An older couple looked on them with concern. The man rolled his window down and asked them if they wanted a lift.

Billy and William hesitated and looked at each other. Smiling, Billy turned back toward the kind couple and said, "Thanks, but no thanks. We're good."

"That was very nice of you though," William added. "But we'll be okay."

Billy grinned. "Hey! Have you ever heard the expression that someone doesn't have enough sense to come in from the rain?" He gestured back and forth between him and his dad. "Yeah, that's us."

Perplexed, the couple reluctantly began to drive again, leaving the Harris' to walk back to Pecan Falls in the tender, warm shower. It might have been for the best though; they probably did not want the two of them making a puddle in their backseat anyway.

As father and son walked, Billy looked up at one of the hills. The details from the woods at that distance were obscured by the low clouds and the falling precipitation. From Billy's viewpoint, it was a great treat walking with his dad – almost even an honor. He suddenly remembered the old days, when he was just a little tyke. Billy always felt safe in his presence. His dad seemed so tall, strong, knowledgeable, and funny back then. It was evident now that those days really have not gone anywhere. In just a few short years though, Billy would be grown and he would most likely not see his dad as often. But for now anyway, he could not possibly imagine anyone with whom he would rather be with.

… well, maybe mom.

And how did William feel about walking home with his son, both of them sopping wet? Well, let's just say that he had something nice to record in his journal that night.

ABOUT THE AUTHOR

A high school teacher for roughly fifteen years, Grant Holland's varied writing resume includes a weekly article, a play, and a paper that was submitted into the United States Congressional Record. He enjoys spending his time with his wife and their two sons and can often be found on the piano bench at his church in central Arkansas.

Printed in the United States
By Bookmasters